Copyright © 2025 by E.K O'Connor

Paperback Edition 2025: 979-8-9919474-3-5
Digital Edition 2025: 979-8-9919474-2-8

All rights reserved.

Dust Jack Cover by Shade of Stars
Book Wrap Cover by Josh (Art of Arklin)
Illustrations by Ramona (Alderdoodle) and Soulafein
Interior Character Art by Soldagarius

Trigger Warnings:
Blood, violence, death, near-drowning, dark water, monsters,
assault (discussed, not included), drinking

This book is for Kel,
without whom, it would never have been published.

I love you.

Author's Note

As a mythologist, I want to briefly acknowledge the source material for this story and some of the inspirations behind this retelling. The epic poem Beowulf has captured the attention of scholars, historians, and writers for centuries, and the sheer volume of content written on and about the epic is overwhelmingly massive.

I suggest anyone with a love for history and myth who is not familiar with it, go and find a translation to enjoy (my favorites are those by Tolkien, Seamus Heaney, and Tom Shippey).

The myth has long been one of my favorites, a passion that inspired this re-imagining, along with my desire to increase queer representation and women warriors in literature. With so many powerful women written out of history, I like to put a twist on classic myths that imagines how things might have been, if women had a more prominent role.

That being said, I in no way intend the contents of this book as a re-write, an improvement, or anything that otherwise infringes on the original myth.

This story is born out of a deep love of the source material that I do not wish to alter or attempt to 'improve'. I simply wish to add to the vast store of literature inspired by this epic, and to those who find a female version of Beowulf—especially a queer one—offensive, this book isn't for you. To everyone else, grab a seat by the fire, and we'll begin our adventure.

Contents

Prologue

H ark! And listen well, to a tale of warriors and kings long past, and one among them you may know.

This story is often told over flickering flames and in high halls, carried by words and hands and deeds. Into the tapestry of destiny it is woven, passing over seas and under the wheeling of the stars until what once was is now only memory.

You may have heard of that warrior of old, monster hunter, dragon slayer; but each story is changed in the telling, and this is a path not yet taken, the whispers of which you have yet to hear.

Part 1

The Coast of Denmark

Chapter 1

The icy spray of the sea filled the air as she grasped the side of their longship and swung herself over, into the frothing water. Waves surged nearly to her waist before her boots hit the sandy bottom, the cold seeping through her clothes and sending knives into her skin. Currents of foam swelled and tugged at her, roiling so close to shore, filling her helm with the smell of salt.

She pressed her hand to the slick side of the boat, steadying herself as some of the other warriors jumped in beside her. The ruddy sail had been drawn up the moment they entered the small bay, and the oars pulled up as they reached shallow water. They would finish the rest by hand. She gritted her teeth against the chill, gripped the side of the boat, and helped heave it as far onto dry land as she and the other warriors could manage. As soon as the prow had been drawn up on the dark sand of the beach, the rest of their party climbed ashore.

The pants she wore were weighed down by water, heavy as the mail under her tunic, and she crossed the sand with heavy strides. They had made their way through the storm at least, and she took some comfort in that as she shivered slightly, shifting her weight to ease some of the warmth back into her legs. The wind still howled around them, whipping a flurry of froth into the waves and swirling the dark clouds that brooded overhead.

Out of habit, her hand found the hilt of her sword at her waist and gripped it tightly as she stalked further up the beach. The ground beneath her feet seemed unsteady, her legs used to the roll of the sea waves, but the cool air of the storm kept her head clear even if her footing was shaky. The thick bear hide draped around her shoulders kept some of the cold at bay, and the leather of her armor was a bulwark against the frigid wind. She could hear shouts among the other warriors as they unloaded what few supplies they carried, but her gaze had strayed to the cliffs that surrounded the small beach.

She had seen the watchman when they first entered the bay, his silhouette a small black dot on one of the cliffs. He had disappeared not long after they passed into the shallows, but she had a feeling they would see him again.

It took only a few minutes to unload their items, and she had already shouldered her small pack and gathered up her shield in one hand when one of the other warriors gave a cry of warning.

Even at a distance, she could make out the hail of wet sand kicked up by the hooves of the watchman's horse. He rode toward them at speed, just beyond the reach of the waves. She shook her shield, brushing sand off the image of the Fenris wolf painted across the front, before she slung it over her back and took a few steps forward. The other warriors gathered around her, well-armed and armored. There were fifteen of them, if she counted herself, and she couldn't help but admire the bravery of the watchman as he rode so swiftly toward such an armed gathering.

Most of the warriors wore thick boots stained dark by seawater, and tunics of boiled leather or blackened mail. Swords and axes hung at belts or across backs, as did an occasional shield, the paint chipped from hard use. Spears stood out black against the white foam of the sea like a bare thicket. The cold seemed not to bother them any more than it did her, all of them wrapped as they were in cloaks, with fur sewn into tunics and the tops of boots or adorning their shoulders in the form of full hides like her own. Most had long hair, tied back in braids or plaits, and more than half their number had beards to match. Some, but not all, wore iron helms. Dark beaten metal covered their heads and noses, their features seeming more pronounced beneath the shadows cast over their eyes as they watched the newcomer approach.

The watchman pulled his horse to a halt not more than ten paces from them, his own face barely visible beneath his helm as he brandished his spear. She could feel a few of those around her tense, but his challenge was little more than a formality against so many. He cast his eyes across them, and she imagined he might be looking for a leader. It came as no surprise that his gaze didn't settle on her. Though she was almost equal to her shield mates in height and possessed a strong build for a woman, she was not nearly so broad as some of the men among them. Still, she knew from the way the rider glanced past her that he had likely thought her a smaller, perhaps younger man. Most who saw her did.

The watchman kept his spear aloft as he shouted above the wind.

"Who are you that would disembark on these shores without asking the permission of the clans here? You who come armed and armored to the realm of my king, Hrothgar, in whose service I watch these coasts for any threat to our Danish lands. I ask your names and your purpose if you wish to pass." He gripped his spear tightly, his gaze combing their ranks.

She took a deep breath and slowly stepped forward. Some of the warriors closest to her stood aside, making way as she walked to the front of their formation. The watchman looked down at her, at the shimmer of her sea-green eyes beneath her helm, as she stood before him and spoke.

"We come from Geatland."

The watchman failed to keep his mouth from falling slightly open as her clear voice cut the air. She managed to keep a wry smile from her lips. It was not unheard of for a woman to wield a sword, but whether it was her helm or simply the way she carried herself, she had a knack for confusing the less observant. When the watchman failed to gather himself in time to respond, she carried on speaking.

"I am a thane of King Hygelac. My father spent time on these shores and was a friend to your king. There are likely many among your elders who would remember him."

The watchman blinked several times and, seeming to regain his wits, lowered his spear.

"By what name are you known, thane of Hygelac?"

She tilted her head slightly, keeping her eyes on the watchman as she spoke.

"My name is Beowulf."

There was a flicker of something in the watchman's eyes, some strange mix of curiosity and suspicion, but it passed too quickly for her to know for certain. She continued, shifting her weight slightly and leaning an elbow on the pommel of the blade at her hip. "We come in good faith to the halls of your king, Hrothgar. Word has reached us of the misfortune that has befallen him and his people."

"You would offer your service?"

"Indeed. We have heard of the beast that haunts his halls. There are few in these lands who have not heard the tale by now, I imagine; ill news spreads far and fast. I come with fourteen of my best fighters to aid your king." Beowulf extended her hands slightly, gesturing to those around her who stood close, their eyes still on the watchman.

The man on horseback frowned slightly as he looked them over with new interest, before his gaze once more settled on her.

"And what have you to offer that my king has not already tried?" He tilted his head slightly as he spoke. "Even the finest of our warriors have long since been sent to the afterlife by this beast."

A few of the newcomers on the beach exchanged glances, but their leader's green-eyed gaze remained locked on the watchman. Her calm seemed to make him bristle slightly, and he failed to hide a small sneer from his lips.

"What makes you think your fates may fare better?" he asked coldly.

One warrior let out a muffled chuckle, and she shot him a sideways glance before turning back to the watchman and giving him a small nod.

"That is for your king to decide. We offer what aid we can. Whether our service is accepted is for your king to determine."

The watchman chewed his lip for a moment before slowly nodding.

"You measure your speech wisely," he said slowly, "and I believe your word, that you come in service to my king. It will be, as you say, his choice to grant you welcome." He paused a moment, looking them over once more, before he glanced up to where the dragon prow of their ship rose from the sand toward the gray sky.

"I have men who will watch your boat while you are on these shores. They will ensure it is kept ready and waiting." He dropped his tone so low even the keen ears of his horse could not have heard as he whispered into his collar, "Should you survive to have need of it."

Beowulf turned back to the other warriors, their nods telling her they had gathered all they had brought with them. She adjusted her shield on her back, taking comfort in the weight of it, as the watchman turned his horse back down the beach at a slow walk. Her own boots traced over the hoofprints in the sand as the other warriors fell in behind her. One last glance over her shoulder was all she would chance, a last glimpse of the ship that had carried them across the raging sea, before she turned her gaze before her and followed the watchman.

Even as she settled into the rhythm of her strides, she felt the ground still seeming to sway unevenly beneath her. Despite sea legs, she and the others kept an even pace as they trudged behind the watchman in a line. They left a trail of tracks in the wet sand, the wind whipping at their backs as they went. The horse's hooves clattered first on the rock of the narrow path leading down from the grassy heights above before finally finding turf, as the company made their way above the reach of the sea. Beyond the protection of the cove, the wind blew more fiercely, pulling at cloaks and hair as it sent waves rippling through the grass that lined the narrow track from the coast.

For all they carried, the warriors traveled at a swift pace, crossing the distance to the King's Hall in only a few hours. The wind died down as they moved further inland, amid the low hills that rolled across the horizon. They passed within sight of hamlets as they went, clusters of buildings where smoke rose into the gray sky, lifted by wind now little more than a chill breeze that gently drifted through the fields. Before long the hills and forests gave way to the sight of Heorot, the great hall of King Hrothgar. It seemed to glow like a beacon despite the gloom of the storm, nestled atop a large hill that overlooked the land on all sides. A murmur rose from the warriors, they beheld the hall, its painted sides shining in the faint light of day as if made of beaten gold.

Surrounding the hall and the hill it stood upon was the village, larger than any they had yet seen on their journey, ringed by a high wooden wall and filled with numerous thatched buildings. Sheep grazed in some of the nearby fields, and the great gates stood open that herdsmen and travelers might enter. The sounds of life echoed out across fields to meet them, the distant clink of a blacksmith's hammer and the bleating of sheep carried on the wind. From here, all seemed well and at peace.

Once they were within clear sight of the hall, the dirt of the path beneath their feet became hard-packed and firm, more of a proper road than a track. It was here that their guide halted his horse and turned to face them.

"As promised, the hall of my king. Go and find welcome there." His gaze settled on Beowulf for a moment as he spoke. "I must return to my post, and see to your ship. All-father watch over you and favor your fortunes, thane."

He nodded, which she returned along with a gesture of her palm as she brought it first to her chest before extending it slightly out toward him in thanks. The watchman urged his horse back the way they had come at speed, hooves thudding on the hard earth as he passed the line of armored warriors. They paused only a moment to watch him go, before they turned back toward the hall and fell into step once more.

Beowulf led the way, her mind on the warm fire that likely burned within the hall, and all else they might find within. The ocean storm had been the easy part, and she couldn't help but feel unsettled by what awaited them. She did not doubt they would find welcome, but alliances were delicate things, and she would have happily preferred a raging storm over politics if given the choice.

They drew stares as they passed through the village gates, first from the guards who watched them warily, then from the villagers within. Hushed words trailed in their wake as they made their way between buildings and up the hill toward the hall.

The warriors behind Beowulf spoke little, most glancing about their surroundings in silence as they walked. She kept her thoughts to herself, eyes darkened and alert beneath a frown as she glanced at the buildings that flanked their path. Despite the sounds of life they could hear around them, the village seemed oddly empty, and many of the houses looked abandoned. A few doors hung open, with no signs of life within. The villagers that watched them huddled in small groups, as sheep do when frightened, exchanging words in quiet whispers. There was fear in the air. It was thick enough to smell under the wood smoke, and it set her teeth on edge. She could feel the hair on the back of her neck stand on end, but she kept her jaw set and her chin up as she led the way.

They made their way up the path that led to Heorot, and to the great door that stood ajar. The mighty hall was even more grand up close, and no small wonder it had become something of a legend, the pride of King Hrothgar's ancestry. The rough-hewn wood seemed to glow a deep gold color, and the intricate carvings of the great door caught the shadows of the fading light as the cloud-covered sun sank lower in the sky. Here, the guards stopped them, and one of their number stepped forward. The dark red-brown hair that wreathed his face matched the color of the cloak he wore over his armor and was tied in a plait like his beard.

"I am Hrothgar's herald. It is my duty to ask your purpose here." His voice rumbled like distant thunder as he spoke, appraising the band before him. "I can tell by your armor and weapons that you are no mere travelers. What does an armed host want with my king?"

Beowulf stepped forward slightly as she spoke. "We are loyal to King Hygelac of the Geats, who rules the lands across the northern sea. I am a thane under his command, and we offer services to your lord and king."

The herald raised an eyebrow and looked her up and down. She continued in even tones. "I am here with those most loyal to me, some of the finest warriors in all of Geatland. We've heard of your misfortune, and that of your king, Hrothgar. I believe your liege will hear us out if we might bring our message before him."

The herald nodded slowly, before raising his chin slightly as he spoke. "And who is it who comes to speak with King Hrothgar?"

She raised a hand up and removed her helm. Her fair hair tumbled free, a mix of loose strands and occasional bone-tied pleats that fell thick and wild just past her shoulders. Her face, no longer concealed, was fair but strong, her jaw sharp and gaze keen despite the softness of her cheeks. She could not have been much older than seven and twenty winters.

"I am Beowulf." She tucked her helm beneath her arm. "Your king knew my father. I should like to speak with him, if he would see us." Her bright eyes met those of the herald and her gaze did not waver. When he continued to stand in silence, she took a deep breath and continued.

"We heard of the monster that ransacked your hall, killed your king's men, and left a bloody massacre in his wake." The air seemed to grow still around her as she finally spoke to the shadow that had drawn them across the sea to those shores.

"Such stories have made it to our lands, and being an ally to your king, my liege has sent me to lend aid."

"I see." The herald nodded, appraising her anew. "I will bring your message to my king and return with his reply." He stared at her a moment longer, before turning on his heel and disappearing through the gap in the great doors, leaving the warriors to wait.

A few of them spoke quietly. Some shifted their weight on their feet or looked back at the village. Beowulf continued to stare at the door through which the herald had vanished, the wind playing with feathery flyaway hairs that ringed her face. She only turned away when one of the members of her band stepped up beside her and leaned close.

"I know that man. Wulfgar, I believe he's called. I have heard he's a fine warrior and wise advisor." The warrior's blue eyes flicked toward the door before settling back on Beowulf.

"Mmm," she responded quietly, one hand absent-mindedly kneading the pommel of her sword, the only subtle betrayal of any nerves, kept carefully reserved behind a flat expression. The thinnest line creased between her brows, and a single muscle moved in her jaw. "I don't doubt we'll be given an audience." She spoke firmly as she turned back to the door.

"Certainly not." The other warrior almost chuckled. "He'd be a fool to turn away help." He snorted derisively as he glanced to the guards at the door, both of whom seemed uneasy in the presence of so many armed visitors.

"Never mind the help, Braggi," she muttered tightly. "There's honor to be found too. This king paid my bloodline a kindness that I may yet return."

"Oh, I know, I know," he whispered back, pushing some of his loose brown locks out of his face as he did so. "But that shouldn't be the only reason."

Beowulf turned and caught the grin that curled on the edge Braggi's mouth as he spoke. She let a small huff of air from her nose before releasing her sword and crossing her arms, regarding him with a raised eyebrow.

"I wish it were as simple as monster-hunting renown. There's more delicate politics at play here, and it would be wise to keep and strengthen what allegiances we can."

"Ever humble, eh?" He elbowed her lightly, though it earned him little more than a scowl. "Still," he continued, "this isn't like fighting giants. You sure you're up for this?"

It was her turn to elbow him. "You have to ask?" she mumbled out of the corner of her mouth. "I've fought plenty of monsters before."

He grinned. "And yet you say you don't come seeking renown."

"I don't." She finally turned back toward the door, before dropping her gaze to the stones at her feet. When she spoke again, it was too quiet for even Braggi to hear, shared only with herself and the wind that played through her hair. "I want to help these people." She would not have told him then, or ever, that he was right. She of all people should appreciate the truth of legends, even when they seem to defy what is possible. Every story could be embellished, but the truth in the stories that had reached Geatland was bloody and brutal beyond compare.

Trolls and giants were danger enough, but this beast had slain even the finest warriors. Beowulf knew Hrothgar's rule was weakening, and neither he nor his fighters had been able to keep the intruder at bay. It was a poor king who could not protect the people under his own roof. The empty houses in the village were proof enough, and the hall, despite its beauty, stood cold and quiet before them on the hill.

It was more than monster hunting, something in which she was already well-versed. This was political as well, and whether or not she could be of help would impact more than her own renown. She had slain trolls, even bested giants, but this was a new challenge. More importantly, it was a chance to help a kingdom whose foundations were crumbling thanks to this creature that made a slaughterhouse of the king's own hall.

Braggi could tease all he wanted, she thought to herself as she looked back to where the great doors yawned ajar. He underestimated her desire to help others, but he always had. As she stood before that door thinking about the journey that brought her there, she knew he overestimated her ambition, but she would be lying if she said it was *only* a desire to help that had called her across the sea. This time she knew the stakes were much higher.

She was pulled from her thoughts by a slight rustle from within the doors. Wulfgar the herald re-emerged, looking slightly less stern. He measured his words less cautiously this time as he regarded Beowulf.

"My good thane." As he addressed her, the murmurings from the warriors around her slowly faded. "My king says he knows of your ancestry, and indeed knew you when you were young. You may enter the hall and speak with him."

Beowulf nodded and the warriors moved toward the door, but a raised hand from the herald stopped them before they could enter.

"Your shields and spears must be left just within the entrance to the hall, until your purpose is made clear."

At that, every warrior among the band looked to Beowulf, who glanced once between the herald and her followers, before nodding in assent. They dropped their shields where they stood, unbuckled their blades from their belts, and set their spears against the wooden walls. They kept only their armor and what packs and provisions they carried, leaving their iron at the door.

The warriors slowly entered the hall, filing in as the door was pushed only a small portion wider, heavy on its hinges. Beowulf led the way behind the herald, blinking slightly in the dim light as the troop entered. The glow from outside still entered through the windows along the sides of the hall, casting long shafts filled with swirling smoke and dust. Sturdy pillars ran the entire length from the open doors to the back of the hall, some hundred feet long. The middle of the roof was open that the smoke from the long flume of a fireplace at its center might escape. Flames crackled there, set down deep into the stonework of the floor, and on either side large wooden tables ran the length of the hall.

A hundred warriors could have feasted there with enough room to stretch their legs. Now, even in preparation for the evening meal, the hall seemed eerily quiet for how thunderous the warriors' footsteps sounded, echoing as they did. Some of King Hrothgar's men lined the hall, interspersed amid the massive intricately carved wooden pillars that acted as the skeleton of that great wooden beast. Images of the tales of kings and gods were carved deep into the dark wood, and torches set in the brackets on each pillar sent shadows and light playing across the stories etched into wood.

The warriors were watched from the moment they stepped through the doors. In addition to the guards, there was a small number of Hrothgar's soldiers within, many already seated at the low tables or near the fire. Others in service of the king walked about the hall, minding the fires, refilling mead horns, or turning the large boar that was roasting over the hot embers in the long firepit at the center of the hall. A pair of dogs, ruddy brown and dark gray in color, trotted toward the newcomers as those within the hall turned their attention to the warriors' arrival.

Beowulf and her followers walked in silence until they had nearly reached the far end and stood before the stone steps at the back of the hall. Here the floor was raised slightly, away from the wooden tables, and a large wooden chair carved and painted in gold wrapped around the figure of a broad-shouldered man who bore a simple gilded crown. Hrothgar watched the warriors' approach from beneath bushy eyebrows of chalk gray, his long hair of a matching color surrounding the stern and lined features of his face before seeming to blend with his beard.

The king stood before the warriors reached him, his eyes on Beowulf. His build reflected his strength as he assumed his full height, his long cloak tumbling free over his fine linen garments. He raised both hands, shimmering with rings, in a gesture of welcome as he addressed the newcomers.

"Welcome, Beowulf, daughter of Ecgtheow, thane of Lord Hygelac, hero of the Geats. Know that you and all who follow you are welcome in Denmark." His voice was strong and clear, but there were deep shadows in the lines of his face, and a weariness that seemed to hang from him like a ghostly shroud.

Wulfgar offered his liege a small bow as he stood aside, and the warriors assembled before the king with Beowulf at their lead. She locked eyes with the king for the briefest moment, before dropping a single knee to the stone floor, braids falling forward as she bowed, and her warriors followed suit. She had barely stood again when Hrothgar spoke to the room at large.

"It is by the blessings of the gods themselves that you find yourself on these shores. Word of your deeds has reached us from across the sea, and we have heard the stories of your feats in battle."

Beowulf's jaw tightened slightly as she stood, her warriors again following suit, and it seemed that for the first time since entering the hall, she was aware of how many eyes were on her. Hrothgar continued, his voice echoing through the quiet.

"We have heard of battles with sea beasts, and the many giants you have defeated single-handedly. It is said you have the strength of thirty men in each arm, and if the tales are to be believed, I think it more akin to forty." He smiled from where he stood, finally looking back down to Beowulf, his arms still slightly open. "Know that if you aid us here, not only will you be compensated with rich treasures from my coffer, but I do not doubt that songs and tales of your deed will spread thrice as fast as the tales of our woe."

There was an excited murmur in the hall. A few of Hrothgar's fighters had shifted to get a better look, some standing at their tables as they peered through the ranks of the Geats to glimpse the warrior at their lead.

"It is true." Beowulf spoke in a voice slightly hollow and distant. She knew this part; she had done it before. It was easy enough to recount her deeds, and a warrior's boast was as binding as a promise. It was tradition, and one that she was loath to uphold for how arrogant it had always seemed to her. She took a deep breath before she began. "I have slain many enemies of the Geats. In my youth I trained among the finest warriors and honed my skills. I battled with my kin against trolls. I have slain sea beasts in the deep and overcome many foes."

There was talking in the hall now, quiet rumblings in the corners of the room, and the occasional scrape of a bench as yet another of Hrothgar's warriors tried to get a better look. The only people in the hall that Beowulf acknowledged, besides the king himself, were the three female fighters she had seen among the ranks of the guards, to whom she gave a fleeting nod.

"We have heard of your plight, good king," she continued, turning back to where he stood. "The elders of the court of Hygelac know of the sufferings of your people. We have heard of the beast that haunts the steps of your hall and reaps blood and grief in his wake."

At her words she heard some of those who stood under that low roof shift uneasily. A few sidelong glances from the guards, or a sharp inhale from one of the warriors. It was as if they feared that to name the shadow would bring it down upon them. Even Hrothgar in all his majesty seemed to almost flinch, so small a movement it was that Beowulf doubted any others saw.

"My fellows and I made this journey with the hope we might lend our skills," she pressed on, "knowing that we might have a chance to aid you, good king. And I for one might repay the debt of kindness you showed my family."

Hrothgar nodded, a wide smile creasing the lines in his face. "I accept your aid, young hero."

Now it was her turn to make her promise, as was customary. It would lay the foundation of the stories that might yet spread from whatever would transpire beneath that roof, for good or ill, as it would be for any allegiance between this king and her own.

"Good king, I ask only that myself and my men are allowed to do this in our own way, without the aid of your swords here." She gestured to some of Hrothgar's soldiers scattered throughout the hall.

"Of course." The king nodded. "None of my warriors will intervene, if that is your request."

"Further..."

Beowulf paused only for a moment, half to gather a deep breath, and half to ensure that the hall was so quiet she could hear the rustle of the flames in the hearth as all within listened to her words.

"I have heard that this beast, Grendel, as he is called, fights without the aid of weapons or armor. As such I will meet him in equal and single combat. My skill against his own. My warriors will only act if I should fall." There was another murmur in the hall as she said, "I will fight him without armor, a shield, or a sword. Grendel fights with no weapons but his hands, so I shall meet him just the same, to the death." At this there was a smattering of hushed chatter.

Braggi caught Beowulf's eye briefly and grinned. *Well played,* she could almost hear him say. He had always been one to enjoy boasting, and the prowess they could wield as warriors. He had, after all, been the one to teach her how to boast when they had been foundlings, so many years ago. The rest of the warriors around her stood silent, some of them smirking slightly, as the tide of mutterings passed through the hall. Hrothgar's brows had raised high enough to almost disappear beneath the rim of his crown, but he remained silent. Only once the hall had begun to quiet once more, did Beowulf speak again.

"If I should perish, good king, I know there will be no need for a funeral pyre." She kept her voice steady and even, despite the tightness her own words knotted into her stomach. Death was no stranger to a warrior, but she had tried to keep from thinking of what kind of fate she might meet at Grendel's hands. Being slain by a sword was one thing, having your limbs torn from your body and devoured was quite another.

She kept her expression stern and ignored the knots in her gut. "I hear Grendel takes his plunder for a meal, and if I die,

I will doubtless be strewn across the moors where he keeps his den. I would ask only that my sword be returned to my lord Hygelac, that he might know of what transpired. The fates move as they will."

"Indeed." Hrothgar spoke solemnly. He had resumed a sterner expression, and nodded as Beowulf finished her request. "You may face this beast on whatever terms you so choose. I do not doubt your strength or skill, and I pledge to do as you have asked, should the battle go ill. But come"—he smiled again, gesturing once more to the hall at large—"you are our honored guests. Join us this night in feasting after your long journey, and may we recount the tales that have brought you here."

A small cheer went up from the hall, shared by some of Beowulf's warriors. The tension in the air drifted away as the hall resumed the pace of the evening. Warriors returned to their seats, mead was poured, and the newcomers found seats along the low tables. Beowulf watched Hrothgar return to his seat as servants drew a small table out before him.

She made her way slowly to the leftmost of the banquet benches, not far from the end of the hall where the king sat. Braggi and some of the others had found seats near a handful of Hrothgar's warriors. Two of the women warriors in service to Hrothgar were there as well, and one raised her mead horn to Beowulf and gestured her over.

Beowulf removed her cloak and set it, bear hide up, on the seat before sitting, grateful to be off her feet. She ignored the sideways glances of some of Hrothgar's fighters. Those who knew her well, her warriors, treated her as they would any other, and in that she now took comfort as she always had. Those who knew of her from story alone or from seeing her on the battlefield always watched her as one might a dangerous animal. Cautious, but curious. She was perceived in attitudes from reverence and disbelief to doubt and scorn, and even fear. She had long since learned to act as if she did not notice. She idly accepted the mead horn offered to her by one of Hrothgar's servants before falling into chatter with Braggi and the others.

The meal in the hall was a customary welcome to guests, nothing overly grand on such short notice, but a welcome comfort after a journey being tossed about on an unyielding ocean. Beowulf breathed deep the warm, smoky air of the hall, wiggling her toes in her boots and savoring the taste of mead on her tongue. If what the night brought with it was as bad as the stories said, it may well be her last feast, and she was determined to enjoy it.

Chapter 2

"**I**t's too quiet."

Braggi spoke gruffly to the mead in his cup. Subdued chatter echoed around them, the fire crackled in the long hearth, and outside the last light of day had begun to fade.

Beowulf looked around the hall again, unsurprised to see no change from the other dozen times she had glanced around between bites of her meal. The warmth from the fire and the sweetness of the mead had smoothed away the rough edges the ocean had scoured on her mind and brought feeling back into her stiff fingers.

"Didn't use to be." It was one of Hrothgar's men who had spoken, looking up from his seat across from Braggi, his shoulders hunched so that his eyes shone from just beneath his furrowed brows. "Used to be filled with laughter and song."

Beowulf leaned forward and met the man's gaze. "So I heard. A hall like no other. Some said fit to rival Valhalla itself."

The man nodded darkly and sucked his teeth. "And now look at us. A dozen warriors perhaps, on our best days. A handful of servants along with whatever villagers are stubborn or stupid enough to stay. Everyone else has fled or been killed. We few loyal remain though..." His voice trailed off.

Beowulf raised an eyebrow, and the man, after gazing shiftily about, dropped his voice and leaned further forward. "Only a fool would stay after dark. I'm afraid you all will be on your own if you sleep beneath this roof."

Braggi scoffed at that, and Beowulf shot him a sideways glance before turning back to the man. "I am sorry for those comrades you have lost. I don't know which is worse, the death of your shield mates, or the betrayal of those who left."

"I don't blame them. I might not agree; we swore vows after all. But this thing is..." he trailed off again, shaking his head.

"We've come to help," she answered flatly, "so under this roof we will stay."

The man shrugged, and the woman at his elbow, the one who had called Beowulf to their table, spoke now to the visiting thane.

"A noble gesture, but even if you succeed, I don't think this hall will ever again be what it was." She looked up then, intently, past Beowulf, toward where Hrothgar sat.

Beowulf turned that she might see the king more clearly. Hrothgar had finished his meal and was gazing into the bottom of the goblet in his hand. He seemed lost in thought, eyes glazed, and he looked suddenly old in a way that Beowulf had not yet fully appreciated. The lines carved into his face were deep and shadowed, and his shoulders hunched as though a mighty weight pressed upon them. Beowulf watched him as the woman across from her continued.

"He failed to keep his people safe. His best retainers were all cut down under his own roof. Some of the finest among us. We've all lost friends to this demon, but I fear our king has lost much more. Our people lose faith, and his power in this realm is but a whisper of what it once was." She sighed heavily, and Beowulf finally turned back to meet her gaze. There was something deep in the warrior's eyes then, something bright and cold as she looked directly at Beowulf and continued speaking.

"He's invited warriors here before." She spoke slowly, her tone sharper than before. "Warriors that promised to slay this beast. They shared our meat and mead and made their boasts of how they would kill the monster when he came in the night. And every time the dawn rose, the hall was slick with their blood."

Whether it was a warning, or a challenge, Beowulf could not tell. She felt Braggi stiffen slightly at her elbow as she looked down into the amber mead in her horn and swirled it in thought before taking a sip. When she spoke, it was slow and measured.

"We've all heard the stories. I make my boast knowing that this ends in blood one way or another. I am prepared for whatever awaits me in the strands of fate." She looked back at the woman, who gave her a small approving nod before turning her attention back to her drink.

Braggi gave Beowulf a knowing look, before glancing up to where Hrothgar sat. His small frown told her his thoughts. A king who could not guarantee the safety of his people was no king at all. Hrothgar's reign had ended the moment the beast first spilled blood in his halls. Hrothgar himself likely knew it, worn and wearied as he was. Sorrow hung about the man like a shawl. What it would mean if Grendel was slain, Beowulf could only guess. Hrothgar had two sons. Perhaps they might rebuild some of the legacy of their house.

She was jarred suddenly from her thoughts by Braggi's elbow in her ribs. She turned as he jerked his head toward the table across the hall from them. A group of Hrothgar's men sat there, and from the rising sound of their voices they were thoroughly enjoying their king's mead.

"That one," Braggi muttered, glancing over his shoulder. "The one with the dark hair who looks like he's got a dagger wedged up his arse."

Beowulf slowly scanned the room, settling briefly on the gaggle of warriors. A few of them stood, most sat, and all of them were growing louder with each passing minute. The one in the center of the group chanced to meet eyes with Beowulf. His hair was a deep earthy brown, plaits plastering it to the sides of his head. His jaw was lined with a thin beard, and his mouth was turned down in a scowl as he glanced at the visitors.

"He looks a bit the worse for wear," Beowulf grunted as she turned back to her drink. She saw something in his eyes, something she had seen many times before, not unlike the scorn she had found in the eyes of some of the warriors who first trained her, or the young boys she trained with as a foundling. There was something hateful in that look that sent a prickle of anger down her spine. She had turned away as soon as she saw it, but it was too late.

A voice broke above all the others at her back, silencing some of the idle conversation in the hall. "I heard a story about you, thane, and I wonder if it might be true."

There was something sour in his voice, almost jeering, and as Beowulf turned to face him, she saw several of her own warriors turn as well. The room slowly silenced, all those within looking to the two figures who now stared at each other. Beowulf shifted where she sat that she might face him more directly, whispering to the woman opposite her as she did.

"And who is this?" she asked under her breath.

"Unferth. Son of Ecglaf." The woman let out a small grunt, almost a scoff. The king's nephew. Beowulf had heard his name before. She placed her horn mug gently down on the table. Her free hand balled into a fist as she forced it to her lap and squared her shoulders with the man opposite the hall. She knew only a small amount about him, but more than enough that she felt she could hold her own should he have a drunken desire for a battle of words.

Unferth glanced at the warriors near his elbows before turning back to Beowulf with a look of derision and disdain.

"It's said that, when you were in training, you and your fellow warrior Breca had a challenge to see who was the better swimmer. Driven by vanity, the two of you waded into the wild sea in full armor and swam there, seeing who could make the crossing in quicker time." He chuckled as he spoke, his gaze briefly drifting up to where Hrothgar sat.

Beowulf could see it as Unferth looked up toward his king, then back to her. Envy. Something small and festering behind those eyes, the same thing that turned the corners of his mouth into a sneer. Hrothgar, for his part, looked slightly pained, his brow deeply furrowed as his warrior carried on mocking his guest.

"It's said that, after toil and struggle in the open waves, Breca out-swam you and made it to shore first." Unferth grinned, and some of the warriors at around him snickered. "You finally floundered ashore having run afoul in your attempt to best him." Unferth drained his mug then and crossed his arms with his chin slightly stuck out, daring any response.

Beowulf made a slow show of swinging her legs around to the other side of her bench that she could fully face him. Hands resting on her knees, she looked him up and down. He swayed slightly where he stood, and she could see the hazy fire in his eyes. She cleared her throat as she glanced over the many faces turned in silence toward her. She had the attention of the entire hall, and she was determined to make the most of it.

"An interesting recounting, Unferth," she said idly, "though I think the mead may be doing most of the talking." A few small chuckles echoed from the corners of the room, and Unferth flushed slightly where he stood, his mouth tightening as his smile turned back to a scowl.

"It's true," she continued, speaking more to the hall than to Unferth. "Breca and I have long been close friends and well matched in our skill. We trained together in the early days, and both of us have long had a love for the water. We made a habit of challenging each other to dangerous feats in the wild ocean."

They were good memories mostly, and she allowed the joy they brought her to show freely on her face as she recounted the story. They had always competed as foundlings, doing reckless challenges to see who could outmatch the other. That day had been a boasting match that ended in dark water and armor, blood on foam, but it held a special place in her heart.

That day was the day that everything had changed for her, the day she became the warrior whose name was known far beyond the shores of her people. She had already been a skilled warrior among her kin, a title she had fought hard for and taken pride in. After that day in the sea, she had become something else. As the story went, and as she would say if asked, the gods had seen fit to gift her the strength that had now made her a legend, though she was not yet thirty.

"We swam out in armor." She gathered her thoughts and pressed on, one hand mindlessly reaching up over her chest where a necklace of iron hung hidden beneath leather and mail. The hall was deathly quiet, and she took her time in telling the tale. "We carried our swords as well, as the deep sea has no shortage of monsters and only a fool would venture there unarmed. We swam for many hours, neither of us making it much further than the other. Back then we were always well matched, Breca and I. We had come within sight of shore when something grabbed me."

She remembered it all too well, the feeling like a vice closing around her ankle, drawing her beneath the waves and down into the crushing black.

"A sea beast, akin to a whale, with sharp teeth and powerful jaws." Someone near the back of the hall let out a small curse, and a few of the warriors exchanged glances. Beowulf's comrades were the only ones not enthralled in the story, so many times they had heard it. They mostly watched the reactions of Hrothgar's warriors as Beowulf continued her tale.

"It dragged me down, and in the dark swirling waters my blade struck its mark, and I slew it, but my freedom was not so easily won. The fiends often hunt in packs, and I killed seven more in that blood-strewn sea before I could make my way to shore."

She remembered the taste of iron in the water, salt flooding her nose and mouth, being blinded by the darkness of the roaring ocean as she hacked and stabbed, struggling against the current. The last beast had pulled her further down, so deep she had lost sight of the light above her as she struggled in its grip. They had reached the bottom, dark rocks like teeth yawning out of the blackness, as she plunged her blade into it. Exhausted as she had been, lungs screaming for air, it had nearly been the end of her. The truth of what she found in that darkest abyss was one she kept to herself. The story continued only with what need be known, that she staggered to shore in torn and blood-soaked armor. Birthed from the wild sea and bathed in slaughter, her legacy had begun on that sandy shore.

"So, yes." Beowulf gave a small nod of her head in Unferth's direction. "I finished after Breca. He made his way to shore, and I slew eight monsters of the deep before following his path."

Unferth looked slightly bewildered for a moment, the mead haze still heavy in his eyes. He seemed unsure as to whether he had succeeded in mocking her, though some of the more sober listeners had already begun to look at him in mild amusement. Beowulf could have left it at that, but the prickle of anger had not left her fingertips, so she stood and gestured toward Unferth.

"But tell me, Unferth, since you seem an expert on my feats, what have you accomplished that stands even close in renown?" She crossed her arms and raised an eyebrow. He had started this, and she was determined to finish it.

He reddened slightly and sucked in air, puffing up his chest slightly as the two of them glared at each other across the hall. She still wasn't done.

"If you are so mighty as you seem to think, why does Grendel still haunt the hall of your king, and why have you not butchered the monster yourself, if you are so confident?"

Unferth blustered slightly at her words, and Beowulf caught sight of a few grins scattered throughout the hall.

Her anger still simmered, and every battle of words was best carried to the death unless her resolve be questioned. She unleashed her killing blow then, as she dropped her tone, her eyes growing cold and hard as she stared unwaveringly at the warrior who offered her insult.

"You've nothing to your name but the blood on your hands. You, a kin-killer, already thrice damned to the depths of Hel for what you have done."

The hall went deathly quiet. Unferth had gone from beet red to white as a sheet in a span of seconds. Beowulf stood still as a statue, glaring at the warrior who seemed to suddenly sober as he dropped his gaze to the table before him. Only then did Beowulf look once more around the room, some of the tension dropping from her shoulders.

"To speak of deeds is one thing; to perform them is another." Her voice was gentler now, and she watched out of the corner of her eye as she spoke to where Unferth slumped back into his seat. Her gaze flicked briefly up to where Hrothgar sat, now looking less distressed and more satisfied. He raised his goblet to her ever so slightly as she resumed her seat, and chatter once more trickled into the hall.

"Well." Braggi snickered. "That was... something."

"Was I too harsh?" Beowulf gave a semi-sincere grimace.

It wasn't Braggi, but the woman across from her who answered.

"Oh, certainly not. Unferth is an ass. Nice to see him put in his place for once. And by a woman, no less." She grinned, a grin that Beowulf couldn't help but return before she drained her mug.

The sound in the hall rose once more as the evening waned, and soon Hrothgar's queen graced the visitors with her presence. She entered from the back of the hall, fine robes of pale brown swirling about her. She was younger than Hrothgar by a span of years, her light eyes bright and her auburn hair tied back, revealing a gilded necklace that hung about her throat. As was a customary welcome, she presented a goblet of mead first to her husband and king, before carrying goblets through the hall and meeting each of the visitors with words of welcome.

She swept through the warmth and idle chatter, offering the goblet to each warrior present. The queen reached Beowulf last, seated at the end of the table as she was, nearest to the king and at the end of the queen's path. Beowulf offered a small bow as the woman held the goblet forward and spoke.

"My name is Wealtheow." She smiled as Beowulf carefully accepted the goblet, the warrior's rough hands only just brushing those of the queen. "I have heard of your feats in service to Lord

Hygelac. You are a most welcome guest on these shores and in this hall. Truly, the gods have blessed us this day and brought you to our aid."

It was a formality, spoken loudly enough for everyone in the hall to hear. As with boasting, there was a sour taste to the back of Beowulf's mouth as she responded in kind. But her boast and her pledge were her word, and both blades and words could win allies and make enemies. Beowulf had long since learned to use both.

"My thanks, good queen. I cannot speak for the gods, but the plight of your people is not one we could suffer to leave unanswered. I have made my pledge, and I stand by it." She spoke loudly, passing the goblet back as she did. Wealtheow beamed her approval before returning to sit at Hrothgar's side as the feast was finished.

Braggi spoke from near Beowulf's elbow. "She seems a kind soul. I know little about her, but she doubtless has the bearings of a fine queen."

"She does," the woman opposite Beowulf answered. "She has always looked after our people. Her sons will make fine rulers one day."

Braggi glanced at Beowulf. The darkness in his eyes told her his thoughts as he looked up to where the queen sat. That lineage was not as secure as any in that hall would like to think. War came often and swiftly between clans, and Hrothgar's failing kingship might welcome other dangers beyond Grendel into that hall. Treachery was never far behind a jealous fighter's heart.

Beowulf looked back at Unferth, seated by the fire and scowling drunkenly into his mug. He was the king's nephew, and should any ill befall the king's sons, he was the next in line for the throne. Even if Beowulf succeeded in purging the monster from that hall, the legacy of Hrothgar's bloodline was weakening, if not altogether spent.

Beowulf pushed the welfare of Wealtheow's sons from her mind. That was for a future she did not plan to linger in those lands to see. She had a boast to carry through, and the night had already descended upon them. The feast had finished, and the chatter in the hall had faded. The long shadows cast across carved pillars and stone flooring had become suddenly ominous, and unlike the usual mead-heavy drowsiness that often descended on a hall after feasting, the air here became brittle with a gnawing fear.

Only once the guards and Hrothgar's warriors within the hall had begun to shift where they stood or sat did the king rise. He made his way to where Beowulf was sitting as those of his house rose and gathered what belongings they had.

"Never have I left the care of this hall to another," he said to Beowulf as she stood slowly amid the sound of movement in the hall. "I name you hall warden for the night. May the gods grant you victory." His expression was stern, his brows knitted. He reached forward and the two clasped forearms briefly, before Wealtheow leaned forward and bestowed her favor in the form of a kiss on Beowulf's forehead.

The king and queen slowly departed the hall, their retainers and warriors in tow, walking out into the moonless night beyond. Beowulf and her followers bid farewell to the warriors they had shared their meal with, exchanging nods as Hrothgar's fighters trickled out into the dark until they were the only ones left in the hall. They gathered their weapons, and each cleared a space on the floor for sleeping. The great tables were pushed aside, opening the center of the hall and clearing space around the fire for whatever the night might bring.

Beowulf threw a hide down on which to sleep and began stripping her armor. The other warriors removed their heavier cloaks, though most chose to wear their mail to sleep, a caution against that prowler of the night that would soon be among them. They kept their weapons close and spoke little among each other as they doused the lights within the hall. Only the hearth fire remained, casting shadows across the floor.

Beowulf peeled off her boots and jerkin, pulled off her ring-mail shirt, and removed the light wool tunic she wore beneath. She had lived her life among warriors, and few things were kept secret when they took rest or tended to wounds. She stripped without shame until she stood topless and barefoot on the stone floor, wearing only a rough pair of leather trousers. Firelight played across the markings of scars on her skin that traced like ropes over her ribs and back, and across her arms.

Anyone who saw her would have guessed she was a warrior, if not for the memories of wounds across her body, then by her sturdy build. Like the others, she looked like one who could swing a sword as quickly and easily as downing a mug of ale, and while her body was not without its feminine curves, it showed an uncommon strength. She pushed her braids back, flicking her thick hair over her shoulders, and sat for a time, watching the others bed down for the night. Many set their shields behind them to lean against, but true to her word, Beowulf went without shield or sword. She handed both, along with her helmet, to Braggi.

"You're certain?" he asked as he placed them by the wall.

Beowulf tilted her head as she regarded him. "Of course. I keep my word."

Braggi glanced at some of the other warriors before lowering his voice. "You're not frightened?" There was something almost mischievous in his eyes and teasing in his voice as he spoke, and Beowulf snorted and pushed his shoulder in response.

"My days of fearing death were over when I became a warrior. When you learn it is not an ending but a doorway, it does not grip you with the dread it once did."

"Wisely said." He chuckled and nodded. "Though even warriors are seldom above fear of dying. Myself included." He shrugged. "Sometimes."

Beowulf flashed a knowing smile. "There is an arrow coming for all of us, Braggi. It's not something we can escape. All we can do is choose whether we take it in our back or in our chest."

He laughed outright at that. "Indeed, but I for one would like to live to see the dawn. I've not yet had my fill of fighting and fucking, at least if I have any say in it."

"Don't forget the drinking," she added with a wry glance.

"Ah, that too."

She felt it then, the faint prickle of fear at the back of her mind. She flexed her fingers and breathed deep the warm air, smelling the smoke of the fire. The fates were not hers to understand, but she felt almost certain that this night would not be her last. It was still not enough to banish doubt completely from her mind. She quieted the small twitch of worry, reminding herself of the vow she had made the first time she ever touched a sword: win or lose, she would always give her all in the face of any odds.

Her hand wrapped unconsciously around the necklace that hung against the bare skin of her chest. The flat piece of iron was smoothed from touch, though the engraved icon of a downward-pointed sword was still visible at its center. She took a deep breath. Fear fled before her as she made her way back to where she had laid out the hide on which she would sleep.

The hall grew closer to silence with each moment, until the hushed air was slowly filled with the steady breathing of those who had already drifted off. She waited for a time, occasionally peering to where the great door of Heorot was left ajar. She could see the watchman's torch, a tiny flickering spot of light in the shaft of night beyond.

Her fingers played with some of the bone beads that fastened the ends of the braids festooned through her hair as she waited for her mind to grow still. Sleep never came easily on the edge of a battle, but it would have been a lie to say she was afraid anymore. Terror might keep even the most stalwart warrior awake, but it was anticipation, not dread, that played through her mind and prickled down her spine each time she gazed to where that mighty door yawned open to the night.

She had brought only her most skilled warriors with her, those she trusted with her life and who she knew would finish the job if the night brought her death. They found sleep, even if it was light and fitful in the face of the night stalker that came for them. There was not a weak heart among them, and the travel-weary war band found rest under that seemingly doomed roof. Even Beowulf, after a time, allowed the weight of their journey to descend on her fully. Sleep pulled at her, drawing her under, and she curled by the fire and drifted into a dreamless slumber.

Chapter 3

Something woke her in the middle of the night, pulling her from fitful sleep. Every nerve in her body seemed to jolt at once, and the hair on her neck and arms stood on end. She didn't move, instead holding cautiously still, taking in as much of the room as she could see without turning her head.

She had rolled slightly as she slumbered, twisting toward the now-dead fire, where the hot coals cast a ruddy glow about the interior of the hall. The light pulsed with the flickering of the remaining embers, throwing long shadows into corners and playing across the carved pillars. She could see most of her band from where she lay, sleeping figures scattered throughout the middle of the room. The chests of her comrades rose and fell as they drifted through the realms of a shallow, expectant slumber.

She could feel her body straining at being kept so still. Something was telling her to move. To stand. To run. As her eyes mostly adjusted to the gloom, she breathed evenly and scanned the hall for any sign of movement. She could still see the door in the faint light from a torch that had been set into the wall by the night watchman. His silhouette was visible where he slumped slightly against the wall. The angle seemed odd, and she looked for a long moment before her breath caught in her throat and her jaw tightened. He had fallen asleep.

The pace of her heart quickened as she glanced through the still hall. Seeing nothing, she turned her attention to her other senses. Alarm prickled over her skin. Beneath the soft snores and the crackle of the coals, she heard it. A long, slow, rhythmic breathing. Slower than any human, it burbled oddly, as though its owner had water in their lungs. She listened, the slow watery sound heralding dread as she looked to the shadows near the edge of the hall, the fire between her and whatever it was.

No moonlight shone through the windows that night, and the darkness in the corners of the hall was deep. Something moved there, the shape of which she could not quite make out as it slowly passed between the pillars, frighteningly silent for its size. She squinted through half-closed eyes. It had not seemed to notice she had woken, and that was an advantage she was keen on keeping.

Then the shadow took shape, and the firelight glinted on wet skin the color of dark moss. Even with its stooped back, it stood some seven feet tall, and it moved with uncanny silence. It was mostly humanlike, but bigger, and somehow twisted. Its shoulders and torso were thick and sinewy, with muscled arms hanging so low that the long claws on the end of its fingers nearly scraped the floor. The flesh that covered its body was slippery looking, and it carried with it the stench of rot and swamp mire. Thick and matted hair hung down past its shoulders and covered portions of its face. Through the dark mane, two glimmering eyes glowed a menacing red, and even at a distance Beowulf could see the sharp teeth in its mouth, so large they protruded out past its lips even when its jaw was closed.

Beowulf held herself still as Grendel emerged from the shadows, looming over the sleeping warriors. The monster surveyed the bodies sprawled before him, and she quietly hoped he would draw closer.

Instead, he pounced like a wildcat.

Terrifyingly quick and quiet for his size, the monster lunged forward, and Beowulf's cry stuck in her throat as he descended on one of the men below. He lifted him like a ragdoll, and he was already in the monster's mouth by the time he woke. His strangled cry, mixed with Beowulf's yell, roused the hall into a frenzied panic as Grendel devoured the man's head and the upper half of his chest, as the rest of his body dropped to the floor in a heap.

By the time the others had found their feet, Beowulf had already closed the distance between them. Leaping nimbly over alarmed fighters, she crossed the stone flooring and sprang over the remains of the fire that blocked her path. Heat bloomed beneath her for an instant, before her feet were on the floor again and the monster was within reach. Caught off guard by her rapid approach, Grendel swung his arms, one after the other, claws raking the air.

Beowulf ducked the first blow and blocked the second, holding her forearms up like a shield against the beast's wrists as he swung toward her. Despite his strength, she stopped all the force behind his strike, his guttural grunt of surprise bolstering her courage as she pushed his arm wide and drove her fist into the soft flesh of his gut. He stepped back before lunging in again, grabbing for her with his long limbs. She deflected both of his strikes, and her bare arms stopped his blows like tree trunks. She was more reserved in her own onslaught, instead observing him and dodging or blocking each swing he made.

The surrounding warriors made no move to intervene beyond safeguarding their own lives. Only one strayed too close, and Grendel struck him with a kick that sent the man tumbling clean over the hearth to crash into where the benches had been moved. No mortal could boast even a fraction of that strength, enough to rip up a fully grown tree by the roots, and Grendel knew it as well as any other. That is, no mortal *should* have been so strong. His sickening glee had faded the moment Beowulf matched him, and his grin had turned to a snarl.

Beowulf, for her own part, could not keep the corner of her mouth from curving into a smile. She could feel the cold ground beneath her bare feet, feel heat from the coals and every muscle that moved beneath her skin as she sprang and dodged. Never did she feel so alive than when she came so close to death. Whether she was fighting with a sword in her hand, or nothing at all, it did not matter. Time slowed around her as her heart pounded in her chest and she exchanged blow for blow with her monstrous opponent. The two of them moved slowly around the hall as he clawed at her, occasionally splintering benches or toppling one of the tables in a great shower of shattered wood.

The warriors kept their distance, weapons at the ready but mostly occupied with staying out of the way of the two combatants. Anyone unlucky enough to get caught by a claw or foot went tumbling as the two foes crashed through the hall. A few of the most daring took a swing with their blades if Grendel drew too close, but the blows glanced off his skin as though it were made of stone. Grendel paid them no mind as their strikes bounced harmlessly off his hide. He was far more occupied with the woman who grappled with him, harrying him with blows as she deftly outmaneuvered him.

As the tide of the fight turned ever more against Grendel, Beowulf carefully positioned herself between the monster and the door, blocking his escape. Though she could hear her warriors shouting, she couldn't discern their words over the pounding of her heart in her ears. Grendel's snarl grew more grotesque with each blow she blocked or dodged, until he roared and lunged forward, driving his entire body weight into her and knocking her back. She kept her footing, barely, struggling against him as he raked a set of claws along the outside of her ribs. Ice-sharp pain turned red hot as she leaped back out of range, her side growing warm where crimson spilled across her bare skin.

Grendel breathed deep, his nostrils flaring and his eyes regaining some of their glow as he smelled her blood on the air. He snarled and leaped forward again, but she was too quick. She ducked under his arm, her hair flying behind her, and brought her knee into his ribcage. Only those closest heard the pop of breaking bones, but all heard Grendel's roar. He struck her across the shoulder in retort, but his claws failed to find purchase as she tumbled and rolled before springing to her feet again.

The monster whirled, eyes now wide with something Beowulf dared to think of as fear, and he lurched sideways, his gaze sliding to the door of the hall. She ran at him before he could flee, taking three great strides across the stone floor before launching herself against him, driving an elbow into his chest. His arms closed about her, but before he could lift her from the ground, she drove her heel into one of his knees, forcing him further down to the ground as he howled in pain. The two strained against each other as she wrapped her arms around his shoulder. He roared and squirmed, his eyes set on the door as he tried to pull away.

Beowulf gripped Grendel's shoulder, her arms wrapped around his as she struggled to keep her grip. His skin was clammy and damp, as if a thin film of algae covered every inch of flesh. She leaned into him, his free arm clawing the air wildly as he reached for her head. She took a deep breath, steadying her feet on the floor, then threw all her strength against his arm and twisted. A mighty yell echoed through her chest and her voice filled the hall as she wrenched with all her might. There was a thick, wet, tearing sound, as with her bare hands she tore Grendel's shoulder, ripping his arm free of his body in a spray of hot dark blood. Grendel let out a scream, a panicked burbling cry that sent a chill through all who heard it. His shriek echoed out beyond the hall and into the night like the wail of a wraith as he howled his pain and fear into the moonless night.

His cry diminished to pained gurgling, Grendel broke free of Beowulf's grasp and stumbled toward the door. No longer the stealthy stalker of the night, his strides were broken and unsteady. One clawed hand clamped over the gaping wound torn in his shoulder as he loped in his ungainly manner from the hall of Heorot. Out into the night he staggered, trailing blood out into the dark as he fled back toward the wild moors from which he'd come.

Beowulf stood, her chest heaving as she looked at the path her quarry had taken. Her skin felt as if it had been touched by lightning and she was buzzing from the fight, her pulse hammering in her ears. A mighty cry went up from her war band, filling the hall with the sound of victory as the fire in her eyes slowly diminished. The muscles of her shoulders loosened, the rise and fall of her chest slowing as her breathing settled. The world around her steadied once more, and the pain from her side finally made itself known in earnest as she wiped some of the blood from her face and walked to a nearby bench.

Braggi came to where Beowulf was sitting and offered her an herb pouch and some rough linen that she might bind the wound in her side. She accepted gratefully.

"That was impressive." He grinned as she set to work packing moss onto the wound. It was long, but not overly deep, and it only took her a few moments to wrap it sufficiently. She left her chest bare, sweat and blood still glistening on her skin.

"Glad you think so. That makes one of us. Wasn't nearly as final as I would have liked." She frowned as she wiped her brow. "I should have liked to give his head to Hrothgar."

"Does it matter?" Braggi grunted. "That wound was fatal. We all know it. He likely did too." Braggi glanced out in the direction of the door, where the watchman who had fallen asleep had entered somewhat sheepishly and was surveying the hall.

Many of the tables and benches were nothing more than piles of splintered wood. The pillars were still standing, but in his haste to escape Grendel had knocked one of the great doors most of the way off its hinges. The hall needed repairs, though all that could wait until morning. There was only one other matter that preoccupied Beowulf, more so than the monster's escape, and she set her attention to it as she stood and crossed the hall to where the beast had first struck.

The body of one of their band still lay on the floor in a pool of scarlet. Beowulf and the others set to work, carefully placing their fallen comrade up on one of the still-intact tables. She did not doubt that Hrothgar would accommodate a pyre. He would likely see it as a small price to pay for the defeat of the creature that had brought such grief and bloodshed to his halls.

A prize had already been won, and Beowulf took the time to retrieve it. Grendel's arm still lay where she had torn it from him, fingers curled and claws reddened by her own blood. She tied it with ropes tossed through the rafters and hoisted the grizzly trophy to hang behind the seat of the king, a testament to her victory.

They cleaned the hall enough for sleep, and Beowulf exchanged brief words with Hrothgar's watchman that the king might know what transpired before he returned at daybreak. Braggi banked the coals of the fire as they settled down around it to seek rest, which this time they found more easily and deeply than before. Beowulf pulled on her light wool tunic, moving it gingerly over her wound, and resigned herself to try to catch what sleep she could before dawn. The others had better luck, and once again she found herself the only one awake, or so she thought.

It was not the claws or teeth of Grendel that played at the edges of her thoughts, not his stench or strength, or the burning red in his eyes. Her mind strayed to the dead warrior, one among them who would not be making the journey back to his home in this world. She had not accounted for the monster's speed, and her mistake had cost her comrade his life. The more she turned it over in her mind, the more it sent doubt flickering in the edges of her thoughts.

"There's something keeping you awake."

Braggi's voice startled her from her thoughts, and she turned to where he lounged on his back, almost within arm's reach, his eyes barely open.

"Have you just been staring this whole time?" she asked, shifting slightly to cross her arms over her middle.

"Tried to doze, but I trust your instincts better than theirs"—he gestured vaguely around him to where the others slept—"and so long as you don't trust sleep, I won't either."

"It's not like that." She shook her head, lips pursed as she looked down toward her feet, her brows knitted in a frown.

"Then what is it?" he asked with a grunt.

A long silence stretched out between them, and Beowulf pulled her arms more tightly over her middle. Finally, after a long sigh, she spoke again.

"It's Einar. I had the chance to wake you all, and I didn't. That beast was faster than I expected, but if I had—"

"Don't." Braggi's voice was firm, but not unkind. He shook his head as he looked over at her. "You always do this to yourself, Wolf."

Her frown deepened. "It's my duty to protect my kith and kin. I've always been proud to be a warrior, but there is more to it than swinging a blade."

"Much more. It is in all our words and deeds, in how we treat others and govern ourselves. But you cannot protect everyone. None of us can."

She sighed again, before offering a small and mirthless smile. She wondered silently to herself if she would ever walk away from slaying a beast without a single doubt in her mind. The world was seldom as simple as good and evil, and though fighting beasts came more easily than fighting humans, it still weighed on her. She was a protector, and she was a killer. While the first was much harder, it was the part that had always mattered the most to her.

"I know you're right." She untangled her arms and scrubbed her hands over her face. "But it still troubles me."

"Save yourself the heartache. This is part of our lives as warriors and I would have thought you were used to it by now."

"I am. Just because I am used to it doesn't make it easy all the time," she replied quietly.

Braggi snorted. "Just some of the time." His tone was light and joking, and though it brought a small smile to her lips, it did little to ease her mind. She stared at the glowing coals a while longer, and Braggi shifted himself onto his back. She had at least seemed to satisfy his concern about lurking danger, and within a few minutes she could hear his snores drifting from where he lay in the gloom. She took a deep breath and rolled onto her side, forcing her eyes shut even if her thoughts were slow to release her from their grip.

***

Fitful sleep found her eventually, not long before dawn light streamed into the hall. Shafts of morning shone through the small windows of the eastern wall, illuminating the destruction of the night before. Already, the followers of Hrothgar had begun to return, and Beowulf and her warriors helped move the unbroken tables to their proper place. Once the worst of the damage was cleared, some of the servants provided them a morning meal. Villagers slowly trickled into the hall as the morning wore on, whispers and shouts echoing as all who entered caught sight of the bloody prize hung above the seat of the king.

Hrothgar finally returned to the Heorot along with his retainers. He approached Beowulf first, as he surveyed the hall, seeming unbothered by the damage beneath his roof. Even the door, swinging precariously as it was, had not seemed to trouble him. He strode up to Beowulf and embraced her, before patting her hard on the shoulder and turning to speak to the hall at large. His voice stopped the work within, servants and warriors alike pausing where they had begun to clear the damage.

"Never has a more noble warrior dwelt beneath this roof. Send the messengers to the nearby clans. Let all know of what has transpired here!"

A boisterous shout from the warriors answered him and the flurry of activity resumed. Despite the work that lay ahead, the mood was noticeably light, and the promise of celebration seemed only to improve it. Hrothgar turned back to Beowulf, his eyes bright for the first time since she had seen him. Indeed, he seemed years younger since only the night before.

"Good thane, you would honor my hall if you would let us hold a feast to celebrate yourself and your kin."

Beowulf felt her ears grow hot. She knew a celebration meant an aggrandized retelling of the battle, and one she would be expected to tell proudly. Tradition was the cost of the king's favor, and it was expected of her as much as any other warrior. She gritted her teeth and gave a slightly stiff nod.

"My warriors and I would be most grateful. It would also be a fitting means to honor the one we lost."

"Excellent! We shall have songs and games to celebrate." Hrothgar clapped his hands, seeming untroubled by the death of the warrior that still weighed on her mind. She could not blame him; her kinsman was the least of his concern. "I will send word to the nearby lords. Many can be here before dark. Tonight shall be a feast to remember!" He clapped his hands and turned on his heel, giving commands to those closest to him to send out messengers.

A throng of villagers made their way to the hall, many carrying wooden planks and hammers that they might repair at least some of it in time for the coming festivities. The warriors, Beowulf among them, left Heorot as it filled with all the hands the village could spare.

Braggi and the others gathered wood for a pyre, while Beowulf and three more of their number carried Einar's body between them. All of Einar's shield mates made their way quietly down from the hill, out beyond the walls and into the fields beyond. Wood was stacked, the fallen warrior's items laid with him, and by midday the flames of the pyre crackled loudly beneath the light of a weak sun. There was no priestess left in Heorot to preside over the rites, so Beowulf and the others spoke aloud together, recounting the man's deeds and calling the All-father to welcome him into the realms beyond.

After the fire had burned low and as the sun began to sink in the western sky, some of Hrothgar's fighters came and joined their visitors beyond the village walls. It was a chance to pay their respects, and to share stories beyond those they had exchanged at the meal the night before. Some of Hrothgar's fighters began short bouts of horse racing for the entertainment of their guests, and they spent what remained of the day away from the flurry of activity in the great hall.

Beowulf sat on the grass, enjoying the breeze and the faint sunlight and watching the horses circling the village, seeming to fly across the green fields. It was still late spring, and even in full daylight the air was cool and crisp, with nights cold enough to leave frost on the ground. The last snows had not yet fallen, but clear days like this brought the promise of summer. Some of the children from the village, who had snuck away from the work at the hall, had gathered to watch as well, though most of them were looking at Beowulf. None approached her, and most fled if she made eye contact, but to those who held her gaze she always flashed a playful grin.

"That was well done," called a voice behind her. It was the woman she had sat across from the night before. The warrior was only wearing a tunic, no armor needed for festivities, and her fair hair was woven into a singular braid which ran along the top of her head and down between her shoulder blades. She sat beside Beowulf with a huff and nodded back in the direction of the hall. "I can only imagine it was quite a fight."

"One of the hardest I've had in some time, I think." Beowulf offered some of the smoked meat Hrothgar's fighters had shared with her. "Remind me of your name?"

"Amma." The woman smiled, before raising an eyebrow. "I hear you ripped that arm off with your bare hands."

"I meant it when I said I would fight him without a sword. Turned out to be a good choice, too; no weapon could cut its hide. Some of my fighters had to defend themselves if Grendel strayed too close in the fight, and every blow they swung glanced harmlessly off that creature's skin."

Amma shuddered for a moment before a look of amusement settled on her face. "Still. I am sorry I missed it. I should have liked to see that. You should have seen Unferth's face when he walked into that hall and caught sight of the arm."

"Took it a bit hard, did he?"

"Looked like he'd been slapped with a wet fish."

Beowulf snorted, trying and failing to contain her laughter, and the wound in her side protested with a twinge of pain.

Amma chuckled and tore off a hunk of the smoked meat. Beowulf leaned back on her elbows, enjoying the warmth on her skin and the smell of the grass as the soft chatter of the other warriors floated around them, accompanied by the distant sound of the horses' hooves. The smell of smoke from the pyre still hung in the air, faintly drifting on the breeze.

It was Amma who finally spoke again as she squinted out across the fields to where the horses ran. "It will be quite the feast tonight. Word has already spread quickly. I don't doubt every great house in the land will be singing songs about this within a fortnight."

Beowulf grunted. "The skalds always exaggerate. Makes for a better story I suppose, but it never sat right with me."

"And yet"—Amma glanced sideways as she spoke—"you tore the beast's arm off with your bare hands. That is not the strength that a mortal possesses."

There was something in her tone that made Beowulf turn to face her directly, her brows slightly furrowed. "I'm not some god in disguise, if that is what you are asking?"

"You may not be one, but you're more than any man here. How is this possible? I would have said it was just stories, but having seen that arm..."

"I was given a gift," Beowulf murmured quietly, picking at some of the grass. "When I was younger. Ironically, after the contest with Breca, which Unferth tried to mock me for. I was a skilled warrior before then, and I do not mean that as a boast. I was as good as any other, if not better. I worked hard, trained hard, fought hard." She looked at Amma, and something knowing passed between them. "You know how it is. It's difficult, as a woman. You work twice as hard for half the recognition sometimes."

Amma nodded. Her jaw tightened, and something in her gray eyes turned hard as steel. "Thankfully, once you prove yourself, it gets easier. You can earn respect on and off a battlefield, just as any other warrior. But you'll often be underestimated."

Beowulf nodded in agreement. "This is sometimes an advantage. But you know how it is. I climbed my way up through the mud and blood of battlefields. I was slaying giants before I was twenty winters old."

"I don't mean to insult." Amma placed a hand on Beowulf's shoulder. "I don't comment on your strength as the only justification for your prowess. I had heard stories, and you had already become something of a legend among your people if not mine as well. That was long before—"

"Something changed. Thank you, for not discrediting what I achieved without my gift."

"Of course. I know what it is like all too well. It's hard won and deserves recognition. Do you regret the... gift... that was given?"

Beowulf thought for a moment. She listened to the distant shouts of the warriors on horseback and breathed deeply, savoring the fresh air. A raven called from somewhere nearby, and a stillness stretched out between them for a time before she answered.

"No. Boasts and songs and stories may be the immortal legacy a warrior can leave behind, but I've always cared more about doing my duty than merely talking about it. This gift has let me help and protect people in ways that I could not before. That, to me, is worth my pride, if people wish to credit the gods for all I am capable of."

"For what it is worth"—Amma sighed and stuck a strand of grass between her teeth—"I think that anyone who isn't a fool knows well enough that gifts of such nature are seldom if ever given by the gods, and if they are, it's only to someone who has proven themselves worthy of the gods' favor." She lowered her voice to a lighthearted whisper. "Which even among fine warriors almost never happens."

Beowulf snorted, and Amma raised an eyebrow, turning to face her, though the thane continued to gaze out at the fields. "What?" Amma asked, "You don't think so?"

Beowulf frowned. "It's not that. I just never much enjoyed all the attention it brought me."

Amma burst into laughter, and Beowulf finally turned back to her, looking slightly confused.

"I have bad news for you," Amma managed between hearty chuckles. "You were a fine warrior before your gifts, and that would have brought you attention enough. As it is, you're bordering on becoming a legend. You might want to get used to the attention."

Beowulf could only scoff and shake her head. Still, Amma's amusement, more so than her words, brought a smile to her lips.

"In fact," Amma continued, dropping her voice in a slightly more conspiratorial manner, "there's been a lot of talk among the warriors about your deeds. That's the actions of a leader there. You protected these people, destroyed that which plagued the hall of our king. Our king who was powerless to stop it."

Beowulf sat bolt upright, her expression darkening as she spoke. "Such things should not be said, even in jest. Hrothgar is a fine king. He has done well for his people, and this monster was not of his making, nor was the misfortune he suffered."

"I do not speak ill of my king; please don't misunderstand. I only wish to let you know that you've earned yourself a great deal of favor and loyalty among the warriors here. Myself included." Amma's gaze searched Beowulf's face before slowly dropping to her lips and lingering for the briefest moment.

Beowulf's brows remained knitted, but the corner of her mouth quirked into a small grin before she looked over Amma's shoulder to where some of the other warriors sat. Amma continued talking, her voice low. "I am sure there are those who doubt you, or who distrust you, but when you prove yourself in battle as you have done, you earn the loyalty of many. You're a fine warrior, Beowulf."

Beowulf chewed the edge of her lip before looking back at Amma. "I fear for the future of this kingdom, I don't deny. I know I am not the only one. The other warriors know and trust you more than they do me. I would ask that you make it known that I serve your king loyally, and I believe he deserves the love and loyalty of all his kin."

Amma gave a small nod, frowning slightly as she did, before the two of them turned their gaze once more to the band of horses racing through the late afternoon light. By dusk the feast would likely begin, attended by any lords who could make the journey in time. Even as they sat and idled in the fields, a shadow grew in the back of Beowulf's mind as she looked out across the grassy hills and forests. Something ill still stirred in these lands, though whether it was beyond the village walls or within Heorot itself, she could not say.

Chapter 4

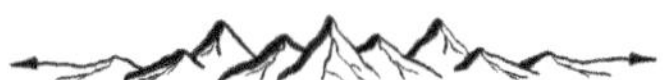

True to his word, Hrothgar procured a feast of special magnificence. The hall was cleared of all remnants of battle, the stone floor scrubbed and cleaned of splintered wood. Some of the broken tables and benches were replaced, as many as could be built in a single day. The scratches on the large wooden pillars and places where stone had been chipped by Grendel's claws remained, a testament to all that transpired beneath that roof.

As the sun sank low in the sky, those who could make the journey arrived with their warriors and kin. Nearly a half dozen lords came, making their way out of the night with their retainers and into the warm and glowing hall. Three skalds came to perform, and while they sang songs of gods and heroes of old, each took the time to compose a tune in honor of Hygelac's thane, slayer of beasts and defender of Heorot.

Grendel's arm still hung high in the hall, a grizzly spectacle for all to see, proof of the monster's demise. For the first time in many months, Heorot was once more filled with laughter and song, the benches and tables crowded the entire length of the hall. Mead and food was shared aplenty and servants threaded their way among the crowd. Children ran between the tables, their laughter ringing off the walls, often accompanied by some of the dogs. All found welcome and joy, untroubled by fear beneath that gilded roof.

Beowulf and her warriors sat as they had before, close to the feet of the king, who dined with his wife and two sons,

Hrothmund and Hrethric. Dark-haired like his father, Hroth-mund, the eldest was making his best attempt at growing a full beard, though he had a few years to wait. He could not yet have been Beowulf's age, likely only just entering his teenage years, but even younger men had become kings in their time. Wealtheow sat beside her husband, all four of them at the head table, overlooking the hall once more filled with the local clan leaders and their finest fighters.

The sound of the skald's voice carried above the chatter, weaving a tune of some of the past kings of Hrothgar's house, praising the deeds of the beast slayer who came to the aid of Heorot. Beowulf, for her part, mostly fixed her gaze on the bottom of her mead horn. One night of boasting had been enough and she was already beginning to feel like an animal in a cage. She could sense the eyes on her in the crowded hall. The voice singing her praise was part of the life she had come to know, but she had never grown to like it. She longed in that moment, more than anything, to be able to breathe the cool air of the night and see the stars, but alas, a warrior's duty was not on the field of battle alone. At least she knew she had done well in securing an ally for her king, and in that she took pride. Beyond that comfort, it helped her mood to see that Unferth had joined the festivities and was wearing an expression that suggested he had a mouthful of raw turnip.

Round after round of mead was shared, until Hrothgar stood and the hall slowly grew quiet. He raised his horn aloft and spoke in a voice far stronger and younger than any Beowulf had heard him yet use.

"Hail to the hero of Heorot, slayer of beasts and protector of my kith and kin. Hail, the thane of Hygelac for her might and her honor. Hail, Beowulf!"

"Beowulf!" the hall shouted as one. Her name echoed in a loud roar that filled the room. She kept her eyes on the king as he looked toward her, forcing from her mind the knowledge of how many were watching her.

Hrothgar once more spoke to the room at large. "Long had Grendel haunted this hall, filling this greatest of houses with blood and slaughter and grief. Agony was upon me, for all wisdom and craft of war failed to stop this or protect those who dwelt beneath this roof. Surely, the gods have favored us, for one came to our aid and did what no mortal man could do. I honor you, Beowulf." He turned back to where she sat frozen, keeping her gaze on him. "I honor the woman that brought you into this world, for she has gifted us with a hero of legends. Often have I honored lesser deeds, and even the mightiest of warriors could not achieve what you have done."

Braggi leaned close from where he sat next to Beowulf and whispered, "You think he's been enjoying the mead a bit too much? Seems a bit... enthusiastic."

She kicked him under the bench and made no reply.

The king continued. "Beowulf, I say this now as king of these lands—you shall want for nothing. You have earned all rewards that I can bestow. I take this vow now before my people that they might know it, and I say that from this day forth I consider you as my daughter. I think of you as my own, and in all ways I might aid you and reward you, I shall."

There was a roar of approval. Beowulf felt something tighten in her chest, a sudden twinge, as she looked up at the king. He had been generous, incredibly generous, and while she had her judgements, she did not blame him for his misfortunes. But the nagging fear at the back of her mind reared its head as her gaze drifted momentarily to the king's sons. The house of Hrothgar had not yet suffered the stain of feuds or betrayal. She quietly murmured a prayer to the All-father that it might remain that way.

Her thoughts whirled so loudly in her own head that she almost forgot her formalities. It was her turn to speak. Conscious of the eyes on her, she stood slowly and took a deep breath. Her voice did not falter as she spoke.

"Good king. You honor me, and I accept. It was a bloody battle in the end, and not without cost. I thank you also for giving us leave to honor the life of the warrior who fell to Grendel and for allowing us a pyre that we could send him to the high hall before we depart." There were several nods from around the room. "I wish only that I might have slain the beast and left you his body on the floor of this hall. As it is"—she gestured up to where Grendel's arm hung—"his wound will be the death of him, and his body will rot in the mire he called his home."

Another cheer went up in the hall, this time accompanied by the hammering of fists against the heavy tables.

Hrothgar clapped his hands together in approval, his voice ringing out as soon as the ruckus had died down. "Now, let us commence with a reward for your services, and let the wealth be shared also among all those here who pay fealty to this great house as a gratitude for their loyalty."

A third cheer went up, the loudest yet. Hrothgar raised his horn once more.

"To the hero of Heorot. Hail!"

"Hail!" The room roared, mugs were raised and drained, and some of the chatter renewed, though in more hushed tones. The offering of rewards was a formal matter, and one to be observed without distraction. The king could display his wealth, while also doling out riches among all those who attended. It was an old tradition, one that helped cement allegiances and ensure a flow of wealth throughout the king's realm. Furthermore, as Beowulf well knew, both her actions and his would strengthen the bonds between Hrothgar's people and her own, the Danes of those shores and the Geats who dwelt across the sea.

With a gesture, Hrothgar called forth several servants, laden with goods to be brought before the hall so that all might see. As a token of thanks to the young warrior, he gifted her a new helm with polished iron in shapes likened to a wolf's ears on either side and gold enamel beaten into the details of the face plate—more a ceremonial possession than something to be worn on a battlefield. Along with it, he gave her a shirt of ring mail and a well-crafted blade. To her warriors, he offered fine spears and swords, before procuring a chest of gold, which he himself presented to Beowulf, who rose from her seat to accept it.

"A wergild, to honor the life of your man who died in service of this hall, for yourself and the king whom you serve. I give this to you with my favor and thanks."

Beowulf nodded her gratitude as she took the chest and stowed it along the bench with the others.

She was about to turn back to her seat when Wealtheow approached. The queen made her way across the front of the hall and met the warrior there amid the quiet conversation of the hall. In her hands she held a torque made of gold, the ends wound into tight spirals that shone in the light of the hall. As she offered the gift to Beowulf, the warrior could see concern in the lines of her fair face.

"An honor, and well deserved." The queen's voice seemed somehow tight, almost strained. "And a generous gesture of the king to accept you as his own. May he rule long and well. When his time comes, his crown will pass to his kin, and gods willing they will rule long after him." Her voice evened out the longer she spoke, but Beowulf could hear her fear and wondered if any others had heard it as well. "All-father favor you, thane, and may luck always find you."

Beowulf knew she wasn't the only one who feared the ways in which the haunting of Heorot had weakened Hrothgar's rule. There was not any distrust that she could see between the king and his nephew, kin-killer though Unferth was, but power twists hearts for ill only too quickly. Wealtheow feared for her sons, and rightfully so. The eldest may have entered manhood but he had not yet been tested by battle or war, and the youngest could not have been more than ten winters. Beowulf glanced up to where the two boys sat in idle conversation. She doubted they knew the danger they were in purely by being alive and being Hrothgar's blood. She feared for the future of that house, though she did not plan to stay.

Beowulf gently placed her hands over the queen's, meeting her gaze and trying her best to say with her eyes what her voice could not utter: *I know.* Wealtheow allowed a trembling smile to ghost across her lips before she nodded lightly and withdrew her grasp, leaving the torque in Beowulf's hands. Beowulf, again aware of how many eyes were upon her, turned and spoke to the hall at large, still holding the torque gingerly.

"I accept these goods with gratitude." She looked around the hall. "Gold and goods may bring us joy and plenty, but no treasure is more valuable to king or warrior than loyalty. Blessed be this house in the eyes of the gods while all company remains honor bound and true."

A soft cheer of agreement went up in the hall.

Beowulf looked once more to the queen, whose smile spoke of gratitude. She held Wealtheow's gaze for the briefest moment, before looking up to the table where Hrothgar sat with his sons.

She spoke slowly. "Further, as the king has taken me as one of his own, know that his sons too are my kin. Any who would pledge their loyalty to me, would pledge also to Hrothmund and Hrethric. They have their father's wisdom and will rule well in their time."

Another cheer, and as Wealtheow beamed and returned to the high table, Beowulf gestured to the two boys sitting beside their father. After a nod from the king, the two of them made their way down to the warriors' table, where Beowulf offered each a seat on either side of her. The two of them seemed more than eager to sit among the warriors, and both regarded Beowulf with a kind of quiet awe as they took their seats beside her and the skald once more filled the hall with the sound of music.

With the formalities concluded, the noise in the hall rose once more. The boys spoke little, mostly listening intently to the idle conversations between the warriors. It was Hrethric, the youngest, who finally spoke, eyeing Beowulf timidly as he did.

"Have you slain many monsters? I've heard the stories. Are they all true?"

"Some of them." Beowulf grinned at him over her mug. "Most of them. Though I don't doubt the skalds exaggerate a bit. They might claim I wrestled a giant for three days on end, when it was likely closer to three minutes."

"I should like to do the same, I think." Hrethric beamed. "I'm less interested in the throne. I would rather be a warrior—that way I could slay my enemies and defeat monsters."

Beowulf felt something twist in her gut at the delight in which the young boy spoke of killing. She remembered that feeling herself. She reckoned many warriors did. It was only after she had taken her first life that her desire for bloodshed had waned and she, like so many other warriors, came to think of it differently. The horror and grief of warfare was all too often left out of the songs. You wouldn't learn the full force of what you had wrought until there was blood on your hands. She had been a foundling, and for her it had come when she was thirteen. There had been a battle between clans in the summer before her first moon. She had killed her first man before she had even become a woman.

"Monsters are easier," she said, her expression darkening slightly as she spoke. "But remember, there is much, much more to being a warrior than to taking a life."

Hrethric nodded. "It's like father always says, being a good warrior is like being a good king. You think before you act, you protect the weak, you look out for your kith and kin."

"Indeed. And you never take a life needlessly. I fight first and foremost to protect, to help others. It's part of why I have made a name for myself hunting monsters. Any warrior knows well enough that they cannot protect everyone, but they do the best they can." She took a deep breath and looked back up to the high table for a moment, before leaning close to both boys. "A good warrior acts honorably both on and off the field of battle and strives to be noble in both word and deed. If a day comes when you sit on the throne, remember first and always your duty is to protect. A wise king never seeks out war and keeps only those who he trusts with his life close by his side."

Hrothmund and Hrethric nodded. Satisfied for the time being, Beowulf leaned back and glanced once more up to where

Hrothgar sat at the head of the hall. Wealtheow looked for once even happier than the king, and as the night waned both occasionally smiled down toward where their sons sat. Beowulf was sure to keep the two heirs close, that all those in the hall might see her with them. Even if they had not won their people's loyalty, she had. She hoped it might be enough, but in her heart she doubted it, and something in her chest grew heavy when she thought about the future that awaited the house of King Hrothgar.

Some measure of her thoughts must have shown on her face, at least enough to be noticed by Braggi, who nudged her from across the table.

"Let's go see what the stars are making shall we?" He winked. Beowulf couldn't help but smile at that. She patted both of Hrothgar's sons on the back before she and Braggi stood and took a meandering path through the hall and toward the door.

"Formalities getting to you too?" Beowulf asked under her breath as they walked through the hall.

"A little. I'm lucky enough to not be the center of attention. I certainly don't envy you, though I think you did well with those lads."

"It's something," she mumbled. "I doubt it will be enough."

Braggi drained his mug and placed it on a nearby table as they reached the door. The two of them stepped out into the night, the cold air meeting them in a rush as they passed beyond the warmth of the hall. Guards stood posted at the entrance, so the two of them walked a short distance out of earshot. The door, restored to its hinges, rested open and cast a shaft of light out into the night beyond. Beowulf blinked as her eyes adjusted to the dim, and she breathed deep the crisp night air. The dark took shape around her, and the early summer constellations winked into existence in the sky above.

Braggi sighed heavily.

"It was a noble gesture. I don't think you and I are the only ones who worry about what will happen here in the years to come. I am sure the queen is grateful for what you did for her sons. Hrothgar seems either not to notice the peril they all are in, or he simply doesn't want to see it."

"I would guess the latter. He is not an unwise king, but he may yet be too trusting." Beowulf crossed her arms tightly over her chest, feeling the pull of her armor at her shoulders. If they stayed out much longer, she knew she would miss her cloak against the chill air.

"Well," Braggi said after a long silence, "I suppose what happens in these lands isn't so much a concern of ours. We've done what we can, you more than the rest of us. We have a king to return home to. One who I'm sure will be most pleased with the loyalties and renown we have helped secure."

"True." Beowulf tugged absentmindedly at the end of one of her braids as she spoke. Something loomed at the edges of her mind. She had thought it merely the messy politics of which they spoke, but now, beyond the hall, it had begun to feel like something else. She could not have explained it if she had tried, the same way she could not have said how or why she often knew she would survive a battle before she even entered it. The weakening of Hrothgar's house hung heavy in her thoughts, but beyond that, something threatening prowled at the edges of her mind. She could feel it now, as she stood beneath the open sky. It was as if the night held its breath. Something was coming.

"You alright?" Braggi's voice startled her from her thoughts.

"Mmm. Something worries me."

"From there?" He jerked his head back toward the hall. "Or something else?"

"I don't know. But I do not think the king and his family should sleep beneath this roof tonight." She frowned into the gloom. Her imagination conjured dim shapes out beyond the edges of the village, where the wind made ghostly waves on the sea of grass.

"We'd best tell him then," Braggi muttered as the two of them turned back toward the hall. He had known her long enough, fought with her often enough, that he had stopped questioning her instincts years ago. She smiled her gratitude at his back as they retraced their steps, once more entering the warm hall and blinking in the brilliance and noise that met them.

Beowulf relayed her message to one of the stewards, for already the skalds had finished their songs and guests had begun to move the tables and benches aside to bed down for the night. She and her band had long since made a habit of sleeping in their armor, and from the looks of it, many of Hrothgar's fighters had done the same. They claimed spaces on the floor, some reclining on their shields, while the company of the hall prepared for the night. Beowulf was relieved to see Hrothgar depart with his family, along with many of the villagers, trailing out into the night beyond as the hall grew quieter. She found a spot to sleep near the head table, a bit further from the fire, and bedded down in her armor with the rest of the warriors. Soft chatter still echoed through the hall as those within slowly dozed off, and the fire burned low.

Sleep was once more reluctant to find her, and agitated thoughts kept her from rest as she glanced about the hall. Her palms prickled as they often did before a fight, and while the death of Grendel brought peace of mind and heavy sleep to many of those around her, something would not let her rest. She kept her sword close, a comfort against her thoughts and worries, until the fire had dimmed to coals and the hall had filled with soft snores and steady breathing. Her eyelids finally grew heavy, and she drifted into a light and fitful slumber filled with strange dreams of half-glimpsed shadows.

Caution had been their best action, and she had hoped that she was wrong, that the worry she felt was some lingering remnant from her battle the night before.

***

She knew from the moment she woke that her instincts had been right. A loud scream dragged her from her dreams, and instinct forced her body to motion before her mind had caught up. She was hardly awake yet she was already standing, her sword drawn as warriors roused around her. Panicked cries filled the hall, and in the dim light she saw something fleeing toward the doors. It was large, larger than Grendel, and it had filled the hall with the smell of foul water, mud, and rot. It crashed through the doors and out into the night, disappearing even more swiftly than it had come.

Beowulf sprinted after it, dodging between warriors and panicked sleepers, trying to survey the room on her way. Nothing seemed smashed or destroyed; it was only when she drew nearer to the great doors that she saw the signs of death. There was a great smear of blood across the stone floor, drops trailing out the way the creature had fled. She gritted her teeth and followed them, the hall a roar of shouts and yells around her as the warriors followed her and spilled out into the night.

Somewhere beyond the hall a bell was ringing, the sound of metal and fear echoing out into the night as the village surged to life in the midnight hour. Beowulf scanned the dark, but neither she nor any of the others could find any sign of their quarry. Even with torches in hand, the only trail left was one of deep clawed footprints and spattered blood. The creature had fled into the night, taking with it its bloody prize, leaving only panic in its wake.

Beowulf cursed under her breath, gripped her sword tightly, and turned back to where some of the hall guards stood. She barked loudly, her voice cutting through the din.

"How is it that no one saw it?"

"We... there was nothing," one of the guards stammered. He looked to be middle-aged, his beard thick and dark. The knuckles of the hands that gripped his spear were ghostly white and shone with sweat. "There was nothing, no sound, none of us saw it. It was too quiet."

Beowulf tilted her head and snarled her frustration.

"I..." Someone spoke unsteadily near the wall to her left, and she turned to see the younger guardsman, propped against the wall and holding himself up with his spear. It looked to be the only thing keeping him on his feet, and his eyes were wide and glazed in the glow of the torches.

He spoke weakly. "I saw it. Not... not before... but when it came out."

Beowulf breathed deeply and let her shoulders drop, relaxed her grip on her sword, and turned back to the older guard.

"Has the king been told?"

"Yes." The man nodded. "He should be at the hall soon."

"Good." Beowulf sheathed her blade as she spoke. "See if you can find out who the monster killed." The man nodded and turned, making his way back toward the hall. The initial rush of warriors had died down amid curses and angry mutterings. Many now made their way back inside, while others began a slow round through the village, searching for any sign of whatever had descended upon them that night. Beowulf turned back to the young guard, still staring blankly ahead as he was, and placed a hand on his shoulder.

"What's your name?"

He turned to her and blinked, as if seeing her for the first time. "Hama," he croaked.

"What did you see, Hama?"

He swallowed hard, his voice trembling as he spoke. "It was big. I thought it was Grendel at first. I saw him that night he fled trailing blood back to his den. It was like him but... bigger. And it—" He broke off, frowning slightly. "She, I think it was. The same way Grendel looked like a man but twisted. She was tall, had claws and long teeth. Hair too, long hair that was wild as a thicket and dark as ink. And her eyes—" He shuddered and fell silent.

"That's enough. Thank you." She placed one hand on his shoulder and offered him her other, guiding him on his unsteady feet back to the warmth of the hall. Her mind raced as she walked and her jaw was tight, the fear in the air setting her teeth on edge. When she had sat Hama down on a bench and ensured he wouldn't tip over, she returned once more out into the night to examine the monster's tracks while she waited for the king to arrive.

She didn't have long to wait, but the panic had almost died down by the time Hrothgar arrived, sword on his hip. Wealtheow was there by his side, hair undone and wild. Both of her sons were close at hand, and they followed the king as he entered the hall and surveyed the damage. The area where blood was spilled had been cleared, and the rest of the hall was filled with warriors, many exchanging agitated and brooding conversation. Hrothgar swept through and spoke with a few of them before turning back to Beowulf.

"This new devilry has wounded me deeply." He spoke quietly, but it was anger, not sorrow, that burned in his eyes. "It has killed Aeschere, one of my oldest and truest friends, one who always counseled me wisely."

"I take fault upon myself." Beowulf spoke through a tight jaw. "You named me warden of this hall, yet one of your men was slain under my watch. I would—"

"Nonsense," Hrothgar muttered darkly. "I took back the mantle of hall guardian the moment you slayed the beast Grendel and freed us from his curse. It was my watchmen this new monster slipped by. My own guests, who thought themselves safe, who were in danger. I do not know what this is; I do not imagine Grendel survived his wounds."

"He didn't." Beowulf lowered her tone as the king looked at her with a raised eyebrow. "This was something else. Something like Grendel. A creature who I would wager took the life of your friend as recompense for my killing of one of her own."

Hrothgar stared, brows deeply furrowed in thought. "Do you think they are family? That they might share blood?"

"If I had to guess." Beowulf glanced briefly then at Wealtheow, who stood by the door, one arm wrapped tightly around her youngest son's shoulders. Hrothgar followed the path of her gaze, fleeting though it was. Realization dawned in his eyes as his expression darkened.

"You don't think... gods be good. His mother? Could it be such a thing?" His voice had become thin, reedy, and even Beowulf could not ignore the chills that the thought sent down her spine.

"It's only a guess. Would not the loss of a child drive any parent to rage and grief?" she asked, and the king's expression darkened. He nodded slowly. "I think," Beowulf continued, "that this killing was an act of vengeance. A single life only was taken, recompense for my slaying her son."

Hrothgar frowned. "That is ill news indeed. I do not know nor can I speak to the nature of these monsters. I know only where they might make their home, and even that is speculation." He swallowed, keeping his voice low. "There is a place, not a half day's ride from here, past one of the forests thick with frost even in spring. The wood there overlooks a lake—dark water even under the sun's light, but at night the whole of the surface burns as if on fire, and a foul smell rises into the air. None who have strayed there have ever returned. It is a god-cursed place, and evil things dwell there. I suspected that Grendel may have come from there. If there is indeed another like him who means to bring bloodshed to this hall..."

He trailed off, seeming lost in thought.

Beowulf opened her mouth to speak, but Hrothgar turned instead toward the warriors scattered throughout the hall, addressing the war band before him.

"Take what rest you can, good warriors. There is a time for grief, but it is not now. Now is a time for retribution. I will not see bloodshed and despair brought to my people again, less than a day from celebrating the restoration of this hall. Now is a time for vengeance."

A murmur of agreement rose among the warriors. Hrothgar looked at them each in turn as he slowly paced before them, hands curled into fists. Beowulf stepped forward. She knew what came next, she knew her duty, but something other than fear made her hesitate for only the briefest moment before she spoke.

"King Hrothgar, I pledge my service once more. As I freed this hall from the terror of Grendel, so I vow I will bring an end to this beast that comes hungering for vengeance for her brood's demise."

All eyes turned toward her, and some among her warriors offered small nods of approval. The promise of bloodshed seemed to banish whatever fear or doubt still lingered in the hall.

"I will take my retainers at daybreak," Beowulf continued. "If the king might grant us horses, we will ride to this creature's lair. There I will best it, as I did Grendel. It is a warrior's duty to win honor and legacy before death, the only semblance of immortality we are granted. I will overcome this she-beast or die trying."

A shout of approval echoed through the hall as the thane riled the room into conviction. Hrothgar had to raise his voice to speak above the cheers, his voice echoing above the chatter.

"Praise be the gods for sending you to us, Beowulf. Do this task and, as before, you will be richly rewarded. I will provide you and your company with horses at dawn, and some of my own fighters to ride with you."

The two clasped hands briefly, then the king turned and strode from the hall. The queen and her children followed, along with a few of the warriors, while the rest settled back into the hall in the hopes of at least a little rest before sunrise. Beowulf returned to her place near the end of the hall and leaned back against her shield.

She did not try for sleep, she knew she had no chance of finding it. Instead, she frowned toward the door and tried to picture in her mind the dark shape she had only just glimpsed as it had fled. She had been able to make out the legs and at least one arm, but even as she squinted at the open crack that led out into the night beyond, she still couldn't reckon the monster's size. It had been bigger than Grendel, certainly, but how much bigger she wasn't sure. Her mind seemed to play tricks on her in the half-light as she squinted, her arms tightly folded across her chest.

She eventually gave up trying to discern the beast's size, her thoughts drifting instead to the deep pool that Hrothgar had described, the lake beyond the frosted woods, where they would ride at dawn. The dark water conjured itself in her mind, still and quiet, reflecting the shapes of the tangled trees at its edge. She imagined diving, feeling the cold, the darkness that awaited her as she descended, and it sent a shiver down her spine despite the warmth of the hall around her. Deep waters and dark shadows swirled, reminding her of her contest with Breca and the fear she had felt when the sea beast had grabbed her ankle and dragged her down into the briny depths.

It was only when the first hinting of light crept softly in the windows and through the gap in the mighty door that her thoughts finally freed themselves from darker things. It would be some time yet before true sunrise, and the hall was still quiet. Only one other person stirred, a warrior, down near the door. He rose carefully and silently crossed the room toward her, careful not to rouse his resting brethren. It wasn't until he was halfway to her that she recognized him, and her jaw stiffened as her arms tightened where she had them crossed over her chest.

Unferth approached carefully, almost on tiptoe, until he stood before her, looking down with an oddly troubled expression on his face. His dark brows were knitted tightly together as his gaze flicked from Beowulf to the floor and back.

"May I sit?" he whispered quietly, and there was an odd hesitance about his manner that made some of the tension drop from Beowulf's shoulders. She nodded, and he carefully turned and sat beside her, worrying the bottom of his tunic with his fingers. He frowned deeply, seeming unsure of what to say, as the two of them sat in awkward silence for a long moment. It was Beowulf who broke the stillness first, her voice barely a whisper lest she wake any of the others.

"Did you manage any rest, Unferth?"

"Some. Not much." He shrugged. "It was nobly done. Your offer to hunt out this new monster." There was something he wasn't saying; his voice was almost pained. Beowulf sighed and sat fully upright. She had half expected him to make some snide comment, but he'd been quiet since Grendel's arm had been hung in the hall. Now he picked at the wool of the tunic beneath his mail, seeming to grapple with his own thoughts. Despite his hesitance, she wasn't about to prompt him. He'd been an arrogant host, and if he wanted to share more words with her he could damn well find them himself.

Unferth finally let out a long sigh and scrubbed his face wearily with his hands. "I've seen it," he said finally. "The place we're heading to at daybreak."

"'We?'" Beowulf raised an eyebrow.

"I'll be going with Hrothgar's men, along with your own. This is the land of the Danes, and we'd be poor hosts to leave you wandering it aimlessly."

"Kind of Hrothgar to lend us some of his warriors for the journey." She continued to stare out at the rest of the room, keeping her voice to a whisper. She waited a few moments while Unferth fidgeted uncomfortably at her side. When he spoke again, his voice faltered slightly.

"I don't doubt your honor—"

"Really? You have given me cause to think otherwise." She spoke tersely, trying her best to keep the vitriol out of her voice.

"Please listen." He turned toward her and she, somewhat irritated, turned toward him.

"Unferth, I understand you were drunk, but making a jealous mockery of a guest in your lord's hall goes against all the laws of hospitality. If Hrothgar hadn't had so many other troubles on his mind, I don't doubt he would have had choice words for you."

"I know." His voice raised slightly then, and it was more of a hiss than a whisper as he struggled to keep the urgency from it. "I know and I'm—"

He broke off and gritted his teeth. Beowulf took a moment to appreciate that the two of them were the only ones awake. She doubted he would have spoken in such a way had anyone else been privy to their conversation. When he found his voice again, it didn't falter and he managed, surprisingly, to hold her gaze.

"I'm sorry. I was wrong to speak in the way I did. Wrong to make a claim about a story I did not know the truth of. I was wrong to insult you when you came to the aid of this house."

Beowulf kept her surprise from showing on her face, but she relaxed her brows a little and softened her gaze as she regarded him. After a moment, she gave a slow and purposeful nod.

"I know I've not given you reason to listen to me," he continued, looking back out toward the hall, "but this place you're going, no one has ever entered those waters and survived."

"I've heard."

Whatever he found in her voice, it wasn't what he was looking for. She couldn't tell what he was pushing her toward, whether it was fear or something else. He sucked his teeth in a frustrated fashion before pressing on.

"I've seen hunts in those woods reach the water's edge. A stag will sooner turn and die facing the dogs than jump in those waters. There is evil there to be certain."

"Evil indeed, if the creature dwells there, which your king and his advisors all seem to think, given that it was likely near where Grendel lurked as well. If it is the creature's den, then of course I'm going. Heorot has seen its share of bloodthirsty monsters. It's time this kingdom had some peace." She regarded him darkly as she spoke, her fear for Hrothgar's sons once more rising in the back of her mind.

"There's a reason no one ventured there to kill Grendel. Even if we knew where the beast bedded down, there's not a mortal alive who could survive a journey into those depths. That was a realm of shadow we could not—cannot, touch."

"So," she sighed, "you mean to dissuade me from my quest?"

"No." He turned then, shaking his head slightly. "You've made your boast, and I wouldn't try to take that from you, I just"—he frowned—"would want you to know something of what you are getting into."

Beowulf raised her eyebrows as she regarded him. The entire conversation still felt odd, and unlike the side of him she had first encountered at their welcome feast. Unferth shifted next to her, and it took her a moment to realize he was unbuckling his scabbard from his belt. He turned and placed the blade, still in its sheath, down on the stone floor between them. The handle was well crafted and worn smooth with use, and the blade smelled of leather and fresh oil.

"Take this. When you make the plunge," he murmured, nodding toward the blade. "It's a fine sword. It will serve you well." When she eyed him curiously, he shrugged with a half-sad smile. "I have no great gifts to give befitting the deeds you have done for this house, and those you plan to do. This is something, however small it may seem. I would ask that you take it with my apology and with my thanks."

Beowulf stared at him. His eyes looked somehow brighter now than in that drunken haze the first night of their meeting. She could see no malice in them, and though she did not trust him, she could hear the wound to his pride in his voice, and in the truth with which he spoke. Alone as they were, she knew his words were meant for her and her alone, with no need or desire to impress, or express anything but that which weighed heaviest on his shoulders. He gestured to the blade as he spoke.

"It is called Hrunting. Never has it failed the hand of any who has used it in battle. It has been called upon in times of great need and always stood equal to the test. May it serve you well."

Carefully, she reached down and lifted the blade from the floor, drawing only an inch from the scabbard and examining it, tilting it in the light. It was well cared for and shone in the half-light of the coming dawn that filtered in through the hall. The handle fit her grip well enough, despite her hand being slightly smaller than the sword's usual wielder. She looked up and nodded her thanks, before placing Hrunting back down by her side. The first rustlings of waking warriors could be heard in the hall, but she dared to speak a bit louder.

"Hrothgar asked you to be part of the journey today?"

"No." Unferth shook his head and shifted, but made no move to stand as the hall slowly woke around them. "I asked to go." He must have felt her eyes on him then, as he turned back with another small smile. "You've done something I thought no man could ever do." He glanced back toward where Grendel's arm still hung above the high table.

She offered him a wry look in return. "I'm not a man."

"Indeed. And I was wrong for doubting. You have become a hero of these lands. If you succeed today, I think you'll become even more."

He stood, smoothing the edges of his tunic as he looked down at her.

"Oh?" she asked, making no move to stand. "And what's that."

He eyed her, his expression flat and unreadable. When he did speak his voice was so quiet she almost couldn't hear it.

"A legend."

Unferth turned and trudged back across the hall, leaving her sitting as the other warriors rose around her. Part of her liked to think he was joking, but there had been no lie in his eyes, and his words had been for her alone. His final words left her with a strange, unsettled feeling. Every warrior seeks glory, but for her it had never been about that alone. And yet, deep down, she felt as though a fire had been kindled deep in her chest. The thought of defeating something that set terror in even the most stalwart warrior's heart, something no mortal could supposedly stand against, filled her with a tingle of excitement like sparks that made her hand itch to hold a blade.

She stood slowly and gathered up her belongings as the last warriors awoke around her. They took a meal together in the hall as the dawn broke. The mood was quiet, less fearsome than it had been the night before. A feeling of anticipation seemed to hang over the party in the growing light of day, as they gathered up their weapons and departed from Heorot. The king, true to his word, provided a horse for every member of their company, and the sun had only just risen above the foothills as they thundered out along the road. The journey would only take a small part of the day, but where they were going none wanted to linger after nightfall. Time was of the essence as they made their way until Heorot was but a gold-tipped hill in the distance.

Chapter 5

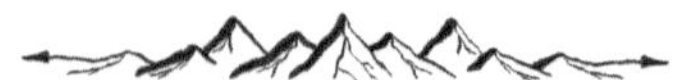

They had been riding for a few hours, leaving the main road behind and taking the narrow tracks that led up into the foothills. The air still had a chill here, and even as midday approached the shaded grasses and trees shone with a light covering of frost. The wind pulled at Beowulf's hair and turned her cheeks pink, and she pulled the fur of her cloak further up by her ears. Steam rose from the horses' nostrils as they slowed their pace, traveling carefully between the wild and twisting trees and winding their way through the gloom, with the smell of sap and cold earth rising around them. Ravens called in the air above, their dark silhouettes blending with the stormy clouds that hung low in the sky.

The light faded under the cover of the evergreens, their branches intertwining as the forest thickened around them. Ash and oak trees, some of them with trunks as wide as the length of a horse, reached their limbs up and out, blocking out much of the sun and dampening sound. There was still a track to travel along, a narrow game path that cut through the wood, wide enough for them to ride in single file between low branches. Even without it, they could have followed the creature's trail easily enough, deep gouges still carved into soft soil by the mark of her claws. And as far as they were from Heorot, there was still an occasional spattering of blood to be found.

Conversation had grown quiet, and Beowulf moved further toward the head of the column as they rode up along a granite outcropping that offered a glimpse of their surroundings. Forest stretched out around them; beyond that, on one side there were green fields and rolling hills, and on the other, the trees gave way to the steep upwellings of the mountains, their sides covered with light snow, the tops of them hidden in a thick bank of low cloud. The sun faded not long after they entered the forest, casting the world around them in graying twilight. The horses knickered nervously in the eerie silence.

Rounding the cliff, they passed through a grove of twisted beech trees, and the ground before them sloped down toward a massive clearing. Even at a distance, the smell of stagnant water wafted on the chilly air. They descended from the outcropping back into the thick cover of the forest, following the path that reached nearly to the water's edge.

A sudden shout went up from the front of the line, and Beowulf urged her horse forward the short distance to where the foremost riders had stopped. A few of them had dismounted, and someone swore loudly as Beowulf pulled her steed to a stop and slid from the saddle.

"Gods be good." Unferth's voice reached her as she neared the group of warriors and saw what they had gathered around. There, not a stone's throw from the water's edge, was Aeschere. His severed head had been placed on the ground before them in a pool of blood, turned to face any who might approach the still and silent lake. His body was nowhere in sight.

Beowulf cursed under her breath, before turning to tie her horse to one of the nearby trees. The rest of the band dismounted, not daring to draw any nearer to the water's edge. Some tethered the horses, while the others checked the nearby area for any danger before they cleared a space in which to wait. One of Hrothgar's men gathered up Aeschere's head, as much to honor the fallen as to put the grisly remains out of sight. Not a warrior among them was at ease, and many hands rested on their weapons. Beowulf began setting down some of her belongings near one of the trees that grew closer to the dark water of the lake. Braggi was the only one to approach her amid the hushed chatter.

"Seems an odd thing to leave behind, doesn't it?" he asked, trying to defuse the tension, as he leaned against a nearby tree and regarded her.

"It's a warning," she muttered darkly as she removed her cloak.

"A warning? You think this thing knew we would follow it? I wouldn't reckon it's so smart."

"Smart enough to sneak past the guards to claim a wergild." She peeled off her boots and stowed her Fenris shield against the tree as she spoke. When she turned to look back at Braggi, he was staring at her with his mouth twisted into a grimace.

"You truly believe that?" She could hear the incredulity lacing his voice and offered him a small shrug. When he continued to stare questioningly at her, she stopped what she was doing and stood to face him directly.

"I don't justify or defend its—her actions." She crossed her arms. "Though I can't help but notice she has abided by the laws of men as we know them. I slew one of her kin, and she took one in recompense. Only one. She could have killed more or done more damage when she entered that hall. Instead, she took only one life and left a warning for any who followed her."

Braggi looked mildly skeptical, though he nodded slowly, glancing back toward the water with an expression of mild disgust. "Well"—his voice croaked slightly—"when you put it that way."

"I do not doubt this creature is evil at heart, but I also respect the purposeful way it has acted. Much more so than its offspring."

"Odin help you, my friend. I don't know about this one."

It was the first time Beowulf had seen genuine doubt on Braggi's face, and she did her utmost to quell the ripple of unease it sent through her.

"Odin and Tyr both," she said. "I would be most grateful for their favor, but I do not fear death."

She passed Braggi and walked on bare feet across the cold ground to the edge of the lake. The other warriors had settled as much as they could, being so close to the creature's lair. Some stood, while others leaned against the nearby trees. Weapons remained sheathed but within easy reach, and not one among them was at ease. She did not think, nor feel, that death waited for her in the depths of that lake. But it was the first time she could remember that she also felt that she may be wrong. The one thing she knew she could not abide was inaction. Even with the path before her clouded in doubt, she reminded herself that the only way out was through.

She reached down and dared to touch the water, her fingertips breaking the oily surface where she crouched at the shore. It was deathly silent. No wind blew in this deep grotto, not a single bird could be heard. The cold water swirled around her fingers, seeming somehow viscous. Even at the shallowest point near the edge, it was inky black. The color, and the dark silt beneath, made it seem like a pit of dark tar that reeked of decay. She seized a stone from the bank and, hefting it for a moment, threw it out toward the middle of the lake.

There was a great splash that echoed around them, ripples shimmering over the surface, before the water suddenly churned with the upwelling of dark shapes. Creatures, their shapes impossible to distinguish beyond scaled sides and an occasional fin, writhed beneath the surface and sent waves to the silty shore. Beowulf leaped upright, drawing Hrunting as she did, and the sound of further blades being drawn rang out around her as the other warriors seized their arms.

There were too many creatures to count, their serpentine bodies twisting froth into the dark water. The smallest was little longer than a grown man's leg, and the largest Beowulf could see had a body at least two feet thick where it heaved and broke the surface.

The warriors had to shout to be heard over the splashes as some of the serpents found the shore, slithering swiftly toward their quarry. Someone fired an arrow past Beowulf, and the shaft sunk deep into one of the larger serpent's sides as it twisted up onto sand. It writhed as the warriors hacked at it, spilling oily dark-green blood onto the ground. They slew at least a half dozen that dared to come onto the land, all the warriors careful to stay out of the grip of sharp fangs and writhing coils. Only when no more creatures would dare the open air did some of the warriors lower their weapons, but the serpents continued to slither and thrash, making the lake seem to boil.

Braggi and Beowulf exchanged a glance, before she turned to the rest of the warriors who stood near the water's edge. Although she had stripped her cloak and boots she had kept her armor, and Unferth's sword was in her hand, its blade already wetted by the serpent's blood.

She took a deep breath. "If I have not returned before the sun is a handspan from the western treetops, leave this place and return to Heorot."

Some of the warriors murmured, and Braggi opened his mouth in protest, but she cut him off. "That's a command. If I don't make it back, all the wealth I have earned is to be delivered to King Hygelac. As well as news of my fate."

She turned to where Unferth stood, close at hand, worry carved into the lines of his face. Her next words gained her some confused looks among the warriors as she gestured to him. "Should I perish, give my shield and the blade I carried from Geatland to Unferth, for he has kindly bequeathed me his own, that I may win honor with it." Unferth, momentarily surprised, managed a small nod.

It was Braggi's voice that answered her. "Beowulf, we would wait until dawn if—"

"Do not linger." She spoke firmly. "No one else needs to die here, and none should stay after dark."

Braggi nodded, though his expression was grim. When he spoke his voice was stiff.

"Tyr protect you, my friend."

She gave him a small nod of thanks as she turned back toward the seething lake. Her fingers gripped the sword in her hand, the weight and feel bringing comfort to her mind as she slowly stepped out into the cold water. Her feet sank deep into soft and sticky silt and the cold chilled her skin as she waded past her knees. She felt coils brush against her legs as she walked, but here in the water none of the serpents made a move to attack her, though she held her sword at the ready.

Beowulf ventured as deep as her waist, before she turned one last time to those standing on the shore. Her own warriors regarded her with nods and furrowed brows, standing so very close to the shore, as if some part of them wished to follow. Hrothgar's fighters looked mostly shocked as they stood back from the water's edge and watched her. She gave Braggi a grin, a genuine one that shone in her eyes despite her heart fluttering in her chest. Turning, she reversed her grip on her blade, and took a long deep breath, feeling the cold air searing her nose and throat. Her feet settled into the silty bottom, then she pushed off hard, closed her eyes, and dove into the lake.

***

The cold water that swirled around her head was almost paralyzing. It sank like knives into her temples, and whole body shuddered as the thick dark water enveloped her and she kicked downward. She had been standing on some edge of a drop-off, and even as she swam, she still could not reach the bottom. The weight of her armor and wet clothes dragged her down as she kicked hard, her movement fighting against the cold. She dared to open her eyes but could not even make out her hands as she held them before her. Her fingers pulled the water past her as she pushed deeper and deeper down. Serpents swam around her, but none attacked as she sank. Their coils bumped against her in the darkness, and she could feel the water they disturbed, but neither teeth nor coils wrapped around her limbs.

Ever further down she sank, her heart pounding in her ears, until the water suddenly surged violently around her. Then something slammed into her side and arms like iron vices wrapped around her, squeezing the air from her lungs as she was yanked first sideways and then down into the depths. She struggled, and cold water flooded into her nose and mouth as the creature drew them both deeper and deeper. It was a powerful swimmer, and its grip remained strong even as it pulled her along. She strained in the monster's grip, kicking out, bare feet knocking against its thick legs, sliding against smooth, slime-covered scales.

The world spun around her, any sense of direction lost in the roaring water and the blood that pounded behind her eyes. Her lungs screamed for air as she struggled, finally managing to pry one of the monster's arms loose, but not enough to escape its grasp entirely. Lights burst in the corners of her vision, and the monster suddenly changed direction, loosening its grasp on her. Beowulf had no time to orient herself, as no sooner had the monster unwound its limbs from around her than it sank its claws into the back of her armor near her collar and yanked her up and backward.

There was a rush of water and suddenly, still half blind from filthy water, she felt air as the world hurtled and spun around her. She could feel the pull of gravity again, but no sooner had she sucked in a breath of air when she slammed against the surface of slippery rock and collided with hard stone. She coughed and gagged, rolling on her side and spitting water as she struggled to right herself, shaking her hair from her eyes. Despite being flung about like a rag doll, she had kept her hold on Unferth's sword and now held it before her as her vision cleared. She found her knees first, and kept one hand pressed against the stone before finally getting her bare feet under her and feeling cold rock beneath her toes.

She was in an underground cave, the walls lined with some kind of lichen or slime that emitted a faint but persistent glow, just enough to see in the gloom. Still gasping, her hair plastered to her head by frigid water, Beowulf dared to look behind her at a small pool of churning water. The creature had dragged her down to the depths of the lake, before yanking her upward into the cave and tossing her like a piece of meat onto the stone as they both burst up into the stale and wet air. Beowulf blinked and looked around her, sword held high, her chest heaving as she regained her breath.

The cave was large, twisting back far enough that the other end was out of sight. Carved from smooth limestone, the sides of it were rippled as if by water and looked more like living flesh than cold stone. There was a smell of death in the air, and from where she stood she could already make out the bones scattered all about the floor. But there was more. Under bones and bog moss, tucked into corners and against deep curves in the rocky wall, there were piles of old weapons. Swords and spears, many rusted, lay in heaps, along with empty and corroded pieces of armor. A tally of the dead, they were a grim reminder of all the lives that had been lost to that dark place, the most recent of which Beowulf made quick note of. There, only a few feet from the water's edge, was a headless body that she assumed was Aeschere. He was twisted oddly, some of his bones broken as he was dragged to that dark pit and dashed upon the rocks.

He wasn't the only fresh body to be found either. A short distance further, along an opposite wall of the cave, Beowulf could make out the distinct shape of Grendel's body. Long since gone cold, it lay with its remaining arm folded over its chest, more carefully placed than Aeschere, its ruddy eyes turned pale and empty like those of a dead fish.

Beowulf had little time to orient herself, and she had only dared to take a few steps further when the beast that had dragged her there once more approached. Grendel's mother had waited crouched in the shadows after she'd dragged her prize to her den, and even allowed the warrior to regain her breath before she attacked. With eyes burning like coals, she stood to her full height, surpassing even Grendel by several feet, her head nearly scraping the roof of the cave above her. Her skin was scaled and slick like that of her progeny, her arms long, and her fingers tipped with wicked claws. A dark hide was tied around her waist, and tucked into one side of it was a rough-shod knife made from the long jagged head of an old spear. Wild and matted hair covered her head. It cascaded over her shoulders, fell down her back, and partially covered her breasts where it hung against her chest. Her teeth protruded past her lips as she snarled, slinking forward, nails scraping the wet ground.

Grendel's mother lunged at Beowulf with a howl of fury, her claws raking the air as she descended on the thane. Beowulf parried the first blow, and her blade knocked the strike wide, keeping sharp talons from sinking into her throat. The second blow she dodged, before retaliating with one of her own. She swung an arcing slash across the beast's torso and felt the blade make contact, but not a mark appeared on the monster's flesh. She ducked and rolled, leaping away from the pool lest she be knocked back into the water. Bones crunched beneath her as she regained her footing and whirled, placing herself with her back facing the deeper part of the cave, away from the water where Grendel's mother now stood.

The monster leaped again. Beowulf blocked what blows she could and dodged the rest, her sword flashing in the half-light as she swung and struck the beast again and again. But no matter the force of her blows, the blade could not bite through the dark, scaled flesh. Beowulf cursed as she narrowly blocked a claw aimed for her head, and sliced at the monster's arm to no avail. Growing impatient, Grendel's mother let out another screech that echoed off the wet walls and threw her full weight against the warrior, slamming Beowulf back into one of the cave walls.

Stone scraped at her mail shirt, and she tasted copper in her mouth as she tumbled, the wind knocked from her chest. She scrambled to her feet again and spat crimson onto the floor, before lowering Hrunting to rest in a pile of bones. Swords were of no use here. Instead, she moved in close, as she had with Grendel, dodging wide swings until she could get near enough to throw her fists and elbows against the creature's body. The monster grunted under the force of her blows and staggered back as Beowulf advanced and drove her shoulder into its abdomen. She was rewarded with the sound of a rib cracking.

Grendel's mother let out a wail of pain and lashed out, one hand wrapping around Beowulf's throat and forcing her backward onto the stone floor with the force of a thunderbolt.

Beowulf yanked at the hand around her neck, kicking up with bare feet as the monster leaped on top of her, its free hand clawing toward her face. She caught the blow within inches of the talons reaching her eyes, and the two stayed locked like that for a moment, both of Beowulf's hands on the creature's wrists. Grendel's mother kept her viselike grip on Beowulf's throat but yanked her other hand free, pulled the crude knife from where it rested at her hip and stabbed downward toward the warrior's head.

Prone, pulse pounding in her ears from the claws around her neck, Beowulf saw the blow as it descended and kicked off the ground, sliding just enough that the blade dropped to her shoulder rather than her head. The ring mail of her tunic kept the blade from sinking into her skin, but the force of the blow sent white-hot pain searing across her shoulder and back. She could feel her heart hammering in her chest as she twisted her hips and swung her legs up to kick at the arm that held her pinned to the floor.

She slammed her heel into the monster's elbow and felt something crack. The hand around her throat loosened and Grendel's mother took a step back, giving Beowulf the room she needed to find her feet again. The warrior pulled herself up with blood in her teeth and fire in her eyes, as the monster again rushed toward her and she lunged forward to meet it. The two collided, claws and fists lashing out at the other. They were matched for strength, and they struggled in the gloomy cave, scattering bones and old mail across the wet floor.

Grendel's mother, unable to so easily tear apart the quarry she had dragged to her abode, let out an enraged shriek before again slamming her weight into the warrior. Beowulf staggered back but this time managed to keep her footing as her back hit the wall and she let out a grunt, dropping into a crouch. The monster made no attempt to grapple her, instead stalking back out of reach, one arm hanging slightly askew and the other hugged around its side. Dark-green blood dripped from one of its flared nostrils. Beowulf steadied herself for another attack, and that's when she saw it. Their fight had knocked loose the pile of debris that had covered its resting place against one of the walls. Tucked beside the splintered remains of a shield was a sword unlike anything she had ever seen.

Time seemed to freeze for a moment as Beowulf looked at the shimmering weapon, resting tip down amid bones and debris. Only half of the blade was visible, but despite the damp and the grime, it shone as if freshly polished. The hilt and pommel looked to be made of gold, the guard was beautifully crafted in the rough shape of a triple spiral, and the circular pommel was engraved with an image of a tree. From appearance alone, anyone would have guessed it was no ordinary sword. The wear of time and damp and the filth of the cave seemed not to touch it, and as Beowulf regarded the blade, she knew she had seen it before. It drifted like the specter of a half-remembered dream, and she could recall the cold of ocean waves and the sand of the ocean floor beneath her feet.

Something stirred in her chest, whether it was fear or elation she could not have said, but she knew that sword that sat against the wall, and she knew deep down it was meant for her.

A shriek from Grendel's mother pulled her back into the present, and the monster lowered to a crouch, ready to pounce. Beowulf gauged the distance to where the sword sat, then took a deep breath and ran, scattering bones as she leaped across the cave. She reached the sword only a moment before the monster reached her, and her hand closed around the hilt. It was warm to the touch and fit her perfectly. She closed her grip and swung the blade upward in a shining arc.

A scream split the air as the blade cleaved through the flesh of the creature's shoulder, forcing it to stagger back, painting the wall of the cave with a splatter of blood. Beowulf felt warmth spread through her limbs as she advanced and lifted the weapon, light as a feather in her grasp. For a moment she felt as though she could sense everything around her. She could feel the cold floor under her feet, the pulse of the water from the lake above and around them, the sound of her own breath and the movement of every muscle in her body as she swung the sword with deadly precision. The blade sang as it sliced through the air, leaving a shimmering arc as Beowulf met her mark and cut through skin and bone. Grendel's mother's head toppled to the floor, and her body, twitching, thudded down beside it.

Beowulf panted heavily and lowered her blade, tasting metal in her mouth as her arms dropped to her sides and her chest heaved. As the frenzy of the fight passed, she began to feel the aches from where she had been thrown against the walls and floor, and a dull throbbing pain in her shoulder where her mail had turned the monster's knife. The hand she wiped across her face came away smeared with blood—her own, a brilliant crimson, and that of the creature, a deep mossy green, some of which must have gotten on her lips, as she realized she could suddenly taste it, a deep, earthy, pungent flavor that she spat onto the cave floor. Later, she would convince herself that she had been seeing things, that the rush of battle had clouded her thoughts, but it seemed for a moment as if the entire cavern around her was infused with moonlight. A soft silvery glow, reminiscent of long winter nights, washed over her, filling the gloom as she stood over her fallen foe. As quickly as it came, it vanished, and she was left blinking as her eyes once more adjusted to the dark.

She felt the weight of the sword in her hand suddenly shift, and looked down to see a piece of it drip onto the stone floor as if it were made of liquid. The monster's blood, though harmless to the cave walls and her skin, was melting the blade as if it were made of ice. Beowulf watched, momentarily frozen with surprise, as the entire blade slowly melted away until only an inch or so above the handle remained. She turned it over in her palm in the light. The undamaged handle still shone, the intricately crafted triple spiral glinting gold. Something about the weight of it was comforting, and she tucked it into her belt before retrieving Hrunting from where it lay in a pile of moss-covered bones. Even with her foe defeated, there was something about the place that set a chill in her bones, turning her stomach as her eyes settled on where Grendel's body lay. The sooner she could leave, the better, but she would not return to the world above empty-handed.

Whatever enchantment or dark boon had been on Grendel and his mother in life seemed to disperse with their demise, for Hrunting cut easily through the fallen monster's flesh. Beowulf carefully severed Gendel's head from his resting corpse, leaving it where it lay on the cold floor. Then she walked the few short strides to where Grendel's mother's head had fallen and, seizing it by its long hair, turned and made her way back toward the pool at the entrance to the cave. She was glad to leave that place; the longer she lingered the more the walls seemed to close toward her, as if the very stone bore her ill will.

Her fist tangled into the monster's hair, heaving the head as she reached the water. Her other hand gripped Hrunting and, holding the blade close, she took a deep breath and plunged into the icy water.

***

Minutes had seemed like hours to the company of warriors who waited above. The moment Beowulf had plunged into the depths, some of them had begun pacing. They stood by the water's edge or lingered near the horses, some glancing up to where dark storm clouds boiled in the sky above. A light spring snow had begun to fall, too thin and fleeting to stick, muting any sound they made. The writhing of the water serpents had lessened the moment Beowulf had dove in, but their bodies still occasionally broke the surface. Time dragged painfully, and what was a span of minutes seemed half a day for those who waited.

Someone near the edge of the water let out a shout, and the others ran to the edge, watching in surprise as the serpents receded, disappearing entirely as the water finally stilled. Unferth leaned close to Braggi as the two stood and scanned the surface.

"They vanished! A good omen, you think?" Unferth asked.

"I can only hope. There is foul magic here. I don't trust any of it."

The party of warriors stood eagerly on the bank, searching for any sign, even a single ripple. Moments later their patience was rewarded, and a great splash broke the surface, no more than a stone's throw from the edge. Water surged as Beowulf burst into the cold air, coughing and spluttering. A massive cheer went up among the waiting warriors, and some even dared to take a few steps forward into the water so that they might meet her as she approached. Her hair was soaked, and a small trickle of red came from the corner of her mouth. Her jaw was set tight and her expression slightly pained as she waded forward through the water, dragging something heavy and submerged behind her.

She splashed forward until she had nearly reached the edge, shaking the water off Hrunting's gleaming edge before stepping up toward the banks. She heaved her prize from the water, and a gasp rippled through the band of warriors as she tossed the monster's head to land heavily on the silty shore. It landed upright, eyes glassy and blank, mouth slightly agape, and a few of the nearest warriors took a wary step back.

"Gods be good." Braggi almost laughed as he surveyed the head with a grimace. "You found her then?"

Beowulf nodded, still catching her breath as she stepped out on dry land. "I did. Or rather, she found me but is all the worse for it." She grinned for the first time since she emerged, though it was fleeting.

They made quick work of wrapping the head in a massive hide, so that it might be slung between the horses, too much of a burden for one rider alone. The weight of it was light enough for Beowulf, gifted with strength as she was, but she had no intent of carrying it the entire way back. Some of the other warriors had started a small fire while she battled below, and she took a moment to warm herself beside it as Braggi and one of the others helped her out of her mail. She had anticipated her journey might get damp and had had the foresight to pack some fresh clothes, which she began to change into as the warriors readied the horses. Wet clothes could mean death, especially so high in the mountains, and even the hardiest warrior would not tempt sickness or cold.

Her skin turned to gooseflesh as she yanked on a fresh pair of breeches, lacing them up with still-numb fingers. She could already see a deep bruise welling up on her shoulder, along with numerous small scrapes and abrasions from where she had been slammed against the walls and floor. They bloomed under the memories of older injuries, standing out where white scars already crisscrossed parts of her body. Mindful of her shoulder, she carefully shrugged into her tunic and pulled on her boots, before gathering up her fur-mantled cloak and swinging it on, grateful for the warmth.

They mounted and departed, Beowulf riding in the middle of the column, enjoying the freedom from the weight of her armor and the warmth of her dry clothes as the feeling returned to her limbs. Her hair began to dry, loose strands trapping the delicate snowflakes as they drifted from the sky. The mood around her was lighter than before, and occasional chatter or laughter echoed up and down the line as they made their way back.

The return journey seemed shorter, and the company's spirits much higher despite the gathering dark. Though the clouds did not break, the snow ceased as they emerged from the forest and dropped back toward the lowlands, winding their way around small groves of trees and along the hunting trails. The ground began to level out as dusk descended, and though they still had some distance to cross, they could make out Heorot among the hills that rose in the grassy fields around them. It glowed like a hot ember, beckoning them from a distance. Soon they reached the road and sped onward on their journey.

It was nightfall by the time they reached the village. Darkness had settled in earnest, but for once Hrothgar's men embraced it without fear, the night terrors that had plagued their land now defeated. Across the landscape, small points of light appeared where villages nestled in foothills and at the edges of scattered woods.

They gathered a small crowd as they entered the village, excited clamoring surrounding them as they made their way to the main hall. Once they reached the great doors, the warriors dismounted amid the gaggle of onlookers that clustered around them. Beowulf went to retrieve her armor but Braggi stopped her with a hand on her shoulder.

"Don't. I've got it. I'll put it in the hall."

She raised an eyebrow, to which he grinned and jerked his head toward the open door. "Go on. You've got an entrance to make."

She snorted and punched him lightly in the shoulder but didn't argue. With one hand she gripped the hair of the creature's head, the other rested on the hilt of Unferth's sword at her hip.

The gruesome trophy dragged behind her, heavy as it was, as she walked inside. A nightly meal had already begun, the air quiet and tense with anticipation that shattered as she strode through the door. The moment she entered, the entire hall surged to life. Warriors rose from their seats and villagers clamored, some letting out gasps as they caught sight of her grizzly prize.

Beowulf walked through the hall in silence, her expression set and stony, pulling the head behind her as she crossed the room. At the end of the hall, Hrothgar slowly rose from the high table, his mouth slightly ajar. Only once she had passed around the great flume hearth and had reached the foot of the high table did Beowulf stop. With a heavy swing of her arm, she tossed Grendel's head to land with a wet thud on the stone before her.

The room erupted with a loud cheer that echoed off the walls, mugs were raised and fists pounded against the table. The rest of the warriors had filed in behind Beowulf, her own and Hrothgar's fighters all standing by her heels as she bowed before the king. Hrothgar beamed at her, his joy echoed in the face of Wealtheow as she looked down at the Geatish warrior. The king raised his drinking horn high and the hall finally fell silent again.

"Beowulf, thane of Hygelac, may the gods favor you and bless you this day, for you have done what no mortal man could do."

A murmur of agreement spread throughout the hall. Hrothgar gestured to the band of warriors. "Come and sit. Replenish yourselves with food and drink. Tonight, we celebrate noble deeds, for the shadow that has long loomed over these lands is finally defeated!"

He raised his horn high in the air. "To Beowulf!"

"Beowulf!" the entire hall roared.

The warriors found their seats, Beowulf once more taking one close to where the king sat, and meat and mead were shared aplenty. It took a group of four stout warriors to loft the monster's head up on the rafter near where Grendel's arm hung. Hrothgar watched Beowulf eagerly, though he waited to press her for the story until she had eaten. Beowulf took her time, savoring the warmth of the mead that helped ease some of the pain in her body. She ate and drank, and spoke little.

She had an easy enough time ignoring the attention directed toward her, focusing instead on her mug and plate. Hrothgar's warriors watched her with a kind of reverent fascination, so far removed from the distrust and disdain with which she had first been greeted. Occasionally, when she looked up from her food and chanced to lock eyes with one of them, they gave a small nod. Amma, the warrior she had befriended, came to sit across from her, wearing a grin that stretched from ear to ear.

"Heard you went for a swim ." She spoke over the rim of her mug. "You fought well."

Beowulf swallowed her mouthful and grunted. "I survived. It wasn't a clean fight by any means."

"Still, you killed two monsters in as many days, a feat once thought to be impossible with anything less than an army."

"That seems like an exaggeration." Beowulf shot her a wry look, before smiling down at the table. "But thank you. I'm just glad to see this hall made safe. Your people have seen far too much bloodshed."

Amma nodded, frowning slightly. "It's true. It is a welcome respite. And what's more, it has done much to strengthen the ties between our two peoples. This kingdom is forever indebted to you. Your king will be proud and pleased, I am sure."

"I believe he will." Beowulf sat back a bit and sipped from her mug. "For my own part I am just happy to have been able to help. To shield a few lives. And to still be alive to tell the tale." She chuckled as she finished.

"I won't lie"—a small grin tugged at Amma's lips—"I wouldn't expect you to be in good shape after a fight like that, but you really do look like shit."

"Ha!" Beowulf's laugh almost sounded like a cough, and she immediately winced as the still-healing cuts on her ribs and the pain in her shoulder twinged in protest. "I feel it."

Braggi, listening in on their conversation, patted Beowulf on the back, perhaps a bit harder than needed. She winced again and shot him a glare to match the wink he offered.

He chuckled. "I'm sure you'll be right as rain in no time."

The three of them laughed, and Beowulf drained her mug.

Hrothgar's voice pulled her from her reverie. The king had stood once more, and the room again grew quiet as he gestured toward where she sat, his voice booming above the low murmur of the hall.

"Come, Beowulf, tell us of your feats! I would hear it from your own mouth what transpired in the deep there. Tell us, so the skalds might begin working on their new song!"

She swore lightly under her breath, keeping her face neutral, before slowly standing and walking toward the table. She looked to where the princes sat, eyes as eager as their father's as they watched her. Her gaze strayed along the hall, to the warriors and villagers watching her closely, and she caught sight of Unferth at the opposite table. He raised his horn a few inches and gave her the tiniest nod, before she turned back to the king.

"In truth, I think it's a tale I would do a poor job of telling." She heard her voice rebound off the walls and ring in her own ears. "I plunged into the lake and was dragged to some dark den beneath the waves where Grendel's mother sought to paint the walls with my entrails. A worthy foe she seemed, less bestial than her offspring. She fought more like you or I than a beast."

Her last comment was met with some whispers and a few shaking heads, some of the warriors frowning incredulously as she, of all people, spared a shred of honor for such a creature. But she could not forget the time she had been given to find her feet when she had first been dragged into that dank cavern, as if Grendel's mother had wanted to fight her fairly. It was only one life the creature had taken. Payment for the death of her son, not the same wanton destruction he had wreaked upon that hall.

Her thoughts strayed once more to all that transpired within Heorot, and she glanced first to the two princes sitting beside Wealtheow, and then to where Unferth sat, his eyes still upon her. Beowulf unstrapped the scabbard from her hip, lifting the blade so that all in the hall might see it as she spoke.

"I was given a boon for my journey to the depths. Unferth, noble warrior among you, gifted me his own blade that I might win glory with it. An honorable gift it was, and it brought strength to my spirits in that dark place." She crossed the room as she spoke, eyes following her as she moved to place the sword on the table before a slightly surprised looking Unferth. "My thanks, friend," she said quietly, before turning back to the hall.

"Unferth helped lead us to that place, and as well as honoring me with his blade, I do not doubt that he will continue to bring honor to this hall"—she slowly began walking back toward the high table—"honor to his king, and honor and glory to his king's sons."

Wealtheow's gaze seemed to burn through her. Their eyes met, and the queen wore the same subtle smile she had before. *Thank you.* A cheer went up around Unferth who, smiling with surprise, retrieved his sword with a nod of thanks. Beowulf stood once more before the high table and turned back toward the hall.

"I had to fight the creature with the strength of my arm alone. In the end, the beast's cunning was a match to my own skill, and the battle may have gone ill, but I saw and seized a rare sword from the monster's treasure hoard, and with it I cleaved its head from its shoulders."

Another loud cheer echoed through the hall, accompanied by the thumping of feet against the stone floor. Satisfied enough with the story, Hrothgar clapped his hands three times, bringing the room back to silence.

"Beowulf, know now that your legend grows. Your feats will be proclaimed in lands far and wide, your deeds beyond those of any warrior this world has known. May your life be long, your troubles few, and may you take pride in the knowledge that you will be forever immortalized in story and song. Hail, Beowulf, hero of Heorot!"

A final thunderous cheer rippled through the room. Beowulf felt her neck prickle and grow hot, and her fists closed as her name echoed around her. She took a deep breath and bowed once more before the king, part of her mind trying to block out the sound of her name as it was shouted in the hall. *This is your path.* She set her jaw and took a deep breath as the energy in the room slowly ebbed, the warriors returning their attention to conversation and drink. Rather than return to her seat, she stood and pondered for a moment, one hand pressed against the hilt of the sword she had found and kept tucked into her belt. She turned back to the high table and, after only a moment's hesitation, approached King Hrothgar.

She bowed and pulled the hilt from her tunic. Only an inch or so of blade remained, the metal rippled slightly where it had been melted by the monster's blood. She wrapped both hands around it, tracing the smooth spiral patterns, before she held it before the king, who regarded both her and it with raised brows.

She spoke quietly. "This is the blade, or rather what is left of it. it's unlike any smithcraft I have seen."

The princes craned their necks to see as Hrothgar took it gingerly from her hands and turned it over and over in his own. He regarded it in careful silence, tilting it under the light so that the gold shimmered. Beowulf spoke again, trying to keep the curiosity from her voice.

"These are your lands, and I thought you may yet know something about this blade or where it might have come from."

She had seen it before and recognized it the moment it caught her eye in the cave. How she knew it was a secret she kept to herself, but it made her even more curious as she watched the king examine it. He turned it over in his hands, tracing the intricate metalwork with his fingertips, his brows furrowed in concentration as he studied the hilt and what little remained of the blade.

"It is truly a fine craft, not like anything I have ever laid eyes upon." He looked up, seeming almost confused, before he gingerly traced the triple spiral. "These, though... I've seen these symbols before. They are old... very old. I have seen them carved into stone, but never into metal such as this."

"Where did you see them?" Beowulf tried to keep her tone measured, lest she betray how keen her interest truly was.

"Old stones," he murmured. "Legend says it's from the time before the alliance between the Aesir and the Vanir. Before the two separate houses of godly beings united and built Valhalla. It was a time when magic was unknown to the All-father, power-ful though he was, when only the Vanir knew the ways of true magic. The Vanir held sway before the warlike Aesir came. It was the powers of earth and magic and women which ruled these lands."

Beowulf felt something prickle down her spine, ending with tingles in her fingertips. She could not decide if she found it pleasing or not, but every word the king spoke settled deep within her mind and refused to budge. She realized after a moment that he was looking back up at her. She cleared her thoughts and refocused her eyes.

"My thanks." She reached out as he carefully handed the hilt back to her. She tucked it back into her belt, finding its weight somehow comforting.

Hrothgar gave a nod of approval. "A fine prize. Though I will send you back with more."

"Good king, you've already—"

"I insist." He gently held up a hand to silence her. "You have done so much for my people and for me. And more than should have been asked of an army, let alone a single warrior. Please allow me to express my gratitude, lest I be in debt for this." He gave her an almost tired smile.

Beowulf hesitated for a moment before nodding.

"King Hygelac will be most grateful for the many goods that will be sent to his court."

To Beowulf's surprise, it was Wealtheow who spoke, leaning across the table, her eyes sparkling as she looked intently at the warrior.

"You have done well by your king indeed. And by this house. You have done much to strengthen the ties between our people. I pray that no ill befalls any in this land or in yours, but should the worst come to bear, I believe this is a valuable alliance for our peoples."

"Indeed." Hrothgar nodded as he sipped from his drinking horn. "Know that you shall have welcome in this house as long as you shall live, Beowulf."

Beowulf bowed her gratitude, but as she turned to leave, Hrothgar's hand caught her own, gently, stopping her as she turned. The king leaned forward and looked at her intently.

"I would share a bit of wisdom, if I might." He spoke softly, looking ever so slightly strained as he did.

"I would be honored." Beowulf turned back to face him, searching his expression. "You have many years as a leader in times of peace and war. You have ruled long and well. There is much you know that I have yet to learn."

He nodded slowly, the smallest smile appearing on his face, though a strange sorrow still lingered in his eyes. When he spoke again, it was very quiet, so much so that Beowulf had to lean closer to hear him over the dim chatter in the hall.

"The strength and pride of all warriors fades with the waning of time. Make the most of what you have now. Seek victory and renown, but do not delight too much in material wealth or goods." His expression darkened and he sighed heavily. "Remember that the truest gift any warrior can hope to win is immortality through the legacy and legend of their deeds. It is only your story that lives on after you. Do what you can while you can, and always remember, death comes for us all."

She considered his words, nodding slowly, before she dared to show a hint of a smile. "We only choose how we meet it."

He regarded her thoughtfully then, the grizzled older king and the young warrior standing in silence for a moment. Beowulf offered a final bow, before returning to her seat, feeling the king's gaze on her back as she went.

She remained quiet at the table, her thoughts claiming her focus as she sat beside Braggi and the others. The quiet drone of conversation mixed with the clatter of bone dice being tossed on one of the tables, and the crackling from the great fire in the heart of the hall. Her hand pressed against the strange hilt where it was tucked against her waist, the metal seeming warm from more than her skin alone. She remembered the moment in the cave, washed in moonlight, some strange brilliance that had inexplicably penetrated that gloom. She thought of the king's words, of the time of the Vanir. A time of women, before Odin learned the magic of the runes, when deep secrets were woven into the very earth itself.

"Beowulf?"

She blinked and looked up to see that Braggi had turned sideways to stare at her expectantly.

"Mmm?"

His expression changed from one of mild curiosity to slight concern, his brows furrowing slightly. "I was just saying we would likely be leaving tomorrow. Are you alright? You seem worried?"

"Just tired." She sighed with a fleeting smile. "And yes, with our work here done, I think we'll likely set out as soon as we can. Hrothgar will likely host another great feast, but we have been away long enough, and I have had more than my fill of celebration. Hygelac will be expecting our return. We may need some help to carry the spoils, but I don't doubt a few of Hrothgar's warriors may see us off. Some of them have been watching our boat, after all."

Braggi glanced at her sideways before grunting his agreement and taking a swig from his mug. He looked almost as tired as she, but then again, it had been a challenging few days. It was still hard to believe it would only be their third night in that hall.

Some of the other warriors had slowly begun to drift from the tables as the hour grew late. Beowulf waited a bit longer before she stood and made her way toward the door. She wanted some fresh air, and perhaps to see the stars before she bedded down for the night.

Beyond the light of the hall, the night stretched under a vast sky littered with small points of light. The moon had already risen, and there was a faint enough light that Beowulf wasn't momentarily blinded when she stepped out of the hall. The cold breeze greeted her as she passed through the great wooden doors and out beyond the shadow of the building. She made her way left, around the edge of the hall, never straying more than a few yards from it, but far enough that she could better appreciate the brilliant white sparks in the sky above. At the edge of the hill she came to a stop and pulled her cloak tighter about her as the wind rippled through the bear fur mantle over her shoulders and tugged at the loose strands of her hair.

Before her, she could see light from the hearth fires of the village below, and above her the night unfurled cloudless and clear. The sound of the hall was muted and dampened, and the wind whispered as it crept past. Somewhere, distantly, she heard a wolf howl into the dark. The sound of it brought a strange comfort to her, not unlike the feeling when she gripped the gild-ed sword hilt still tucked into her belt. Despite its now-useless state for battle, she kept it close beside her own sword. Already an idea had taken root somewhere in the recesses of her most private thoughts that she might get a new blade fashioned for it.

She breathed in the night air, one hand straying to her chest as it had her first night in Heorot. Beneath her clothes, she could feel the pressure of her pendant against her skin, and she kept her hand there as she whispered a quiet prayer of thanks into the night. She thanked Tyr, god of warriors and battle, for guiding her blade and for aiding her in keeping her wits about her. A warrior is courageous in word and deed, and the one-handed god reminded all that judgment must align with justice. Njord, god of the seas, was the one to whom she spoke next, praying that they might have a safe return journey.

She might have been satisfied to end her prayers at that, but something in Hrothgar's words still lingered in her mind. Her prayer was silent, barely a whisper into the night, but she hoped Freya might hear. She may have been a goddess of beauty and fertility, not one Beowulf was accustomed to addressing, but there had been a time before many of the gods had arrived, when only the Vanir had been known in that land. Beowulf couldn't help but wonder if perhaps, once, Freya's domains had been different. Surely, the goddess who watched after one of the realms of the afterlife, Fólkvangr, would know something of battle. Beowulf could only wonder as she shared her quiet prayer with the night and hoped it was heard.

Caught up in her thoughts as she was, she didn't hear foot-steps behind her. She was caught off guard as someone spoke quietly behind her.

"You'll be returning home tomorrow then?"

Beowulf whirled, her braids whipping around her, one hand instinctively close to the hilt of her sword. Amma materialized out of the shadows behind her, looking slightly sheepish. Beowulf let out the breath she had been holding and relaxed her shoulders, and Amma gave her a light smirk.

"Apologies," Amma said as she closed the gap between them, coming to stand beside Beowulf. "I didn't mean to startle."

"My own fault for not being attentive." Beowulf shrugged as the two exchanged a glance. A heavy kind of silence seemed to hover around Amma, and she fidgeted slightly as she looked out over the village rooftops.

"It's a shame. Would have been nice to have you all here a bit longer. Perhaps get to play some games and celebrate for more than a single night." As Amma spoke, one hand fidgeted with the bracer on her opposite arm.

"I wouldn't ask any more of your king. He's been a most gracious host."

"It was the least he could do, given what you've all done for us."

"Still." Beowulf took a long breath of night air before she continued. "I would ask no more of him nor any others. And besides, my king would likely want us to return before too long."

"Mmmm." Amma nodded. "I imagine he's somewhat loath to be without his finest warrior for any longer than he has to."

Their eyes met for a moment and Amma grinned, a look that Beowulf couldn't help but return as she answered. "Peace never lasts long in our kingdom nor any other. There's always a battle or a blood feud being fought somewhere. Having me there helps... dissuade those with ill intent."

"This is true. As much here as there, I am sure." Amma sighed. "I suppose your renown is quite a boon in that way. Helps protect your kin without you even needing to spill a drop of blood."

"Exactly. I've always found the practice of formal boasting to be a bit..." Beowulf frowned, searching for words as Amma watched her intently. "I'm not sure. It's just that I've always found actions to speak much more than words. But, if my reputation is a shield for my people, I have no complaints. I'd rather have my legacy be a bulwark than have to take lives to protect. There's enough of that in the world already."

Amma nodded thoughtfully, and Beowulf sank into a pensive silence. It was true: the greater her reputation grew, the greater the protection for her kin and allies, and that, to her, had always been the biggest reward. She hadn't wanted admiration, or even to be praised in the songs of skalds, but for all her deeds and reputation did to protect her people, it was well worth it. She sucked her teeth and tucked her hands into her armpits for warmth.

"It's easier with the monsters," she mumbled.

"Gods, really?" Amma sounded genuinely surprised. "I would rather face a human foe. At least then I'd have a good chance."

"It's been easier with the monsters because it feels... well it doesn't feel the same way when it's a monster. The only lives I've ever regretted taking were humans. Even if a warrior is my enemy, if they fight with skill and honor, there is more weight to taking that life, I think." She looked at Amma, who was regarding her with an almost quizzical expression. "At least for me."

Amma nodded thoughtfully. "I understand. Truly, I do." She sighed. "I would only fear facing monsters because I haven't the same skill or strength as you. But I suppose if I did, I would likely feel the same as you do."

"Perhaps. But don't dishonor your abilities. I cannot say, as I've not seen you fight, but Hrothgar chooses his closest warriors carefully."

Even in the half-light of the stars and moon above, Beowulf could see the slightest hint of color creep into Amma's cheeks.

"I should hope so." Amma smiled as she spoke. "It would have been nice to have more games with you all, that we might have sparred."

Beowulf chuckled. "It would have been fun, certainly. I have quite enjoyed the company here."

Again, that strange silence crept around Amma as she returned to fidgeting with her bracer. Something prickled in Beowulf's palms, sent a bit of heat creeping up the edges of her ears. She watched Amma intently, until the warrior let out a heavy sigh and glanced back toward the hall.

"Some of your warriors will be seeking out company tonight," she murmured.

"All the better. It's been a long journey, and with our task done I don't doubt some of them may want someone to warm their bed before we make our return."

"Will you be joining them?" Amma asked lightly.

Beowulf almost laughed, feeling her ribs twinge as she did. "Gods, no. I think if I do more than lie down at this point, I'll reopen a wound. I'm stiffer than a frost giant's beard."

Amma laughed, and Beowulf might have joined had her mind not suddenly caught up with her words, with Amma's fidgeting, with the tentative way in which she asked.

"That is—" Beowulf spoke quickly, feeling her neck grow hot as her words stuck awkwardly in her throat. "If you were wanting company, any of my warriors would treat you well, as I am sure you would them."

Amma laughed again, more in earnest. "I don't doubt it, but that had not been on my mind. I was not planning on sharing anyone's bed tonight. I was purely curious if you had plans to."

A small wave of relief rippled through Beowulf as some of the tension dropped. "I had no plans to."

"Weariness aside, if any of the men were to your liking, I could gladly tell you which might be the best pick." Amma flashed a mischievous grin. Beowulf felt the heat return to her ears. It was her turn to fidget, and she picked at some of the fraying thread on the edge of her cloak as she spoke.

"I would most certainly trust your judgment in that regard, but I do not think any man in this hall would be to my liking. I would fight beside any of them but invite none to my bed." She looked up, offering her own wry look and searching Amma's face for her reaction. The warrior looked oddly pleased as she regarded Beowulf and took a few steps forward, drawing close enough that Beowulf could almost make out the reflection of the stars in her eyes.

"I think you have good taste indeed." Amma's smile broadened. "Speaking for myself alone, I have always preferred to have a man in my bed." She paused and glanced downward for a moment, her gaze straying to Beowulf's lips. "But, I've always preferred women for kissing." Her last words were a whisper, the ghost of a smile still lingering as one of her hands moved to rest on the furs at Beowulf's shoulder. The smell of woodsmoke swirled between them. Beowulf allowed a hand to gently stray to the edge of Amma's jaw, fingertips only just touching her skin, as she leaned forward and their lips met.

Beowulf could taste the mead they had been drinking, made somehow sweeter by Amma's lips. The kiss was fleeting, and after a moment they pulled apart, Amma grinning as she let her hand drop from Beowulf's shoulder. There was a wry gleam in her eyes as she spoke.

"Goodnight, thane of Hygelac. If I do not see you again, I wish you a safe journey."

"Farewell shieldmaiden." Beowulf felt a small buzz of warmth seeping through her chest, easing the last of the tension from her bones. Exhaustion slowly sank on her like a thick fog bank. "Fortune favor you." The two of them looked at each other a moment longer before Amma turned and made her way quietly back to the hall.

Beowulf waited a few minutes, welcoming the feeling of weariness after so many long hours on edge. She took a few deep breaths of the cool night air before she followed in Amma's footsteps, tracing her path back into the warmth and fading light of the hall. The fire had died low, and the chatter had mostly grown quiet. Many of the warriors within were already staking out a place on the floor to sleep, and unlike the nights before, Beowulf had neither intent nor desire to be the last one to slumber. True to Amma's prediction, several warriors were missing. Some of Hrothgar's fighters and a few of Beowulf's band all looked to have found lodgings elsewhere for the night.

Beowulf threw down her cloak and furs at a spot near enough to the fire, before pulling off her boots and lying down, her body grateful to be horizontal, her limbs seeming to sink into the floor. The quiet sounds of the flames and the last whispers of conversation washed over her. Her thoughts offered only one small onslaught before rest, as they again drifted to the sword handle still tucked against her waist, and she thought for a moment of woods and wolves and a woman's magic. Sleep dragged her off like a thief into the night, and she finally found deep rest for the first time since they had landed on those shores.

Chapter 6

Dawn broke clear and cold as the first rays of light shimmered through crystals of hoarfrost on the grass. Steam rose from the chilled earth and thick mist enshrouded the valleys, making the hall of Heorot atop its small hill seem like an island in a sea of fog. The sounds of the village waking were dampened and muffled, but the air had a lightness to it that the kingdom had not felt in many years. Windows were opened to greet the dawn, and all who dwelt there stepped out into the day without fear of discovering a night's slaughter.

The hall itself was slower to rouse, the company there steeped in mead-laced dreams as light filtered through the windows, sending motes of dust dancing. The fire was rekindled as the warriors slowly stirred and gathered up their belongings. It would be a long day's journey, and as such chatter was little and quiet. The Geats, those hardy warriors who had come from across the sea, broke their fast before the king entered the hall, that they might set out with the day still ahead of them.

Hrothgar said little beyond wishing them all well on their journey and praising the deeds of their leader once more. He arranged for five of his own warriors to accompany Beowulf's band back to the beach, not only for the sake of formality but also to help carry the gold and goods they would be taking back with them. The hall became a flurry of activity as the visitors prepared to depart, all the while still beneath the hanging trophy of Grendel's arm and his mother's head, a reminder of all that had passed in those few days.

Beowulf ensured all among her gathering were accounted for, including those who had slept elsewhere for the night. She herself had been slow enough to rise, stiff from her wounds but better rested than she had been in days. Already only a single night of peace and the morning daybreak had her itching to move, and she welcomed the thoughts of the sea breeze in her hair. She gathered up her belongings, and led the way from the hall with the others at her back.

Near the great doors, the king and his family bid them farewell. Hrothgar embraced her as he would his own. His eyes still seemed weary but nonetheless bright as he spoke into the morning light.

"Fare thee well, Beowulf. May the winds be at your back and see you and your kin safely to your own shores. Know that you will always find welcome here."

Beowulf bowed her thanks deeply, before briefly making eye contact with the queen. Wealtheow had one of her arms wrapped around the shoulders of her youngest, and her eldest offered his hand. Hoping that many eyes were on them, Beowulf clasped his forearm and clapped him on the shoulder, bringing a warm smile to his face. His mother offered only a small bow as she spoke her thanks.

"Fates favor you, Beowulf. My thanks for all you have done for this house and family."

"Thank you for your hospitality." Beowulf returned the bow. "I wish all the best to your family. May your sons grow strong and healthy. I do not doubt they will make fine rulers one day."

Beowulf could not help but notice the queen's eyes were not free of fear, and while it saddened her, she reminded herself that she had her own homeland with troubles enough to worry over. She had done what she could for the house of Hrothgar. At least, she hoped she had. Her gaze drifted up to the edge of the roof. Somehow, though she could not have explained it, she felt deep down that she would never see the inside of that Heorot again, and whether that realization came with relief or sadness, she couldn't seem to decide.

The Thane of Hygelac pulled her cloak tight against the chill air, before raising her voice above the crowd to call the attention of her fighters. They turned to follow, and the small troupe slowly made their way from the hall. There, at the edges of the path leading down to the houses below, some of Hrothgar's warriors had gathered with the villagers to bid them farewell. Amid the crowd, Beowulf briefly caught sight of Amma, who raised a hand and flashed a broad smile. Beowulf returned the gesture in kind as she turned toward the road, following Hrothgar's warriors who would lead them back to the beach.

They passed the broad fields as they went, where the wind rippled the grasses and sent the low clouds skittering across the face of the sun. Once or twice Beowulf chanced a glance over her shoulder, watching as Heorot shrank behind them until it was only a small bright point atop one of the rolling hills that scattered across the landscape. Small woodlands and forests darkened the green fields on either side as their path wound toward the sea. It was not long before the smell of salt was heavy on the air, and the wind around them grew ever fiercer. The road had long since become more of a track, until they walked single file past the line of the hills to where the ocean stretched out beneath the horizon.

Hrothgar's warriors led them back down the way they had come, the path turning to loose and stony shale as they cut down through the cliffs surrounding the protected cove where they had first come ashore. Their boat waited for them on the beach, guarded by three soldiers, one of whom Beowulf recognized as the watchman who had first approached them when they made landfall. She and her warriors had help loading the boat as they stowed the chests of gold and goods they would be returning homewards with. Both companies exchanged farewell, and the Geats clambered into their longship with the rising of the tide and pushed out over the waves.

Hrothgar's warriors lingered only long enough to see their visitors leave the shore, then turned and made their way back up and along the stony cliffs. The boat caught the wind as it eased out from the cove, and the red sail unfurled. Beowulf gazed over her shoulder, watching the warriors as they shrank, and the Danish coastline slowly fell away behind them. The sail snapped in the wind above, and the sky seemed far more favorable than the storm that had brought them to those shores. She breathed the sea air, savoring the feeling of the spray of salt on her skin, as they stowed the oars and let the wind carry them on their way.

Despite her desire to return to familiar lands, she could not help but feel a small sadness for all that she left behind. The kingdom she now departed was not without its troubles, but the people had treated her and her warriors with honor, and something in the land there felt old and somehow secret in a way that settled deep within her bones. That moment in the cave stuck with her, and she continued to turn it over in her mind, all the while resting one hand on the ancient sword hilt still tucked into her belt. The open space of the sea gave her thoughts freedom to roam far and wide, and their departure left a strange taste in the back of her mouth, one of bitter blood and sweet mead.

She walked forward to the helm and rested a hand on the polished whorl of the ship's prow. Wind pulled at her hair and cloak, and the open ocean stretched out before her. She let her mind wander as she gazed out at the water, satisfied with all she had fulfilled in their time on Danish shores, yet still uncertain of what was to come. The fragility of Heorot had unsettled something within her, and not just for the sake of Hrothgar's sons. War came quickly, and even in her own homeland the future was always uncertain. She comforted her worry with what protection this new legend in the tapestry of her legacy might bring, as the sea bore them home.

Part 2

Geatland, five years later

Chapter 7

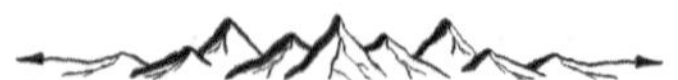

The messenger rode into camp well after the sun had set, cold winds at his back as his hard-pressed steed frothed, hooves thundering on the frosted ground. A light snow had begun to fall, though the hush that it brought was quickly overrun by the messenger's panicked arrival. He leaped off his horse at the edge of the camp, half jumping, half falling from the saddle, words tumbling from his lips. Lucky for him, and luckier for the beast that bore him, one of the men keeping watch at the edge of camp took charge of the weary animal. Permission to pass didn't slow the messenger's approach, and he ran at a steady clip through the camp, gathering a small crowd of curious armored onlookers as he went.

Some warriors had already gone to bed, but most were still up, grouped around the fires that burned steadily in the night, keeping the chill at bay. The ground underfoot had become a sloppy mire amid the damp and the many footfalls of fighters and horses, and more than once the messenger nearly lost his footing. He was breathing hard by the time he reached the large tent, his breath causing ice crystals to gather in his beard. He yanked his hood back with one hand, while the other held tight to the roll of parchment he carried, and the two warriors at the entrance to the tent stood aside, that he might pass.

The air within was warm despite the soggy ground, and the canvas was large enough to encompass space for a small fire. The modest flames cast light across the tapestries that hung on the sides of the tent and on the helmets that had been stowed amid furs on top of three cots. A poor excuse for a table was set out in the center with a few stumps around it to serve as chairs, and though the evening meal seemed long finished, there were still three people seated there in quiet conversation.

The messenger came to an unsteady halt, breathing hard, his appearance startling all those within to their feet. He took a deep breath, pushing long dark locks from his face with a free hand and holding the scroll forward with the other. Those now standing around the table looked at him with a mix of surprise and concern. The man and two women there, warriors all of them, waited for the intruder to speak.

"He's fallen," he panted. All those around the table exchanged glances and one of the women, dark-haired and bright-eyed, unconsciously slid a hand to cover her chest. The other woman, standing opposite the messenger, regarded him with piercing green eyes, her face stoic aside from a muscle in the side of her jaw that twinged before she spoke.

"Where. When." It wasn't spoken like a question, her voice grim and level.

"Frisia." The hand holding the scroll had begun to tremble lightly as the messenger continued to hold it out. "Some of the Geatish forces survived, but were defeated less than a week ago."

She frowned deeply then, her eyes fixing on some point near the messenger's feet, her brows knitted tightly. The other woman, her hand still on her chest, exchanged another glance with the man sitting in the tent before speaking tentatively, her question breaking the hesitant silence.

"What does this mean?"

The messenger looked back to the green-eyed woman, still staring at something only she could see. When she failed to answer the question that hung between the four of them, the messenger found his voice, albeit somewhat unsteadily.

"Kingship would go to one of his children, but they are too young. His queen is from a different tribe, and is not of our people. Rule would go to—"

"Leave us." The green-eyed woman spoke curtly, her voice cutting through that of the messenger like a knife.

"But—"

"Now." She looked up at him, her eyes burning with an emerald fire that froze him to the spot. He hesitated, before placing the scroll carefully on the table and retreating back out into the cold of the night. His message delivered, he allowed exhaustion to consume him, and made his way to the nearest fire that he might find food and drink.

The silence that lingered in the messenger's wake hung heavy in the war tent, and the dark-haired woman glanced expectantly back and forth between her fellows as they stood frozen. Finally, she turned in mild frustration to the man, gesturing to where the scroll lay innocuously on the table.

"Braggi, does this mean what I think it does?"

Braggi shot a sideways glance to the third among them, before sighing heavily and carefully lifting the scroll off the table and unfurling it. Light flickered across the runes as he slowly read the message's contents. He sighed again before lowering it, using his free hand to scrub his face in a weary fashion.

"Ravna, I think you should leave us for a little while."

The dark-haired woman looked for a moment as though she might protest, but thought better of it. She grabbed her cloak off her cot, wrapped it around her shoulders, and stepped out into the night. The tent flap fluttered slightly in her wake, letting a few stray snowflakes swirl in. Braggi grunted and sat back down heavily, idly picking at the edge of the parchment with his thumb.

He finally spoke as he stared at the table. "Well. Fuck. Guess that makes things a bit complicated. Should I call you Queen now, Beowulf?"

Beowulf stood still as a statue, her eyes fixed on some distant point, her jaw tight. *I should have been there.* Hygelac had seemed a permanent fixture, king since the time she was a foundling. It seemed odd, to be told of his death but to see nothing of it. She wondered if they had even recovered his body or if he had become a feast for the crows of Frisia like so many other Geats. It was strange to fathom that with little more than some etchings on parchment, he was now somehow gone. She had not even begun to consider the implications of his death, merely that it had somehow happened. And that she had missed it. Braggi seemed to read her thoughts, or at least know her well enough to guess what she was likely thinking.

"Don't blame yourself, Wolf. You were needed here. Can't fight on two fronts at once. If you'd been in the raid in Frisia we might not have been able to defend our own lands here against the Swedes."

"True." She finally blinked and looked at him, her body unlocking from the strange paralysis she had seemed trapped in. She sighed and held out her hand for the parchment, which Braggi gingerly placed in her palm. "Somehow, I thought he would live forever. Nonsense though it is."

"A warrior should know better. There's an arrow for all of us."

"Indeed." She unfurled the parchment carefully and read the news of her king's demise written there. "We only get to choose whether we take it in the back or in the chest. He died in battle, and honorably, I am sure. He would have wanted it that way, I don't doubt."

She tossed the parchment onto the table where it curled tightly of its own accord, then sat back down heavily, rubbing her temples.

"So, you know what this means, right?" said Braggi.

"It means I wish Hygelac had never made me a chief or given me the lands he did when I returned from Denmark," Beowulf said bitterly.

"After the alliance you won with Hrothgar those years ago, he'd have been a fool not to give you half his kingdom. That was one of the most important alliances this kingdom has ever made. The Danes and the Geats together have done well in times of conflict and peace, thanks to that."

"I know." She frowned. "And I knew what it meant to accept. Looking after my own people as a chief has been a task enough, but now..."

"Well, if nothing else your reputation is a boon. There's not a warrior in all these lands who wouldn't follow you into hell itself at this point."

She shot him a dark look, and he managed a light but slightly forced laugh, before placing a hand on her shoulder and leaning a bit closer.

"Listen, you're always saying that above all else you want to protect people, especially those who can't protect themselves."

"Always."

"What better way?" His question earned him a quizzical look from Beowulf, who frowned slightly as if waiting to be the brunt of a joke. "Think about it." He shrugged. "Your reputation is a shield that lets you protect these lands without much violence."

She snorted and gestured to her armor. "You say that while we're neck deep in war."

"Yes, we're defending our lands, quite successfully I might add, but think of all the many others who might incite violence if your reputation did not hold them at bay. You said it yourself—it's a legacy by which you can protect your people."

"I did." She sighed heavily. "And to that I hold. But—"

She winced, seeming almost pained by the flurry of thoughts that raced through her mind.

"But what?"

"I am a warrior, and I enjoy that freedom. Being a chieftain is already more than I want. But now the whole kingdom..."

She returned to rubbing her temples. Braggi allowed the silence to stretch between them, filled only by the occasional rustle of the tent flap or snap of sparks from the fire. After a while, he spoke.

"It may not be what you want, but for what it is worth, I think you'll make an excellent queen." He spoke softly, almost too quiet to hear. Beowulf turned to him, slightly surprised. She kept her voice measured.

"I hope so. I want to serve and protect my people." She sat back slightly, her thoughts only just beginning to settle. "If this is the will of the fates, so be it."

Braggi snorted. "So serious as always."

"Should I not be?"

"Not saying that, but you needn't always speak as if you're on trial before the gods." He winked, which earned him little more than a snort from Beowulf. But it was enough to break the stiffness of the air, and tension slowly dropped from both of their shoulders. Silence moved freely between them for a short while, before Braggi's eyes sparked with a realization and then swiftly darkened.

"Though, there will be a bit of unpleasantness with his son and daughter," he said. "Their mother too, most likely." His normally cheerful expression had grown remarkably grim. Beowulf sat more upright, searching his features as she spoke.

"What's your meaning? Hygd is from a different tribe and bloodline. Though she is queen by marriage she does not have the lineage to sit on the throne."

Braggi grimaced slightly. "That's not exactly what I meant."

"Then what? Her children? Her eldest daughter isn't yet old enough for the throne." Beowulf muttered. "Unfortunately."

Braggi picked up his mug and stared into it, weighing his thoughts. Beowulf, still distracted, turned his words over in her mind. Something loomed in the space between them that she couldn't quite put words to, but it made her feel somehow blind, as if there were something obvious that she had somehow overlooked.

"Braggi." She spoke slowly. "I admit my wits are not at their sharpest right now. There's something you're guiding me toward, but I either cannot or will not find it. Speak plainly."

Braggi looked up from his mug, his eyes still dark, searching Beowulf's expression for something, as if he could speak with his gaze rather than his words.

"I admit you always did scoff at politics, despite how adeptly you've navigated them in the past." He grunted as he lowered his mug. "The children. Hygd too. If you're to rule, you'll need to kill them."

The silence that chased his words was deafening. Beowulf froze, every muscle locking in place, holding her face in an expressionless mask. She waited for a long moment, for Braggi to crack a grin and admit his joke. Her mind, still wrestling with the news of the death of their king, was upended entirely. Her knuckles went white, and her hands, resting on her knees, flexed as she dug her fingers into her legs. She had no reckoning of how much time passed between them, only that Braggi held her gaze through the entirety of it, and only when she could trust her voice to stay even did she find her words.

"Why"—she inhaled slowly—"would you suggest something like this?"

Braggi looked momentarily surprised, and Beowulf felt a prickle of anger from somewhere deep within her chest.

"It's the only way for you to protect our people," he replied, sounding somewhat puzzled.

"What, by killing the wife of our king?" Anger rose, and she struggled to keep it from her voice as she continued. "We haven't even had time to mourn and you're suggesting we butcher his wife and children?"

"If you want peace, yes!" Braggi's voice rose slightly, slight confusion still lingering in his eyes as he looked at her, as if he somehow could not fathom why she didn't understand.

"Hygelac's children are the heirs to the throne," Beowulf bit back, managing to keep most but not all the venom from her voice. "I'd sooner die than see harm done to them."

Braggi scowled. "Now isn't the time to be bound by naive ideals."

"Is that what you think I do?" She felt fire flare in her chest, spread down her arms, and send needles through her fingertips. "You think I make my boasts and profess my loyalties, only to backstab those I have given my word to protect the moment it seems opportune?" She couldn't keep her voice from rising.

Braggi raised his hands up slightly, as if they might dampen the vitriol of her voice. Still frowning, but looking almost more sad than angry, he lowered his voice again and spoke in a measured tone.

"Listen, I mean no insult to you. I have always known you to be an honorable warrior. I would never insult that—"

"You just did."

"Just—" He let out an exasperated sigh. "Let me explain, please."

Beowulf shot him a grim look and crossed her arms tightly, digging her fingers into the fabric of her tunic. Braggi observed her cautiously before he continued.

"War is on all sides of us. Tribes and kingdoms get into conflicts as quick as the turning of the seasons. You want to protect our people, more than anything, yes?" He looked at her expectantly, and after a moment of hesitation, she responded with a small, stiff nod. "Good. I know this about you."

Beowulf still sat coiled like a spring. Outside, the wind had picked up, and the tent flap fluttered with each gust, snapping in rhythm with their spoken words.

"If you sit on the throne, Hygelac's wife—"

"Hygd," Beowulf interrupted. "She has a name."

"Hygd." Braggi held his hands up apologetically as he pressed on. "Hygd and her children will be displaced. It is your duty to find yourself a husband and produce blood heirs to continue your line. Hygd has no right to rule, she isn't of our tribe. Her children may be heirs, but neither is old enough to sit on the throne. If you take the mantle of queen, you'll need to produce your own line."

Braggi traced his fingers carefully across the table before them, illustrating each statement he made with a different hand placement, his fingers drawing invisible lines of ancestry through the grain of wood. Such it was that he didn't see the grimace Beowulf failed to hide from her face as she listened to his explanation of what her queenship would require. She understood what he meant. Surviving heirs would be a rallying point for dissent. Two competing houses would easily split the kingdom. Regardless of how widespread her reputation had become, if she ruled and had her own heirs while Hygelac's children lived, there would always be unrest. Another threat of war to add to the list.

Beowulf frowned as her thoughts caught up with his explanation, and he detailed past examples in their own history of so many kingdoms that had collapsed through conflict for the throne—kin pitted against each other, and the breaking of all vows of loyalty that held the fragile realm together. Braggi didn't mention Heorot, but for a moment Beowulf felt herself dragged back to that warm, bright hall, watching Unferth sitting beside Hrothgar, watching how Wealtheow never strayed far from her children. There had been a look in that queen's eyes, something between fear and rage, something measured but somehow desperate, that Beowulf doubted she would ever forget.

Her mind dragged her back to the present as Braggi finished explaining and looked at her expectantly. The full meaning behind his words had finally sunk in, and she felt the anger drain from her body, leaving a heavy sinking feeling in its wake. She slumped slightly and sighed, leaning forward to rest her face in her palms, listening to the storm outside.

"I suppose it's too much to hope that I could rule only until one of Hygelac's children was old enough." She didn't phrase it as a question.

Braggi snorted, though his voice was empty of humor as he replied. "The most legendary warrior in remembered history? Not likely. I reckon most of our people would be more than happy to see you on the throne. If you stepped down for the children, I don't think their rule would last long."

Beowulf could only grunt in agreement. Once she was there, she would have to stay. More than that, she knew what awaited her where her duty was concerned. She would need to make a strategic marriage to strengthen their alliances with the

Danes most likely, someone from Hygelac's lands perhaps. She would need to produce children of her own bloodline. All once her hands were stained with the blood of Hygelac's family, metaphorically or otherwise.

"If I were smart," she mumbled, "I would avoid the whole thing entirely. Maybe cede this right to another one of the clan leaders. Just stay out of it."

"If you think our people would be content in knowing that you allowed someone else to claim a throne that was rightfully yours, then I worry you may have been hit on the head in our last battle." Braggi tried a forced laugh, but it sounded more like a cough.

Beowulf sighed again. Every path that presented itself seemed a bad option. She scrambled internally for a little longer, before she resigned herself for the moment. Perhaps there was something she had not yet thought of. In fact, she was almost sure there was, but she doubted she would find it in the middle of the night after a day on the battlefield that had drained her strength.

When she spoke again, her voice was quiet. "With this fight won, I think a handful of us can afford to return to Hygelac's hall. There will be a ceremony, no doubt. And if I do take the throne, there will be something to mark it at that time." She scrubbed her face with her hands. "That gives me a few days to figure out what the fuck I am going to do."

Braggi eyed her thoughtfully for a moment and shrugged. "I suppose. I think it seems straightforward, even if it's not the most honorable path. You want to protect our people. Your reputation has already done much to that effect, but as a queen I think you could do even more."

"Perhaps," Beowulf mumbled quietly. Weariness had descended on her, and for the first time that night she finally felt the edges of a slow sadness creeping in, trailing in the wake of the death of her king and friend. "For now, I think I just want to sleep." She sighed and stood, stretched, and walked to her cot.

Braggi stood slowly. "I'll find Ravna and then turn in for the night." He walked to the tent flap and stopped. "For what it's worth"—he turned where he stood, speaking over his shoulder in a quiet voice—"I think you will make a fine warrior queen."

It was said gently, and something about it was both comforting and painful in the wake of all it meant, and all it would mean. Beowulf had never wanted it, she still didn't, but the way Braggi glanced over his shoulder made her wish she could find some words to offer him in exchange or gratitude. Finding none, she gave him a sad half smile and a nod, before he vanished out into the night and she collapsed on to her cot, swearing silently.

Her thoughts drifted back to Heorot, then to Hygelac and his family. She twisted where she lay to rest her hand on the hilt of her sword leaning beside her. It always brought her comfort. The familiar gold hilt she had found deep in the monster's den felt as perfectly crafted for her hand now as it did then, and the weight of the new blade that had been forged was as balanced and light as air though it cleaved through wood and leather like soft butter. Naegling, she had named it, and as she gripped the handle in the dim candlelight of the tent, she thought once more about when she first saw it and seized it in that cave.

She shut her eyes and whispered into the half-light. It was not Tyr, the god of warriors, to whom she spoke, though he doubtless could have offered wisdom on the roles of honor and duty. She remembered instead the goddess who taught Odin magic and the wisdom of women's ways, the goddess who presided over an afterlife not found in the great mead hall of Valhalla, but in a wilderness unending. She, who took her chosen share of warriors who fell in battle. The goddess who presided over love, but also war.

"Freya, goddess of magic, goddess of love, please help guide me," Beowulf whispered quietly. The sense of heaviness sunk still deeper in her chest. She offered a second whispered prayer to the All-father, that he might grant her king safe passage to Valhalla, before she turned on her side and sought sleep.

Braggi and Ravna returned not long after, and Beowulf feigned slumber, her back toward them as they stripped and got into their respective beds. She curled beneath warm furs and sought rest, but even as the hours passed, it remained elusive. Her thoughts were her only company, and they circled like ravens over a battlefield. Her mind harried her long through the dark hours, until she eventually drifted into a fitful sleep rife with troubled dreams.

Chapter 8

The smell of smoke mixed with the salt-kissed air that blew over the hills from the western ocean, swirling high into the overcast sky as the darkening plume of smoke rose up toward the heavens. There was no body to burn, for neither Hygelac nor any of his warriors had returned across the sea from Frisia. The ashes of the pyre would be buried along with weapons and gold, the best recourse left to honor the fallen king. He had ruled long and well, and the grief of his loss was evident on the faces of all those who stood atop the windy cliffside as the flames danced before them.

The heat from the fire cut through the cold winter air, melting the snow closest to it and breaking the bleak white of the landscape. The path from the cliffs wound back down through the trees to the hills below, where the great hall of the Geat king was a dark smudge on the land. Ash danced on the wind under the thick clouds above, and the threat of snowfall loomed as the wind swirled through cloaks and hair.

The high granite cliffs, their faces too steep to hold snow, had long been the chosen spot for last rites for kings and lords. Many pyres had burned here, overlooking the lands below. It was a sacred place dotted with standing stones, their carved runes long softened by the wear of time. They stood like sentinels amid the scattered oaks and evergreens at the edge of a forest that continued up into the high mountains to the north. The peaks, dusted white, were lost in a sea of low clouds, the weather seeming to share for a moment in the loss of those lands and all who dwelt there.

The king's cliffs, as they were called, were wedged between the mountains and the foothills, offering a view out to the west to the expanse of the great ocean. The air smelled of salt even more so than in the lowlands, where the Hall of the King and the village around it sent a small trickle of smoke into the air from hearth fires. It was the place of kingship for all the lands of Västra Götaland that expanded out as far as the ocean to the south and west.

In the north, the vast mountains and rivers formed the border of their land. The hills over which the sun rose in the distant east belonged to the eastern kingdom of the Geats, ever allies to their brethren along the western shores of the continent. Late King Hygelac had ruled the vast land of the western Geats for nearly three decades, presiding from his seat in the Hall of the King that sat nestled not far from the base of the great cliffs.

For Beowulf, that hall would always carry special meaning. She had been raised there, had trained there, and had fought her first battles in the nearby lands. It was the closest thing to a home she had ever had, and she had often climbed the king's cliffs to survey the land and sit among the standing stones, listening to the calls of ravens.

Now she stood among so many others, her cloak pulled tight about her, the wind ruffling through the furs wrapped about her shoulders. The boiled leather of her armor, the weight of her mail, and the furs she wore all kept her warm even as she stood still. The mourners who had gathered, villagers and warriors alike, formed a throng in a half circle around the pyre, facing the edge of the cliffs and the distant sea.

Priestesses tended the flames as those in service to the king stood in silence, or stepped forward to leave offerings among the rich grave goods. No fewer than six horses had already been sacrificed, and a wealth of armor and weapons and beaten gold was stacked as gifts to honor their king as he journeyed to his afterlife in the halls of the All-father.

Over a hundred of them gathered there, a crowd so large they were intermingled amid the standing stones and the silent snow-covered pines that slowly encroached from the forest's edge. Some of the mourners slowly began to leave as the fire burned low. With offerings made, prayers spoken, and the pyre nearly spent, those who had come to honor their king made their return journey down the cliffs. The crowd dwindled slowly but surely, though some of the warriors lingered longer.

Beowulf could see Hygd standing near the pyre, wrapped in a cloak with snowy fur about the shoulders. She was younger than her husband had been by a span of years, but that was not uncommon. She could not have been more than a few years older than Beowulf, somewhere in her mid-thirties or slightly older. Her hair was a rich brown, tied into a single thick braid that fell past her shoulders. Beneath a heavy cloak, Beowulf could just make out a dress of a pale woad-stained blue, with gold inlay on the edges that flashed in the light of the flames. As was custom, Hygd wore a thin gilded circlet for a crown, and a small sword at her waist, the shining pommel only just visible through the folds of the heavy cloak that danced about her in the wind.

The queen wore an expression that seemed carved of stone, perfectly still and measured, her jaw tight and her sea-blue gaze piercing. One hand clasped the other, resting down and in front of her, as she looked from the earth at her feet to the fire, up to the heavens and back again. There was a grief about her, a sorrow unmistakable, but it seemed stiff and cautious, and Beowulf was painfully aware of the occasional glance that Hygd directed toward her. Only once did their eyes meet, and the queen gave her a look that seemed to pass through Beowulf's armor, so piercing it was.

Beowulf frowned up at the smoke that swirled higher in the sky and wished for a moment that this death could simply be honored as it was, without grief being so closely chased by the politics of it all. It was simpler when an honorable warrior died, and she could not help but feel a pang of sorrow for Hygelac, so fine a king he was, that his death should be marked by fear and distrust amid those who loved him most.

Hygd's two children, Heardred and Halga, stood beside their mother, wrapped tightly in their cloaks, their shoulders raised against the chill. Halga was the eldest, and looked to be only just entering womanhood, still small and slight as she was. She had her mother's dark hair, pulled into braids that fell past her shoulders, and her father's light-brown eyes. Her brother was her opposite in appearance, and nearly a foot shorter. Ocean-eyed Heardred could not have been more than ten winters, close in age to his sister. His fair hair was still short, and was tucked neatly behind his ears, which had already turned red from the cold. Both he and his sister had rosy marks around their nose and eyes, signs of tears already spent, though fresh ones still occasionally left a shining line down one of their cheeks.

Hygd stood close by them both, the three of them in silence as the pyre burned low. Most of those who had gathered for the funeral had already made their way back through the stones and trees, along the path as it wound down from the cliffs. The crowd slowly dwindled until only a handful of warriors, the king's family, and the priestesses remained. A few of the king's loyal retainers would help move the grave goods into the large pit that had been dug beside the pyre. Once it had burned to ash, all that was left would be placed in among the bodies of the horses and the offerings of wealth to be buried in the cold earth.

Beowulf stood and watched the smoke a while longer, her gaze occasionally drifting out to the distant line of the sea. She held the handle of Naegling tightly, finding comfort in the weight and warmth of it. *Freya, goddess of war, goddess of magic, goddess of love, guide me.*

"Beowulf." One of the warriors spoke, a herald of Hygelac's court. Beowulf recognized him but could not recall his name. "You'll need to return to the hall soon. The elders want you crowned before sunset, lest the realm be left leaderless."

Beowulf frowned, daring a glance back to where Hygd stood in silence beside the dying pyre. "Must it be done so swiftly?" she asked, already knowing the answer.

"I am afraid it cannot wait. The other leaders have all gathered, all who could make the distance in time."

She heard the implication in his words. It was true; the land that Hygelac had ruled over was vast, stretching so far and having so many souls within it. The jarls who had come to pay her their allegiance could not be kept waiting. She pushed it from her mind and focused instead on the next words he spoke.

"The elders would see you crowned before the end of the day. It would be wise to return and prepare."

She stood for another moment, looking up now at the sky as the clouds threatened a storm. Daylight had only just come, but here in winter it would pass before long, leaving them in the long dark of the winter's night. Not finding any way around it, Beowulf turned back and nodded.

"Very well." She paused then, glancing back at Hygd. "If I might, I would request to speak to the queen before the ceremony occurs."

The herald nodded. "You needn't make a request. You can order it. And Hygd is no longer queen." He looked pointedly at Beowulf as he bowed. "You are."

Every word he spoke left a sour taste in Beowulf's mouth, though she did her utmost to keep it from showing. Her eyes blazed as one hand curled into a fist by her side, but she spoke in even and measured tones.

"I would not *order* the queen"—she looked back at Hygd as she spoke for emphasis—"in her own home. Please let her know I *request* to speak with her beforehand."

The herald opened his mouth to speak again but, seeing the fire in Beowulf's eyes, clamped it shut and nodded.

"Good." Beowulf turned, her cloak whipping about her, and walked along the path back between the standing stones. She wound her way through the scattered trees, under the bare branches of a large ash, listening to a raven that croaked from within its branches. *Goddess, guide me.* She made her way slowly back toward the hall and village below.

Her journey down from the cliffs had painted color back into her cheeks by the time she emerged from the forest in the lowlands. Braggi met her at the edge of the village, and Beowulf couldn't help but notice that the somber mood from atop the cliffs had somehow been broken. A small crowd awaited her near the outskirts of the scattered buildings. Conversation bubbled quietly, and a dissonant mix of lingering sorrow and excitement seemed to pass amid the warriors and villagers as they parted for her to pass through.

"What's going on?" she asked Braggi as they stepped through and then beyond the crowd, which trailed in their footsteps.

"They're about to get a queen," he muttered.

Beowulf frowned down at the ground as she walked. The snow in the village had been thawed under feet and hooves until it had formed a slushy mass that they walked through on their way up to the hall, and Beowulf glared down at her boots almost the entire way. Finally, as they drew nearer to the hall, Braggi stopped and put a hand on her shoulder.

"Is it wrong that the people might be excited to have you as queen? You have a reputation that is known well beyond the borders of the sea, among our allies and our enemies both."

Beowulf continued to frown. She had no argument to counter his. Being able to protect her people through renown was something she had always sought. But she hadn't wanted it like this.

"I am still grieving the death of my king," she said flatly, to which Braggi tilted his head apologetically. "And I would not see his loss taken lightly."

"He has been honored by the rites of our people as is custom. He will be honored in songs and stories all through the night." Braggi kept his hand on her shoulder. "And"—he tilted his head again—"the people will celebrate the crowning of a new queen, one who is the finest warrior in all living memory."

She felt another surge of anger, but the simple kindness she could see in his eyes quelled it like cold water. Instead, she sighed, before reluctantly meeting her friend's gaze.

"Thank you." She tried for a weak half smile. "Truly, Braggi. I am grateful for your guidance but also for a chance to better serve and protect our people. I didn't want this, but since it is my intention to bear it regardless, I will do my utmost to do it honorably."

"You will." He smiled.

"I just wish"—she broke off, frowning for a moment, eyes cast downward—"it could have been different. That the politics and fragility of all these kingdoms had not tarnished the mourning of our king with thoughts of treachery. I would rather his wife and children..."

She felt the fingers of Braggi's hand on her shoulder flex slightly as he searched her expression. When she offered him nothing, he drew closer and dropped his voice.

"I know what you must do. The herald already informed me you would be speaking to the queen."

Beowulf made a note in her mind to replace the herald with one who spoke less and listened more at her earliest opportunity, but otherwise said nothing. After a lengthy pause, Braggi leaned past her and whispered.

"Myself and some of the others, we are armed and ready. It would be best if it was not you alone. It would be wise to deal with the queen first and then her children. We will meet you in the war council chamber near the back of the great hall once the queen has been brought there."

When he stepped back, his expression was grim but determined. Beowulf regarded him for a moment, wary of the eyes around them, though thankfully no one was in earshot of where they stood at the doors of the hall.

"You went ahead and planned all this." She didn't phrase it as a question.

"You didn't share your plan the entire journey back here. I figured you had decided to do it alone, but it would look better for you if someone else held the knife." He shrugged.

Grim though his words were, Beowulf couldn't help but feel a sudden desire to embrace him. She hadn't shared her plan, because even she herself had thought it half mad. She still wasn't sure if it was a wise idea or one even more foolish than going swimming in an ocean full of sea beasts, but it felt somehow right. Her choice aside, Braggi had revealed the levels of his loyalty. He was someone she trusted as a fellow warrior, one she knew would have her back if she needed it. And here, to save her reputation, he was easily prepared to sacrifice his own. To shed innocent blood so that she would not have to.

The thought of it made her stomach twist slightly, and at the same time filled her with an odd and conflicted sense of gratitude. She couldn't find the words to explain it, or even to thank him, and she knew, given their topic of conversation, that neither of those options were something she wanted to do aloud even if she could. Instead, she placed her own hand on his shoulder and squeezed, looking level in his eyes.

"Your loyalty means more to me than you know." She looked at him with piercing eyes, but he held her gaze unwavering and nodded. She declined to share her actual plan, keeping it close to her chest, so fragile and wild it was. Instead, she turned from Braggi and walked into the vast hall with him at her heels, through the crowd that had already gathered within.

The hall was vast, much in the style of Heorot with mead benches and tables, a high table at the end, and a great hearth in the middle. It was less ornate, and the wood that comprised it was rough and worn. The air inside was warm, and filled with light from the hearth fire and the many torches along the walls. The tables had already begun to fill with warriors, and many villagers had begun slowly trickling in. The chiefs who could make the journey for Beowulf's coronation had already begun to arrive. The hall would be filled to bursting that night.

Eyes and whispers followed Beowulf as she walked, the crowd parting like water around rock as she made her way through the hall, past guards who nodded at her approach. She passed from the main room into the network of rooms at the back of the great hall, making her way toward the largest. The council room was where the tribal leaders gathered in times of peace and war, and she was relieved to find it empty when she got there.

It was strange to be in the room in which she had often attended the king's council, only now it was *hers*. The whole hall was, and the thought was more than a little unsettling. It would take getting used to. She already planned to spend less time there than any of her forebears. Her home was on a battlefield. The throne could be an afterthought. She was already turning the ideas in her mind, pondering how she might keep her warrior ways even as a queen. With one hand she closed the large door at her back, and with the other she flung her cloak onto one of the chairs at the table. The small fire that burned in the hearth along the wall filled the room with welcome warmth, and she moved to stand before it as she waited alone with her thoughts.

She could only hope the queen would accept her request and could do nothing but wait until then. The sound of the crowd in the hall trickled through the door and set her teeth on edge. Music mixed with chatter, and Beowulf found some small comfort in knowing that those in the hall would at least be entertained with song and drink while they waited for the feast to begin. She passed the time by pacing before the fire, her thoughts swirling like snow flurries blown by a biting wind. She had her back to the door when it opened, and she spun on her heel to see Hygd enter.

A momentary burst of sound slipped in from the hall beyond before the door closed, and Hygd stood there, unmoving. It was an odd moment, every pop from the fireplace seeming cacophonous in the empty air between them as they regarded each other. Beowulf searched the queen's expression for something... fear, anger, anything. Hygd's visage looked carved from stone. The lines of her face were quite beautiful, the shadows cast by the fire dancing across her cheeks and lips, but there was a coldness there that revealed nothing. Only the thinnest line, delicate as gossamer, ran between her brows.

Without the cloak and furs, the rich blue of her dress was all the more apparent, the gold along the edges of the sleeves and hem sparkling in the light. Her circlet glinted, as did her sea-blue eyes, and her gaze was clear and bright. Beowulf was painfully aware that one of her hands was still on the hilt of her sword. If Hygd had seen it, she showed no sign. The warrior couldn't fail to notice that the blade the queen wore as a formality for her husband's funeral was still strapped to a fine leather belt that cinched at her waist over the blue of her dress.

"You requested to speak with me." It wasn't a question.

Beowulf remembered her manners then and offered a small nod before gesturing to the table. "I did. Would you like to sit?"

"I'd prefer to stand."

"Just as well."

A long silence stretched out between them, and Beowulf would have given anything in that moment to know the queen's thoughts, but Hygd's face and eyes remained clear and cold. Beowulf let her hand slip from the pommel of her sword to rest at her side.

"My condolences for your loss." She almost added *my queen*, but thought the better for it, less Hygd be called upon to correct her.

"Thank you." Hygd offered little more than a small nod of acknowledgement. Beowulf, struggling to convince herself that her plan was not entirely foolish, searched for words for a moment and, failing to find them, spoke the next best thought that came into her mind.

"Were you close?"

Confusion flitted briefly across Hygd's face, and she regarded Beowulf oddly for a moment.

"He was my... husband." It sounded almost like a question.

Beowulf felt her ears grow hot. She had never been one for small talk, let alone stalling. It wasn't a battle she faced now, of words or of wit. It was something half mad, and she found she wasn't quite sure how to approach it. Thankfully, something must have shown on her face, as Hygd suddenly spoke again and saved her from her embarrassment.

"That is... we grew close, you could say." Hygd's face softened slightly for the first time, and she clasped her hands in front of herself, her gaze drifting downward as she spoke. "It was an arranged marriage, yes. But between you and myself, I would say that I grew to love him, though perhaps not in the way you are thinking."

It was Beowulf's turn to raise an eyebrow.

Hygd looked back up, worrying one of her thumbnails as she spoke. "He became very close to me. I loved him as a friend, as the father of our children."

She offered no more in explanation and Beowulf did not press. Hygd had at least shared something beyond the cold mask she hid behind, so Beowulf did her utmost to return the favor. She leaned back against the table, resting her palms against the rough wood.

"He was a good king. I will always be grateful that he took me under his wing as a foundling. He always encouraged me to pursue my life as a warrior as soon as he saw it was what I truly wanted."

"He was someone of purpose," Hygd added, before leveling a measured gaze on Beowulf. "As are you."

Unsure how to respond, Beowulf simply stared into the dancing flames of the hearth, brows knitted. Hygd regarded her, before shifting her weight slightly and crossing her arms.

"Why did you ask to see me?"

"I wanted to apologize."

Again, confusion clouded Hygd's features. Beowulf shrugged and gestured broadly around herself.

"All of this..." she pointed in the direction of the door. "A king's passing should be celebrated with both mourning and joy, not hampered by thoughts of treachery or..." She paused for a moment, remembering suddenly the hall of Heorot, and

Unferth. The words tasted sour on her tongue as she spoke. "Kin-killing."

Hygd stiffened and lifted her jaw slightly. "I see. I regret to inform you that I do not think your apology will be of much consequence."

"For my own part in all of it, I am sorry."

"This situation was not of your making." Hygd spoke matter-of-factly. "None of this was your choice. I know you to be an honorable warrior."

"I only want what is best for my—*our* people. I want to keep this hard-won peace."

She stared up at Hygd as she spoke, the tiniest tone of pain dancing through her words. She wanted no ill will and no warfare, at least as much as she might have the power to prevent it. She had never wanted to be a conqueror. She fought to protect, but her battlefield had suddenly changed to one where she didn't know the terrain, and she felt blind and lost. She sighed and stared for a moment up at the high beams above them.

"I have never had much of a mind for politics. I never lusted after the things so many others do. As a warrior, I make my boasts and oaths and I fight to uphold them or die trying, but this..." She trailed off.

The fire popped and fizzled, sending a small cascade of sparks out onto the stone floor. Hygd spoke clearly and plainly, with such a lack of emotion in her voice that Beowulf at first almost did not grasp the gravity of her question.

"Are you going to kill me?"

Beowulf felt something hard and sharp deep in her chest as the queen's words confirmed the caution and coldness that Beowulf had seen in her face. Of course, any apology would seem meaningless. Hygd had likely already considered all the options. She had a keen mind, and Beowulf often wondered how much of the success of Hygelac's rule was due to the political skills of his wife. For reasons she could not explain, it filled Beowulf with such sadness to imagine that this woman's first thought upon hearing of the death of her husband was that she and her children would soon follow. Sorrow was chased by a flicker of something akin to respect, as Beowulf acknowledged why the queen still wore her blade when she entered that room.

"No."

"No?" Hygd sounded more wary than surprised. Beowulf simply shook her head.

"I have no intent to harm you, or your children. Nor will I allow any harm to be done to any of you."

Hygd turned her head slightly away, regarding Beowulf with a sideways and mistrusting glance. The warrior pushed off the table she leaned against and took a few slow steps forward.

"You do realize," Hygd asked slowly, "what this means?"

"That I cannot rule while you all live, and that I cannot rule and then cede the throne to one of your children? Yes. My reputation has helped me protect our people in many ways, but here it is suddenly a hindrance, and while I am grateful for our people's support, I know I could never cede the throne without starting a war."

Hygd crossed her arms, still regarding Beowulf with an air of mistrust. "So, you have considered options and found them all to be shit." She spoke flatly.

Beowulf almost laughed, caught slightly off guard by the direct manner in which the queen spoke. Somehow, calling it what it was seemed to drain some of the tension out of the air, and despite the gravity of that which they discussed, Beowulf couldn't help but grin. A grin that she was surprised to see briefly reflected in the smallest curl of the corner of the queen's mouth.

"Well." Beowulf shrugged. "It seems we understand each other."

"Indeed. And yet you asked to speak with me, which tells me you have more thoughts on the matter."

Beowulf nodded and sucked her teeth. She did, and admittedly they all seemed ridiculous, but it was her best chance. What was more, it was the only way she could achieve all ends without bloodshed.

She spoke slowly, suddenly aware of her heartbeat in her ears. "I think there is a way to keep the peace. I can rule without any harm coming to your children or yourself. By the laws of our people, I would not need to continue my own line, but your children could rule after me as if they were my own heirs." Her palms had begun to sweat slightly, one hand drifted to the handle of her sword, and she took a slow breath.

Hygd frowned in confusion but took a few steps forward until they were within arm's reach of each other. She regarded Beowulf warily still, but in her eyes there was the slightest flicker of hope. It flashed for only an instant, but long enough to affirm in Beowulf the path she now took, and her certainty helped steady her.

The last demons of doubt fled as the queen asked in a quiet voice, "How is this possible?"

"That's why I wanted to speak with you. In truth, the plan depends on you."

They regarded each other for a moment. Beowulf stood firm, her heart and mind steadied, seeing finally the glimmer of hope and the determination in Hygd's eyes.

"What must I do?" There was still caution in the queen's voice, but any fear had vanished, temporarily buried by her quiet determination, that strength which had brought her before Beowulf expecting death and which had armed her with a blade rather than see her beg. Beowulf could not help but respect it, and she sighed in an almost apologetic fashion before she answered.

"Marry me."

A jumble of expressions chased each other across Hygd's face, and she looked at Beowulf as though she thought the warrior was joking. When Beowulf said nothing, Hygd's mouth fell slightly ajar.

"You're serious?"

"Yes. It would mean I would claim your children as my heirs by law. I would rule, they would be safe to rule after me, and the kingdom would not be split." Beowulf answered flatly. Hygd stared into the fire for a moment, working it through her mind, before she nodded slowly.

"I see your reasoning in this. And I do not disagree. If anything, I feel a bit foolish for not considering it myself. It's just not common seeing that..." She trailed off awkwardly.

"I'm a woman."

"Yes. And I know it has been done before, it's just less common when it comes to royalty. I hadn't considered..." Words seemed to evade her again, and her cheeks flushed slightly as she looked back at Beowulf, then down at the stone floor.

Beowulf let out a mirthless chuckle. "Not what I had expected or planned."

Hygd tried for a small laugh, and though it sounded more genuine, perhaps it was the relief in her that almost turned it to a sob.

"Nor I." She looked back up at Beowulf, and for the first time there was something that faltered in the rigidity of her features. The queen had hidden her fear well, and with a plan that could work, unusual though it was, that fear suddenly swayed under an onslaught of tentative relief.

"It is," Hygd said slowly, "something that would certainly work to address the fears we both have on how to settle the issue of succession. I understand now why you wanted to speak to me privately. This is..."

For the third time, she faltered into silence. She kept still, turning her gaze back to the fire, still precise and measured in the way she moved and the stiffness of her jaw.

"It is"—Beowulf sighed, leaning back on the table—"certainly not what either of us expected."

Hygd turned back, a calculating curiosity in her eyes as she asked, "Why did you not order this when the right to rule was yours? Why even bother asking? With the throne you could have married me regardless. Why ask me now?"

Beowulf couldn't help but frown, feeling a slight affront on behalf of the queen. She stood up once more and crossed her arms over her chest.

"You were already in an arranged marriage. And power or not, regardless of whether I think this is the right choice or not, it has a significant impact on you. I would not act on this without your blessing."

Hygd studied her, her eyes piercing, and whether it was approval, respect, or gratitude that hid behind those sea-blue irises, Beowulf could not have said. Only that Hygd looked at her in a way she had never done before, with a kind of quiet contemplation that struck Beowulf to her core. Hygd opened her mouth again to speak, but the silence was suddenly shattered by the sound of the door being thrown open. Hygd spun reflexively, but Beowulf, without thinking, had already leaped forward, her hand on the pommel of Naegling. She took a stride, moving instinctively between Hygd and the door, trusting the armed woman behind her not to plunge a blade into her back.

Braggi stood in the doorway, a man and woman with him, armed and armored with weapons drawn and faces grim. They stopped short as Beowulf moved to meet them, her off hand raised palm out like a shield.

"Hold!" Beowulf called, her voice mingling with the chatter that flooded in from the hallway and the great hall beyond.

The warriors in the door paused, uncertainty on their faces, as Braggi faltered for a moment where he stood and looked at Beowulf questioningly. Beowulf's eyes blazed as she stared at the three of them, a small snarl on her face as her hand hovered near her sword, daring any advance. Braggi slowly relaxed his stance and sheathed his sword, and the others followed suit, confusion still etched on their features.

Somewhere behind Beowulf, Hygd found her voice, stepping forward as she spoke until the two of them were abreast of each other, squared off with the three warriors.

"What is the meaning of this?" Hygd's voice cut like a knife, sounding assertive although Beowulf did not doubt that Hygd knew exactly the intent that Braggi and the others had carried when they burst into the room. Beowulf took a moment to regard the queen with a sideways glance. Hygd held her chin high despite having no weapon in her hands, and quite pointedly walked until she was level with Beowulf, refusing to remain behind her. Beowulf relaxed her stance and cleared her throat.

"Forgive me, my queen." She turned and nodded apologetically to Hygd, the three warriors exchanging a few glances between them as she spoke. "I had informed them I would only be here a moment before returning to the hall. Doubtless my warriors meant only to ensure no harm had befallen me."

The two warriors at the back exchanged a small side-glance and then nodded unsteadily, as if unsure what they were agreeing too. Braggi stared at Beowulf, caught somewhere between confusion and frustration. Beowulf stepped forward and placed a hand on his shoulder.

"You have my thanks. I would be grateful if you could ensure some guard would accompany Queen Hygd as she prepares for the handfasting."

Braggi's eyes bulged for a moment as he looked at her.

"Hand—"

High though the tension ran in the room, Beowulf couldn't help but take a small amount of amusement in the shock that showed blatantly on his face as he gawked like a fish.

"This isn't just a coronation tonight." Beowulf smiled as she spoke, genuine this time, as the shadow of doubt and dread that had lingered over her dissipated. She had been given two impossible choices but had opted for neither, and dared to hold out hope that her third choice might yet work. "It's a marriage as well. And no ill shall befall my future queen if I have any say in the matter." She finished, and her eyes scanned over the warriors before settling back on Braggi.

Surprise and disbelief were quickly followed by something that looked almost like admiration, though it flitted across his face for only the briefest moment. He clamped his jaw shut and gave a nod that made his beard shake, then turned and walked out. The other warriors followed. When Beowulf turned back to Hygd she was surprised to see the queen staring at her contemplatively. The warrior offered one more small bow.

"I should leave. I'll be wanted in the hall. Please take what time you need before joining me there." She turned to go, but Hygd's voice stopped her in her tracks.

"Wait."

She turned back, still unable to read the strange curiosity in the queen's eyes. Hygd smiled then, the first genuine smile Beowulf had seen on her face since the death of Hygelac, as she stepped forward and placed a hand on Beowulf's arm with a feather light touch. When she spoke again, her voice was barely a whisper.

"Thank you."

Had it been a warrior she had known or someone she was closer to, Beowulf might have hugged her. Instead, she gently took hold of the queen's other hand and raised it to brush her lips gently across Hygd's knuckles, before turning and walking from the room.

Chapter 9

B eowulf was crowned queen before the sun set on the day of Hygelac's funeral. A simple circlet of iron was placed atop the dirty blond braids that ran through her wild hair, and her face was marked with blood by the same priestesses who had kindled the funeral pyre. The warriors of the hall hailed her with raised blades, their shouts echoing through the hall. Mead was poured in plenty as all those who dwelt in the village and all the chieftains who had come from across the western lands celebrated the crowning of their most renowned warrior as their queen.

A coronation and a funeral was cause enough for celebration and songs, but the night was made all the more festive with the inclusion of a wedding. Hygd stood beside Beowulf at the head of the hall, her chin held high, her expression proud and austere as the two of them interlocked hands and a thick braid was wound around their grasp. Beowulf kept her thoughts to herself and her emotions from her face. She whispered a quiet prayer of gratitude as the priestess invoked Freya to preside over the union of the two queens as they were married in the eyes of the gods.

The hall was a raucous cacophony of celebration, as warriors and villagers alike shared food and drink and listened to the songs of skalds. Although all those present knew that the wedding festivities would run the full length of the month, none made any attempts to pace themselves as the moon rose over the snow-kissed landscape on that winter's night. The warmth of the hall kept the chill well at bay as the hearth fire roared, and music filled the air.

Beowulf kept her eyes down for much of it, staring at the half-eaten food on her plate, or the swirls of mead in her cup. Her thoughts had tied knots in her stomach even before Hygelac's funeral, and her appetite had refused to return in full force despite the worst of her worries being put to rest. She sipped her mead and tried to savor the feeling of relief, now that the immediacy of war or bloodshed had been quelled. She found some comfort in the boisterous song and laughter that filled the hall. It was a proper way to honor their fallen king, with a celebration of his deeds and a coupling of grief with joy.

The people were happy, at least that she could see, and there was no small amount of celebration taken in her coronation. Though she might not have openly admitted it, knowing that her rule was heartily welcomed brought her a tentative happiness and even a bit of cautious pride. Despite it all, she still felt a glimmer of dread that refused to relinquish its grip.

War had been her biggest fear, seconded by the thought of having the blood of Hygd, Heardred and Halga on her hands. She was admittedly still amazed that her plan to ask for Hygd's hand had actually worked. Hygd had a cunning political mind, but Beowulf's plan had been a bit unusual, and she hadn't known what to expect. Now, with the weight of her coronation settling on her shoulders as she sat at the head of the feasting hall, she had a sinking feeling that the hardest challenge yet lay ahead.

They had peace, and it was a commonly held belief in a land so rife with conflict, that the best kings and queens were those who were fine warriors. Whatever way she broke it down in her mind, killing monsters was one thing, but leading an entire kingdom was another, and while she did not doubt her skills as a leader in battle, she was aware she was entering a realm of dealings she knew very little about. There was one comforting thought that stayed with her, that while she may lack the knowledge, Hygd certainly didn't.

Beowulf cast a sideways glance to where the queen sat. *Your wife,* she reminded herself, looking carefully at the woman who sipped her mead while looking out at the hall, her face as impossible to read as ever. Beowulf had at least resolved in her mind how to face the rest of the evening, and when the call went up from the crowd for the newlyweds to retire, she was ready.

Many of those who sang and cheered at the call were already deep in their cups. A few had already fallen asleep on the tables, and the night's festivities promised to carry on for a few hours more. Tradition had to be upheld; the couple were expected to depart together for their own more intimate celebrations, and Beowulf didn't hesitate. She stood, holding her hand out to the side that Hygd might take it, as the celebratory crowd in the hall pounded their fists against the oak tables.

Hygd glanced down at Beowulf's hand for the briefest moment before their eyes met, and there was something between hesitation and doubt that ghosted across her face before she took Beowulf's hand and allowed herself to be led from the hall. Cheers followed them as they departed, passing through the doors at the back. A few of the warriors closer to Beowulf made lewd gestures and flashed grins at the warrior as they disappeared. Beowulf gave the hall one last smile of her own before the doors closed behind them, leaving them in the hallway near the council room.

It was a short distance to where the queen's chamber was, near the end of the hall, and here there were no guards nor servants that followed them. They walked as far as the council chamber, Hygd's jaw tight and her posture rigid yet not ungraceful, before Beowulf stopped.

"This is where I leave you." She spoke quietly as Hygd turned to her, confusion written on her face.

"Are you not to…"

Hygd glanced further down the hall to where her chamber was. The same chamber she and Hygelac had shared the night of their wedding, or so Beowulf guessed.

Beowulf shook her head. "I'll have the council room as my own. It's large enough to serve a dual purpose. There are plenty of furs I can sleep on tonight, and tomorrow I'll have a small bed put there for myself."

"You're queen. By rights you and I have a room already," Hygd said somewhat stiffly.

"I know." Beowulf sighed, before allowing a small and somewhat sad smile to dance across her lips. "You are queen as well, and you have as much right to your own autonomy. You being my wife does not make you beholden to me. At least not by my own reckoning. I would never want any woman bound to me to feel as though she did not still have her freedom."

Hygd considered her for a moment, confusion slowly giving way to something that looked almost like respect, though doubt still lingered in her eyes.

"I would have you sleep where you will," Beowulf said softly. "Just because you are my wife does not mean you owe me anything, nor do I expect it."

"But it's tradition." Hygd sounded half confused, and half as if she was trying to test Beowulf.

The warrior let out a single short laugh. "I normally wouldn't say this, but fuck tradition." Hygd's eyes widened slightly but Beowulf pressed on. "You are my queen, and I am yours. I wish to lead only as your equal. You are not beholden to me now or ever."

Hygd held her gaze as her eyes lost their cold chill. She looked for a moment as if she wanted to speak, to ask something, and her brows tilted slightly upward. She hesitated only a moment before closing her mouth and shaking her head slightly, as if banishing the thought, whatever it was.

"Thank you." Hygd spoke softly.

Beowulf offered only a small nod, before once more bringing the back of Hygd's hand to her lips and brushing a kiss across the queen's knuckles. She released Hygd's hand and turned away. Beowulf did not look back to see the queen looking after her, but walked instead to the council room, closed the door, and leaned against it heavily. She let out a long huff of air, the wind leaving her as she slid down into a seated position.

"Well, fuck," she murmured into the empty room, the sound of her voice accompanied only by the crackle of the fire in the hearth.

The floor was comfortable enough, and she had slept under the stars on the cold ground on many a night. Once she had stripped to her shirt and breeches, she settled in amid the furs, the tension of the last few days finally relinquishing its grip. What she had feared the most was, for now, averted, and she could sleep soundly for the first time since the messenger had brought news of Hygelac's death.

She expected she would find very little alone time in the coming weeks, and resolved to get rest and solitude where she might. The feasts and celebrations for a wedding, particularly a royal wedding, would carry on for near a full month.

***

Thankfully, Beowulf only had to sleep on the floor that first night. A visit to the small sauna behind the main hall on the first morning helped clear her head, and by that night a bed was brought to the council chambers, and it became a slightly more welcoming living space. She didn't doubt that her somewhat untraditional arrangement with her new wife had likely sparked at least a small bit of gossip among the servants of the hall, but Hygd's safety, and that of her children, was foremost in her mind.

The more she thought about it, the more Beowulf reckoned that marriage seemed an odd thing, at least when it was arranged. Hygd's comment about "learning" to love her husband, and loving him almost like a good friend, seemed strange. Beowulf was acutely and suddenly aware that, despite her status, Hygd had at least begun her queenship living in a cage.

It gnawed at Beowulf the more she thought about it, for their current arrangement seemed a recurrence of what Hygd had already experienced. The queen had been given even less of a choice than Beowulf herself in their marriage, given that an alternate option had been likely death, or a lifetime of leading one half of a split and warring kingdom.

Beowulf did her utmost to give the queen not only her privacy, but also anything she could to make her more comfortable, not the least of which included her freedom when it came to the two of them sharing a bed. It irked her that there seemed so little she could do, and during the long feasts in the weeks following, it nagged at her. She had little to attend to insofar as leading the realm. Winter would soon be over, and the entire realm was still sustained by a bountiful harvest from the fall prior. There wasn't much need to worry about hunger or sickness, and aside from the recent battle with the Swedes to the north, it had been a time of peace and plenty. With warfare at least temporarily abated, the realm took it upon itself to celebrate the coronation of its new queen in full force.

For Beowulf, this meant precious little time away from the hall, and she very quickly began to feel like a wolf in a cage. Daytime involved more menial affairs, followed by feasting that began well before the sun had set. Beowulf, for her own part, reveled little, and drank her mead in measured amounts, keeping her thoughts as her own council, even as they slowly began to eat her alive.

It was near the end of the third week, when celebrations were finally showing a faint indication of slowing, on one of the first days with some decent sunshine, that she had snapped at some of her warriors in council. Braggi and some of the others had suggested they make a show of strength to the Swedes, and Beowulf had refused in less than measured tones. She immediately apologized then excused herself to the hallway beyond. She was walking quickly on stiff legs, fists clenched, heading toward one of the back doorways of the hall, when she rounded a corner and nearly walked straight into Hygd.

"I'm sorry." Beowulf startled slightly, stepping aside so that her wife could pass.

"Are you alright?" Hygd paused. They had spoken little, occasionally at the feasts, and then not much more than sharing memories of the hall or briefly asking how the other was doing. There was a strange feeling that they were both enduring some kind of trial, rather than celebrating a honeymoon, and Beowulf doubted that it wasn't the first time that Hygd had needed to adjust to something new and perhaps a bit jarring. But the queen was experienced in the ways of court, more so than Beowulf, and had spoken and attended most of the scant council meetings that had occurred in those weeks, and Beowulf was always grateful for her insight. Her question now seemed more genuine and less a courtesy, and Beowulf allowed herself a frustrated grunt before she responded.

"I feel a bit like an animal in a cage. I've been stuck under this roof for too long and I'm certainly not"—she paused before offering an awkward chuckle—"not my best, shall I say."

Hygd gave a knowing nod and a slightly amused smile, before gently taking one of Beowulf's hands and slowly uncurling her fingers, melting the clenched fist.

"You do remind me a bit of an animal that might bite anything that prods at it," she said, slowly letting go of Beowulf's hand. "It's not what you are used to, and I imagine you're not one for having your freedom stymied."

"You're one to talk," Beowulf snorted, and then quickly followed with, "Apologies, that sounded a bit rude. I don't mean it as a criticism, only that you've had to get used to... well, being in a cage of sorts, I would imagine."

Hygd stared at her intently for a moment, her eyes no longer as icy as they had been during those first days after Hygelac's death. She seemed to weigh something for a moment, before she glanced over her shoulder to one of the small back doors of the hall.

"I have. But we find our own ways. Would you like to get out for a bit? We could go for a quick ride. I could use some fresh air myself."

Beowulf, caught slightly off guard by the offer, blinked a few times before she answered. "Out? I mean…"

Her words jumbled slightly in a race to escape her lips, so she took a deep breath and tried again.

"I would be very grateful for some fresh air. Please lead the way." She smiled slightly, still a bit surprised by her queen's gesture, but not one to turn it down.

Hygd led the way to the door, taking only a brief detour to retrieve her thick winter cloak, lined in snowy white fur. Beowulf was already armored, and the leather she wore would keep her warm enough so long as she was not out for too long. The two of them slipped from the back door out into the dim daylight beyond.

It was a short distance down the hill from the hall to the stables, and they walked in silence, the two of them abreast of each other as they passed a few of the hall guards. The smell of dry grass and the sound of nickering animals greeted them as they entered the building, weaving around some of the stable hands as they worked to clear out the stalls. Beowulf's ash-colored gelding, Tordenvejr, was always eager to stretch his legs, and patiently waited while he was fitted with his barding. The two young men who readied the horses for their queens asked no questions and offered only an occasional curious glance. The two wives drew little attention as they climbed atop their mounts and rode out onto the track that led down toward the village.

The great hall was slightly offset inside the circular ring of the buildings and habitations around it, and they took the shortest road, to the western and much smaller gate. They passed carts and horses on their way, as well as occasional children dodging along the earthen roads. The air was crisp and cold, the snow in the lowlands still inches thick on the ground, the roads a muddy mire. The horses' hooves splashed through as they left the town at a trot and finally passed beyond the gates. Beowulf gave only a small nod to the guards stationed there as they departed, their mounts picking up speed as they went.

Out beyond the walls, Hygd urged her silvery steed onward, and Beowulf gave Tordenvejr more of the reins, letting him stretch his neck out, his hoofbeats drumming ever more rapidly. The cold wind under a slate gray sky smelled of fresh snow and cold ice from the mountains. Beowulf breathed deeply, savoring the fresh air as her horse's pace quickened. Tension fell from her shoulders the further they flew from the hall, both of the horses now galloping, Hygd's cloak tumbling about her like a restless storm cloud.

Beowulf's laughter was lost in the wind as she hunched slightly, letting Tordenvejr break into a full gallop and thunder over the flat and snowy path, ice flying as they went. It was only when they reached the scattered evergreen wood that marked the start of the steeper foothills that she slowed. The forest speckled the landscape here, stretching up into the mountains and surrounding all sides as the path turned further upward until the cliffs rose high and proud and the steep track turned to switchbacks.

Hygd took the lead, though where she led them, Beowulf could not have said. Just beyond the edge of the wood she took a narrow hunter's path that Beowulf herself had not even seen until they were already on it. Their route led them away from the cliffs and through the trees, the world silent around them under a thin blanket of snow. Here they walked their steeds, the ground more dangerous and uneven underfoot. With the roar of the wind no longer in her ears, Beowulf could hear the faint call of a raven, and the whispering of the wind through the army of pines they slowly moved through.

Their path opened suddenly into a clearing, filled with the gentle sound of running water. A small waterfall tumbled down through the rocks, the stream above and below coated in places with a thin sheet of ice. Where it flowed freely, the water that fell over the rocks burbled loudly and chortled. The clearing itself was nearly a hundred feet in diameter, broad and open beneath the sky. It was dotted with several large ash trees, bare of their leaves, that stretched their limbs up toward the heavens.

Hygd dismounted and led her horse to the stream, and Beowulf followed suit. The air around them was still and quiet, the clearing protected from wind on all sides by the thick wall of pines they had moved through. There was something deeply peaceful about it, and Beowulf took a moment to look around her as she tied her horse and breathed the chill air.

"I've never seen this place," she said softly, turning back to see Hygd dipping her hands in the icy water before placing a droplet on her brow.

"I found it many years ago when I was out riding."

"It's beautiful."

Hygd nodded her agreement and stood, before making her way to a large fallen log and clearing off some of the snow that she might sit. "It is. I come here often. I always have."

She seemed poised to say more, and Beowulf, not wanting to break what stillness had made her queen wish to share, quietly came and cleared a space to sit a few feet from her. Only when Hygd failed to continue, leaving them for a time with the sound of the stream, did Beowulf speak again.

"Do you ride often?"

"When the season permits. I find it freeing." She said with a small but genuine smile. Beowulf had sensed a stiffness about her, one that hid in the corners of her mouth and eyes, rendering her face a cool and expressionless mask, but away from the eyes of the hall, it had somehow vanished. There was a sparkle to the blue sea of her gaze that Beowulf had not seen before, and somehow it felt oddly intimate, and it made the warrior's ears grow hot as she glanced away to where the horses stood tethered.

"Do you find the hall confining?" Beowulf asked carefully.

"No more so than you," Hygd said, and Beowulf let out a short laugh.

"So that's a yes."

Both she and Hygd laughed; the sound was muted by the soft snow about them, but it seemed to lift a weight from both of their shoulders.

"It's not so bad," Hygd said after a short pause. "I think I find it easier than you. It is home, after all, and I care for that place as well as those beneath its roof."

"It's not what I am accustomed to." Beowulf frowned slightly as she spoke. "I am used to a bit more freedom. A warrior may spend much of their life at any given hall, but time out in the wilds, and out further on the fringes of the realm—that is what I miss."

"That's more the ways of a monster hunter, I would think," Hygd said, and Beowulf turned to her, but the queen was gazing out across the clearing. She kept speaking, her eyes fixed on some point in the distance. "Journeying to the fringes of the world of men, venturing out into the wilds. I would imagine that being without that would feel..." She trailed off before turning back to Beowulf, something almost sad in her eyes. "Limiting."

"I suppose so. And I do miss it. I should think I will try to get out a bit more, even if only for a day at a time where I can manage." Beowulf chewed her lip as she thought, savoring the clear air as she did so. "So long as it would not interfere with my responsibilities, I think it would do me well to stretch my legs a bit more often. If not for my sake than for anyone who trains with me in the yard. I get a bit irritable when I am kept pent up." She snorted, and Hygd laughed lightly.

"What was it I heard your friend say? A wolf in a cage?" the queen asked.

Beowulf grinned and rolled her eyes. "Yes. Braggi likes that one. Hearkens to an old nickname. When I was training as a foundling, they called me 'Little Wolf.'"

"I like that." Hygd looked Beowulf up and down. "It's fitting."

"He's not wrong, I suppose." The warrior shrugged, unable to hide her smile as silence descended on them once again. A very light snow had begun to fall, and in the stillness of the clearing it made a faint rustling sound as it drifted down about them. Beowulf began to feel the edges of the chill creeping through her armor and caught herself wishing she had brought her cloak. Hygd pulled her own tighter about her, the snowy fur around her shoulders brushing against her cheeks. She regarded Beowulf for a while before she spoke again, and when she did her voice was much softer and her tone more measured than before.

"It is my duty to rule as much as yours, and any time you would like to get away from the hall for a measure beyond a day, know that you leave it in good hands." The gesture was unexpected, and oddly kind. At first, Beowulf was not entirely sure how to best respond. She did not want to give the impression it went unnoticed or unappreciated.

"That's a generous offer." She returned the queen's smile as she spoke. "And one I would be sorely tempted to take you up on, but I fear it would be recklessly irresponsible of me." She looked out across the clearing again, as the wind picked up faintly and stirred the trees around them, making the bare branches of the ash trees tremble slightly as the pines whispered. "I would not leave unless duty, whether it be warfare or monsters, called me away. Such would not be the actions of a wise queen."

Hygd nodded. "I understand."

"Please don't mistake me though," Beowulf followed quickly, reaching out and placing a hand on the stump in between them and leaning slightly toward where the queen sat. "I am incredibly grateful for the offer. Moreover, you are experienced in the more delicate aspects of ruling, and I most certainly am not. The people know it, and trust you for it." She paused for a moment, until the queen's gaze met her own. "As do I."

Hygd gave a small and faltering nod, before Beowulf continued.

"I extend the same favor to you, but more so. It has been on my mind lately, and I kept meaning to speak to you about it, but the time never seemed right." The warrior turned her gaze downward as Hygd's expression changed from one of tentative kindness to one of slight curiosity.

Beowulf took a deep breath. "I want you to know beyond a shadow of a doubt that you have your freedom. You are not bound here, not even to these lands, and I would not have you stay if your heart called you elsewhere."

Hygd blinked several times, wearing a similar confusion on her face that Beowulf had seen the night of their marriage. Less a look that betrayed a lack of understanding, and more one that showed Beowulf that her words, actions, or both had surprised the queen.

"I have never felt trapped here." Hygd's expression reordered itself, and she took a deep breath. "Yes, my marriage was for an alliance, but this place is my home. I ride out to escape the noise and press of the hall, but I would never want to leave. This land, the hall, all of this is my home. All of it is the nearest and dearest of things to my heart, after my children."

Beowulf nodded her understanding, before reaching out toward the queen who, after a moment of hesitation, took the warrior's hand. Only when the queen's eyes once more met her own did Beowulf speak.

"I am glad, truly, that this place is your home. More so that you do not feel trapped. But I want you to know that I wish for you to have freedom in all things." When Hygd once more looked confused, Beowulf continued. "Should you ever want to return to your homeland and take your children. Should you ever wish to spend more time away from the hall."

Beowulf paused for a moment, a smile tugging at the corner of her mouth, before she continued. "You have the freedom to choose whatever you desire to fulfill your needs. Such is only right."

When the Hygd still looked slightly confused, Beowulf let out a cough of a laugh before squeezing the queen's hand slightly.

"What I am saying is please take whoever you wish to your bed, anyone you want or would choose."

"Oh!" Hygd's eyes widened slightly, and her cheeks flushed before she laughed and withdrew her hand, putting her fingertips to her lips.

"It may not be the standard arrangement, I know." Beowulf couldn't help but grin as she spoke. "But it is one I would like to make clear between us."

Once Hygd had recollected herself, she frowned slightly, down at a spot in between them on the log, before she answered.

"It's not a standard arrangement, but not unheard of by any means, though not one that I have ever considered or dealt in." She looked back up to the warrior beside her. "Still, this is a liberty I am grateful for."

Beowulf shrugged. "Seems the least either of us could do. Everyone deserves their freedom, and the right to follow the desires of their heart, if it does no harm to others."

Hygd studied her as the two of them sat in silence. Snowflakes drifted down and settled in the strands of their hair, the wind whispering faintly. It was the first time Beowulf felt that something of importance, something close to the heart, had passed between them. The very fact that Hygd had chosen to share that glen with her, and that the two of them had been able to speak comfortably about matters without the stiffness that had plagued their conversations before, all added to ease that settled slowly between them.

Hygd reached out as Beowulf had done before, and when the warrior offered her hand, the queen wrapped it in both of hers.

"Thank you, Beowulf." She spoke softly, her eyes as bright and piercing as ever though the ice in them seemed to have melted. "Truly." She gave Beowulf's hand a small squeeze and released it. Beowulf could only nod, finding no words that seemed right for the moment, and instead they sat in the stillness as the snow fell heavier, until finally they both sensed the time that had passed.

"We had better return. It would be wise to be back well before dark," Hygd suggested as she stood.

"Agreed and—"

Beowulf broke off unsteadily as Hygd turned back to look at her. Then she smiled as she spoke. "Thank you for sharing this place with me."

The queen offered a smile in return, as the two of them made their way to their horses and departed the grove.

The ride back felt longer, likely in part to a slower pace as the storm picked up around them. Beowulf was thoroughly chilled by the time they returned, and after leaving the horses for the stable hands to brush down and feed, she welcomed the warmth of the hall that awaited them as daylight faded.

It felt like the beginning of something. Small, but significant, a seed of trust had been planted. What passed between them was fragile, and as winter turned to spring it would doubtless be tested when the realm faced a greater threat of war. Beowulf quietly hoped it would continue to grow, unable to shake the feeling of the queen's hands around her own, nor banish from her thoughts the way Hygd's eyes had shone where she sat free under the open sky.

Chapter 10

Warmth spread gradually across the western lands as the long nights grew slowly but surely ever shorter. The snow began to melt, though the air remained crisp and clear and the nights bitterly cold. As the seasons turned ever closer to summer, the snow began its retreat back up toward the mountains, and the path of the sun rose higher from where it had dipped low to the horizon during the heart of winter.

The great hall of the western lands was known by a new name, and though it had not been given its new title in any official manner, all who dwelt beneath the roof and the surrounding lands of the Geats called it the Great Hall of the Queen. With it came the hope and promise of prosperity, for the legend of Beowulf had spread far enough to make any neighboring tribes consider twice before invading those lands. Peace, albeit tenuous, had lasted through winter and the beginning of spring. The very land itself seemed to celebrate, and as the fields warmed under the bright sun, they were painted with splashes of color from wildflowers.

The village surrounding the great hall came alive as fields were tilled and seeds planted, and the herdsman could once more take their flocks far into the hills for the best grazing of fresh green grasses. Even in times of peace, the training yard of the great hall was full of activity, and those warriors not scouting or roaming the borders of the land would practice their arts through the hours of the day.

Of the two queens who ruled there, one in particular often made use of the training grounds. It was no secret that Beowulf preferred it over the quiet of the hall or the new, smaller and more crowded queen's council chamber that had been built now that the old one was otherwise being used as her personal quarters. Those who lived within the village had often come to watch her practice at first, her legend inspiring curiosity, but the attention had somewhat quieted after the first few months. Now, it was only the usual crowd of excited children or other warriors who would lean on the wooden fence that encircled the grounds, sometimes placing bets.

A gentle breeze carried the warmth of the sun through the village, riding above the cacophonous sounds of life. Sunlight glinted on blunted iron as the warriors practiced, and at the far northern end of the yard arrows flew from archers' bows. Today's crowd was on the smaller side, mostly comprised of other warriors. They gathered in one corner of the yard, stand-ing idly beside the wooden fence, watching as Heardred and Halga swung blunted blades in practice.

Beowulf leaned with her back against one of the posts, her arms crossed tightly over her chest as her eyes followed the movements of the two children and the warriors they were sparring with. She had always believed that the more fighters helped train a fighter, the more skilled they could become. It was something she had learned in her own training, having seen and fought against a variety of opponents. The two warriors who stood toe-to-toe with the children both restrained their prowess, moving with more purpose and slower speed so that they might better match their small opponents.

As soon as the snow had grown thinner on the ground, the children had resumed their regular lessons. It was custom that all leaders, regardless of gender, be trained in the art of combat from a young age. Nothing forbade any individual from par-ticipating in warfare, and thanks to the prevalence of conflict, many knew how to swing a sword, even if not to an expert degree. Heardred and Halga had each begun their lessons before they were ten winters old. Beowulf was not surprised but was nonetheless touched when Hygd asked that she help oversee her children's training. It was both a compliment and a gesture of trust, and one that Beowulf was still unsure how to repay. For the time being she was determined to train both of them as well as she possibly could.

It had been a rough start earlier that spring, for she had spent little time with either Heardred or Halga on their own. Thanks to her reputation, she had acquired something of a legendary status in their eyes, and both of them had balked at the idea of crossing blades with her, even training ones. The first few times they had come to the training yard, Beowulf instead sparred with some of the other warriors and simply asked the children to watch. She advised them on what to look for, how to be mindful of their opponent's movements, and asked them to explain everything they saw.

Once, when a sparring match with Braggi had been particularly ferocious, a piece of a splintered shield had cut into her skin just past her bracers, near her elbow. She had made a point of showing both Heardred and Halga that she bled just as anyone else did. She could be beaten just as anyone else could, and she could be killed just like anyone else. After that bout, she had put training swords back in their hands and set them against some of the more seasoned warriors who were used to training.

On occasion, and only as much as both Heardred and Halga seemed comfortable with, she would lightly spar with them. She always found it easier to teach by doing, and while both of the children still got nervous when they crossed swords with her, it seemed they slowly but surely had begun to see her to be as human as the rest of them. Today she had resigned herself to mostly spectate, and leaned back enjoying the fresh spring air as it wafted through the yard.

Halga was quick on her feet, and surprisingly swift for being a wiry teen. She had shown less interest in the use of a sword but begrudgingly went through the training. Her bow was a different matter, and she had already proven herself as an accomplished archer. Beowulf had switched her from the sword and shield combination she had previously been training with, as it had proved cumbersome. Halga's speed was her strongest trait, and since she had swapped to wielding a shortsword and a long knife, she had fared much better. Still, she always grumbled about her training, unless it was with her bow.

Heardred was a slightly different matter, and small though he was at only twelve years of age, he showed promising strength. He seemed to relish his sword lessons, even as he struggled against opponents so much larger than himself, and his small arms quickly tired under the weight of the light sparring sword and shield he carried. He was not so agile as his sister, but he had a fierce determination about him, one that seemed to shimmer in his eyes, which were the same bright blue as his mother's.

Beowulf was watching Halga closely as she sparred with one of the warriors. Her dark hair was tied back in a braid that whipped about her as she swiftly parried an incoming strike, responding in turn until the warrior's shield made hard contact with her side and sent her sprawling onto the well-trodden turf. She scrambled up with an angry grunt and huffed her frustration.

"You're forgetting to watch your opponent's feet," Beowulf called from a short distance away, and Halga turned. "You're so focused on where you want to strike that you are missing when your opponent shifts their stance."

"And how am I supposed to watch their feet when I am also supposed to watch their eyes? And their arms?" The girl huffed again in an exasperated manner. "I don't have three pairs of eyes."

"It would be funny if you did!" Heardred called from a few feet away as he swung his blunted blade fiercely at his sparring partner's legs. "Beowulf, can you imagine if—Oof!"

He went tumbling, and just as quickly scrambled back to his feet, before stubbornly charging his opponent again, not even waiting for any comment from Beowulf.

She chided him. "Focus, Heardred! You can chat about your sister's eyes all you want when you aren't in combat. Distractions can mean death."

Heardred grunted his affirmation as he swung his sword. For his small stature and minute strength, he was incredibly stubborn, and it made him in equal parts a rewarding and frustrating student. Halga, on the other hand, had turned toward Beowulf, looking somewhat irritated.

"You say to watch too many things. How can anyone be expected to do it all at once?"

"You can see things without fixating on them. Try and maintain a thorough awareness of your surroundings."

The only response Beowulf got was a snort as Halga turned back to her opponent and closed the gap, iron blades ringing against each other.

"You're so eager to strike. Focus a bit less on hitting until you are more skilled at avoiding being hit yourself." Beowulf's raised voice carried over grunts and the clash of weapons. She watched the child squaring off and darting around her larger opponent and was pleased to see that she pressed her attack less recklessly, if only slightly. Beowulf was watching so closely she barely heard Braggi as he approached at her elbow and leaned on the post beside her, pausing for a moment to stretch like a cat in the spring sunshine.

"She's doing well?" he asked.

"Better. She's a bit overeager but she's learning. Heardred as well." Beowulf answered without taking her eyes off the two sparring matches in front of her.

"He's wonderfully stubborn." Braggi chuckled. "Reminds me of you a little."

"I certainly got knocked on my ass nearly as many times as him." Beowulf snorted. She would have said more, but a frustrated shout caught her attention, and she looked back in time to see Halga fling her sword to the ground in exasperation and stamp a foot against the hard ground.

"It's too many things!" she half shouted, crossing her arms tightly, her long knife still tightly clasped in one hand. "There's no way I can watch them all. How am I supposed to focus on hitting someone when I am trying so hard to not get hit myself?"

Heardred and the warrior with him slowed to a stop as they both turned to look first at Halga, then Beowulf.

Braggi grunted, "Teenagers."

But Beowulf paid him no mind and instead straightened from where she leaned on the post and crossed the distance between her and Halga. A typical trainer would have strong words about throwing a sword, as well as her attitude, but Beowulf knew better than to assume that a firm hand was always the best approach. The way she had been trained was the best way to train anyone. Beneath Halga's anger, Beowulf could see the redness in her eyes where she lingered on the verge of frustrated tears.

Beowulf sighed heavily as she reached the princess, and she knelt down to pick the shortsword off the ground, before rising only just high enough that her head was level with Halga. The warrior training Heardred seemed to sense the delicacy of the situation and carefully recaptured the boy's attention to begin drilling blocking techniques with his small shield, while the warrior training Halga excused himself to a different section of the yard. Beowulf locked eyes with Hygd's eldest child, and reached out to place a hand on her shoulder over the small leather training tunic she wore.

"It's a lot, I know. You'll get there, but it takes time. We can only ever do our best and be diligent."

Something in Halga shifted, the anger flaring through her seemed to fade slightly, and her eyes grew damp as she pulled some of her tunic sleeve from the edge of her bracer and pressed it to her nose and sniffed.

"Easy for you to say," she mumbled softly. "You could beat any warrior here if you wanted."

"Perhaps, but I have been doing this for many, many years." Beowulf shook her head and brushed the flat of Halga's discarded sword against the side of her breeches, cleaning off the dirt.

Halga pouted. "That doesn't matter. You could crush someone's skull with your bare hands if you wanted. I've seen you toss a man like he weighed less than a piglet."

Beowulf frowned slightly and looked down, nodding as she did. "Yes, I have been gifted extraordinary strength in this life, and I can do things other mortals cannot. But I have been made no quicker, and no smarter, by any means other than my own. I bleed like everyone else. I can't outrun an arrow, and I heal just as slowly from my wounds."

A few silent tears rolled down Halga's cheeks as she stared intently at her feet. Beowulf very gently moved her hand from the child's shoulder up to the side of her face and delicately used her thumb to brush away some of the tears.

"It wasn't always like this, Halga." When she said the child's name, those brown eyes once more met hers. "I wasn't always gifted with strength. I was a foundling, and I learned to wield a blade as soon as I could walk. I trained, I still do, but it was hard at first."

There was a new curiosity in the child's eyes, and she regarded Beowulf as the warrior stooped slightly to speak with her. Her tears slowly stopped, and though her brows stayed furrowed, she looked intently at Beowulf, who kept speaking.

"I trained just as you are now, and I was knocked down. I wasn't the biggest or the strongest, or even the fastest. What was more, I was a woman, and goddess knows we often must work doubly hard before our skills are not doubted."

"You weren't the best?" Halga asked in a small voice.

"Not at first, no." Beowulf grinned. "I was knocked down. Over and over again I was shoved down into the dirt. But I got back up. I *always* got back up, even if I was tired or aching or knew I would only get knocked down again. If I had the strength to stand, I stood."

Halga looked at her quizzically then, and it seemed she saw her with new eyes. "Then why keep getting up?" she asked tentatively.

"Because I loved it."

The look Halga shot her was outright incredulous. "What, getting knocked down?"

"No. But fighting." Beowulf had a gleam in her eyes now as she spoke, and her hand, back on Halga's shoulder, gave a gentle squeeze. "I loved it. I still love it. Nothing made me feel more alive and more free than when I had a sword in my hand."

She carefully handed Halga's shortsword back to her, and the child took it after only the briefest hesitation, her arms finally uncrossing.

"I kept getting up because I knew in my heart that I wanted to be a warrior, and I refused to give up on that. I trained through rain and snow and fought beside the other warriors. It took time, and no small amount of dedication and perseverance, but eventually there was no one who could knock me down. I could match blows with the best warriors of our people and hold my own. Maybe even win. That was no gift from the gods, that was something that I gave myself."

"So..." Halga spoke slowly, looking down at the blades in her hands. "You're saying that I could do that too? That I could get that good?"

Beowulf chuckled softly and smiled, raising her other hand so they both now rested on the child's shoulders. "What I am saying, princess, is that you can become great at anything you *choose*. If you're willing to persevere, to keep rising when you are knocked down even if the odds seem impossible, you can accomplish greatness."

Something started to burn brilliantly in Halga's eyes as she looked at Beowulf. She seemed riveted by the warrior's words, as the two of them stared intently at each other.

"We train you in the ways of the sword, myself and the other warriors. It is my duty and my privilege to teach you how to fight and defend yourself. What you choose to strive for, though—that is your own choice to make in this life."

Halga sniffed and nodded.

"Just remember"—Beowulf gestured to the blade in her hand—"a warrior acts honorably on and off the battlefield. Don't throw your blade again."

Halga nodded again, this time somewhat sheepishly, as Beowulf straightened and patted her on the shoulder. "That's enough for today, I think. Go put away your weapons and armor and clean yourself up."

Halga gave a last nod and trotted from the training yard; Beowulf's gaze followed her as she jogged up the hill, passing her mother. Hygd walked down to the training yard, and briefly clasped hands with her daughter as the two of them met, before the queen continued alone toward the gathering of warriors. The pale green of her dress seemed to blend in with the grass about her feet as she walked the rest of the distance down the hill and was greeted by Braggi near the fence at the bottom.

Beowulf in the meantime had turned her attention back to Heardred, who was currently doing his utmost to take out his sparring partner's kneecaps. His arms already looked to be tiring, and he narrowly avoided being struck in the head by a half-hearted swing from his opponent. He raised his small shield at the last second to deflect the blow, before stepping back, arms hanging down by his sides. Beowulf chuckled as she called to him.

"Heardred, that's enough. I promised your mother I would train you, not knock you out flat before dinner."

He turned and gave a wry grin, his short fair hair damp with small beads of sweat. He was at least twice as filthy as his sister for all the rolling around on the ground he had done. Beowulf stepped up to him as the other warrior picked up the last of the training gear and headed toward the edge of the yard. Heardred only came up to the bottom of her chest and looked up expectantly as she approached.

"I can keep going," he said matter-of-factly, even though both his arms had all but gone limp at his sides.

"You've done plenty." She chuckled and patted him on the shoulder, before pausing to adjust his leather jerkin slightly. "You'll need new armor soon, though. You've all but outgrown this set."

Heardred puffed his chest out slightly at that, before turning to look to where his mother and Braggi stood talking by the edge of the field. Hygd didn't always come to watch the training sessions, but occasionally she could be found on the periphery of the yard.

"I know Halga doesn't want to be a warrior," he said as he turned his gaze up to where the hall stood high and proud at the top of the hill above them.

"No?"

"No. She always says she wants to travel instead. See more of the world."

Beowulf nodded contemplatively. "I hope she may get the chance. I just want her to be able to defend herself, but her dreams are hers to chase."

Heardred turned to look at her, puzzlement written across his features. "Father always said she had to marry, that was her duty."

Beowulf snorted. "What her duty is, is up to her to decide. I don't doubt she'll have your mother's support with whatever she chooses." Her jaw tightened for a moment, before she added quietly, "As she will have mine."

Heardred looked back up to the hall, still seemingly slightly puzzled, before he turned back to Beowulf with bright eyes and a broad smile.

"I want to be a warrior. I want to be one of the best." He might have brandished his small sword as he spoke, had his arms not been so tired.

Beowulf laughed. "And a fine warrior you will doubtless make. You have the resolve of a stubborn bear." She patted him on the shoulder again as he giggled. "Now go take care of your weapon, remember to clean it, and get yourself out of your armor before the evening meal."

Heardred nodded his assent before skipping off toward where his mother stood, his arms still flapping at his sides, sword and shield clasped in tired fingers. Hygd stood at the edge of the fence. Whatever conversation she had shared with Braggi seemed to have run its course, as he now walked slowly across the short distance to where Beowulf stood. Braggi grinned at Heardred's back as the child passed him and ran to his mother briefly, before trotting up the hill following in his sister's footsteps.

"That went well enough. Seems you shared some helpful words with Halga." Braggi glanced over his shoulder as he spoke. Hygd remained at the fence of the yard, and a few of the other warriors ambled over to join their queen for idle conversation.

"One can only hope. Still, they are both doing well."

He grinned. "You make for a good teacher."

Beowulf snorted at that, and Braggi feigned offense. "You think I jest?" he asked, placing a hand over his chest.

"I think you're being an ass."

He laughed briefly, before his expression turned serious. "Honestly, though, I think you've done a fine job with both of them."

Beowulf shrugged but couldn't hide a smile. She wanted it, desperately, to be true. There was enough danger and death in the world as it was. If she could give someone even the barest tools by which they might defend themselves, that could see them through all kinds of danger...

She was thinking like a monster hunter and she knew it.

It had been several years now since she had faced something that wasn't human. Though she enjoyed a good fight, she knew too well the cost of war. Being a protector had always been preferable to only being a killer. She knew she missed the wilds as well, being cooped up in the hall, with only a few days here and there that she might escape, had made her itch to get out. Hygd's grove was a blessing, but not enough.

Braggi must have sensed something of her thoughts, as he reached out and boxed her lightly on the shoulder.

"Care for a match?"

"What, now?" she asked. She was hardly wearing sparring gear, and her light armor over linen pants and tunic was already keeping her more than warm enough in the spring sunshine as the day began to wane.

"Yes, now. There's plenty of us in the yard. We should go for a few rounds." He winked and leaned a bit closer as he added, "don't want my queen to lose her edge, after all."

She raised an eyebrow, but he already knew he had won. Braggi let out a laugh and called over one of the warriors who was talking with Hygd, as well as one more from the far side of the yard. The man and woman gathered up blunted sparring blades, one of them taking a shield as well.

"Trollspawn," she muttered at Braggi, who merely grinned at her as he pulled off his cloak. Beowulf picked up a blunted sparring blade in one hand and a battered wooden training shield in the other.

"Three on one? Seems fair enough." Braggi laughed and lunged. Beowulf didn't even have time to quip a reply before she narrowly managed to block his swing from striking her neck. What words she had meant to speak or thoughts that had filled her head vanished instantly, her world suddenly hardening into crystal clear focus. The three warriors leaped at her, and it took all her speed and concentration to avoid their blows.

The day melted around her, anything beyond her immediate surroundings blurring into nonexistence as she became acutely aware of the movements of her body, the breath in her lungs, and the ground under her feet. She jumped and dodged, ducked and sidestepped. With all three of them she would have little chance to get a blow in edgewise, so she instead focused on her footwork, maneuvering so that the warriors would get in each other's way, one of them shielding her from the others.

She ducked a swing aimed near her head and rolled to one side, keeping the closest warrior between her and the other two as she landed a blow on the back of the man's knee, dropping him where he stood. As he scrambled back to his feet, Braggi and the woman converged on her and she took a strike to the ribs as it snuck below her shield. She turned her body at the last moment, avoiding the worst of it, though it drove the air from her lungs as she coughed and staggered back.

All three advanced toward her, and again she used one as a shield against the others as they attempted to move around each other to reach her. Dodging another swing, she closed the small gap between herself and the other woman, driving her shield against the woman's side with enough force to send her hurtling backward. The woman took Braggi down with her when she fell, and Beowulf leaped forward toward the remaining warrior, taking advantage of what little time she had bought herself.

The man swung his blade first, followed by his hand ax. Beowulf parried the first blow and blocked the second with her shield, the wood shuddering as she braced against the blow. They traded swing for swing, and already she could see the other two scrambling up from the ground, so she pressed her attack. Stepping forward, she struck out with blows he neatly parried or managed to dodge, as each came closer to striking him. He swung toward her, and as his sword made contact with her shield, she caught the blow and swung her own blade in turn, catching his sword between wood and iron and sending his weapon clattering from his grasp.

Beowulf ducked another swing from the man's ax and side-stepped, swinging her blade as she passed him and pulling her force as she contacted the length of his back. The blow was gentle enough as she controlled the swing, only giving him a light knock, but her aim was over his spine. He knew as well as she that the wound would have been fatal, and he briefly threw up his hands to yield before running out of the way of the other two warriors and excusing himself from the fight.

Two against one were much better odds, but Braggi pushed her defenses. It was more difficult now to maneuver one of them in front of the other, and she risked the two of them flanking her. Beowulf adjusted strategy and retreated slightly, rolling out of the way of a blow and leaping back as soon as she found her feet and Braggi's blade came whistling at her chest. She relied heavily on her shield, blocking the incoming blows with wood and iron both.

She could feel the sweat already prickling across her skin, the heat spreading through her muscles, and the shudder that every block and parry sent through her body. The corners of her cheeks ached from the grin that spread as she swung and lunged, her heart pounding in her ears. Her breath came heavy, and the world beyond their small patch of rough-trodden ground little more than a blur.

Though Braggi pushed her, she could tell he wasn't giving his all. Nor was she, for that matter. That was something she saved for any fight where more than her pride was on the line. Braggi, like her, was grinning, and for the briefest moment her mind flashed back to their earliest sparring matches, when she was but a foundling and he had only just managed to grow a scraggly beard.

She let out a short laugh as his blade sang past her and she sidestepped just beyond his range. The woman charged her, shield forward, blade held high. Although she had the stamina to go a bit longer, Beowulf saw her chance to end the fight and took it. She pointed the tip of her blade toward the earth and brought it across her body, parrying a blow meant for her stomach, before she set her feet in the earth and twisted hard. Keeping her blade pointed down, she yanked it back across her midline, leading with the heavy pommel, which she drove into the woman's shield.

There was a deafening crack as the shield nearly splintered, bits of wood flying, and the woman tumbled back and nearly lost her footing. Beowulf was already on her, and the woman barely managed to parry her blows until one finally broke through—a glancing blow across the ribs, much like the one Beowulf had been dealt, and not enough to take her out of the fight. It was the second blow, though, that would have been fatal, as Beowulf knocked the woman's sword wide and swung, stopping her blow at the last moment to only tap her on the collarbone, right at the base of her throat.

The woman, breathing heavy and grinning, threw up her hands and hopped backward out of the way. She shook the nearly broken shield from her arm and stepped out of range.

Beowulf, on the other hand, had to duck and take several skittering steps backward to narrowly avoid Braggi, who had come up behind her. The two of them matched blade for blade, more for fun than in any seriousness. With only one foe remaining, Beowulf felt her battle senses soften. The movements of her body and of her opponent lost some of their crystal clarity, and the force of her heart hammering against her ribs lessened.

The fight came to a close when Beowulf swung low and knocked one of Braggi's knees out from under him, before knocking his shield wide when he held it above himself in defense. He let out a breathless laugh and held up his hands in surrender as she pressed the tip of her blade against his chest. She flashed a grin before she tucked her sword under one arm, using her free hand to clasp his and haul him to his feet.

The other two warriors had stuck around to see the end of the fight. Breathing hard, sweat beading on their faces, all four of them clasped forearms before the other two moved further down in the yard, leaving her with Braggi. He was grinning ear to ear.

"Good fight. You've gotten slow," he said as he raised an eyebrow.

"You're one to talk. You had a good shot at my back you could have taken more than once."

He chuckled. "Guess I've gotten a bit slow myself."

"With training the little ones, I think I may have neglected some of my own practice. I need to get back into daily bouts."

"I'm always happy to cross blades with you. Though next time I won't go easy on you." He winked. She knew he was joking, but he was one of the few people who had never treated her differently even after her gifted strength. Even though he knew as well as she that he couldn't match her, he would always talk as if he could, and despite how it annoyed her sometimes, she was grateful for it.

"I don't know how I'll manage," she said somewhat melodramatically, before picking up some of the shield pieces still on the ground and walking with him toward the edge of the training yard. The sweat on her skin made her tunic stick to her beneath her light armor. She was still itching to move, and it seemed the sparring match had instilled a greater desire to swing her sword rather than appeased it. She made up her mind to work her muscles a bit on some of the wood and straw dummies not far from where she and the others had been training the prince and princess that morning.

Braggi followed her most of the way before ambling off toward the fence, where Beowulf was surprised to see Hygd still lingering. One of the archers, a young woman who had only just cut her teeth in real combat the year before, was idly talking with her. Braggi went to join the little gathering as Beowulf tossed the shield pieces aside, hefted her training sword, and squared off with one of the dummies.

It wasn't nearly as satisfying as fighting a living opponent, but it could take quite a beating, and it held up well as she swung at it time and time again. Her strength never needed work, but her speed was something she could always practice. She swung high, then low, then high again, paying mind to the position of her feet and wrist. She swung from the shoulder, twisting her hips each time she landed a blow, ensuring the chunks of wood she sent flying came from exactly where she had aimed for. When her arm tired, she switched to her off hand for a time, before drilling a final few blows with a two-handed grip.

The movement cleared her head even as it sent her blood pounding in her veins. She breathed deeply, her flyaway hairs plastered to the sides of her face where her braids didn't keep them from her skin. It felt unbelievably good to move, to swing, to simply to have a sword in her hand. When she finally stopped, breathing hard and muscles burning slightly, she felt light as a feather and her fingers no longer itched the way they had before.

Satisfied, she handed off the training sword and shield she had used to a group of about a half dozen other warriors who were practicing within the bounds of the yard. The archers had mostly finished for the time being, and the sun was slowly dipping lower in the sky. Thinking of the evening meal, she wiped some of the sweat from her brow and turned back toward the hall, surprised to see Hygd was still leaning on the fence.

The queen rested on her elbows, looking as if she had been there for some time. Braggi and the others were nowhere to be seen, and the queen stood on her own, her eyes on Beowulf. The back of the warrior's neck grew momentarily hot as she wondered briefly how long the queen had been watching her like that. She pushed it from her mind as she walked toward Hygd, stretching some of the stiffness from her arms as she went.

"You know you smile quite a lot when you train," Hygd said with a small, amused grin.

"As you do when you ride," Beowulf returned with a small bow.

"I'm surprised you noticed."

"Impossible to miss."

Her comment drew a light laugh from Hygd, whose smile spread a bit wider as she regarded the warrior standing before her. Beowulf felt a light flutter in her chest, something almost akin to nervousness, but warmer.

"I suppose," Hygd said after a moment's pause, "that when we do things that bring us joy, it shows. Though not everyone may have the attentiveness to spot it."

Beowulf shrugged. "You watched some of the training today."

"I watched you, yes."

That wasn't what I said. Beowulf didn't speak it out loud, but felt the strength of Hygd's gaze more strongly, though she did not break it. Entirely unsure what to say in response and aware of how hot her ears had become, Beowulf cleared her throat. Looking into those ocean blue eyes was suddenly surprisingly challenging, and the words in Beowulf's mind jumbled around an unexpected wave of happiness that the queen's answer had sparked. It was not the first time Beowulf had felt gripped by a sudden desire to tell the queen how beautiful she was, but like every time before, she thought better of it. Instead, she spoke the first sensible question she could conjure.

"Do you ever train?"

"What, here?" Hygd turned and looked back out across the yard, brushing a stray strand of her hair behind her ear as she spoke, and Beowulf couldn't help but notice the line of her jaw as she lifted her chin slightly and looked across the expanse of well-trodden turf where the warriors trained.

"Sometimes. I learned just as any other queen or warrior, training from a young age, though I cannot say I have ever had your aptitude for it."

"Training and having the skills differs from making a life of it."

"Indeed. But yes, to answer your question." She turned back, her color in her eyes dazzling in the fading light of day. "I do still know how to swing a blade. Well enough for myself if nothing else."

Beowulf grinned outright. "I would like to see that sometime."

"I'm sure you'll get the chance. Though I would tell you not to expect much." Hygd smiled down at her feet for a moment. "It's not exactly a spectacle." When she looked back up, there was that same expression Beowulf had seen before, as if she wanted to say something, but either couldn't find the words or the means. "Your skill with a blade is..." She trailed off awkwardly for a moment. "Well, it's beautiful to watch. I can only imagine what you must look like on the battlefield."

Beowulf felt heat spread up her ears for a moment, but it vanished quickly under the threat of a darker and more brooding thought as her brows furrowed and she spoke in a quiet voice.

"I pray you never have to."

Hygd merely nodded, as some of the strange tension dissipated from the air around them. After a moment, she cleared her throat and smiled again, though it was fleeting this time.

"I understand your journey on the path to warriorhood was an interesting one, to say the least."

"Not so different from many other young warriors, I should think," Beowulf mused, grateful for the slight shift in subject. "Though I suppose once the trolls and sea beasts got involved it got a bit more interesting." She winked. Hygd let out a light laugh.

"I would love to hear a bit more, if you would be willing to share."

"Certainly. If my queen would in return perhaps tell me a bit more about how she came to these lands?" Beowulf asked wryly.

"Seems only fair." Hygd spoke in a lightly teasing tone, before gripping her dress and swinging her legs up so she could sit on the thick beam of the wooden fence. Beowulf wiped some of the stray hairs from her face and joined her, the two of them looking out across the yard.

"What would you like to know?" Beowulf asked, painfully aware of how close they sat.

"Braggi." Hygd pointed out to where he stood near one edge of the yard, exchanging slow swings with some of the other warriors, though all of them seemed to be doing less fighting and more talking. "How did you two meet?"

"I broke his nose."

"You what?" Hygd let out a short burst of laughter. "Really?"

Beowulf grinned and shrugged. "We were both kids. Foundlings, training for the first time. He made some comment about me being a weakling because I was a girl, despite the fact that many women train to be warriors. Doesn't mean they're always respected the way the men are."

"So," Hygd asked with a small smirk, "you broke his nose?"

"Only after he made some comment about sending me back to my weaving."

"I suppose that's one way to end an argument." The queen looked back to where Braggi stood.

"I would have preferred to use my words, believe me," Beowulf said, "but when you are a child in the foundlings, the weak are quickly weeded out. If you want to be respected, you strike first and you strike hard."

"So, you beat him in a fight, and that was how you met?"

"Oh, certainly not." Beowulf laughed, and Hygd looked at her with mild surprise as she continued. "I lost the fight. I broke his nose, yes, but he had three other friends with him, all of them bigger than me. One of the warriors broke up the fight, but not before I had a split lip, a terrific black eye and a few cracked ribs."

"I am curious how such a horrible first meeting led to such a close friendship." Hygd laughed. "You two seem very close."

Beowulf nodded thoughtfully. "I came back. And I wasn't scared of him. We kept our distance from each other for a bit, but I think he learned to respect my stubbornness as I respected his skill, and the way he looked out for others. Wouldn't have thought it from our first encounter, but anyone he considered a friend he was always sure to have their back."

"And you trained together all your lives?"

"Mostly. By the time we were in our teens we had become good friends. We were evenly matched too, until a bit before my twentieth birthday. He would jest that it was all downhill for him after that. From then on, I was the more skilled fighter."

Hygd nodded thoughtfully before glancing sideways to where Beowulf sat beside her, appraising the warrior as Beowulf's gaze still roamed across the training yard.

"You are very dedicated. I have known very few warriors to have your skills."

Beowulf looked back, seeming surprised for a moment by the sudden shift in conversation toward her. "Thank you."

"I understand," Hygd said slowly, turning to face Beowulf as she spoke, "that even before whatever gift befell you, you were one of the finest warriors among our people. That is no small feat, and I hope it is one you can take pride in."

Beowulf nodded her thanks. "You are too kind. I do not think my skills deserve such praise, though I confess myself glad that you think so." She looked back out toward the yard, a light smile forming on her lips. "I never set out to be the best, or to achieve the renown that I have. I did it because I love it." She turned back to Hygd, feeling suddenly exposed under the blue-eyed gaze of the queen as she spoke of her heart's path. "I have always loved being a warrior. Above all things I love possessing skills that allow me to protect those I love."

The light smile still played on Beowulf's lips as she and Hygd regarded each other, the queen's eyes searching her face as she spoke.

"That is noble." Hygd spoke slowly and let out a small sigh. "As a mother, the desire to protect is one that I understand only too well. More than that, when I became queen, I understood what it meant to protect beyond one's own blood. I have always admired the honor of warriors that binds them to protect. Not all follow such a path; I have met some who enjoy the power to take a life."

Beowulf grimaced. "It's a necessity as a warrior, sometimes. I have always found it one of the hardest parts. It's why I prefer hunting monsters."

The queen regarded her strangely then, a smile trying desperately to form in one corner of her mouth, but her gaze so intent that it banished any mirth.

"That is something I have noticed about you." The queen spoke slowly. "You are not just exemplary in your physical feats, though those are impressive enough on their own. You act and think in a way that is unique, that I think this world needs more of. It is something that I respect in you."

Beowulf felt her cheeks flush slightly, and she picked intently at one of the fraying leather straps on her bracers. "My queen, you are far too kind. I am glad that you think so, but I think you give me far too much credit."

"Perhaps." Hygd spoke quietly, looking back out across the yard as she did. "But a warrior who prefers to risk themselves against monsters rather than men is already something admirable."

"They are often easier, I find. Not to overcome in battle—in that regard I think they are more of a challenge. But killing monsters does not weigh on me as heavily." Beowulf gathered herself, the heat easing from her cheeks as she spoke. She looked up at the sky for a moment, before turning her gaze earthwards as her expression darkened. "That's not to say that humankind is not capable of monstrous things."

Hygd nodded in grim silence, and the mood about them changed as the late afternoon wore on. She frowned into her palms where they rested in her lap. Beowulf, not wanting to have placed a weight on either of their shoulders, cleared her throat, before shifting slightly to face Hygd more squarely.

"If I may..." she began, and only continued after Hygd looked up and nodded. "You mentioned protecting people, the desire to protect one's own people, as I have expressed."

"Of course. A people and a home both, as one is often not without the other."

"And what are those to you?" Beowulf asked carefully. "I mean no offense by this, nor am I testing your loyalties. You merely said that becoming queen gave you a new understanding of your role as a protector."

Hygd seemed to ponder the question for a moment, before she turned and looked out across the village. When she spoke, it seemed more to the air around her than to Beowulf.

"I came here when I was very young. Not much more than a teen. My mother and I came to live in the court of King Hygelac when war came to our homeland. It was for the purpose of an alliance, as the Geats are renowned fighters and would make powerful allies. My kin warred with the Franks and were losing. I was promised to Hygelac as a bond between our peoples—"

"Did you want it?" Beowulf asked, interrupting.

Hygd looked at her in surprise, and Beowulf wondered for a moment if anyone had ever asked her such a question.

"I—" She turned back to look out across the village. "I was not opposed. What I wanted was something I never felt I could consider. I wanted to do the right thing, and to me, at the time, that was marrying the king."

Beowulf nodded thoughtfully, unable to miss the line, thin as gossamer, that had appeared between Hygd's brows. There was something almost sorrowful about her, and for a moment Beowulf wanted to reach out and take one of the hands that rested in that lap. She curled her fingers into fists instead, and let the queen continue when she was ready.

"I married when I was not yet twenty winters. Later than planned or expected, but the Geats had gone to war with the Swedes yet again and the wedding was delayed by a few years as a result. By then I had spent so much time here that it had become my home."

She lapsed into silence, and Beowulf let it linger around them for a moment before she asked her next question.

"Do you miss it? Your home? And would you want to return?"

"If this is you trying to tell me to take my children and return to my homeland again..." Hygd asked wryly, but a smirk had cracked in the corner of her mouth. Beowulf laughed and held up her hands.

"No, I'm just curious, I swear."

Hygd let out a small snort, something Beowulf had not yet heard from her, before she answered.

"There was a time when I may have. But that land gave me up and left me on my own. I always had to find my own way here, even at court. Even when I was surrounded by others, I felt lonely. I found comfort in the wilds first, in the hills and flowers and little rivers of the land itself. It took time, but eventually I found it in the company of others, and my husband was one of the first. Hygelac was always kind and gentle to me, and learning to love him was easy."

She smiled wistfully across the training yard, to the corner where some of the warriors still sparred, and beyond to the roofs of the stables and the blacksmith nearby, where smoke curled from the chimney into the spring sky. When she turned back to Beowulf, she looked almost sad, despite the brightness in her eyes.

"This land became my home. I came to know it, as it came to know me. I found people I grew to love, and now I truly feel that this place is my truest home. These are my people." She leaned slightly toward Beowulf and placed a hand between them on the fence beam on which they both sat. "*Our* people."

Beowulf nodded, still mildly lost in the ferocity of Hygd's gaze. The gravity of what Hygd had said slowly dawned on her, and she knew by the way the queen spoke how deep within her heart the truth that she had shared dwelt.

"Thank you." Beowulf spoke softly. "And I know it is no small thing to share the journey of one's past. Is there anything you might wish to know of me that I have not yet thought to share?" She wanted suddenly to repay the favor, to reciprocate the queen's act of trust, but had the realization that she hadn't a clue where to begin.

After looking the warrior up and down with a thoughtful expression, Hygd tilted her head slightly and asked, "How did it come to pass? Your gift?"

Beowulf weighed her answer for a moment and turned to look back out across the yard again, conscious of the queen's eyes following her every move.

"How did I acquire the strength of more than a dozen men, you mean?"

"Yes. I've heard you wrestled with Grendel and his mother both. I've heard you can uproot a grown tree with your bare hands." She gestured out across the yard. "I've seen you train, how carefully you restrain your strength, and even then I've seen you send fighters twice your size tumbling."

Beowulf nodded and weighed her thoughts. A gift from the gods, she had called it, and so had everyone else. It was likely the truth, but the exact details had never passed beyond her lips, not even to Braggi.

"If it is too personal a question..." Hygd began, Beowulf's demeanor betraying the weight of what she had asked.

"No," Beowulf said quietly. Her fingers found the hilt of her battle-hardened blade at her waist. That same hilt still fit her hand as well as it had when she'd first found it in the cave of Grendel's mother those years ago. Even in its scabbard, Naegling had a familiar and comforting weight, and the feel of that intricate gold hilt in her palm cleared her thoughts. The tree and spirals on the pommel and handguard were known to her before she had taken it up in her defense, far more than coincidence, and were intricately tied to the history Hygd had asked her to share. Somewhere up above, the shrill cry of a hawk split the air, and Beowulf looked up for a moment as her hesitation slowly melted. She looked around them briefly, and once satisfied there was no one within earshot, she leaned in closer to the queen and began her tale.

Chapter 11

Cold water pulled at her clothing, her leather armor weighing her down as she swam hard against the briny current. The sky above had long since clouded over with thunderheads, and a light rain had begun to fall. The waves grew higher, and white foam fluttered into the air on the cold wind, each swell seeming to hit harder than the last. Beowulf spat water and kept dragging herself through the icy ocean. In between waves she could glimpse the distant shore, though the sea threatened to throw her off course with each new wave that heaved around her.

Breca was behind her, she knew that much. She pushed the exhaustion in her limbs to the back of her mind, sucked in frigid air and kicked her legs. She would reach the shore soon enough. All she had to do was keep going. She didn't dare imagine the warm hearth of the training hall, or even the feeling of solid ground under her feet. Not yet. Instead, she pushed forward, her hair plastered to her head as she cut through the water.

There was no warning, nothing that broke the surface, not even a swell beneath her. Something closed around her foot like a vice, a sharp pain stabbed in her ankle, and suddenly she was yanked downward. She had only a moment to suck in what air she could before the waves closed on top of her. The rumble of thunder and howling wind was replaced by the silence beneath the sea. Salt water clouded her vision, but she could see the massive body of the sea beast, some twenty feet in length, and its mouth around her ankle. It could have easily taken her leg off in a single bite, but it had chosen to toy with its meal first, its teeth only just puncturing through her skin. A small swirl of crimson trailed up past her as she was pulled ever downward in the beast's jaws.

She could feel the warmth of the creature's mouth around her bare foot, and see its massive yellow eyes as its dark and shimmering body twisted, pulling her deeper. Her sword was already in her hand. She used its hold on her to leverage her blow, curling her body downward and driving the blade into the soft meat near its eye. She pushed it as deep as it would go, and the creature writhed violently as its jaws released her ankle.

Beowulf retracted her blade and watched as the creature thrashed horribly in the water, blood pouring from its head as its death throes sent it back into the abyss. But it was not alone. There were more of them, their bodies blending in with the depths below her, their presence betrayed only by the glow of their eyes.

With legs too cold to feel any lingering pain from where the creature's teeth marked her skin, she kicked upward toward the faint light above. A thin swirl of blood followed her like a thread as she ascended and broke the surface with a gasp, to be once more tossed about on the stormy sea. She sucked in air and strengthened her grip on her blade, being sure to orient herself. The land was close now, painfully close. She could clearly see the cliffs and the breakers along the stony beach. Smoke rose, likely from a fire the others had started as they waited for the arrival of the two contestants. She hoped Breca had found a safer path, or perhaps her blood would lure the beasts away from him. Either way, reaching shore was no longer her priority as the creatures converged on her from below.

She took a deep breath and plunged, holding her sword out before her as she dove and letting its weight lead her downward. She could see the sea beasts clearly now, at least three of them near enough that she could make out their bodies. They circled her slowly as she stopped her descent and treaded beneath the surface. The silence was deafening as they swam in ever tighter circles around her.

One of them surged forward, only just visible in the corner of her vision as it moved with alarming speed. She turned at the last moment, moving her body to one side and holding her blade out. She could get little momentum behind a blow as the water slowed her every move, but the beasts moved fast enough to do the job themselves. The edge of the creature's open maw caught on the edge of her blade, and she twisted, the force of its approach burying her blade deep into its throat.

The next was already on her, and she twisted again, only managing to catch it on its side as it passed. Its tail hit her on the way by and forced out what little air she still had in her lungs as the barbs on its tail ripped through her mail. Her skin was so cold she couldn't tell if it had drawn blood, but if it had, it was a glancing strike. She risked taking her eyes off the creatures long enough to surface for air, gasping as her head broke the surface. When she looked back toward the depths, she could see rows of teeth rising from the darkness beneath her.

She plunged again, blade first, her arms disappearing almost to the shoulder in the creature's mouth as her blade punched up through the top of its skull. More of them were coming, she could see the dark shapes around her. Her already weary limbs protested as she kept her blade close and caught herself wishing Breca was with her. At least if there had been two of them, they might have stood a better chance.

She slew three more, resurfacing between each for air, before the seventh caught her other leg and dragged her downward. It seemed to have learned from the death of its fellows and was less intent on ripping her apart than it was on drowning her. She stabbed at it as best she could, struggling against the water that rushed by her, her blade piercing through scales but not far enough to do real damage.

It drew her ever downward, and she fought the panic in her chest that rose with every stroke of the creature's tail as it took them both deeper. Her only hope was the very jaw that held her, and she curled her body and eased her blade between the rows of teeth where her leg held them apart. One quick thrust sent the tip of her sword through the brittle bone of its skull, and she felt the beast jerk and heave before it released its grip and stilled.

The last one descended on her from above. Beowulf barely raised her sword in time, catching its teeth as it snapped for her head. She might have lost her sense of direction entirely, unable to determine which way was up or down, had not the storm above finally reached its full fury. A sudden flash of lightning filtered down into the murky depths, illuminating the surface of the sea above her. The distance seemed painfully far, and it grew ever farther as the last monster pushed her downward. All she could do was hold it at bay until her feet suddenly struck something hard and her legs buckled.

They had reached the bottom. Large rocks and patches of graying sand were strewn about them, and seaweed swayed like grass in the half-lit world beneath the waves. The monster had swum off when she struck bottom and had turned in a wide circle for another assault. Jaws gaping, yellow eyes wide, it moved with alarming speed toward her. She set one boot against the surface of a hard rock beneath her and twisted the other into soft loamy sand. Her feet planted, she held her blade by her side for as long as she dared, until the creature had reached her.

Using its momentum against it, she thrust her arm out, ducking her head at the last instant as its jaws partially closed around her and her sword plunged into the flesh of its open mouth. The tip of her blade jutted out one of the large gills of its throat, just as some of the teeth from its nearly closed jaws split through her mail and into her shoulder.

She gritted her teeth as the monster jerked violently, pulling its teeth free and trailing crimson from where it bit her. Its body whipped frantically, stirring up sand until the world around her was obscured, and its dark blood pooled like smoke, so even after its body was reduced to twitching, she could still make out little of the world around her.

Her lungs ached, her bones screamed with pain and fatigue, and the cold felt like a knife in her skull. She needed air, desperately, but her limbs had become as heavy as if they were made of iron. She needed to push off the bottom, and she turned her gaze up as she felt her lungs seize. High above her, another flash of lightning sent shafts of splintered light down into the murky ocean waves.

Push off. Push off now, her mind screamed. But the weight of the water and her own exhaustion pushed down on her, and she dropped toward the soft sand on which she now stood. Her pulse hammered in her ears, and pinpoints of light began to spread in her vision, closely followed by a growing darkness. The terror in her mind seemed for a moment to be a far-off thing, as cold shadow descended around her and her body buckled slowly toward the ocean floor.

You're dying. Her own voice spoke softly in her head. There was no panic, no dread, only a strange curiosity as the darkness enveloped her. The watery world around her seemed, for a moment, to go black. Her hands, one still gripping her sword, dropped toward the soft sand. Then in an instant, her vision returned, and she found that what she had dropped onto was not sand at all, but soft, warm grass.

Delicate blades of green tickled her nose and face where she had fallen flat, her arms underneath her. She sucked in a lungful of air, not bothering to try to stand, and her body shook as she gasped and heaved on the grass. A few loose strands of hair, perfectly dry, tumbled across her face, and around her was a soft twilight that dazzled after the dark depths of the sea. She pulled her arms awkwardly from beneath her, alarm prickling in the back of her mind as she realized she no longer held her sword.

As soon as her breath had returned, she scrambled to her feet. Her hair and clothes, even her armor, all of it was dry. The places where her mail had been ripped and her skin punctured by the teeth of the sea beasts were now perfectly unharmed. She looked no different than she had earlier that day at the beginning of the swimming contest, when she and Breca had made their respective boasts before plunging into the sea. Only her sword and boots were missing.

Beowulf finally looked up and around, confusion and fear warring in her mind and the absence of her blade making her fingers twitch. The grass was soft and smooth beneath her bare feet, and it grew all around her as she stood in the sea of green. Nor was the ground flat, for that matter, but it undulated ever so slightly, dipping off to her left where she could hear the burbling sound of water. There were trees too, a small line of them that likely followed the creek she heard as it snaked through the green fields. Young oaks and ash trees were scattered here and there in small copses all around. Wildflowers peeked up from the grass, an occasional berry bush dotted with fruit could be seen, and birds flitted through the scrub and low branches of trees. It was beautiful, and though the smells and sounds were familiar, it looked like no place she had ever been.

Something pushed her forward, so she walked. She had thought it fear at first, but she also felt a strange sense of urgency. It descended on her as if in a dream, the way the mind becomes so certain of something it cannot fully explain or even find the source of. Grass swished about her feet as she crossed the meadow, as the ground rose slowly beneath her toward a slight slope. There was a tree at the top, and it drew her like a moth to flame. What reservations or confusion occupied her thoughts seemed somehow dulled, the world around her feeling like something from a dream.

The half-light of the setting sun painted gold across the clouds scattered in the sky above, as the strange world around her took on the soft quality of the gloaming hours. The air was just cool enough to be comfortable, and it carried the smell of wildflowers as it danced through her hair. Her feet drank in the lingering day-warmth of the earth as she walked.

It didn't take long to reach the top of the hill where the tree, a mighty ash, stood waiting for her. It was bigger than any she had ever seen, its limbs reaching up so high to the heavens she almost lost sight of them. Its trunk was over ten feet in diameter, and its bark old and wizened. At its very center was a great gash, like a wound in its core. It stretched from just above the ground where its mighty roots sprawled to just above her head, and was wide enough that a person could have climbed into it should they have desired. It reminded her of the scar of a lightning strike, dark and almost black on the inside, a great living cave that stretched open before her.

The tree seemed healthy enough, and grew with and around the great opening in its body as if it was of no consequence. The lowest branches grew so great and heavy that in some places they dipped to rest on the ground before twisting back skyward once more. Beowulf reached out and traced her fingers gently against the warm bark, as somewhere above her a hawk shrieked from its perch. A moment later she saw it, a flurry of black and white and brown, as it settled on a limb just beyond her reach and gazed at her with gold eyes.

What do you seek, Beowulf? The voice echoed softly all around her, and she spun, trying to find its source. It was neither above nor below, nor in any other direction she could tell, but seemed to emanate from the earth and sky and trees all at once, carried on the wind. The dream state of her mind quelled some of her fear as she reached out once more to touch the tree.

"To serve as a warrior, to protect the land and people that I love."

To protect from what? You have already fought in the wars of men.

The hawk studied her from its perch, and she could feel its scrutinizing gaze follow her as she took a few steps back from the tree, the wind rising slightly around her.

"Beyond the wars of men. There are things that kill without discretion or remorse. Even a seasoned warrior stands little chance against the horrors of this world."

You wish to kill, then?

"I wish to protect." She felt heat prickle on the back of her neck. "Being a warrior means more than conflict and battle alone."

The hawk regarded her, its gold eyes bright as it tilted its head. The air around her seemed deadened somehow, as if the dream world around her was holding its breath. There was a flurry of feathers on the branch above her as the hawk descended. If she had blinked, she might have missed it, so fast its transformation was. Its wings lengthened as it dropped, and the gilded feathers of its head became hair.

Beowulf staggered back in surprise. By the time the hawk had reached the ground, it was no longer a bird at all, but a woman. She was close to Beowulf in height, if not slightly taller. Her garments were of light leather armor, yet she wore a rough skirt, that looked to be an animal hide, that dropped to her shins. Her hair was pulled back into almost a dozen braids that shone brilliantly gold and were inlaid with vines and feathers. The cloak that hung over her shoulders and draped down her back was crafted from the feathers of a hawk, and they reached so far down as to trail slightly behind her as she stepped forward.

The woman's eyes shone bright gold. She was neither young nor old, but for all the youth of her appearance there was a wisdom in her gaze that cut Beowulf to the bone. She was stunningly beautiful, her very presence seeming to fill much more space than her physical form alone. Brows knitted slightly, her expression somewhere between austere and imposing. To the warrior, it felt like standing in a lightning storm, the woman's presence sending a light prickling across her skin.

The warrior stood for a moment rooted to the spot, her mouth agape as she stared at the figure before her. The cacophony of questions from her waking mind were distant enough that she need not heed them. Like so much of this dream space, she found her thoughts seemed somehow separate, and instead she felt a kind of certainty from somewhere deep within herself.

Instinct guided Beowulf's actions, and she immediately dropped to one knee in the soft grass and turned her gaze earthwards. When she dared to look up once more to the figure above her, she saw the slight frown was gone. Though she looked no less imposing, there was a softness to her eyes as she looked down at the warrior and nodded. The feathers tucked into her fair hair danced slightly as the breeze picked up once more, and she spoke.

"Rise, young one." It was the same voice that before had echoed all around Beowulf, coming now from the woman's mouth. Beowulf stood slowly, still somewhat dazzled.

"I have watched you for some time now," said the woman as she regarded the warrior, "as it is my duty to watch over warriors and women who are in my keeping, that I might choose who will call this place home when their mortal life has ended."

"This place?" Beowulf asked, her voice sounding oddly small and far away.

"Fólkvangr. This is my domain, as suitable if not more so than the All-father's great hall. Some prefer the open sky and the wilds for their spirit to roam." She looked out across the green fields and dotted woodlands that seemed to stretch out endlessly in the perpetual warm twilight. Only after a long moment did she turn her gaze back to Beowulf.

"You say that being a warrior means more than conflict and battle."

"Yes."

"So, tell me, Little Wolf"—she gave a wry smile—"what does it mean to you to be a warrior?"

Beowulf frowned in thought for a moment, trying to transmute all she knew from feeling, instinct and wisdom into something she might capture with words. All the while she could feel the woman's gaze pinning her to the spot. Beowulf opened her mouth to speak, but the woman held up a hand.

"Speak carefully," she cautioned. "Our time is short, and she who can say much with few words is wise indeed."

Beowulf closed her mouth again, clenching the fist that usually held her blade. The wind stirred around them, rustling the leaves of the mighty ash, and she couldn't help but notice how closely the woman seemed to study her as they stood there on the hilltop in the shadow of the tree. Beowulf took a deep breath, and looked up at the woman, meeting her golden gaze even as it threatened to envelop her completely.

"Just because I am fierce does not mean I cannot be gentle. Just because I am strong does not mean I cannot weep. Just because I am a warrior does not mean I cannot soften myself by sharing love in all its forms. In fact, it is my duty to do so."

The woman looked, for the briefest moment, almost surprised. The expression flitted across her face so quickly that Beowulf almost missed it, but she could not fail to notice the small smile that followed it. The warrior waited for a moment and, when the woman showed no sign of keeping her from speaking, she spoke again.

"Being a warrior means dedicating yourself to a path, to training yourself and others, and understanding that you are bound by your word. All bonds of fellowship and every boast you make must hold true. It means treating others honorably, even if they are your foes. It means protecting the weak, honoring those who choose to fight beside you, and facing your fears."

"And do you believe that the finest warrior is without fear?"

"No."

The woman raised an eyebrow.

"I believe that true bravery means doing things even if you are frightened. You are only a coward if your fear governs you."

The woman surveyed her, that same subtle smile still resting on her lips. Beowulf met her gaze without faltering, those piercing gold eyes like pools of sunlight. Finally, the woman gave an approving nod.

"I have watched over you as you have grown into your warriorhood and womanhood, Beowulf. I have seen your skill; moreover, I have seen your honor and your dedication. You have had to prove much. It is a warrior's duty to prove their mettle, to make their boasts and uphold them. But"—the woman turned back to her with a wry and calculating look—"that is not your only reason, is it?"

Beowulf wasn't sure if she expected an answer, and only after a long pause did she reply.

"No. I fight to protect those I love. I fight because training and the thrill of battle make me feel as free as a hawk high in the sky, as unfettered as a wild wolf."

The woman smiled broadly, and Beowulf couldn't help but share it. The air around and between them grew suddenly warm, and they stared at each other for another moment, before the woman stood to one side and gestured to the mighty ash tree.

"By your own determination and the strength of your heart, you have become a fine warrior." Her hand stretched out toward the great gash in the tree, darker than night within, as if it held within it an emptiness as vast as the night sky. "You have and will achieve all that you have set out for. But I can offer more."

A dim light flickered within the opening, a single point of gilded starlight that sparkled, growing brighter and larger as the woman spoke.

"Stubborn and hotheaded though you may be," she said with a raised brow, "you are worthy of my favor, but that choice is yours to make."

Beowulf could see it now, where the light had sparkled into the form of the hilt of a sword. The blade pointed downward, disappearing into the tree, the handle visible within that dark opening. Gold inscribed with the symbol of the world tree formed the pommel, and the cross guard was crafted in the stylized form of a triple spiral, two forming the guard itself and the third merging with the handle. The blade seemed to float suspended there, shining from within the tree.

"If you choose this blade, know that I will grant you the strength to become more than any man who has come before you. You will have the might of twenty within your bones. But it is more than strength that makes a warrior, and your choices and actions will determine the extent of your renown."

Beowulf took a step forward, aware of the woman's eyes on her as she crossed the short distance to the tree. The blade shone before her, and once more the air became still and electrified.

She could feel something about the blade, feel the woman's gaze, something that made her stop and turn.

"What must I give in exchange?" she asked slowly.

The woman regarded her with an approving if not somewhat mischievous look.

"Wise. Your destiny is yours to craft. Death comes for all of us eventually, and know that if you choose this, it will come for you before your time." Her expression looked, if only for a moment, almost apologetic. "But know too that if you choose it, and you live by your code, you will have the potential to become a great legend among mortals."

"Will it—"

"Yes, it will give you the strength you need to protect others against worse than humankind. You will have the might to face beasts that could destroy an entire war band." The woman answered as if she had read Beowulf's mind, before falling silent and watching her.

Beowulf turned back to where the sword hovered within the tree and flexed the fingers of her hand. She whispered softly, more to herself than anything else, but would not have been surprised if the woman had heard her. *Destiny is an arrow that comes for all of us. It is up to us whether we take it in the back or in the chest.* Her mind settled, and she turned back to the woman, holding that powerful gaze once more.

"You have made your decision." The woman said, her eyes sparkling. "Why do you hesitate?"

"I have only one question."

The woman nodded, and Beowulf, feeling certain and steady for the first time since she entered that strange place, lifted her chin slightly.

"Who are you?"

The woman beamed a smile more dazzling than the dawn.

"I take many forms. Some are gentler than others. You know me as a protector of women already. In time you will come to know me in this form as well, Little Wolf."

Knowing that was as much of an answer as she would receive, Beowulf took a deep breath, reached out, and wrapped her hand around the hilt of the blade. Darkness crashed around her with a deafening roar as the dream world disappeared. The warmth on her skin was replaced by an icy chill that pierced her to the bone, and the ground vanished from beneath her feet.

Her hands and knees hit something solid, weight crashing down on her as light returned to her eyes, and she blinked. Water surged around her, salt burned in her nose, her lungs ached. She coughed and spit seawater, and her hands and knees sank into the sands of the beach as another wave crashed over her back, forcing her tumbling forward.

Her fingers dug into the soft silt, and numb and aching with cold, she dropped onto her forearms and hauled herself forward as the water surged around her. The roar of the sea was accompanied by the rumble of thunder above her and the wind howling as rain pelted down onto the beach, rippling in the sand. She dragged herself further, eyes streaming and lungs burning. She coughed up the last of the seawater and heaved herself forward again until she was beyond the reach of the waves. Only then did she dare flip onto her back, her chest heaving as she regained her breath.

She could feel her pendant beneath her tunic, the metal against her chest, the mark of the warrior god Tyr. She whispered a quiet thanks to the heavens above, to any who listened. Normally she might have spoken his name, but the image of the woman by the tree was still burning in her mind, and she had a feeling it was not the god of warriors that she had to thank for her survival.

The sky above was mottled with purple thunderheads, and lightning periodically bathed her surroundings in brilliant white light. Her armor was ripped and tattered, and she could feel the warmth of her own blood where the sea beast's fangs had pierced her flesh. There was no sign of her sword, and how she had come from the depths off the coast to the safety of the beach, she could not have said.

Beowulf had only barely regained her breath when she heard the faint thudding of approaching footsteps. On shaky arms she pushed herself upright, rubbing the water from her eyes as the figure of Braggi materialized, crossing the sands toward her at a dead run. She half managed to rise before he reached her, and he skidded to a halt, his boots turning up the sand as he offered an arm and helped haul her to her feet. She wobbled unsteadily and gripped his shoulder tightly.

"Nine hells, Beowulf. What happened? You look like shit."

"Thanks." She managed a mirthless grin that turned to a wince. Blood had already begun to trickle onto the sand from the wound in her ankle.

"Are you alright? Breca made it to shore a few minutes past. I knew when he made it before you something must have gone wrong."

"I appreciate your confidence."

"Honestly." He shook her slightly, his tone agitated. "What happened?"

His usually lighthearted nature was suddenly strained, and genuine worry was written across his features.

"Sea beasts," she muttered. "Eight. I think. Maybe more."

"All-father, protect you. You killed them all?"

"I think so." She nodded and took a slight step back to stand on her own, but her ankle gave a sharp twinge of protest and she kept her hand on his shoulder.

"Never mind losing the swimming contest, that's impressive enough as it is. Now come on, let's get that leg seen to."

He pulled her arm across his shoulders so that she might use him as a crutch, before they both turned to face back down the beach. Beowulf could see the light of a bonfire a few hundred feet away, several figures standing around it. She was chilled to the bone and even at a distance it looked wonderfully inviting.

Braggi grunted. "I'd offer to carry you but—"

"Not on your life. Though I'm glad your sense of humor is no worse for wear." Beowulf snorted, and Braggi chuckled.

"Only so long as you're alright. You gave me quite a scare there. How about next time you don't go dancing with sea monsters when you go for a swim, yes?"

"Didn't do it on purpose."

"Not enough to have a contest alone. Let's make it deadly."

"Shut up."

He laughed, and had not every inch of her ached, she might have joined him.

As soon as he fell silent her mind drifted back to the great ash tree, and the words of the woman she had seen there. Had Braggi not been beside her, had she not still been bleeding from her fight, she might have wondered if she had not in fact met her death down beneath the waves. Yet here she was, and how she had got there, she could not have guessed.

She remembered, above all else, the feeling of the sword in her hand, the warmth that had spread from it like fire the moment she gripped the hilt. It had been a perfect fit for her. She could still remember the gilded pommel and cross guard, and the words the woman had spoken. *Death comes for all of us eventually, and know that if you choose this, it will come for you before your time.*

It would take less than a day for her to find she could toss a grown man as if he weighed little more than an ale mug, but it would take years before she would ever see that sword again. Only when she found it did she know that day beneath the waves had been more than her imagination, and she had made a choice that would shape not just her own destiny but the course of history as well.

Chapter 12

The last light of day had begun to fade by the time Beowulf finished her story. The warm breeze still lingered, but the training yard had gone quiet, and smoke was rising from village chimneys and the roof of the great hall. The air around them had grown pleasantly hushed and still, the world falling away for a time as Beowulf recounted her tale. Hygd sat in silence, brows slightly furrowed, as she listened. She waited a long while after Beowulf had finished before she spoke, and when she did, her voice was quiet and measured.

"That blade you spoke of..."

She trailed off, and Beowulf shifted slightly where she sat beside the queen on the fence and patted the gilded pommel of Naegling that rested at her hip. Hygd eyed the blade in a way she never had before, something between fear and reverence hiding in the edges of her features.

"So," she whispered, "your strength truly was a gift from the gods, or more specifically the goddess."

"Goddess. Yes. At least, that is all I can fathom."

"But it wasn't lightly given. You earned that with your own dedication and heart, and that is something I hope the legends remember."

Beowulf flushed slightly and dropped her gaze. "I suppose, yes."

"And that is why"—Hygd's eyes suddenly widened, and a subtle smile crossed her lips—"I have seen you leave offerings at the shrine to Freya in the village temple. I thought you were a patron of Tyr, and wondered why a warrior would make prayers to a goddess of fertility and guardian of women."

Beowulf nodded, pressing her hand against her chest, her necklace warm from her skin. "Tyr will have my sword, now and always. I offer him my prayers. But my heart belongs to the goddess in her many guises, be it Seyr, Gefn, or as I know her—Freya."

"I had not known her as a warrior goddess, though I somehow do not find it surprising."

"Her older guises were unknown to me until I journeyed to Denmark. Before the coming of the Aesir, Odin and his kin, there were other gods that ruled the lands. Freya was goddess and queen, one who watched over women and children, but also one who guided warriors and claimed those slain in battle for her realm."

"Fólkvangr."

"Indeed."

Hygd looked down at the blade again and paused for a moment before she spoke again.

"She gave you your strength."

"She offered it, and I chose."

Hygd nodded slowly before she finally looked back up at Beowulf's face. Something in her gaze was searching, and she looked at the warrior with an intensity that Beowulf had not yet seen in her eyes.

"This story, of how you earned your strength. How many have you told it to?"

Beowulf's lips curled into a small smirk, as she placed a hand around the pommel of her sword for comfort. She finally looked out and away over the rooftops to where the light of the gloaming hour still shone in the west over the hills.

"No one."

Hygd stiffened slightly.

"None? Not even Braggi?"

"No."

"Why? Surely no one would disbelieve you. Even without you telling the story, it is commonly believed that your gift is a boon of the gods. Would you not want them to know which?"

Beowulf shook her head, still gazing out at the twilight. She could feel the chill of the evening subtly approaching as the sea-born wind shifted about them.

"Whatever happened beneath the waves, the choice I made, it was all a part of my destiny. It always felt too private. I don't know how else to describe it. I feel it is a truth for me to hold in my heart, known only to myself and her." She looked back at Hygd. "And any who I could truly trust."

It was Hygd's turn to blush, and her ever-present proud expression seemed to crack for a moment, her brows turning slightly upward, her mouth ajar.

"I fear I underestimated how much I asked of you when I requested this story." She sounded almost bashful, and for all the world acting very unlike the stern and slightly cold queen that Beowulf knew.

The warrior laughed lightly. "If I wasn't willing, I would not have told it."

Hygd stared intently and smoothed out the front of her dress with her palms, before turning back to Beowulf. She too smiled, small but genuine, her eyes bright and her gaze much softer than Beowulf had ever seen.

"Thank you. Truly. I do not underestimate the level of trust you have shown me, and I am grateful to know the story."

"Thank you," Beowulf replied softly.

"For what?" Hygd asked, surprised.

"For seeing me as more than a god-given gift." She offered a half-sad smile.

Hygd let out a small laugh, then rearranged her expression into a slightly more serious and familiar form, though her smile remained.

"How could I not? I've seen enough warriors in my day to appreciate the skills you have honed even without your strength. Those same skills I admired only earlier today." Her tone was light and playful, almost joking, but it still made Beowulf's ears grow hot. She let out a laugh of her own, the tension easing from her shoulders. Only then did both of them seem to realize how well and truly the day had been fully spent.

"We ought to return before the evening meal is entirely finished," Hygd suggested as their laughter faded. Beowulf nodded, and the two of them stepped down from their perch on the fence. The cry of a hawk pierced through the last fading light as they walked, side by side, slowly making their way back up to the hall in silence.

Inside was warm and bright, and the smell of roast meat and woodsmoke filled the air. The tables were not as crowded as at a proper feast, but several warriors sat at the long tables, and the sound of chatter mixed with the crackling of the fire. The two queens took their meal at the head table with Hygd's children, as servants made the rounds with food and drink.

Heardred and Halga were having a heated debate about the hunting habits of trolls, and Beowulf couldn't help but smirk as she listened. She kept her thoughts for company and ate her meal in silence, aware of a few sideways glances from Hygd but making no sign she had noticed them. For all the fear that sharing her tale had first stirred in her, there was a strange comfort in someone else knowing. And more than that, Hygd had been curious and kind in her asking. It still made Beowulf's chest grow warm to think that the queen had stayed at the training grounds to watch her. She didn't quite know what to make of it, but each time she turned it over in her mind, it brought a smile to her lips.

Beowulf was deep enough in her own thoughts that she didn't notice when the chatter in the hall suddenly died. Nor did she hear a set of hurried footsteps on the cold stone. Only when Hygd stirred in the seat beside her did she look up to see the villager as he staggered to a halt before the high table. Blood stained the side of his face, and he trembled like a leaf where he stood. All within the hall had quieted and turned to watch him.

Beowulf stood so forcefully she almost toppled her chair. Hygd, slightly more graceful, slowly rose as Halga let out a small gasp. The guards at the great doors who had let the visitor pass trailed behind him, fear seeping through the air in the man's wake.

"Speak." Beowulf gestured toward the man. He nodded, his head shaking, his movements jarred and jittery.

"I come from the village of Vänersborg, on the shores of the great lake," he stammered, his eyes wide with shock. Beowulf knew it; it was not far, a decently sized village that thrived on the edge of the massive lake that formed the northeasternmost border of their land. She nodded, waiting for him to continue.

"They—we—had no warning. They came across the lake—they never..." He trailed off, his mouth opening and closing, eyes unfocused.

"Speak!" Beowulf said clearly, and perhaps a bit loudly, but the fear in the room had set her teeth on edge, and the warriors in the hall had already begun to rise. She could see Hygd beside her, her hands on the edge of the table, knuckles white. The man startled slightly and then nodded.

"The Swedes... My queens, the Swedes have attacked. I rode my steed nearly to death to bring the news."

A roar went up within the hall as warriors began to shout. Those that weren't already standing found their feet, and a general frenzy of rage rippled through the room. Hygd held herself perfectly still, her expression sharp and cold, but Beowulf could see how tightly she gripped the table. The warrior felt her thoughts swirl about her, confusion, anger and dread at the forefront. She took a deep breath and raised her hand, letting the air in her lungs echo through the hall as she shouted above the din in a cry like a dragon's roar.

"Enough!"

The hall fell abruptly silent. Beowulf could see Hygd watching her out of the corner of her eye as the warriors turned their attention to their queens. She took another deep breath, her hand on the hilt of Naegling, steadying her.

"Tell me, what is your name?" she asked the villager, who was still trembling before the high table.

"Gunnar," he answered haltingly.

"What can you tell me about this attack?"

"They"—he swallowed hard—"they came in boats. There was a storm, and visibility on the lake was poor. We didn't see them until they nearly reached shore. By then"—he shuddered violently where he stood—"by then it was too late. It happened so fast. There were plenty of warriors among us, but I fear not enough. I managed to find a horse, and rode here as fast as it would carry me. I had to warn—some of us escaped, but most..."

He fell silent, his gaze dropping blankly to the stone floor.

Another ripple of anger coursed through the hall. Beowulf finally lowered her hand as the warriors kept their silence.

"Gunnar, thank you for bringing this news. I will have the healers see you, and then you will tell me everything you can about this attack." Beowulf's voice was stiff as she spoke, and her body was rigid, aware of the many sets of eyes that followed her. She was surprised when Hygd spoke up from beside her and addressed the hall.

"We are no strangers to war, but it is not to be taken lightly. I will organize the villagers so that we might prepare to receive any survivors and wounded."

Beowulf gave her a small and appreciative nod. "I will gather a war party to reclaim Vänersborg once we know what we are up against. We will depart at dawn. All of you." She gestured to the warriors. "I know you are as angered by this news as I, but the best you can do is get a good night's sleep and be ready to leave at daybreak."

It was Beowulf's first real test as queen, and she knew that every word she spoke would shape how her people saw her. Hygd stepped slightly closer to her and spoke out across the room, in a voice loud and clear.

"We have defeated our enemies to the northeast before, we will do so again. This act will not go unpunished."

Beowulf felt a sudden urge to take the queen's hand as she stood beside her, to interlace their fingers as they both prepared themselves and their people for what lay ahead. Instead, she turned her focus back to the hall, her voice carrying above the angry murmurings that filled the vast room.

"Steel your hearts. We will petition the gods for their favor on the morrow and ride to find victory against the Swedes."

This garnered a loud roar from the hall and more fists hammering against the tables. Beowulf watched Hygd out of the corner of her eye; the queen held her chin high, her eyes burning with icy fire, fists clenched at her sides. If there was any fear in her heart, it did not show on her face.

Beowulf could feel her own dread, the niggling edge of it, stirring in the back of her mind. It was not the thought of death nor battle that crept over her shoulders like a dark shroud, but what it would mean for her people. She was no longer just a warrior. She had a kingdom to protect. The prospect of war had very suddenly become much more costly and complicated.

She gripped the hilt of her sword tightly as the room stirred into activity, most of the warriors departing to make whatever preparations they needed before the dawn. Beowulf called to the guards who followed Gunnar and gave orders to take the man to the healers. The hall slowly emptied while servants cleaned up what was left of the evening meal. Hygd sent both of her children to their chambers before meeting with some of the village elders to prepare for the arrival of any survivors. Beowulf exchanged few words with the queen, but couldn't ignore how seamlessly they both moved to action. They had ruled together long enough to know how the other would likely act, presiding over both welfare and warfare. Beowulf gathered messengers and sent them out to the nearest villages in the dark of night, each of them carrying a warning as well as a summons for able-bodied warriors.

The night had ended very differently to how it had begun, and by the time Beowulf made it to her own room and began stripping down for sleep, the conversations from earlier in the day seemed a lifetime ago. She had already made up her mind to go with the war party, even if it was a bit unorthodox for a queen to ride with the vanguard. Sitting idly was a far worse option, and she knew it would drive her mad. Her mind was too agitated for sleep, and as the minutes she lay awake slowly became hours, she doubted she would get much rest at all.

Worry kept her thoughts going in circles. It was springtime and they had only just begun planting; the food stores from overwinter were all but depleted. It was a poor time for war. She had seen conflict many times over in her life, but the cost of innocent lives had a different weight now. Her responsibility had changed, in ways she hadn't even thought to consider until the threat of invasion had so suddenly descended. She chased her thoughts through the night, until the fire in the hearth had burned low and she finally found sleep.

When she woke, it was still dark outside. Someone had opened her door, and her senses, never fully dulled even during sleep, roused her. She blinked in the gloom of the coals as someone slowly entered the room.

"Beowulf?"

It was Hygd's voice. Beowulf grunted and lifted herself up from where she had sprawled on her stomach beneath her furs. Hygd crossed the room without a word, moving to the fireplace and placing a few more logs atop the embers. As soon as they caught, light bathed the walls and floor. Beowulf watched the glow play across the queen's face where she knelt by the fire, staring at it intently as it slowly grew. She wore a simple dress of pale blue, one that matched her eyes, and as per tradition in wartime she carried a sword on her hip.

"Dawn?" Beowulf asked gruffly, rubbing sleep from her eyes and flipping her loose braids over her shoulder.

"Nearly. I thought you might want a slightly earlier start, the priestesses will—"

Hygd turned as she spoke and abruptly stopped when her gaze fell on Beowulf. The warrior realized it was the first time the queen had seen her wearing nothing above her waist, and though all her years among fighters had made her comfortable wearing only her skin, she felt oddly bashful for a moment. She grabbed her linen shirt off the edge of the bed and pulled it over her head, unable to ignore the queen's eyes as they traced across her upper body.

"The priestesses will perform their blessing at sunrise," Hygd finished, her voice steady and careful.

"Thank you." Beowulf pulled her boots on and began donning her leather armor as the queen made her way back to the door.

Hygd spoke over her shoulder. "The warriors will likely gather at the door of the hall. I will go wake the children." Before she could close the door behind her, Beowulf looked up from the bracer she was tying on and called after her.

"Hygd."

"Yes?" She looked over her shoulder.

"Thank you for waking me."

The queen gave a small nod and a half smile before disappearing, leaving Beowulf to finish putting on her armor. It didn't take her long, as familiar as she was with it. She strapped Naegling on her waist and pulled her furred cloak around her before making her way through the hall and out to the great doors.

There was a flat span of hard-packed earth at the front of the hall which slowly sloped downward the further it got from the building until it reached the village below. Points of light shone from hearth fires, and the dark of predawn still lingered. Warriors had already begun to gather, and the three priestesses had come from the village temple. A place of worship for the many gods, it was adorned with icons of the various deities, three of which the priestesses had brought with them. Wooden statues of Tyr, Odin and Thor stood beside the hall. The gods would require a blood offering in the time of war, and a goat had been tethered beside the statues for that exact purpose. The smell of incense filled the chilled air as the stars began to wink out and the eastern sky turned pale gray.

Beowulf watched the steam from her breath swirl like smoke as the warriors assembled. More of them trickled slowly up from the village and the training yard as dawn drew closer. Chatter was quiet, a low murmur. Some of the warriors watched her where she stood near the priestesses. As she looked out across the many faces, she was pleased to see she knew almost all of them and had fought beside many in the crowd before her. The one she knew longest and best of all slowly approached her, and even through his beard she could see the smile on his lips.

"You look still half asleep," Braggi mumbled as he stepped up beside her and looked her up and down.

She smirked. "Thanks."

"I would have been amazed if you had actually gotten any rest," he said apologetically. He stood beside her and crossed his arms tightly against the cold, bringing his fur-covered shoulders up beside his ears.

"Did you?" she asked.

He grinned. "Of course. Slept like a hibernating bear." When she frowned back, he dropped the smile. "But I'm not queen, and I have a lot less to worry about."

Beowulf took some small comfort in his admission as they watched the warriors assemble. Hygd appeared not long after with both of her children, bleary eyed but dressed and armed for ceremony's sake. As the dawn broke, the priestesses began their invocation and called the gods to lend their might. The blood of the goat was drained into three bowls, one for each priestess, as they invoked the blessings and favor of the gods before the crowd of silent warriors. Nothing would go to waste, and the animal would be the meal in the hall that night. Each warrior would receive a mark on their forehead, a thin line drawn in blood by one of the priestesses. Beowulf went first, and the others followed.

As the warriors passed by the statues, Braggi and Beowulf spoke. His advice was always a boon, no less now that she was queen. They both knew speed was a necessity, and in this instance more important than the size of their forces. Everything they had learned from the survivor suggested that the invaders were a smaller party, likely the first wave. Stopping them in their tracks was a necessity, and to that end they kept their numbers smaller. Some forty of their best fighters was all she would take, all of them on horseback so they could make the journey more swiftly. It was just over fifty miles to Vänersborg, and with any luck they could make it there before they lost the light.

When the last warriors received their blessings, they dispersed toward the stables to ready their mounts. Beowulf turned to follow Braggi, but Hygd surprised her by catching her hand as she passed.

"We'll tend to the survivors here and await your return."

Beowulf gave a stiff nod, aware that the queen still held her hand tightly. She wished for a moment that she might stop time, just for an instant, as she savored the feeling of the queen's hand in her own. She was pulled back into the moment when both Halga and Heardred piped up from where they stood beside the queen.

"All-father watch over you." Halga gave a tight smile.

"Good luck." Heardred's smile was more genuine, but he was newer to the ways of war than his sister and seemed not to grasp the somber mood that settled as the warriors prepared to depart. Beowulf, unable to hide a grin and mildly surprised, gently placed her free hand first on Halga's shoulder, then on Heardred's, before looking back to Hygd. The queen gave her a knowing look and gently squeezed her hand before letting go.

"Goddess protect you, Beowulf." Her smile was thin but genuine, and her gaze lost its ice for the briefest moment.

Beowulf could only whisper her thanks, her mind utterly driven from the topic of war for a fleeting moment. She gave them one last glance before turning, setting her shoulders and following in Braggi's footsteps.

The words of the queen lingered in her mind as she took the reins of her gelding Tordenvejr and climbed into the saddle. The other warriors had begun to form up near the gates of the village. As she rode down with Braggi, they parted in a sea of snorting and stamping horses.

By the time they rode from the village, the sun had begun climbing into the eastern sky. Gray clouds gathered over the northern mountains, threatening rain. The warriors urged their mounts onward, falling in behind their queen, as Beowulf led the way. They left the Great Hall of the Queen in their wake as their path took them east of the great cliffs.

Through forest and field, under an ever-darkening sky, they rode, storm clouds bristling above them. More than once they passed survivors on horseback, those lucky few to escape with horses. Doubtless some would make it to the villages between the great hall and Vänersborg, but the hall held a promise of safety in wartime that wasn't afforded to outlying villages. Those who lived through a raid, unless they were warriors, were often eager to get as far from death as they could manage. Beowulf knew they could not afford to stop, and could do little more than offer meager food and water to some of those they passed.

"We'll be helping them by retaking the village," Braggi said to her the first time they passed a group, and Beowulf wondered if her anger had shown on her face. Either way, she kept his words in her mind and urged Tordenvejr onward. Through forest and field they went, traveling from the main roads to the less maintained outlying paths. Beowulf pushed the horses only as much as she dared, and every few miles they slowed to a walk. They stopped only three times to rest their mounts and stretch their legs before continuing. By the time they neared their destination, the sun had begun to dip into the west, the sky darkened not only by clouds, but also smoke.

The forest that surrounded the outskirts of the village gave them enough cover to make their approach as the sunlight faded. The edge of the lake looked like an ocean at a distance, so vast it was, wind rippling waves over its surface. Hills and woodland ringed the shore, and Vänersborg sat nestled in a low point, built right onto the water's edge. They halted before they drew too close. Though fighting at night was far from ideal, it did give them an advantage.

Beowulf split their party into two roughly equal groups that fanned out on opposite sides of the village, so they might keep the element of surprise despite being on horseback. They moved in from both west and east, catching the village between them.

Scouts were a luxury they could not risk, so close they were to the village. At their queen's orders, they went in blind. Surprise and the advantage of horseback was their best chance, and as their troop crossed through the bracken, they picked up speed. Beowulf could see the village in the twilight as they approached, and the bodies that lay strewn haphazardly around the outskirts. Many who had fled were cut down, and more than a few arrows still stuck out of the backs of corpses.

She urged Tordenvejr onward, feeling his hooves thundering beneath her. A loud cry had already gone up among the warriors that rode around and behind her, weapons drawn as they descended on the village. By the time the warning horns of the Swedes were blown, the Geats had already descended in all their fury. The invaders, in the process of making camp amid the burned husks of buildings, were caught off guard. Makeshift tents toppled as they scrambled for their weapons and the riders came crashing through.

Beowulf was used to the chaos of battle, the shouts and screams and frenzy of animal and man running amok. Having their forces on horseback made it easier to tell friend from foe, a boon as the sun sank and darkness crept through the trees. She swung to either side, hacking low to reach her enemies on foot. The Swedes rallied as best they could, and their arrows toppled riders from their mounts.

Beowulf urged her horse onward, ducking as an arrow sailed painfully close to one of her ears. Only when she had reached the center of the village did she dare slow, her breathing heavy, blood spattered hot and wet across the side of her face. Here, the other group of their riders converged with them, both troops piercing straight to the heart of the village. Satisfied with the initial charge, Beowulf caught brief sight of Braggi in the fray as he dismounted, gesturing first to her, and then to the water. Some of the invaders were likely trying to flee by the boats that had brought them.

She nodded, before dismounting herself. There was no shortage of both friends and foes around her, and with many of the Geats dismounting, it was harder to distinguish sides in the dim light. Beowulf narrowly parried a spear thrust for her chest, driving her blade into the throat of the attacking man, as her forces began to spread out from the center of the village. On foot, they were able to search the buildings as they went, while the remaining riders chased down those Swedes who tried to flee. Beowulf caught one last glimpse of Braggi before the pack of warriors he was amid disappeared toward the shores of the lake.

She occupied herself with searching through the remaining structures, keeping her blade and shield close. Although many of the outlying houses had been burned, some of the larger buildings, including the small hall and nearby temple, still stood. The din of battle from outside followed her as she kicked in a door and immediately crossed swords with another Swede. She could see two more men behind him in the first room. The first she cut down, and the second she kicked into the fire. The third swung for her throat, but she stepped back just beyond his reach before hitting him with her shield so forcefully that he slammed into the opposite wall before sliding down to the floor in a motionless heap. More of her warriors were behind her, and they moved through the buildings room by room.

By the time she had helped clear three of the structures, the battle had begun to die down, and she could pause long enough to catch her breath. Even with the torches and the fires that burned in the makeshift tents set by her warriors, it was difficult to see. Their attack had been swift and sudden, and the last light of day was still fading when the worst of it finished. Someone shouted her name, and she squinted through the mass of silhouettes near the center of the village.

"Beowulf!" It was a familiar voice, and from someone who knew her well enough to omit her title. She took a few strides into the gloom, pausing only to give a clean death to a groaning invader sprawled on the ground beside her path.

"Beowulf!" This time the voice was closer. Something whistled, and suddenly it felt as though she had been struck in the chest with a hammer. The breath was knocked from her, and she staggered back, the shaft of an arrow buried just below her left shoulder. Her shield arm grew heavy, and she clenched her fist, heaving her arm up high enough to lock her elbow until she was sure she wouldn't drop her shield.

She couldn't spot the archer, but no other bolts flew her way. Someone was still looking for her, and she gritted her teeth against the pain as she straightened and shouted her reply.

"Here!"

"By the water!" came the return cry, from the same warrior who had called out before. "There's more of them coming!"

Something in her stomach tightened. It was a good thing they had attacked when they did, if reinforcements were indeed so close. Now they risked being outnumbered. Beowulf grunted against the stabbing pain in her shoulder, blinking away the red spots that popped in her vision. She rested Naegling against her leg only long enough to reach up and snap most of the shaft from the arrow in her shoulder, wincing as she felt the head twist where it was buried, before she lifted her sword once more and cried out above the din.

"To the beach! Warriors of Odin, to the beach!" The cry was echoed by others, floating above the lingering shouts. Beowulf turned and ran, keeping her left arm close by her side. Some of the other warriors had put torches to the Swedes' camp, and the blaze from the tents made it easy enough to see as her boots hammered against the ground. She stepped over the fallen, weaving between buildings, moving to the vast expanse of the lake where it stretched beneath the gathering night.

She was nearly to the water, close to the remains of some of the small huts and the remains of demolished smokehouses.

There was a yell ahead of her and a warrior appeared out of the gloom, her shield painted with unfamiliar colors. Beowulf ran full bore at the woman, slamming into her sideways, shield to shield. Pain ripped through the wound in her shoulder, searing down her arm and across her chest and clouding her vision momentarily as the two of them collided. The woman toppled back nearly a dozen feet, crashing into the wall of one of the huts and collapsing. More were coming, and Beowulf suddenly realized these fighters were fresh. They fought with a renewed vigor, and if they had reached her here, there were far more of them at the water's edge.

"Reinforcements!" she shouted. The Geats who had gone to the shore had likely been overrun, and her focus narrowed as she sprinted toward the water, her mind on Braggi. Beowulf's strikes were reckless as she ran, no strength held in reserve as she sent any who stood in her way toppling. She ran haphazardly toward the water's edge, her warriors following in a throng behind her.

The ground grew slightly rocky, turning to sand, and the shouts in the air were accompanied by the sound of waves on the beach. The water's edge was swarming with Swedes. She could see two boats that had landed, their curved prows pulled up onto the sand. One was empty, the other had only just made shore and already some dozen warriors were jumping over the side into the shallow water. There was another boat approaching, only just visible, and beyond that it was impossible to see.

The Geats rushed onto the shore and the two sides collided. Had the water not seemed black as ink, it would have churned crimson where the fallen floated on the waves. Beowulf ducked and swung, her eyes searching the beach each time she had a moment to spare in the fray. She had already recognized some of her warriors among the fallen, and as she ran across the sand, cutting down foes, she searched until she found him.

Braggi. Her lips formed his name, but no sound escaped them. She could see him on the beach, not ten feet away, sprawled on his side. Half a dozen Swedes lay scattered around him, and his torso was still pierced with the spear that had killed him. Beowulf froze, the world seeming to stop around her. Disbelief hit her like a wall, and her mind struggled even as her body recognized what had happened. Her fists clenched as she began to tremble.

She could not have stood there for more than a moment, but it dragged out for what seemed like an age as she stared at him. His eyes had already glazed over, and blood covered one side of his face. His mouth was slightly ajar, and for all the world looked frozen in a half smile.

She screamed. Not a pained, wracked cry, but a roar that shook her very bones. Her voice seemed to split as she yelled so loudly her throat became almost raw, and the entirety of her body shuddered as the sound escaped her. Fear flickered on the faces of the Swedes closest to her as they continued their advance as she turned on her enemies with fire in her eyes. Her disbelief had broken, and all she felt was transformed into a white-hot rage that boiled from inside her, making her blood run hot.

She forgot the wound to her shoulder and dropped her shield to thud into the sand. Her boots splashed into the water as she waded in among the disembarking forces. She swung Naegling with enough force to split the nearest foe clean in half at his middle. The corners of her vision turned scarlet as she hacked and slashed, splintering shields and bones.

The first boat on the beach was already in flames, her warriors making quick work of destroying it. They ran with torches toward the second as she and those at her back slew the warriors still jumping into the water to meet them. Only when she was surrounded by floating bodies, and satisfied the ship would soon be alight, did Beowulf turn toward the last boat she could see. She waded toward it, moving past where the others had been, the water rising to her waist as she struggled against its force.

An archer onboard fired two arrows at her. She ducked the first before flinging a dagger from her belt at the man, and his second shot went wide as her blade sank into his throat. Some of the Geats had begun to follow her, but not so deep as she had gone. She reached the ship first, the great prow giving her some cover from the warriors onboard as she gripped the side of it with her free hand. There were cries above her as some of the Swedes began to jump over the side, plunging into waist-deep water.

She swapped Naegling into her off hand, confident it would take a few moments for the nearest wading opponent to reach her. Gritting her teeth, she unleashed the rage burning in her bones, clenched her right fist and swung. Her body twisted as her knuckles hit the prow of the ship with enough force to splinter wood as if it was fragile icicles. She gripped anything solid she could reach before twisting back the other direction, ripping another massive chunk from the boat as water flooded in and it slowly began to tip forward.

A shout went up from those onboard as they were forced to jump, the ship sinking in the shallow water as its entire prow was splintered. Beowulf waded in among the invaders, filling the water with their blood. Those few that passed her or tried to flee found themselves on the blades of the waiting Geats. The longboat sank, until only the curled prow and topmost edge of the sides stood above the water. The mast and sail still rose toward the night sky over shallow water that flickered brightly as the other ships burned, heat radiating across the waves. Bits of wood and debris floated in the gentle current, drifting around Beowulf as she stood in the waist-deep water. Her shoulders still trembled, her breath unsteady and hard.

The light from the fires on the shore and the burning boats reached far enough out across the water that they could see the single solitary ship that remained. Those onboard had decided against the carnage, and the craft was only briefly visible from shore as it disappeared back the way it had come. A cheer of victory went up among the Geats on the shore, but Beowulf's voice did not join them.

The last celebratory shouts slowly died down behind her, replaced by the crackle of scorching flames. She stood for a moment longer, water and blood dripping from her face and hair, before she turned and waded back to shore. The warriors there were already at work clearing the destruction of the battle. They would set a watch on the village and allow the wounded to rest as best they could. Those with injuries needed tending to, and the dead would be gathered for a small pyre.

Beowulf's feet felt heavy as she splashed back up onto the beach, her arms dragging by her sides. She wiped Naegling across one of the furs near her shoulder, the only part of her that wasn't soaked. Then she sheathed her blade and continued across the beach to where Braggi lay. The frenzy from the fight was wearing off, and the pain in her shoulder stabbed harder with each step she took. By the time she reached him she couldn't lift her arm.

Beowulf dropped heavily to her knees in the wet sand, watching the firelight flicker across his face. It felt surreal, strange like a dream she was desperate to wake from. She reached out and rested a hand on his shoulder, her jaw tight as something closed in her throat, and her eyes began to burn from more than just the smoke.

"Braggi." His name was thick on her lips as she knelt looking down at him. She might have stayed there, but the mantle of queen rested heavy on her shoulders. Duty forced her to her feet as some of the warriors began to gather.

"Find any survivors." Her voice sounded strange, as if it came from somewhere far away. Only the searing pain in her shoulder kept her grounded. "Tend to the wounded. Burn the fallen Swedes. We will make a pyre for our own at dawn."

Those around her nodded, passing the word on as they dispersed back through the village. She made herself follow, forcing her feet to move. Those with skills in medicine would already be tending to wounds, but she was in no hurry to seek one out. She knew there were others worse off than she. Instead, she set about helping the other warriors, for they had fires to douse and a watch to set. She gathered the most able-bodied among them to watch the village during the night, while others put

209

out fires and combed through the wreckage. Beowulf joined in among them, movement being the only thing keeping her from collapsing as she allowed her mind to go completely blank.

They worked through the buildings as night descended around them, collecting the bodies of their slain foes. Beowulf's steps felt heavy, and the world around her seemed painfully muted somehow. She felt as if she had been knocked from her body by a crashing wave that she could only now trail behind as she moved methodically through the structures. Pain seemed her only anchor, keeping her from drifting away entirely.

It was only in one of the larger storehouses that her senses finally returned to her, and only out of surprise. She had gone into one of the back rooms where mead was usually kept. The heady smell of alcohol wafted from the many shattered barrels, dark liquid mixing with the blood on the floor. She counted two dead and was about to move one of the corpses when she heard something from the far corner. Instinct cleared her mind in an instant and her hand reflexively drew her sword. She stepped slowly, listening again for the soft thud she had heard as she made her way toward a few still-intact barrels in the shadows.

She took a deep breath, lifted her blade, and kicked off the top of the nearest barrel. She had expected a Swede, or an animal perhaps. Instead, the wide eyes of a child peered up at her from the darkness. Beowulf sighed heavily and lowered her weapon. There was at least one survivor left.

"It's alright," she said slowly, taking a step back. "You're alright. We're Geats, all of us."

There was a long pause, during which she retrieved a torch from the front of the storehouse and returned in time to see a small boy crawling from the barrel. He could not have been more than nine or ten years old, his short brown hair scraggly and unkempt. His light-brown eyes were wide with fear and his movements shaky as he crawled from his hiding place. In one hand he held a long dagger that looked more akin to a sword in comparison to his small frame. He clutched it tightly as he stood and trembled before her.

She knelt, holding the torch aloft as she looked at him. He was too well dressed to be a fisherman's son, and even at his small size he had a healthy build and strong stature. He watched her with wide eyes and drew no closer until she raised her left hand as much as she could manage and held it out to him.

"Come on. Let's get you warm. You're safe."

He eyed her hand for a long moment before stepping forward, still clutching the dagger close. Tentatively, he took her hand, and the two of them slowly walked from the building. As soon as they emerged and began passing other warriors, the boy pressed himself to Beowulf's leg as closely as he could without tripping her.

She stopped the first warrior who passed her within arm's length. "There are two in the building back there. Where are the healers?" she asked. The woman pointed back toward the heart of the burned-out village as she answered.

"There's a camp set up near the center for the wounded. There's fire and food there as well, my queen."

Beowulf nodded her thanks, and the woman briefly looked down to where the boy stood before departing. The child had looked up at Beowulf again, his eyes wide, but this time with more than just fear upon hearing her title.

"Unfortunately, yes." Beowulf tried for a smile but felt it falter on her lips as she led the two of them toward the village heart. Her senses had cleared, and though pain still burned through her shoulder and ached in her bones, she no longer felt as though she had been knocked from her body and trailed behind it.

There were small tents set up around the fire that burned in the open space at the center of the village, and the wounded sat or lay nearby. Those warriors with healing skills tended to them, and one of them accosted Beowulf as she approached.

"My queen, your shoulder." The young man placed a hand on her arm.

"It didn't go clean through," she muttered, before placing a hand gently on the young child's back and scooting him slightly forward from where he stood glued to her leg. "This one likely needs some food and any spare hides that might get the warmth back in him."

The young man looked down at the boy, then he nodded and led them both to some of the stumps around the fire. There, he draped a sheepskin over the boy's shoulders, and helped remove the furs from Beowulf and take off her tunic. He offered her some willow bark for the pain, which she chewed as he examined the end of the arrow shaft still protruding from her shoulder.

"You're lucky. A little higher and you might have lost use of that arm."

She merely grunted, allowing her mind to drift as she sat. The reclaiming of the village was already in motion, and for a short time there was little she would have to do. She was pleased to see someone bring a small hunk of bread and a piece of smoked fish for the boy, who ate ravenously in silence. The only words Beowulf spoke for the next hours before she slept was a slew of curses when the arrow was pulled from her shoulder.

Her wound was packed with moss, the splinters were extracted from her left hand where she had ripped apart the boat, and a salve was rubbed over the wounds before they were bandaged. Weary though they all were, they didn't dare leave their position unguarded, instead cycling watches through the night. Beowulf stayed up with the first watch, keeping by the fire. The child beside her refused to go more than a few feet from her, and eventually fell into a fitful sleep, his back pressed against her where he lay curled, wrapped in sheepskin.

She took her rest there, and when she woke the next dawn, she found the boy had nestled beneath her arm and huddled against her for warmth. He still slept, and she guessed his exhaustion had finally caught up with him. She woke him so he might eat, then she organized her warriors to make a pyre for the fallen. Half of their forces would stay in the village to make what repairs they could and protect it from any new attacks. The rest of them would return to the Queen's Hall. This was only the first battle of what she knew would likely be many, and already she had sent warriors to scout the lake and warn of any oncoming attacks. They would need to strike back against the Swedes soon, but first they had to regroup.

Once the sun had well and truly risen, she stood beside some of the others near the water's edge, listening to the rush of the waves and the crackle of flames as smoke from the pyre rose high into the sky. She stood still as a statue, watching Braggi's body disappear in the inferno. The boy, never having strayed far from her, had surprised her by reaching up to grab her hand as they stood among the warriors.

He was staring blankly at the fire, and though he made no sound, she could see the shimmering lines of tears down his small face. It occurred to her then, with a new and sudden weight, that he had likely lost everything. Any family he had, the entire world he knew, all of it was gone. He squeezed her hand tightly, and she couldn't help but give it a small squeeze back as she watched the body of her oldest friend burn.

The mood was somber as they packed up what little belongings they had, half their forces preparing to leave, with Beowulf among them. Her wounds ached, her shoulder protested every movement, and her mind felt somehow dulled as her thoughts lingered on Braggi. She left the other warriors with orders to repair and protect. Once they reached home, she would send out more riders with reinforcements and supplies for those who remained behind. Only when they were close to departing did the child speak the first words she had heard from him.

"Can I come with you?" His voice was small, and he looked up at her where she adjusted the saddle on Tordenvejr. She paused and knelt down that she might be level with him.

"You don't want to stay? This place will be rebuilt in enough time. You don't have to leave your home if you don't want to."

He shook his head and pointed at her gelding's back.

"You're sure?" she asked. "You are our kin, so any house that can provide would likely take you in, but you needn't leave."

He seemed to think for a moment, before he looked up at her inquisitively.

"Your house?" he asked.

"You want to live in my house?" She let out a small chuckle, and he nodded vigorously. She looked up and sighed, wondering how Halga and Heardred would react. When she finally looked back at him, his eyes wide with expectation, she reached out and placed a hand on his shoulder. "I suppose there's no harm in asking. Goodness knows there's more than a few misfits among the warriors and servants in that hall. Such it is in wartime, I suppose."

He didn't seem to understand much of what she said beyond the possibility of him staying, but he gave a hesitant nod before she hoisted him up into the saddle.

"You think you could at least tell me your name, that we might make a better first impression?" she asked as she climbed up behind him.

"Wiglaf," he replied in a small voice as they rode out, some two dozen warriors in all, thundering toward the road to the Queen's Hall.

Chapter 13

The village around the Queen's Hall slowly filled with refugees. Those who had survived the initial attack and traveled far enough came on the promise of food and shelter, both of which were provided. The half of the initial war party that returned took three days to cover the distance, since they were no longer pressed with the same urgency and were carrying some of the wounded with them. They brought news of victory and death, as well as a call for supplies, and fresh warriors who could make the journey back north.

Before she had even dismounted, Beowulf was already eager to depart again. The threat of war still loomed heavy in her mind, and there was work to be done. With reinforcements trickling in from nearby villages, they could soon strike out again in force. But beyond battle, there was much that required her attention as queen, and coordinating the entire war effort would, for the most part, require her to remain at the Queen's Hall. She knew the gravity of the responsibilities that came with her title, but to her it felt like sitting idle, and she chafed at the thought.

Like a wolf in a cage. She heard Braggi chuckle in her mind, and immediately an iron vice knotted itself into her stomach. She jumped from the saddle and used her uninjured arm to help Wiglaf down after her. There would be plenty of room for him among the survivors in the hall, though he seemed reluctant to leave her side. He stayed close to her leg the entire way up and into the great doors, only departing when one of the servants whisked him away for food and rest.

Beowulf passed through the hall and headed for her own chambers, her mind already on the maps spread across the table. She had no way of knowing where or when their enemy would strike next, but they were likely already on the move, and the thought quickened her steps. The news of victory had inspired jubilance among warriors and villagers alike, but Beowulf felt no desire to celebrate. They had won, but she had lost. She leveled her gaze on the floor as she walked amid the cheers that echoed through the hall.

She had only a handful of moments to herself once she reached her room, and she threw off her cloak before gingerly removing her leather jerkin and mail. It was difficult, and her shoulder protested as she moved. Her bracers were much easier to remove, and she tossed them on one of the chairs with the rest of her armor. The chill air wafted through her linen tunic as she rolled up the sleeves and splashed some water on her face from the bowl in one corner. No fire burned in the hearth, and the stone floor was cold even through her boots.

The torches on the walls cast enough light that she could see the maps on the table, and as soon as she wiped the water from her face, she began pouring over them. Even knowing that she probably wouldn't be able to leave the hall as soon as she would have liked, planning gave the illusion of movement, and it helped quiet her mind. More importantly, it kept her thoughts off Braggi.

A knock on the door made her look up, brows still tightly furrowed.

"My queen?" A man's voice echoed through the door.

"Come in."

Three warriors entered, all of whom either she or Hygd had appointed as leaders within the ranks. Braggi had been the fourth. They circled the table, and she was quietly grateful that none of them commented on either their victory or the loss of one of their number.

"We've already sent messengers to all of the border villages." The dark-haired woman to her left, Ravna, gestured across the map as she spoke.

"Good." Beowulf's tone was tight as she spoke. "We need to send out riders and call for swords. One rider to each of the jarls all the way down to the southlands, to request as many warriors as they can send."

The trio before her nodded in agreement.

"And supplies?" Beowulf asked.

"We've already sent some carts to Vänersborg," one of the men chimed in, "but there are likely to be refugees from more battles to come."

"Indeed." Beowulf frowned down at the map. "We'll offer as much of our own food and supplies as can be managed. Any of the jarls southward who are protected will send what supplies they can."

"Agreed." All three spoke in unison.

"And the scouts?" Beowulf asked.

"All along the border," Ravna replied. "When the Swedes come, we'll know."

Beowulf nodded. She knew that meant waiting, for now, until they had amassed enough fighters to strike into enemy territory. It would be a few days at the quickest, depending on how swiftly the jarls responded. She frowned down at the table.

"Good," she said flatly. "If the Swedes move, we attack. If not, we amass enough swords that we can move against them in their own lands."

A murmur of agreement passed around the table, before the sound of the door made them turn. Hygd entered and crossed to join them at the table. Her eyes settled on Beowulf for an instant, before she addressed the others.

"I assume you discussed supplies as well as gathering warriors?" she asked.

"We have," Beowulf replied. "Riders will be sent to the jarls."

Hygd spoke slowly as she looked down at the map. "It might be wise to ask for what supplies can be spared from the southlands. There will be many who need shelter in wartime."

Beowulf watched her as she spoke. The queen had lived and led through many wars. She perhaps knew less about actual battle than Beowulf, but much more about caring for the kingdom at large. Moreover, and this was something Beowulf had always appreciated in times like this, they had always treated each other as equals regardless of their varied strengths and weaknesses.

"Agreed." Beowulf held the queen's gaze as she replied. "We will ask the jarls for whatever might be spared."

The three warriors nodded, then Beowulf dismissed them with a nod and a wave of her hand. Hygd remained a moment longer, watching them go, before turning her gaze to Beowulf as the door shut behind them.

"Are you alright?" she asked, gently placing a hand on Beowulf's shoulder. "I heard you had been wounded."

Beowulf tilted her head nonchalantly to the side, trying to ignore the sparks that spread across her skin at Hygd's touch. Even with her mind largely elsewhere, Hygd's hand on her shoulder brought an unexpected comfort.

"I've seen worse. It'll heal."

"The bandage should be changed," Hygd said matter-of-factly, as her hands moved to the front of Beowulf's linen tunic and her fingers teased apart the laces. Beowulf tried to ignore the slight flutter in her chest as the queen helped remove her shirt, lifting it gently from her injured shoulder. The cool air raised gooseflesh across Beowulf's torso, and Hygd frowned as her touch traced over the cloth wrapped tightly over her wound. The warrior could not keep herself from staring, though Hygd was too occupied with her task as to meet her gaze. Beowulf watched the queen as she slowly began to unwind the wrappings. Even with her mind largely elsewhere, time stood still for a moment, and a current like a thunderbolt rooted Beowulf to the spot. She could feel the heat creeping up the back of her neck.

"I also heard," Hygd said slowly as she raised an eyebrow, "that you sunk a boat. With your hands."

Beowulf let out a mirthless chuckle, trying to ignore the flush of warmth across her skin. "That might be exaggerated."

"The wrappings on your hand say otherwise."

"Is that all you heard?" Beowulf asked, eyeing the queen carefully. Hygd hesitated for a moment, her hands stopping their work as she searched Beowulf's expression, concern hiding in the corners of her face.

"All that matters for now, I think." The queen gently finished her task and set the loose bandages aside. "We ought to change the moss," she said flatly before Beowulf could protest. Hygd had what she needed on hand, and since the arrival of the first refugees, she had taken to keeping several pouches of medicinal herbs on her belt.

"I think your skills might be more needed elsewhere," Beowulf said thickly.

"Nonsense. There are plenty of healers here. You needn't do everything on your own, you know."

The queen's words caught Beowulf slightly off guard and stung, if only just a little. She fell silent, aside from a singular wince when Hygd pulled the moss from the wound before packing in a fresh bundle. She completed the rest of her work in silence, and Beowulf tried and failed to tear her gaze from Hygd's eyes, the curve of her lips, and the soft lines of her face.

Only once the queen had tied the bandage back on did she step back, looking at Beowulf tentatively.

"I heard..." she started, then fell silent.

Beowulf frowned, feeling something sink in her gut. She turned and grabbed her linen tunic and pulled it carefully back on.

"Beowulf..." Hygd's voice was soft, and Beowulf felt something hard and sharp rise in her throat. "I'm sorr—"

"Not now, please." Beowulf turned away and clenched her fist, driving the nails into her palm. "Please, I just—"

She swallowed hard, her shoulders rising toward her ears. "Not yet."

Hygd watched her, something small and sad in her gaze, then she gave a knowing nod, and quietly left the room. Beowulf was left in silence, and until one of the hall servants brought food and kindled a fire, she had only her thoughts for company. She passed the night knowing that all she could do for the time being was heal and wait.

Resting was not something she did well. She kept herself busy enough the first few days by helping around the hall, finding space for the last of the refugees, and gathering news from those who had fled. Occasionally, she caught sight of Wiglaf, and more than once she saw him with Heardred. It was a small silver lining, and one she took comfort in as the days passed under that roof. Beowulf spoke with the warriors, and helped organize another group to reinforce Vänersborg. Only when the nights descended did she feel unease rise in the back of her mind. She slept poorly, and what sleep she did manage was filled with painful dreams, more than one of which confronted her with the image of Braggi sprawled on the ground.

As the days passed, more warriors arrived from neighboring villages, and their numbers at the Queen's Hall grew. Their enemy remained silent, and no further attacks came. Beowulf sent small groups of warriors and scouts northward, as the remainder of Geatish forces amassed in the village surrounding the hall. With enough warriors, they could risk an attack beyond their borders, and they made plans to move against the Swedes less than a fortnight after Vänersborg.

It was three days before their planned departure when Beowulf felt she had very nearly lost her mind. Despite getting enough sleep, exhaustion mingled with agitation so deep it seemed to burn in her bones.

She stood at the table, staring at the maps spread before her and willing time to go faster in her mind. There was something in her that wanted out, that threatened to break through her like steel shattering ice. It seemed that if she did not find some way to break it free, it would break her instead. Beowulf clenched her fists and leaned over, squinting down at the maps and the various lines drawn on the hides in charcoal, marking their possible approaches to the northern border. She heard footsteps behind her, but didn't turn, so familiar they were.

"You need some rest." It was Hygd's voice. Beowulf sighed heavily.

"I've tried."

The queen came to stand beside her, looking down at the maps, her finger tracing along some of the lines etched there. Beowulf, suddenly seeing an escape for her train of thought, turned to the queen with a small, forced smile.

"It seems Wiglaf has found his voice again."

"Indeed." Hygd smiled back. "He has made himself quite at home here in the hall. Heardred and he have been spending a fair bit of time trying to climb onto the roof lately."

"I'm glad." Beowulf's smile was genuine this time. "I don't know if the horror of what he saw will ever leave him, but the chance that it will not dominate his destiny is more than a little heartening."

"Won't come to much if he breaks his neck on a dare." Hygd frowned down at the table.

"At least Heardred has some more kindred company for now. I haven't seen much of him or Halga lately."

"All the people in the hall, everything to do with wartime..." Hygd trailed off before looking back up at Beowulf. "I think it brings back some unpleasant memories for both of them. They've mostly stayed in their rooms or outside. They won't go near the main hall."

"I see," murmured Beowulf quietly. It had been well over half a year since Hygelac's death, and so much had changed since then. She often forgot how short that stretch of time could be for a child who had lost their father.

"Beowulf." Hygd placed a hand on the warrior's shoulder as she spoke, startling her slightly. "Our people need our strength right now. I understand that better than most. I have ruled through enough wars."

She stared intently at Beowulf, her eyes bright and piercing, the hand on her shoulder gripping firmly. She seemed to be searching the warrior's features as she spoke, half pulling her away from the table as she looked her up and down. After a moment, she continued.

"But you and I are equals in this, and I would not have you ignore your wounds under a mask of duty, whether they be physical or otherwise. I hope that you trust me enough to speak to what weighs on you when we have only each other for company."

Beowulf frowned slightly, and Hygd finished in a quiet tone. "Braggi."

Beowulf allowed herself to slump into one of the chairs, sliding out from under Hygd's grasp. Then she leaned over and scrubbed her face with her hands, as Hygd sat quietly on one of the chairs beside her.

"I just—" Beowulf stopped abruptly as something hard rose in her throat and threatened to choke her. She breathed deeply, staring down at her palms in her lap. "As a warrior, I have seen the face of death so many times." She spoke steadily, slowly, aware of Hygd watching her. "But Braggi was always there, and he and I made it out of so many battles worse than that. He was the closest thing I had to family. It's so strange to try to understand that he's gone."

Her voice cracked on the last word, and her vision blurred as silent tears escaped the edges of her eyes in burning heat. Hygd reached forward and took hold of one of her hands, giving it a small squeeze.

"I know," she said softly. "I cannot pretend to know your grief, but I know what it is like to lose someone you are close to, who you have known for so long. Someone who seems so... constant."

Beowulf dared to raise her head, the lines of tear tracks still burning into her cheeks. She was surprised to see that the queen looked on the verge of tears herself, as their eyes met and she held Beowulf's hand tightly. Hygd must have seen the surprise on Beowulf's face, as she sighed and explained.

"Hygelac was the person I had always been closest to. For all the complications of the start of our relationship, he was my oldest friend. Someone who I came to care for deeply and trust wholeheartedly."

"I'm sorry." Beowulf swallowed, something about the queen's sorrow making her own easier to bear, if only slightly.

"We cannot cheat destiny." Hygd sighed. "Death comes for us all one day. It's hard to lose someone you love."

Beowulf nodded, feeling more tears burn down her cheeks. She laughed then, more of a cough than anything else, as she thought of Braggi.

"You know," she said, staring at a point on the far wall, "he could be a real shit sometimes."

Hygd laughed lightly. "The way he was with you," she said slowly, "reminded me of Heardred and Halga. You may not have been siblings in blood, but you were in bond."

Beowulf nodded again, trying to take a deep breath without her shoulders trembling. "I miss him. It's only been a week or so. It was a good death though." She swallowed hard. "I like to think it was what he wanted."

Hygd nodded and squeezed her hand again as the two dropped into a heavy silence for a few moments.

"I am sorry for his passing."

Beowulf nodded her thanks, before disentangling her hand and wiping her cheeks. She breathed deeply and allowed her back to straighten, blinking the last of the tears from her eyes. Hygd sighed and slowly stood.

"I know we must carry ourselves a certain way, as is our duty." She looked at Beowulf intently. "But I will do my utmost to share my weaknesses as well as my strengths. I am grateful for the trust between us."

Beowulf stood as well, a small and half-sad smile playing in the corner or her lips. "Thank you for"—she wasn't exactly sure what to say—"reminding me to put down my sword, as it were." She gestured vaguely to where she had sat, unsure of how to thank the queen for her invitation. It was rare that Beowulf trusted someone enough that she might share her heart's pain, and having been given the room to speak with Hygd had already made her feel as if a weight the size of a mountain was lifted from her shoulders.

She was suddenly painfully grateful for the queen. Grateful for her strength and honesty and the unabashed and unafraid way in which she could and would speak so directly. She could not put words to it, so she merely took the queen's hand and gave it a small squeeze as they shared a knowing look, then Hygd turned and departed from the room.

Beowulf slept deeply for the first time in almost a week that night, her dreams notably untroubled by fire and war. Instead, she dreamt of the tree. She saw the great ash standing high on the hill, and the goddess in the form of the hawk, only this time when she grasped the sword she heard Hygd's voice calling her name as she awoke.

The dawn brought the promise of movement, and the sound of a horn blowing woke Beowulf before first light. She dressed quickly and pulled on her armor before grabbing something to eat and departing the hall. The air was fresh and clear, and smoke rose from the fireplaces of the village and the many tents belonging to the warriors who had gathered there. Each jarl had sent almost a dozen fighters, and there were well over two hundred in and around the village.

She blinked against the graying dawn as she stepped through the great doors of the hall and into the cool morning air, her breath curling in steam around her head. The shouts of warriors and sounds of horses rose on all sides, the village a flurry of activity as their forces prepared to depart. Beowulf was eager to ride, her steps swift as she walked toward the training yard where the leaders of the smaller war bands awaited her. The path down from the side of the hall was short and steep, and she might have taken it at a trot had not something caught her eye.

She spotted Halga. This was slightly surprising given the early hour, but Hygd's daughter had been enjoying walking among the ranks of the warriors. All the new faces in the village brought no shortage of handsome ones, and she was clearly intrigued. There was a small pack of girls she usually traveled with, some from the hall and a few from the village, and they chattered like hens wherever they went. But Halga was alone today, standing near some of the warriors at the edge of the training yard as Beowulf approached.

Immediately, warning prickled on the back of the warrior's neck. Something about the way Halga moved was wrong. The girl took a sudden step back from one of the warriors talking to her. Whether it was her hand or part of her dress she yanked from the man's grip, Beowulf could not tell. Whoever he was, someone Beowulf did not recognize, threw his head back and guffawed, the two men beside him exchanging a laugh as he did. Halga turned quickly, her shoulders rigid and her arms locked to her sides. The men's laughter carried after her as she walked stiffly away.

By the time the girl looked up and saw Beowulf, the two of them were almost within arm's reach. Halga startled slightly, her tear-filled eyes going wide, before she flushed red and turned away, then she dropped her gaze to the ground, her speed renewed as she moved so stiffly she looked as though she might shatter. Beowulf reached one hand out for the girl's shoulder, trying to slow her, but Halga walked through it and made her way toward the hall.

Beowulf's worried gaze followed her for a moment before she turned back to the training yard, set her shoulders, and stalked on her original route toward the three warriors at the bottom of the worn footpath. Fire had already begun to burn in her chest, and she clenched her fists as she walked briskly, her long strides carrying her swiftly to where they stood. The one who had laughed saw her first, and he and his fellows fell out of their amused conversation to give small nods as she approached.

Beowulf locked eyes with him, her chin up, her pace steady as she closed the gap between them. He smiled a genuine greeting as she approached.

"My queen—"

He didn't have the chance to finish his sentence before her fist slammed into the bridge of his nose. The two men on either side of him startled, and their hands moved close to their swords before they seemed to remember exactly who she was. Both took a wary step back as the third, doubled over and clutching his face, dripped red onto the soft earth. He slowly straightened, blood dribbling into his thickly braided black beard, and his eyes blazed as he lowered his hand.

"Hells! What was—" he began in a dark tone, but again Beowulf cut him off. She stepped forward until their faces were only a few inches apart. Even though he was somewhat taller, he genuinely recoiled as she stepped up to him, her mouth twisted into a snarl that showed her teeth.

"You..." She spoke slowly and calmly through gritted teeth, her presence seeming to dwarf him, though he was physically larger. "...have forgotten your honor." She almost hissed, feeling herself shake slightly as she spoke, rage burning white hot within her.

He blinked a few times, as both of his fellows took another step back and exchanged a nervous glance. A few other warriors within earshot had also turned to watch, but they were still and silent as statues, not daring to move as she glared at the man. There was emerald fire in her eyes.

"I didn't..." He began thickly, trying and failing to hold eye contact with her before he dropped his gaze to the ground. "I didn't mean anything by it. I didn't hurt the girl—"

Beowulf spoke slowly, with deadly calm, as she stared at the man as if her eyes might cast spears through him. "If you *ever* touch my daughter in such a manner again, I swear to the All-father I will personally relieve you of your manhood." She allowed her gaze to trail down below his belt to emphasize her point as her words sank in, and he gaped at her.

"Your—"

"*My* daughter," she finished in quiet tones, still unblinking as he seemed to buckle slightly before her. She hadn't thought about it until the words left her mouth, with hot protective rage burning in her chest. There had been no cause to say as much before now, but she knew it in her heart as her lips spoke the words. The man swallowed hard, before nodding shakily and taking a few more steps back. Only when she finally turned away, took a deep breath, and turned back toward the hall did he and his fellows retreat. The tension in the air melted away, and that small corner of the yard was no longer frozen as the onlookers returned to their tasks.

They needed to depart, and she needed to help organize their forces, but it could wait a few more minutes. She had something she needed to attend to, and she crossed the short distance back up the hill toward the hall. She had expected she might have to do a bit of searching, but instead she found Halga before she had gone more than ten steps back into the hall. The girl was inside one of the nearest doorways to a side room, and Beowulf very nearly passed her by. It was the sound of a small sniffle that made her turn, and she spotted the princess where she sat with her back to the wall and her knees to her chest.

Her arms were wrapped tightly around her legs, and as Beowulf stepped into the room, Halga startled slightly before hastily wiping her hands across her face and turning to look away. Beowulf stopped in the doorway, rested one hand against it and sighed loud enough for Halga to hear.

"I'm fine," Halga said curtly, keeping her head turned away. Beowulf didn't answer, but slowly stepped into the room, leaned against the wall, and slid down to sit beside her, moving her cloak to one side as she did. She said nothing, and Halga, after a moment, spoke again.

"I've dealt with that sort of thing before," she said tightly, still turned away.

"I wish I could say otherwise"—Beowulf spoke slowly, her voice quiet, as she stared at a point on the floor between her boots—"but I don't doubt it."

Halga tried for what might have been a laugh, but it came out shakily, her shoulders trembling slightly as she squeezed her arms around her knees. Beowulf turned to look at her. Only the side of her face was visible, but she could see the tear stains on the girl's cheeks.

"Did he hurt you?" Beowulf asked slowly. Halga shook her head. "That's something, I suppose."

Silence stretched between them, heavy and worn. There was a knowing that seemed to pass unspoken. Would that they lived in a world where that sort of thing didn't happen. But it did. And it would happen again. Beowulf felt her stomach tighten. It was Halga who broke the stillness, speaking quietly as she wiped the back of her hand across her face again.

"Does it ever happen to you?"

"What, unwanted advances? Someone making a grab for me?" Beowulf scoffed. "Not so much now unless they don't know who I am. Being a warrior makes it less likely to happen. People aren't as keen to grab someone who has a sword."

Halga tried again for a laugh, and this time was slightly more successful.

"Did it used to though?"

Beowulf sighed, and Halga finally turned toward her. The girl's eyes were red, but her face had been mostly scrubbed of tears. Her usually bright expression was somehow dimmed, and she seemed to sink in on herself slightly, as if she was trying to shrink as she sat beside the warrior. Beowulf met her gaze with a sad half smile.

"Yes. More so when I was younger."

Halga nodded. "I would imagine. As I said, that wasn't my first." Her jaw was tight as she spoke.

"When I was your age, and training as a foundling, there was an older man amid the warriors who tried to do far worse than place hands on me." Beowulf's expression darkened as she spoke, and Halga's eyes went wide.

"What happened?" she asked in a small voice.

"I put a dagger through his hand," Beowulf answered flatly. "What he tried to do to me was against the laws of our people, and for his crime he was stripped of his status as a warrior and cast out of the village." She turned away as she finished, her brows tightly knit. "If only all crimes of that nature were punished in that way."

Halga's breath came a bit more steadily as she nodded. When Beowulf looked back at her, the spite in her eyes was gone, and there was something deeper in her gaze. It was as if she saw the warrior with new eyes, a hidden appreciation in her gaze. Beowulf turned away from the wall to face her directly.

"Your body is the house of your spirit. It is the first hall you learn to defend. Anyone, be they man, woman, or anyone else, has no welcome there unless by your permission." She stared at the girl intently, and Halga gave a shaky nod. Satisfied, Beowulf moved to stand, but Halga reached out and grabbed her hand, stopping her.

"Beowulf..." she began slowly. "I saw what you did, when I left." She traced a finger over Beowulf's knuckles as she spoke, as if to emphasize her point. "I know that that man violated the warrior's code, but I was sure you would have disciplined him differently." She looked up and, realizing suddenly that her words might be taken as offense, stammered slightly and continued hurriedly. "It's just that I have always known you to be measured in all matters, and I have never known you to do something so... impulsive?" She finished timidly.

Beowulf cracked a grin, causing relief to wash over Halga's expression. The warrior gently took the girl's hand in her own.

"Word of his actions will pass to his jarl. A warrior does not act in such a way toward anyone, especially a princess. Why did I punch him, though?"

Halga nodded, and Beowulf gave Halga's hand a small squeeze. She remembered her own words from in the yard, the look of shock on the man's face, the fire that still simmered low in her chest.

"As a queen, I can ensure his actions will be dealt with as is custom, and will leave the disciplining to his jarl. But—" she began, and faltered as she looked at Halga. The girls' eyes searched Beowulf's face, and the warrior wasn't exactly sure what words to use for a moment as the two of them looked at each other and sat in the quiet of the room.

"Halga," Beowulf said slowly, "I have always believed that the bonds we choose are equally if not more important than those of blood, for no bonds are stronger than the ones we make ourselves. This is true whether you are a warrior or a farmer, a fisher or a herder. You may never think of me as a mother, and I would never change that."

Halga looked suddenly puzzled but remained quiet and stared intently as Beowulf continued to speak.

"Regardless of what I am to you, you and your mother and brother are all family to me. These are bonds I have chosen. So why did I strike that man?" She snorted, before looking intently at Halga. "I struck him because he harmed my daughter."

Halga stared at her, her eyes searching Beowulf's face as a dozen tiny expressions flitted across her own, until finally settling into a smile. Her arms and legs had relaxed, and she looked less at risk of collapsing in on herself as she leaned forward and gently wrapped her arms around Beowulf's shoulders.

The warrior froze for a moment, caught off guard in the girl's embrace, before she gingerly returned her hug.

"Thank you," Halga whispered, and Beowulf gave her a squeeze before letting her go. Rising once more to her feet, she waited only long enough to ensure the girl no longer looked shaken, before she turned toward the door. Halga scrambled up after her.

"And Beowulf..." Her voice caught Beowulf mid-turn as the warrior paused and looked over her shoulder. "Be careful. All-father protect you."

Beowulf gave a nod as she departed the room and made her way once more to the side door of the hall, wrapping her furs a bit tighter around her shoulders as she went. The cold air greeted her, the sky a pale orange as the sun crept over the hills. Dawn had already broken, the warriors had assembled, and it was time to depart.

Chapter 14

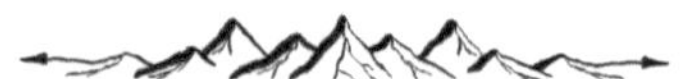

Summer stretched towards fall, the days growing slowly shorter, and blood watered the grasses that grew green on the mountain slopes of the northern borders. The Geats made their war against the Swedes, striking hard into the northern lands near the high peaks. Many among the Geats were eager to fight behind the monster hunter who had won her renown across the Danish sea. At their queen's call, they had rallied enough warriors to sweep the invading forces clean from their lands.

The war promised to be short, and Beowulf had her hopes that it would be over before the turning of the leaves in the lowlands, well before the first snows. She passed the weeks between battles traveling to the encampments all along the borderlands. Unlike her previous experience in wartime, she had been called upon to spend far less time on the field of battle than she would have liked. Leading a host to war meant a great deal more strategy than she had accounted for, and though she had opportunities to meet the Swedes in combat, she spent a great deal more time in council with jarls and the leaders of her war bands.

Beowulf had lost track of how many hours she had spent poring over maps, conferring with scouts, or sending messengers between camps. She had not returned to the great hall in nearly a month, so when the time came to gather fresh forces and return for a war council, she oddly enough found herself looking forward to it. The hall that in some ways had seemed a prison before, now offered privacy, familiar faces, and a comfortable bed that she had admittedly begun to miss.

At least, that is what she would have said if anyone had asked, and it was the truth even if it wasn't all of it. She did not dare admit, let alone even recognize, that she missed the queen's company. Beyond wise counsel alone, Hygd was someone she felt unusually comfortable being utterly herself around. More than once, the queen had crossed gently through Beowulf's dreams, and lingered quietly in the back of her mind, subtly enough that the warrior could ignore it. She didn't dare let her thoughts linger, even as the weight of the war began to wane. The Queen's Hall was home, and that was reason enough to miss it, or so she repeatedly told herself.

She rode with two jarls and a mix of nearly thirty warriors and scouts, their horses thundering across the road as the sun passed its zenith and the Queen's Hall came into view. Smoke rose from chimneys into the clear sky, so bright a day that the thin line of the distant ocean was visible along the westernmost horizon and the riders turned up dust in their wake beneath the summer sun as they entered the village from the east.

The watchmen beat the iron bell that hung at the gate in the great wooden wall, signaling their approach, and a small gaggle of villagers watched them enter. The band made their way up to the hall, Beowulf at the lead, shield across her back over a dark cloak that fluttered in the wind. Even from a distance she could see the small form of who she guessed was likely Heardred hiding near the carved dragon heads that formed the front of the roof of the hall. He wasn't alone; someone slightly smaller crouched beside him, and they both ducked down out of sight when Beowulf's glanced up toward them as she pulled Torden-vejr to a halt.

"Wiglaf! Heardred!" she called, half startling the guards at the door of the hall. "Neither one of you will make a fine warrior if you break your neck or continue to disobey your queen." She shouted, but her tone was light, and she couldn't keep a small grin from her lips. Satisfied they had heard even if they continued to hide, she dismounted and handed off the reins to one of the guards before she strode inside.

The air inside was as warm as the day beyond, but it smelled sweet, like a mix of mead and dry grass. She breathed deeply as she crossed through the hall, her footsteps echoing on stone. A servant tended the great hearth, and a handful of warriors sat at one of the tables playing dice. The hounds, some six in total, all rose from their sleeping places near the fire to greet the warrior as she arrived. She stopped long enough to scratch behind several ears, and she was momentarily lost in a mass of fur and wagging tails before she continued on her path.

Beowulf made her way straight to her chambers, hoping to strip off her armor and clean herself off from her journey. Aside from a few mountain streams, there hadn't been many opportunities to get rid of the dirt and grime during her weeks on the road. She stripped to her linens and made her way to the sauna near the back of the hall. The small structure was crafted of spruce and built down into the ground slightly. It had room for roughly five people at a time, and usually had at least one other person in it. Beowulf pulled off her linens at the door and stepped into the damp, dark room where steam rose from fire-warmed rocks. She used the scraper to peel the heat-softened dirt off her skin, feeling the ache from her time in the saddle slowly easing out of her body.

Outside the sauna was a large tub of cold water that was regularly drawn from one of the nearby streams, and she dunked herself in it quickly, gritting her teeth against the cold as it raised goosebumps on her skin. Once out, she squeezed the water from her hair, pulled her clothes over her still-damp skin and returned to her room for a quick meal before council. She had seen no sign of Heardred or Halga, aside from the former's brief foray onto the roof, and Hygd was nowhere in sight. The queen usually spent the afternoons weaving, but would always be at the war council, though the same could not be said for her daughter.

Four jarls had come, and two of them needed some convincing that lending more warriors would mean a swifter end to conflict. Hygd arrived before any of them, sweeping into the room in a dress of green-dyed linen, a gilded belt at her waist and her hair falling in dark waves past her shoulders. She had several pouches on her hip, and the smell of healing herbs wafted around her as she walked.

The queen crossed the room and gently pulled Beowulf into a brief embrace. The warrior held her tightly, as the smell of the queen's hair swirled around her. The mix of faint woodsmoke and sweet grass, the same scent that lingered around Hygd wherever she went, washed over Beowulf and eased the tension from her like a balm. She held Hygd only as long as she dared, savoring the feeling of having the queen in her arms. When they broke apart, Hygd let one hand linger on Beowulf's shoulder and smiled, her eyes bright and captivating as ever.

"Glad to see you're safe and sound," she said as she looked the warrior up and down. "I hadn't expected any of you would arrive before nightfall."

"Glad to know I was missed." Beowulf dared a small wink and tried not to focus on the small flush of color that spread across Hygd's cheeks, or the feeling of the hand that still rested on her shoulder. "We left before dawn. Though I don't think it will matter too much. I don't imagine the meeting will be finished before dark." She sighed, before returning Hygd's smile. "It's good to see you. How are Heardred and Halga?"

Hygd pursed her lips. "I know Jarl Igni will likely take some convincing." She trailed her hand gently off of Beowulf's shoulder, tracing it down along her arm, as she moved to take her seat at the table. "As to the children, they're all doing well enough. They've kept up with their sparring lessons, and Halga continues to improve with her weaving. Wiglaf has begun training as well. I hear he shows promise, as much as one can, being so young."

Beowulf couldn't hide the approving smile that crept onto her face at the news of Wiglaf. Nor the quiet happiness it brought her that Hygd had, without question or prompting, counted him alongside her own children.

"Good news all around, it sounds." Beowulf grabbed the chair closest to Hygd and sat within arm's reach of her at the table.

"Aside from Heardred and Wiglaf getting into a bit of trouble by letting some of the horses loose, yes."

Beowulf shook her head and laughed lightly. "And what of you?"

"Busy enough helping supply the warriors who have passed through. We've had to move some of the smokehouses to make room for more temporary lodgings with more refugees in the village."

"Hopefully it won't be needed much longer." Beowulf frowned down at the map.

"You believe so? I've not heard news of the war camps aside from what scouts have brought back."

Beowulf turned to look pointedly at the door, her mind already conjuring the images of the jarls striding through it. "If we can convince the jarls to send more warriors, I believe we can strike deep enough into the Swedes' lands that they will sue for peace."

Hygd nodded slowly. "I assume that 'if' depends largely on our friend Jarl Igni? She has thus far refused to send more fighters."

"Indeed." Beowulf chewed her lip and looked once more down at the map, before her eyes strayed to where one of the queen's hands rested on the table. Her mind drifted away from the jarls as she wrestled with the desire to take it in her own. There was friendship between them, and trust, and Beowulf had to remind herself that anything beyond that was impossible. Even when she pushed away all thoughts to the contrary, the queen's gaze and light touch still stopped the warrior dead in her tracks. She was almost tempted to say something but wanted no risk to the friendship they had forged.

Beowulf had convinced herself that the lingering touch of Hygd's hands on her own, and on her shoulders, was nothing but a kindness. The same kindness that made the queen's eyes settle on Beowulf so often. Unsure of what to say or ask, but wanting the quiet moment they shared to linger, Beowulf surrendered to her desire and rested her hand carefully atop Hygd's, trying to find her voice.

"Hygd..." She began slowly, before the sound of the door made them both look up, and Beowulf withdrew her hand like she had been burned.

The queens both stood, and the Beowulf felt heat color her cheeks for an instant, but she took a deep breath and collected herself as the four jarls entered. She avoided eye contact with the queen as the newcomers bowed and approached the table, where they all took their seats. They exchanged brief formalities, before diving into their discussion, and Beowulf took the opportunity to focus her thoughts elsewhere, lest they linger on the queen who sat so close by her side.

Time slipped by, the room only disturbed when a servant came to kindle the fire in the hearth as the last light of day faded outside, and the faint chill of the coming fall settled in. When it became apparent that they would not come to terms in time for the evening meal, Beowulf sent for food and drink for all of them, and they ate around the circular table where firelight flickered across the maps. It was after dark by the time they finally gained ground.

"I only agree if the warriors I lend are held in reserve." Igni, the young jarl with a temper as fiery as her hair, slapped her hand down on the table as she spoke. It was the fourth time she had made her demand and she refused to budge.

"We've spent an hour discussing this, It's only fair that—" one of the other jarls began.

"Absolutely not." She crossed her arms tightly over her chest. "I've already told you all, I've lost twice as many good fighters to this conflict as the rest of you. If it keeps up, we won't have enough hands for the fall harvest."

"As if that's a struggle for you!" the third jarl huffed. "You bring in more grain than the rest of us."

Igni snorted. "I've already agreed to lend the warriors, though you all ask for more than I would like to part with."

Beowulf gestured to the map, where each of the Geatish camps and Swedish villages along the border were marked by carved figures.

"If we can take the outlying villages, which we can if we have enough fighters, the Swedes will sue for peace. We need every warrior we can get. The sooner we finish this the better."

Igni raised an eyebrow. "The Swedes have never been ones for long peacetimes. They waited less than a year after killing our king before they attacked this time."

The third jarl piped up again. "The Swedish king was killed shortly thereafter, deposed by the man who sits on the throne now, and he seems to have had some different feelings about our peace terms. I don't doubt after this we may well have a long-lasting peace."

Beowulf gave him a skeptical glance, surprised by the man's confidence in the promises of their neighbors. She said nothing, but Hygd must have seen the confusion on her face, for the queen spoke up with a small smile.

"I think having a legend for a queen might keep them well at bay. Especially after you sank an entire ship with your bare hands at the battle of Vänersborg."

Beowulf blinked several times, flexing the fingers of her hand as she remembered the splintering wood. A small flutter of shame stirred in her gut. She hadn't lost control of her temper in such a way since she was a foundling, and it wasn't something she overly wanted to be known for. Still, if her legend alone could help protect her people, it was more than worth it. Her discomfort must have shown, enough for Hygd to see it, as the queen's smile faded. Still, Beowulf hoped the queen was right as she turned back to Igni.

"I cannot promise to hold your warriors in reserve. That will be the decision of the leaders of each war party. I can, however, control where they are sent." She reached down and pointed to the map, tapping the southernmost marker along the border, two days from the great hall on horseback. "Based on what our scouts say, it's likely that this war party will see the least combat, but I cannot make any guarantee."

Igni stared at her for a long moment with her arms tightly crossed and her brows knitted. The other three jarls waited in silence, all eyes on the two of them. Had they not already been discussing for a few hours, Igni might have pushed back harder. Instead, she finally let out a huff of air, seeming to deflate as she dropped her arms to her sides.

"Very well," she sighed in a defeated manner. "I don't like it, but I can agree to these terms. I'll send my warriors out at dawn."

Beowulf looked to the others. "And the rest of you, gather your fighters and head toward the camps as we discussed. You should all be there within three days."

A murmur of agreement and a few nods passed around among them. Beowulf lifted her chin slightly and pressed her hand to her chest, before extending it out toward all of them as she spoke.

"All-father watch over you."

The jarls responded in a singular voice. "All-father watch over you, my queens." Then they filtered out of the room, leaving their leaders in silence.

Beowulf leaned over the table and studied the map. She could feel Hygd's gaze on her for a moment, before the queen stood and departed without another word, leaving Beowulf to study the maps in the silence of her chambers.

She stood long enough that a twinge slowly formed in one shoulder where she leaned across the table, though she didn't move until the door suddenly opened again. When she looked up from the table, she was surprised to see Hygd standing in the doorway, her garments entirely changed.

The queen strode up to the table as she spoke, her hands finishing tying her thick dark hair into a singular braid that fell past her shoulders. Beowulf had never seen her in anything but a dress. While the leather tunic she now wore looked almost like a dress, the bottom stopped higher in an asymmetrical line. One side ended just above her knees, the other just below, and the sides were cut all the way up to the belt just below her waist to allow for movement. She wore breeches and boots, and the sleeves of her linen undershirt were pinned to her arms near the wrist by a pair of leather bracers. Her sword was strapped to her side, the hilt freshly polished and glimmering in the firelight. Beowulf raised an eyebrow as she looked the queen up and down in appreciation, unable to keep her eyebrows from rising, nor a grin from curling in the corner of her mouth.

"That went better than it might have." Hygd sighed as she stepped up to the table. "I didn't expect Igni would agree, regardless of her terms."

Beowulf had momentarily completely forgotten the meeting that had concluded less than an hour before, and she shook her head to refocus her thoughts before responding, trying to keep her eyes on the table rather than the queen. "While most of the time was wasted on unproductive bickering, it seems that the end result is what we hoped."

Hygd smiled before folding her hands before her as she stood near the edge of the table. She seemed to hesitate for a moment, eyeing Beowulf as she did.

"Was there something you wanted to discuss?" Beowulf asked slowly, daring to watch the queen, one of the most poised women she had ever seen, as she fidgeted slightly awkwardly. Hygd had never seemed shy, even for a brief moment, and it caught Beowulf almost as off guard as seeing her in armor.

"I wanted to ask you to spar," Hygd said quietly.

Beowulf's thoughts seemed to collide in her head as she blinked in surprise. She knew Hygd could handle a blade and certainly trained occasionally, though nowhere near as frequently as Beowulf herself. Still, it was never something she had strongly associated with her, let alone the two of them crossing swords. Oddly enough, it had never even occurred to her.

"I'm sorry, what?" she asked thickly, her tongue turning to cotton in her mouth as her mind skittered through thoughts of the two of them matching each other blade for blade like a dance. The answer was an unequivocal yes, but something in her refused to even grasp that the offer had been made in earnest.

"You heard me," Hygd said with a subtle grin.

"Really?" Beowulf asked, her mouth still dry, feeling an odd mix of panic and elation rising in her chest.

Hygd let out a small laugh, placing her hands on her hips and shifting her weight slightly onto one leg as she stared across the table at Beowulf, who tried desperately not to stare anywhere besides at the queen's eyes.

"I'm nothing to match yourself, but I figured it would be better than nothing, and there's few others who would want to spar at this late an hour unless they were in their cups." Hygd seemed to regain some of her confidence as Beowulf failed to conceal her interest in the offer, flustered though she was.

Beowulf cleared her throat, her arms supporting her where her palms rested on the table. "I—I mean I suppose that's true, but why now? As you yourself pointed out, it is oddly late for a sparring match."

Hygd looked her up and down where she leaned over the table, those piercing blue eyes seeming to assess her. A wry smile spread slowly across her lips as she held Beowulf's gaze.

"When was the last time you sparred, or fought without deadly outcomes?"

Beowulf counted the days back in her mind. "I think it's been just past a week, almost two."

"That's why I offer." Hygd continued to smile, something in her eyes almost mischievous and entirely disarming. Beowulf, feeling somewhat stupid, still looked at her questioningly, before Hygd pressed on. "It helps you think," she explained. "You've told me as much, and I figure that between all of the councils and meetings you have had to lead, your head might crave the clarity that comes when you swing your sword."

Beowulf couldn't think of a single word to say. She wanted to, as the meaning behind Hygd's offer clicked into place in her thoughts and she finally understood exactly why the queen made it. It was a gift, and more than that, it showed how closely Hygd had observed her, and seen things that Beowulf herself had perhaps not thought to share. She felt heat rising on the back of her neck as Hygd looked at her, her chin held high, expectant in an almost daring way.

"I—" Beowulf began, then faltered, and laughed down at the table. When she looked back up, a broad smile had settled onto her face, one that she could feel all the way to her ears. "Thank you. I would love to spar."

Hygd gave a satisfied nod before turning on her heel and walking on swift strides from the room. "I'll set some torches in the yard and meet you there," she said over her shoulder before disappearing through the door without so much as a single backward glance. Beowulf stared after her a moment, still slightly dumbstruck. She shook her head, gathered up her shield and pulled on a mail shirt with a grin still plastered on her face. It didn't take long for her to armor herself, years of practice guiding her hands and fingers as she laced her leather tunic over her mail shirt. She followed the path Hygd had taken, walking from her room along the side passage to one of the many doors that led outside.

It was truly dark beyond the hall, the stars already shining in the night sky above. A lingering warmth hung on the summer air and carried with it the smell of grass and earth. The training grounds were unsurprisingly empty, and Hygd had made a circle for them where she had shoved almost a dozen torches into the soft ground. It gave them enough space to maneuver and cast enough light to see easily by.

The queen stood waiting in the circle, her sword in one hand and a rough training shield in the other. Beowulf took advantage of the time her descent from the hall took, and studied the queen in an appreciative manner. She had never seen Hygd like this in their time together, and found she quite liked it.

The queen, graceful as she was, had strong shoulders and a calculated manner to her movements that reminded Beowulf of a cat. While Beowulf wouldn't dare bring herself to say it, Hygd looked quite stunning in her armor, light though it was, and much more comfortable with a sword in her hand than Beowulf would have guessed or assumed.

Beowulf walked slowly to the bottom of the hill, slung her cloak over the fence of the yard, drew her training sword from its sheath and stepped into the firelight. Hygd flipped her braid over her shoulder and shook out her arms slightly, testing the weight of her sword as she and Beowulf began ever so slowly circling each other.

"You're sure?" Beowulf asked.

"Of course." Hygd smiled. "Though I must warn you, I'm afraid I'll not be much of a challenge for you. Certainly not if you can break a tree with your bare hands."

Beowulf snorted. "Strength doesn't make a fighter. You asked me to spar. You needn't discredit your own skill."

"Perhaps you should wait until you see." Hygd stepped slightly closer.

"Indeed." Beowulf opened her arms, enticing Hygd's attack, which the queen made without hesitation. She was fast, more so than Beowulf would have guessed, and Beowulf barely dodged her first swing, before blocking her second and countering with a blow that slammed against the queen's shield.

They were both mindful of the torches, and the ring of fire kept their steps close, forcing them to rely on quick and care-ful movements. Beowulf pulled her strikes and took her time with her attacks, far more interested in seeing what the queen was capable of. She wasn't disappointed. While Hygd certainly didn't fight like a warrior who trained hard and often, she was nonetheless skilled with a blade. Speed was her ally, and she did indeed move like a cat as she leaped, dodged, swung, and parried.

It wasn't long before they both were breathing hard, flyaway hairs plastered to their skin with sweat. The night provided a welcome breeze that blew cool and quiet through the yard as the sound of clashing swords rang out into the darkness. The light from the torches obscured all beyond their fiery border, and it seemed as though there was nothing beyond that circular patch of earth where they circled each other and exchanged blows.

Beowulf could feel herself grinning as the queen pressed her attack and their blades whistled through the air. The warrior's boots dug into the soft earth as she moved, breathing hard, feeling the heat of her blood rising. The pressing worries around her mind lifted like fog burning away under a hot sun, the world becoming crystal clear as she moved in rhythm with the queen. Wild green eyes locked with icy blue as the two of them continued their dance, firelight flickering all around them.

Hygd didn't appear quite as elated as Beowulf, her brows furrowed as she concentrated on the moves she made. Nonetheless, when she held Beowulf's gaze, a smile crept onto her lips, which widened as she made a particularly vicious advancing attack, swinging blow after blow. Beowulf could feel her elation turning to giddiness, and she began to laugh as she dodged and blocked, narrowly keeping up with the queen's strikes. Her laughter was replaced by a broad grin as she took a skittering half step back, circled wide, and looked for an opening.

The pauses each time they parted and circled each other grew slowly longer and longer as their breath came hard. Beowulf had the strength and wind to continue, but the queen was beginning to tire. Beowulf knew she wouldn't say as much, but her arms dropped lower each time they paced around each other, and sweat shone on every bare patch of her skin.

Beowulf rocked for a moment on the balls of her feet, waiting for Hygd to take her next step, before she leaped forward and swung for the queen's head. The warrior's blows came high, then low, driving Hygd back on her heels and pushing her slowly toward the flaming barrier that separated them from the black emptiness beyond. Hygd spun at the last second, leaping out to one side, but Beowulf was on her heels and gave her no chance to regain her footing. She trapped Hygd's next strike between her blade and shield, twisted the sword from Hygd's grip and sending it skittering onto the ground.

Hygd didn't yield; instead she swung her shield arm toward Beowulf's head. The warrior was caught by surprise, battle nerves making her laugh once more as she took a staggering step back just in time to avoid the blow. Hygd frowned in concentration, holding her shield before her, her other hand balled into a fist as she resolutely squared off against Beowulf. They slowly circled each other, and Beowulf felt a spark of admiration bloom in her chest as she locked eyes with the unarmed but resolutely unyielding queen.

Beowulf leaped forward, keeping Hygd's attention high as she swung at the queen, forcing her to duck and block behind the battered form of her training shield. Hygd didn't see Beowulf step in deep, their legs crossing, before Beowulf knocked Hygd's shield arm wide with a high strike, pressed her own shield into the queen's chest, and shoved. Hygd was flung to the ground, and Beowulf followed, the edge of her shield hitting the earth beside the queen as she dropped into a kneeling position over where Hygd lay prone.

They froze like that, Hygd on her back with her shield arm on the ground above her head, Beowulf leaning over her, sword tip pointed very carefully at the queen's throat, no more than a foot of space between them. The queen's chest rose and fell rapidly, and their breath was the only thing that filled the silence for a moment as they stared at each other, before a small wry grin formed on Hygd's lips.

There was a sly smugness in the queen's eyes as she looked suddenly downward toward her opponent's stomach. Beowulf followed her gaze, looking down to where the queen's free hand held a dagger, the tip gently pressed against Beowulf's tunic just below her sternum. Beowulf felt her mouth open slightly in surprise as she looked down at the blade. She hadn't even seen Hygd draw it before she fell, let alone felt the tip of it when she dropped on top of her.

Beowulf stared at the blade for a moment as surprise turned to amusement. She could feel the warmth in her chest tingling all the way down to her fingertips as she burst into laughter. Hygd joined her, the tension of the match seeping out of them as they laughed, before Beowulf stood and offered a hand to the queen. Once she was pulled to her feet, Hygd placed a hand on Beowulf's shoulder to steady herself, her laughter subsiding slightly as the two of them looked at each other.

The air seemed to grow strained between them, and Beowulf felt the need to speak, to say something, but not a single word her mind provided seemed suitable. One of the queen's hands still rested on her shoulder, the other clasped her forearm, her touch light. Their eyes had locked, and the captivating sea blue of Hygd's irises was the only thing that kept Beowulf's gaze from straying to the queen's lips, where a small smile still lingered. The warrior stood frozen as the moment dragged out, until Hygd finally gave a nervous laugh and turned her gaze earthward.

Beowulf could only stand like a statue, her mind still scrabbling for words as she tried to ignore what she felt, like a lightning bolt had just struck her. Hygd disentangled herself, and even in the dim firelight Beowulf could see an unmistakable flush coloring her cheeks as she walked to retrieve her sword. By the time she brushed the soft sand from the blade, Beowulf finally managed to speak, her smile evident in her voice.

"My queen, I regret I must inform you that your talents are thoroughly wasted on weaving."

"You're far too kind." Hygd laughed and shook her head, already dousing some of the torches, trying to keep her eyes off the warrior as she grinned at the ground.

"I don't say it lightly," Beowulf continued, aware that though her breath had begun to settle, there was a burning heat that lingered on her neck and ears.

"Well." Hygd doused all but the last torch. "Thank you."

"Thank you for the match," Beowulf said, and sheathed her training sword. Hygd took the last torch to light their way as they walked back up toward the hall. Beowulf could not have said what time it was, all she knew was that she wasn't tired. Her skin felt like the air in a thunderstorm, and seemed to prickle as they walked in a tense silence back toward the hall. Once they were inside, Beowulf turned to bid the queen goodnight, but Hygd gently took her hand before she could speak.

"Beowulf." She spoke softly, taking her time, as if it was the first time she had spoken her name out loud, and something about it sent a small flutter through Beowulf's chest. Hygd refused to meet her gaze, instead staring down at their joined hands.

"I—" Hygd's voice faltered as she spoke, and she frowned downward, carefully running her thumb over the back of Beowulf's fingers. "There's something I have been meaning to tell you." She sighed, and Beowulf felt an odd mix of worry and elation tremble through her limbs. The queen's discomfort was more than a little concerning, and Beowulf stepped forward and placed her free hand on Hygd's shoulder, wanting to offer what reassurance she might. At Beowulf's touch, Hygd trembled slightly, still holding the warrior's hand tightly in her own. Finally, the queen let out a small, forced laugh as she continued to stare down at their hands.

"I have tried. Goddess knows, I have tried to say something. My courage always fails me, but—" She looked up, and her eyes pierced Beowulf like brilliant blue shards of ice, cutting to her core and making the world around them seem to shrink. "Our friendship and your trust means so much to me, I did not—do not want to risk it, but I have to tell you."

Worry turned to fear, and Beowulf's mind raced, trying to anticipate what ill news the queen might share, what had made one of the most collected and clear-headed women she had ever known feel so unsure of herself. Her grip on the queen's shoulder tightened slightly as Hygd's thumb gently traced across the back of her hand. The queen fell silent, and Beowulf felt her heart fluttering anxiously in her chest as Hygd gazed at her. What was mere seconds seemed painfully long as they stood like that, Beowulf's breath caught in her throat and Hygd looking at her with a sudden and strange tenderness that was absolutely shattering.

A small, tentative smile flickered momentarily on the edge of the queen's mouth as her free hand found its way to Beowulf's cheek. Her breath trembled slightly as she spoke in a voice so quiet Beowulf could barely hear her words.

"May I kiss you?"

Beowulf's mind went utterly blank for a moment, before the first thought it conjured was that she had somehow misheard. Perhaps the entirety of the evening had been some odd dream. It was unlike Hygd to ask to spar, and Beowulf began to wonder if she had fallen asleep at the table. Yet Hygd's hand was warm and held her own tightly, and the places where the queen's fingertips brushed her cheeks felt like flame. She felt heat bloom in her chest, tingling all the way to her fingers and toes, as though something warm and bright that she had kept so deeply locked away was suddenly free.

"Forgive me..." Hygd spoke softly, looking back down at their hands, and Beowulf suddenly realized she had left the queen in a very long silence while her own head and heart spun wildly. "I know our relationship is of a strictly political nature, and for that I have been grateful. You have always valued my insight and treated me as an equal, and despite my intentions otherwise, I find myself increasingly attracted to you."

"To me?" Beowulf said thickly, her words coming slowly as her mind struggled to catch up and the feeling within her chest grew until it felt as though a bonfire crackled within her ribs. She had a thousand things she wanted to say, many of which she had thought more than once but kept carefully buried, and they all jostled each other, none of them escaping her lips.

"Yes," Hygd said softly, looking back up, and for a moment Beowulf felt she drowned in the blue of the queen's eyes. "You are one of the most honorable warriors I have ever met. And yet despite being a powerful fighter, I have also known you to be incredibly kind and gentle. There is a beauty to you that reminds me of the winter storms. I am sorry if I speak beyond what is acceptable, but I feel as though this will burn through me from the inside out if I do not give voice to it."

"Please." Beowulf struggled to find words, unsure of how to answer, still half lost in the queen's gaze. "Please do not apologize. I didn't—" she stammered, her mind still struggling. "I didn't expect..." She trailed off, but her curiosity must have shown on her face.

"I have always found both men and women attractive." Hygd smiled sheepishly. "But I had few chances with the latter, and I've never felt like—" She faltered as her gaze slowly dropped from the warrior's eyes down to her lips. Overwhelmed, Beowulf again struggled to find words, as so many thoughts she had carefully tucked away seemed to erupt deep within her.

Hygd let her gaze drop back to their hands. "I understand if you don't feel—"

"Hygd." Beowulf said her name softly, forcing her thoughts to settle as the world around them began to fall away. Hygd looked up, her eyes bright, and Beowulf dared to brush a strand of dark hair from the queen's brow before gently cupping Hygd's face in her hands. She leaned in slowly, aware of the queen's own hand as it moved to her shoulder and their lips met.

Hygd tasted like sweet mead and the smell of summer grass, and her kiss sent a lightning storm coursing through Beowulf's chest. The queen's lips were gentle at first, her approach tentative as she pressed herself closer. One of Beowulf's arms wrapped around Hygd's middle, pulling her in, as their torsos entwined and their kiss deepened. They remained tightly together even after their lips parted, Hygd's forehead gently pressed against Beowulf's own as the warrior breathed in the smell of her, lips still tingling with sparks. Hygd let out a small and nervous laugh, her eyes unbelievably bright as the two of them looked at each other.

"I didn't think—" Beowulf began slowly, feeling all the nervousness ebb out of her in a tide, and a weight dropping from her shoulders that she didn't even know she had been carrying. "I didn't *dare* think that you felt—" She faltered again, searching Hygd's face as she held the queen close to her. "I have felt it for longer than I would care to admit. I did not dare say anything, did not want you to feel I would take advantage of you in any way. I understand the terms under which we came to know each other were less than ideal."

"I tried," Hygd admitted, struggling to hide the smile on the edge of her lips. "I tried to fight it, for reasons not dissimilar from your own. Goddess knows you had enough to worry about, and I didn't want to assume—"

"I did not either. I did not even allow myself to fully recognize it, though now that I have the freedom to do so—" Beowulf laughed, and the space between them grew slightly as she took a step back, holding the queen's hands in her own. "There have been so many times that I have wanted to find a way to tell you how stunningly beautiful you are, to tell you how easily and often I get lost in your eyes. There are so many things that I want to tell you, things I have thought about you, but not dared to let myself speak."

Hygd positively beamed, and Beowulf thought for a brief and dizzying moment that it was the happiest she had ever seen her in all the time they had been in each other's company. She squeezed the queen's hands tightly.

"It's a lot to think about." Hygd spoke softly, as if she could hear Beowulf's thoughts. "Had I the courage I might have chosen a better time." As if to prove her point, she looked down the empty hallway, quiet for the late hour, lit only by a few flickering torches.

"At least it gave us a bit of privacy, even in the yard." Beowulf let out a small laugh as they stood there in the quiet of the night. It was as if a floodgate had burst between them; so many unspoken things seemed to fill the air between them as they stood in the hall.

It was Hygd who broke the short silence first, quiet and tentative.

"Would you prefer not to sleep alone tonight?"

Beowulf's eyes met the queen's, and the warrior failed to keep a subtle smile from spreading across her lips. In answer, she leaned forward and kissed the queen again, deeply, speaking her desire through the strength of her embrace. She took small steps, the two of them moving ever so slightly as they remained pressed together. When Hygd's back gently made contact with the wall she let out a small, muffled sound into their kiss, sending fire racing through Beowulf's core. She could feel the queen's smile on her lips, and it remained even after they broke apart.

Hygd took her hand gently, and slowly led Beowulf down the hall. Firelight danced across the queen's face, her eyes bright as blue stars as the two of them walked in silence to the queen's chambers.

The queen's room was the original home of the royalty in the hall, and just as grand as the council room that Beowulf had made her own. There was already a warm fire kindled in the hearth, and the table at the back was entirely covered in yarns for weaving. A few large bundles of wool hung from the ceiling, filling the room with their light smell. A massive rug was laid out over the stone floor, and the dark wood of the bed frame shone in the light. It was rough cut, the shape of the tree still showing where the bark had been peeled away and the wood smoothed to a dark shimmer.

Hygd shut the door before beginning to unlace Beowulf's bracers. She had not offered, nor had the warrior asked, but she set to it without hesitation, carefully removing her armor as the two of them slipped out of their boots and removed their cloaks. As she removed Beowulf's garments, Hygd's touch sent heat racing across her skin where her fingers brushed over old scars. Beowulf moved slowly, removing the queen's rings first, then carefully helping her out of her training tunic, pausing only to steal an occasional kiss.

Once they had stripped, Hygd kissed Beowulf deeply, her fingertips pressing into her bare back as she pulled the two of them down onto the thick furs of the bed. Beowulf couldn't help but wonder if Hygd had ever lain with a woman, and as such she moved with less speed and more care than she otherwise might. Each time she moved to trace her fingertips over Hygd's skin, she asked with her gaze first, only moving when the queen nodded. Beowulf followed her fingers with her lips, exploring every inch of the queen that she could find, slowly getting lost in the smell and taste of her.

The outside world seemed to melt away. It was only the two of them, warmed by the fire and by each other as time unraveled and the night deepened. Beowulf fell asleep that night with Hygd wrapped in her arms, their bodies entwined beneath the furs, and a peace in Beowulf's heart that she had long missed. Dawn would bring its duties and troubles, but for that night there was nothing in her world but Hygd.

Part 3

12 years later

Chapter 15

Erik had not seen the entrance to the cave, so deeply covered in snow it was. He had walked in the mountains often in his younger years, and his memory of the old game tracks was something he had counted on as he fled into the dark that night. Escaping the hall of his master had been the easy part, but he knew now that freedom depended on his ability to survive, and the first snows of autumn had fallen deeper than he had expected. Wrapped in furs, with nothing more than moonlight to guide him, he had made the slow journey up toward the distant peaks.

He had gotten lost somewhere along the way, he knew that much, but he followed the stars and kept moving north as he climbed ever higher. Dawn would break soon, heralded by the gathering glow in the eastern sky. It was just as he made up his mind to rest that he took a step further, and the thick snow gave way. He could only briefly cry out in alarm as he tumbled down, tucking in his arms and legs as he dropped into the darkness.

The crevasse beneath him had a steep and sloping side; had it been a straight drop he surely would have perished. Instead, he rolled and tumbled down, scraping himself on hard rocks and ice until he came to an unsteady stop, the echoes of falling stones clattering around him. As he groaned and lifted himself into a crouch, taking note of the pain that shot through his limbs, his eyes adjusted to the dark around him. He quietly thanked the gods as he looked up, relieved that the slope he had tumbled down was shallow enough to climb back up and that he could see the lighter patch where he had fallen through the cover of snow high above.

He scanned the walls for the easiest route up, surprised to find that the opening above him was much larger than it had at first seemed. He had fallen in at the very edge of an area nearly twenty feet in diameter; a small hole was punched through the snow at one side where he had dropped through. The walls were similarly far apart, giving the space he stood in the appearance of a large cavern. To his left was more rough stone, but off to his right the cavern continued further into the mountain, twisting back into the darkness. It slowly dawned on him that he had fallen into the mouth of a very large cave, and one that, he realized, was slightly warm.

The air that wafted past had a heavy metallic smell to it, and a faint reek of something like sulfur. Combined with the warmth of the air, it might have meant a hot spring, and the thought of warmth was painfully tempting as he shivered slightly where he stood. He weighed his options for a moment, then turned and walked toward the current of warm air, his steps taking him deeper into the darkness of the cavern.

As he made his way slowly through the cave, the air grew warmer, and his surroundings were ever harder to make out in the gloom. He passed a hand along the wall, feeling his way as he went, until he reached a massive open space, and there he saw something that made his blood turn to ice.

There was a faint glow that pervaded the large cavern, not quite enough to see the ceiling or the full extent of the walls, but enough to make out what lay at the center—a massive pile of something that shimmered like thousands of tiny waves on the ocean's surface. It took a moment for him to realize they were coins. Coins and cups of gold, torques and fine blades, along with goblets and jewelry that glinted like thousands of tiny stars. But he didn't recognize the treasure hoard at first, as his eyes were drawn to what rested atop it.

Crowning the pile of wealth like a black shadow was a massive shape. He could see a curled body, covered in scales like chainmail. Sharp spikes ran along its spine all the way to its tail, which was tipped in a wicked barb the length of a sword. Its head, with massive backswept horns and a large snout, rested at the topmost point of the gilded mountain it lay upon. Tiny wisps of smoke drifted upward from its nostrils, disappearing into shadows of the cave above. Its head was as long as Erik's height from head to toe, not counting its horns, and even from a distance, Erik could see the closed lids of its massive eyes as it slumbered.

Its neck was thick and long, the exact length impossible to determine since the creature lay curled so tightly. Thick and powerful back legs were tucked beneath its massive body where it lay, and though its size was difficult to judge as it slept, it would have easily spanned forty meters from snout to tail. Perhaps even the length of a small mead hall. Most terrifying of all were the huge wings, dark and leathery and folded on either side of its thick body. These were its forelimbs, and it had no front legs to speak of. Where the bones joined at the front of its wings were three finger-like claws, each curled into the pile of treasure as the serpent slumbered.

Erik had never seen a dragon. Dragons were things of stories, nightmares, and nothing more. He stood dumbfounded, barely daring to breathe as he watched the great beast's body slowly rise and fall with its deep and steady breathing. Terror rooted him to the spot as he stared, his eyes discerning the source of the faint glow that pervaded the room. The creature's chest seemed somehow illuminated from within; a fiery glow shone from the cracks between its scales, ebbing and growing in brightness in time with its breath. It inhaled deeply, its chest glowing like a kiln of hot coals, and Erik could feel himself tremble.

His first thought was escape, but even as he took a tentative step back, his gaze drifted down to the pile of wealth beneath the slumbering dragon. The ember glow from its chest flickered on the shining surfaces of cups and coins, illuminating a mountain of wealth greater than a king's hoard. Even if he survived the mountain, he had nothing but his wits and what he could carry, and not a single coin. It seemed silly to even consider when he was within spitting distance of a living dragon, but his fingers began to itch as he stared at the glittering gold. Even though he hadn't yet convinced himself that he wasn't imagining it all, he found with each moment that passed he was more preoccupied with the gold.

He scrubbed his cheeks as he stared, drawing his hands across his thin beard as his eyes settled on the gold. He could see a goblet, nothing too grand, but easily within reach at the very edge of the pile before him. It rested atop a small pile of torques, and he knew he could pick it up without disturbing anything. Only fear made him hesitate.

He took a deep breath, slowly daring to tiptoe closer, watching the dragon carefully as he did. Only when his foot was mere inches from the great mountain of wealth did he dare to look down. He picked up the goblet gingerly, the gold warm to the touch, and lifted it from the pile without so much as a sound. His fear ebbed only slightly as a mild giddiness flushed through him, and he stuffed the goblet into his tunic.

He walked backward out of the cavern, occasionally looking back over his shoulder to see where he was going. He kept his eyes mostly on the dragon and moved slowly, watching its great lidded eyes. Dawn must have broken outside, for a faint gray light had filtered in from the way he had come, and he let it guide him back to the cave's entrance. Only once he lost sight of the dragon did he dare turn around, his pace quickening to a run as he reached where he had fallen through and scrabbled back up the steep wall. Elation and fear pressed him onwards as he climbed with renewed vigor and pulled himself up and out into the light of day.

He rolled onto his back for a moment in the snow, laughing up at the sky and the tension drained from his limbs. Only once he caught his breath and sat upright in the snow did he take a moment to mock his own foolishness. It couldn't have been a dragon; such things did not exist. Never mind what his eyes saw, dark shadows and the gasses that come from the earth could make men see strange things. But the goblet tucked in his tunic was real enough, and only fear kept him from considering another attempt at stealing from the pile.

He withdrew his prize and admired it in the light of the newly risen sun. It glimmered like no gold he had ever seen and still felt warm as he turned it over in his hands. It was beautiful to look at, and once more he thanked the gods for his fortune before tucking his prize back into his tunic. He found his feet slowly, resigning himself to rest once he got further from that dark cave, and continued his trek into the mountains.

The cave would be covered with the next snow. The entrance that had lain for hundreds of years undisturbed would be once more a secret of those peaks. Deep within the cavern, the treasure still shone like starlight, one of so many priceless pieces now missing. Nothing had been disturbed save a single goblet, yet a slow rumble echoed through the cavern. It rumbled like faint thunder from the breast of the great beast, sending a shudder through the mountain of treasure, loose coins jingling as they tumbled and shifted. The dragon's lungs drew in a massive breath, and the glow within its core grew as its brilliant amber eyes slowly opened.

Chapter 16

Wiglaf was breathing hard, sending steam curling around his head in the frigid morning air. Ice gathered in the thin beard that lined his face, and despite how much he was moving and the thickness of his leather armor, he could still feel the bite of the cold. Winter wasn't far away, but they made the most of the lingering light of fall while it lasted, and this day was no different.

He swayed slightly where he stood, testing his footing in the hard earth, keeping his shield before him. He held his sword at the ready as his opponent circled and the cheers of the onlookers nearly deafened him. Speed was his advantage, and that was quickly fading as his legs and arms tired. Sucking in a deep breath, he quickly feigned a leap to one side, before moving in the opposite direction and bringing his blade to bear against his opponent.

Heardred's ax smashed the blow aside, the prince grinning as he nimbly dodged the second strike, and Wiglaf retreated back.

"Getting tired, little brother?" Heardred asked, his laugh a deep rumble.

"Just warming up." Wiglaf smirked despite the heaviness of his limbs. "I'll have you on your ass yet."

He leaped forward again, the two of them exchanging blows as the small gathering of warriors around them let out another cheer. It was no secret that wages had likely been placed on their match as soon as it started that morning, drawing much of the focus of the training yard. Wiglaf doubted anyone had bet

261

on him. Heardred had always been a better fighter, and Wiglaf could not match him in strength or size.

Heardred was still grinning, his blue eyes sharp, as he shook his mane of thick blond hair like some kind of wild beast. He hefted his double-bladed ax, watching Wiglaf closely, waiting for the next strike. Wiglaf took what time he could buy, keeping the distance between them as he tried to wiggle some feeling back into his fingers. He knew the fight was almost over, but he'd be damned if he wasn't going to make Heardred earn it.

The prince leaped at him like a bear, moving his massive ax with surprising speed for how large it was. Wiglaf narrowly blocked the first strike with his shield, feeling it shudder dangerously on impact. His return strike nearly found its mark, but was stopped by the butt of Heardred's ax before the prince slammed his torso against Wiglaf and sent him sprawling. Even on the ground, Wiglaf managed to block another strike before Heardred knocked his shield from his hand and stood over him, ax raised high.

"Yield!" Wiglaf held up his hands, and Heardred grinned.

"You'll beat me yet, little brother." He laughed as a small ripple of applause scattered through the onlookers. He offered Wiglaf his hand and hauled him to his feet before patting him soundly on the shoulder.

"Well fought." He grinned, still breathing hard, as Wiglaf rolled his eyes and punched him on the shoulder.

"I'll have you yet." Wiglaf snorted as he gathered up his training sword and shield, and the small crowd around them slowly dispersed. That was more than enough excitement to start the day, and as the training yard resumed its usual activity, Wiglaf and Heardred went and sat on the fence. They had been watching the new foundlings training, a group of some four or five youths, all of whom showed promise. Heardred stared intently at the corner of the yard where one of the warriors had the newcomers swinging weighted wooden blades at a bale of hay.

"You know," the prince said slowly, "sometimes it seems only yesterday that was us."

"Sometimes it does." Wiglaf smiled as he turned to look at the prince. Everyone said he had grown into his father's bearing, but Wiglaf had never seen Hygelac. Still, he couldn't deny that his older brother had grown into a strong man. Heardred had the air about him of nobility, and one who had yet to know some of the greater hardships of the world despite having been tested in battle. Wiglaf didn't hold it against him, but despite all their years together there seemed sometimes to be a gap between them that words could not cross. Heardred didn't appear to notice, and Wiglaf hoped for his brother's own sake that they might never share that knowing.

The prince had little preoccupation with the throne and had stuck with his childhood aspiration to be an accomplished warrior. He had more than tripled in size since then, his hair a shaggy curled mane of bright locks that fell to his shoulders, matching a finely groomed beard that lined his jaw. His piercing blue eyes were bright and clear like his mother's, and they burned with fire when his ax was in his hands. He was a solid six feet or more in height, taller than Wiglaf by a few inches, with broad shoulders and a body like a bear.

His elder sister, Halga, followed much more closely in her mother's footsteps, and no one doubted that one day she would make a fine queen. She had grown even lovelier as she had gotten older, and more similar in appearance to her mother as the years passed. Her build was ever so slightly sturdier than her mother's, a trait of her Geatish heritage, along with the stubbornness of her father's bloodline that still lingered in her veins well past her teens.

Wiglaf had never grown to match his brother in height or strength. His dark hair had grown long, and he kept it managed in several braids. His beard was no less impressive or thick than Heardred's, and the color was dark enough that it hid some of the youth of his face. Finding his place as a fighter had taken more time, envied friend of the prince as he was. His skills finally earned him the respect of some of the older warriors, and he had been welcomed among them ever since. Much had changed in the twelve years he had spent at the Queen's Hall, and almost all of it for the better.

Wiglaf took a moment to enjoy the peacefulness of the morning, despite being knocked on his ass. The air was sweet and cold, and the promise of winter carried through the late dawn as the sun climbed higher toward midday. The sound of blades rose up from the training yard as the two of them took time to sit and watch the day unfold. It wasn't until the horns of the village guards sounded that they were startled from their reverie.

The two of them exchanged a grin before leaping down from the fence, half running from the yard along with a small handful of other warriors. The riders had already entered the village by the time they reached the front of the hall. A light cloud of dust was kicked high into the air as a dozen of them on horseback made their way through the village and up to the gates of the hall.

One of the queens was at the lead, her fair hair only faintly streaked with scant lines of silver, thick locks intermixed with an occasional braid that fell past her shoulders. Her face had retained its beauty and strength through the years, with the addition of deeper lines and shadows that betrayed her age. The dark furs across her shoulders made her emerald eyes stand out even more, and the gilded pommel of Naegling shone where it was sheathed at her hip.

Beowulf pulled her horse to a stop before the hall and slid to the ground, a smile playing on her lips as she saw both Heardred and Wiglaf.

"You two are a sight for sore eyes." She laughed before looking Wiglaf up and down. "Why are you covered in dirt?"

"Don't ask." He laughed, then stepped forward to embrace her as the other riders dismounted around them and servants gathered to take the horses to the stables. She hugged Heardred next and patted him on the back. The boy who had once stood only as high as her hip was now taller and wider than she herself.

"We hadn't expected you back until later in the day. It's a long ride from the eastlands," Heardred said as the three of them made their way into the hall. Inside was warm and bright, with light flooding in from the windows, as warriors and servants made their way through the vast space. They walked together across the room, Wiglaf on one side of the queen and Heardred on the other.

"We departed early," Beowulf explained as she pulled off her gloves. "Jarl Igni was a very hospitable host and we came to terms quicker than expected."

"So, she agreed?" Wiglaf asked as they walked.

Beowulf let out a dry chuckle. "It took some convincing, but she agreed to the new tithes if we agreed to train a larger number of the foundlings from her village each season."

Heardred grunted, and Wiglaf gave a small nod before he spoke again.

"I am glad it was a success. And it gave you a chance to stretch your legs."

A voice called from the end of the hall, making all three of them look up. "Goddess knows she might go mad otherwise."

Hygd was walking from the back of the hall, her silver dress swirling around her with each step as she approached. Her long hair had a small amount of gray running through it, seven and forty years of wisdom in the corners of her brilliant blue eyes. She had lost none of her poise and walked with her head held high and her steps measured and even. Halga emerged behind her, a young woman who had her mother's strength in her shoulders and the surety of her steps. Her hair was tied back in a single elegant braid, and she wore a beautiful green dress of dyed linen, the gold embroidery of which brought out the brown in her eyes. She beamed and broke into a light jog, passing her mother to throw her arms around Beowulf.

Heardred tapped Wiglaf on the shoulder, and after a brief smile and a nod to their queens, they walked off toward the training yard once more. Halga disentangled herself from the hug and took a step back, beaming as she did.

"Welcome back."

"Thank you." Beowulf smiled. "And please forgive me, but I am obligated to bring greetings and well-wishes from Jarl Igni's son, Aemund."

Halga groaned and rolled her eyes before dissolving into laughter.

"Don't worry," Beowulf said, grinning, "I made no promises nor enticements on your behalf."

Halga smiled as she stepped back and Hygd passed her. The two queens wrapped arms around each other and exchanged a brief kiss.

"Welcome home, my love." Hygd beamed, then turned to Halga. "And I think we should perhaps begin telling these overeager jarls that our daughter will rule all on her own if she so chooses. Anyone who is interested in her hand can take it up with her."

"I couldn't agree more. There's no rush. I was thirty when I married." Beowulf winked at Halga, and Hygd's cheeks colored slightly.

Halga laughed again, before giving Hygd's hand a small squeeze and turning to walk back the way the two of them had come. The two queens lingered a while longer, and Beowulf enjoyed a moment of getting utterly lost in Hygd's eyes.

"Three weeks' journey done," said Hygd. "I trust that each of the jarls you visited was a kind host?"

"Indeed. We managed to come to some new agreements regarding lands and tithes. Not as well as I had hoped, but certainly well enough." Beowulf nodded thoughtfully. "Good to stretch my legs, as the lads said, and good to be back."

"Good to have you back." Hygd smiled, and the two of them slowly made their way to the council chamber so Beowulf could put some food in her stomach and the two of them could catch up on all that had transpired in their weeks apart.

It was late in the day by the time they were done, and the sunlight had already begun to fade in the shortening fall days as night swiftly approached. There was no great feast that night, and though some of the warriors ate in the hall, the queens shared a meal amid conversation on their own.

Once the sun had set and night had begun to close in, Beowulf took the opportunity to walk the circumference of the outside of the great hall, breathing in the clear air. Laughter carried from within the hall where some of the warriors dined, the smell of woodsmoke and cooked meat drifting through the windows. It promised to be a cold winter; the breeze was chilled, but not frosty as it had been in the morning. Soon enough the snows would come to stay, but not yet.

Daylight was fading as all those in the village prepared for their evening meals. There was a silence that slowly descended, soothing and still, as Beowulf walked around the hall. She trailed her fingers over the wood, breathing in the smell of smoke and enjoying the stillness.

When she reached the eastern wall she saw it. The mountains stretched out dark and tall along the northern horizon, but off to the east, there was a faint glow.

The nearest town was less than a day's ride, and even over the hills and the edges of the forest, a dim but unmistakable light could be seen. It was barely visible, a faint orange color that hugged the horizon line. Beowulf knew what a wildfire looked like at a distance, but this was the wrong time of year, and never had any burned so big or bright. She could feel a small fear begin to tighten in the depths of her chest as she looked to the skyline, her hand instinctively closing around the handle of Naegling.

She wasn't standing long before her wondering was answered, and the horn of the gate guard called out into the dark. Beowulf was already at the front of the hall by the time the rider reached it. His horse was frothing, its nostrils flared wide and its sides heaving, and it skidded unsteadily to a halt, the man half falling from the saddle. He looked at first as if he might run into the hall, when he caught sight of Beowulf and immediately dropped to his knees before her.

"My queen," he gasped, hands clasped together before him so tightly that the knuckles turned white. "My queen, something terrible has happened. The wrath of the gods—" He shuddered, his breath heaving.

Some of the hall guards had been drawn by the commotion, along with a few of the servants. Beowulf leaned down and gripped the man by his elbows, lifting him effortlessly back to his feet as he stammered and shook.

"What is it?" she asked, trying to keep the urgency from her voice.

"A serpent," he gasped. "A serpent of Niflheim, bane of the gods, destroyer of man—"

"Speak sense," she said firmly, giving him a small shake. A small crowd had begun to gather around them.

"I do." He balked, wide-eyed. "A dragon has come. Our town—destroyed. It was like nothing I've ever seen. Enough fire to torch a mountain. Turned our warriors to ash where they stood. It destroyed everything. Some of us escaped, most weren't so lucky."

Beowulf knew it could not be true. Dragons were the stuff of legends and nothing more, so they had always been. But something in her chest seemed to sink, and a dread cold seeped in as she thought of that distant glow on the horizon. Something had happened, and though she was loath to believe the man, something had burned that village, whether it was a dragon or no. She could hear murmurs in the surrounding crowd, along with a few light laughs, as she released the man's shoulders. He still stared at her wide-eyed, his mouth opening and closing like a fish. Someone from the crowd spoke up.

"Had a few too many drinks, friend?"

It was followed by another smattering of laughter. The man blinked and looked around the faces at the front of the hall, wincing as if he were in pain.

"Please," he stammered. "You must believe me!"

"No such thing as dragons," someone else chimed in, and their comment was met with a small ripple of assent that passed through the gathering. Beowulf had remained silent, her eyes fixed on the frightened man and her feet rooted to the spot. He looked around himself once more, before turning back to her and trying to sink to his knees again.

"Please, my queen, you must believe—"

She gripped him by the shoulders and hauled him back to his feet, this time keeping her hands there so that she might keep him from collapsing again.

"Enough. Whether you speak the truth or not is of less concern," she said firmly, before turning to the rest of those present. "Something has happened, and whether it was man or beast has yet to be determined."

"It was a dragon, I swear to the All-father it—"

"Enough!" Her voice rang out, silencing the man and the chatter that had passed through the small crowd. She turned to one of the guard captains who had emerged from the hall. "See this man has somewhere to rest, and if he says anything that makes more sense, let me know."

The guardsman gave a nod, before grabbing one of the man's arms to steady him on his feet and slowly walking him in toward the hall. The small crowd parted for them, whispers following in their footsteps as the man was taken inside. Beowulf turned to the assembled crowd before her as one of the warriors spoke up.

"My queen, you don't actually believe him, do you?"

"I don't know," she said flatly, her arms crossed over her chest as she stared the way the man had gone. "But dragon or no, something has caused destruction."

"The Swedes?" another warrior asked, and Beowulf frowned.

"I would not think so. We've had peace with them for nearly twelve years now. I see no reason nor means by which they could strike so deeply into our lands without being seen or stopped." She placed a hand on her sword and spoke to the group. "Gather the warriors after they break their fast once the sun has risen. I'll take two dozen volunteers and ride out to see what has become of this town."

"Two dozen?" someone asked.

"Better more hands than is needed. I can see fire on the horizon, and I would rather not risk the lives of my people. I would rather bring too many fighters than too few, even if it is just a fire and nothing more." Once she saw a few nods, she felt satisfied that she could re-enter the hall, letting the small crowd disperse.

Beowulf walked back down the length of the hall, nearly empty as it was, and made her way toward the room she shared with the queen. She might have enjoyed the night a bit longer, but a gnawing worry had settled within her, and she had a feeling she would need her strength for whatever the next day brought. She sought sleep instead, but when she reached her room she found Hygd awake and sitting by the fire.

The queen looked up as she entered, frowning slightly when she caught sight of the worry that showed on Beowulf's face.

"What is it?"

Beowulf shook her head and pulled off her cloak, slowly stripping her tunic and clothes. She spoke as she undressed, her brows furrowed as she tried to reconcile the truth her mind claimed with the dread that slowly crept into the corners of her heart.

"Something struck the nearest village to the east, burned it to the ground. A survivor just came into the hall."

Hygd frowned and stood, taking a few steps closer as she spoke. "That village belongs to Jarl Gunnar. It was destroyed?"

"It would seem so, but we won't know until we ride there tomorrow."

"And survivors?"

"Beyond the one, I do not know."

Hygd hugged her arms about herself, staring for a moment into the flames that flickered in the hearth.

"What or who could do such a thing? Another jarl? The Swedes?"

Beowulf shook her head as she pulled her boots off. "I think each of those is as unlikely as the other. The man claims it was a dragon."

"What?" Hygd turned suddenly, one eyebrow raised, her expression something between skeptical and confused. Beowulf could only shrug.

"That's what he says. I can only hope we'll find out more when we go there."

Hygd frowned deeply, keeping her arms about herself as she watched Beowulf pull off the last of her garments and climb into bed. The warrior's wife waited a moment before following suit. Only when she had climbed in beside her love did she speak again.

"I would say that's only nonsense, but I have seen strange things in my days, and to burn a whole village..." Hygd trailed off. She rolled slightly onto her side, wrapping an arm around Beowulf, their heads nearly touching as they leaned toward each other where they lay. The warrior rested her arm over the queen's, holding it across her chest.

"I know. I refuse to believe he was telling the truth, but at the same time..." Beowulf looked up at the ceiling, still feeling the seeping dread in her chest. "Something about it just feels... I'm not sure."

"I trust your instincts as much as mine," Hygd said softly, her fingers tracing over one of the scars on Beowulf's shoulder. "And you are not one to idly feel fear. Will you be taking many warriors?"

"I hope for two dozen. We'll need to ride on horseback to make good time."

"That's fewer than I would like," Hygd sighed, before sighing and tracing her fingertips down Beowulf's arm, stopping when she reached her hand and interlacing their fingers.

"I feel the same. But whatever this is, we must find it. We must find it quickly."

Beowulf held Hygd's hand tightly as the two of them fell silent. They lay for a time in the dimming light from the hearth, until only glowing coals remained, and Hygd's breath was steady and even. Beowulf stayed awake a short while longer, unable to chase away the fear that slowly grew in her. She turned to where Hygd lay, her face serene and untroubled in her sleep. Beowulf could not have said why, but the fear in her chest made her wish she could slow the passing of time, the queen's hand still in hers, the two of them just lying there together in the dim light.

She rolled and wrapped an arm around the queen, pulling her close. She was gentle enough not to wake her, though Hygd stirred slightly in her sleep as the warrior brought their bodies together. Beowulf kept her arm around Hygd, holding her close as if she might lose her if she let go. A fitful sleep slowly crept up on her, and she finally drifted into dreams, the two of them wrapped in each other's arms.

Chapter 17

Beowulf dreamt of fire. Ash and smoke choked the air, and cinders drifted on hot drafts that rippled through her hair. She was walking among corpses strewn across the ground. So badly burned were they, that she could not make out anything beyond their shape; no hair or garments or even unseared skin could be seen. She walked slowly, as one who was lost, picking her way across an endless plain of the fallen, the burned ground crunching beneath her boots.

Her heart ached as she walked, each step feeding a growing certainty that she was wading through the end of her people. The air burned in the back of her throat, and as she finally tore her eyes from the carnage by her feet and looked up, she saw before her the charred husk of her own home, the Queen's Hall. The building was blackened and burned, the roof and walls entirely gone. Only the support beams along the walls, the pillars of the halls, and one or two of the roof beams remained. It looked like some strange creature, gutted with its black ribs poking toward the sky.

She walked through the great gaping hole where the doors had once stood, the ruddy, ash-filled sky seeming to shrink down upon her. Coals blazed on all sides as her boots slowly tracked a path on the stone floor. She made it only as far as the center of the hall, and the pain in her chest grew with each step. It was failure that carved a hole in her, her own failure for not managing to protect a single life among her people. All that she loved, everything and everyone, was now merely ashes and beyond her reach.

Agony welled up from within her chest and crashed over her like a tidal wave. So strong was her heartbreak that it felt as though her insides had been ripped out. Beowulf trembled and shook, crumpling toward the ground as her knees gave way. She wrapped her arms about her and hunkered down on herself where she knelt, as if she was trying to keep from being torn apart from the inside out. Her sobs came silently and without tears, shaking her entire body until the pain within her pitched past what she could contain, and she threw her head back and screamed.

Her voice echoed around her as if she might expel the pain that burned within her bones. So forcefully did she yell that her voice cracked as all her strength and air was expended. Every ounce of agony she felt split the air and exhausted her until she fell silent and dropped to her hands and knees. Now the tears came, and blurring her vision and scorching down her cheeks. Only when she heard footsteps in the rubble beside her did she finally look up.

The woman's face was familiar, and just the sight of her felt like a cool stream entering her mind, soothing the pain that radiated through her. She finally managed to sit upright, still on her knees, with her hands in her lap.

"What is this?" Beowulf croaked hoarsely, as the ageless face of the goddess looked down on her. Freya was dressed in her hawk-feather cape, her hair tied in a single braid, a sword sheathed at her hip. She looked down at the warrior, something almost apologetic in her features as she spoke.

"What may come to pass."

Beowulf felt dread and agony sink deeper into her chest. She might have asked after those whose names rose to her mind, but she knew deep down that none survived. The goddess looked about her slowly, before turning her gaze back to the warrior.

She spoke softly, her eyes on Beowulf. "This is the most likely future that awaits."

Beowulf looked up, clenching her fist. "Can it be prevented?" she asked, not even trying to hide the desperation in her voice. Freya regarded her for a moment, then slowly nodded, and Beowulf scrambled to her feet.

The goddess looked her level in the eye, her irises burning gold like a bird's. "There is a way this fate can be prevented." She regarded Beowulf with something almost like pride as she reached out and gently took a lock of Beowulf's hair between her fingers. A muscle moved in Beowulf's jaw, and she took a deep breath.

"How?"

"I told you once, many years ago." Freya spoke lightly, and something in her eyes looked almost sad, before her gaze dropped to the warrior's waist, where Naegling shone. Beowulf followed her gaze, dropped her hand to the hilt, and gripped it tightly. The familiar warmth brought a small comfort to her, and she breathed deeply, thinking back to the last time she had seen the goddess.

She knelt slowly and scooped a small amount of ash into her hands. Fine grains ran through her fingers, staining them black, and she stared for a moment before standing once more, setting her shoulders and staring squarely at the goddess.

"What must I give?" she asked flatly, though in her heart she already knew the answer.

The goddess smiled briefly, then her expression turned sorrowful, and she placed a hand gently on Beowulf's shoulder. Blackness crept in around them, the sky above slowly darkened, and the bones of the charred hall disappeared around them. The world melted away, ash and smoke fading, until it seemed the two of them stood alone in a soft blackness. When the goddess spoke again, her voice was quiet and sad, and she squeezed Beowulf's shoulder tightly.

"Everything."

Darkness closed like a soft blanket as the dream drifted away, and consciousness flooded Beowulf as her eyes opened. She woke slowly from the pain of her dream, coming back to the world raw. She felt as she had all those years ago, washed up on the beach, as if she had been dragged over stones.

It was nearly dawn, and light was filtering through the small single window as she sat and blinked the sleep from her eyes.

Someone was shouting outside; she could hear voices calling, though Hygd still slept soundly beside her. Beowulf carefully climbed from the bed, pulled the furs back up over Hygd's shoulder and kissed her gently on her brow. The queen stirred gently, bringing a small smile to Beowulf's lips as she pulled on her clothes and slipped quietly from the room.

The hall was already full of movement, and as she entered she took a deep breath and surveyed all the night had brought with it.

Some half dozen villagers she did not recognize were in the hall, some of them lying on blankets, their burns already wrapped. Others huddled beneath furs, and the warriors in the hall wore stony expressions as they moved beneath the vast roof. The skeptical expressions that had met the survivor who first came to the gates were nowhere to be seen, and the word "dragon" could be heard amid the whispers of those present. One warrior greeted Beowulf as she walked toward the front of the hall.

"My queen."

"What happened?" she asked, scanning the hall. There was panic on the faces of the survivors. War and death brought pain, but this was something else. This was a terror she had seldom seen.

"More survivors. Some from the same village, but at least two of them are from the next village to the north. There are likely more who haven't yet made it here."

Beowulf nodded. "See that their wounds are tended to. We have enough food and can find places for them to rest."

"My queen—" the warrior began, before frowning. "They all say the same thing."

"Dragon," Beowulf said, and he gave a slow nod. "I know. I do not think we can dismiss it as a mere fairy tale anymore.

Two villages, perhaps more, were burned to the ground in one night."

The man's frown deepened, and Beowulf could see the uncertainty on his face. But he kept his composure and squared his shoulders as he looked at his queen. All around them the hall was hushed, and Beowulf could feel the eyes of some of the other warriors on them. The fear the survivors had brought with them seemed infectious, and it seeped into the hall, slow and cold.

"What can we do?" he asked plainly.

"The only thing we can." She turned to the hall at large, where a small cluster of warriors was slowly beginning to form around them. "At least two villages in one night, and who knows how many dead. If we cannot stop this, all our lands will fall, and more besides." She looked around at the stony faces on all sides of her. The air in the hall grew still, even the smallest footsteps sending thunderous echoes around them. She knew the weight her words carried, and she could feel the tension in the air.

Beowulf lifted her chin as she looked at the warriors in turn. "I do not ask any of you to go with me if you do not wish to. No one will think less of you."

"And for those who would come with you?" the man asked.

Beowulf gave an approving nod. "We'll take as many riders as we have horses for, we will need to travel at speed. All those who would join me, assemble before the great hall after sunrise."

She saw a few nods, then she turned and headed back toward her quarters as the remainder of the hall, and the village itself, began to wake in earnest. It wasn't the thought of her sword and armor that gifted speed to her steps as she passed back through the hall, it was Hygd. She couldn't have said if it was relief or sorrow that welled in her heart as she opened the door to find the queen awake and placing another log on the fire.

Something of Beowulf's thoughts must have shown through her eyes, as Hygd stood and stepped to meet her.

"What is it?"

Beowulf reached out and took the queen's hands in her own. "It would seem the rumors are true, difficult to believe as they may be."

Hygd searched Beowulf's face in silence. When she spoke, her voice was deathly quiet.

"You're going after it." It wasn't a question. Beowulf nodded, and felt Hygd's grip tighten on her hands. Their eyes met, Hygd's a brilliant blue as she looked at the warrior, her features seeming to tremble for a moment before she settled into a sad smile that made Beowulf's heart ache. Hygd nodded slowly.

"I know," she said softly, "and I would not try to stop you, but I wish more than anything that it was not so."

"I have faced monsters before."

Hygd lifted a hand to Beowulf's cheek and looked her level in the eyes.

"Can you promise me that this time is not different?" It was a test, not a question. Hygd already knew the answer as much as Beowulf, who tightened her jaw and let her gaze drop to the floor. She had felt it from the moment she had seen the fire, though she had not known it until her dream. Each battle she had faced, each creature she had defeated, she had always been able to keep her fear at bay. She had trusted in her own abilities, and even in the face of possible death she had always felt certain of her own destiny as a warrior with whatever end it might bring.

This time, no matter how hard she tried, she could not quell the fear that had seeped into her chest. She held Hygd's hands tightly, and it took all her strength to look her in the eyes once more.

"It is different. I do not know but I feel..."

She trailed off unsteadily before taking a deep breath, barely managing to keep her voice even.

"I am afraid," she said quietly, and felt Hygd step closer, their foreheads pressing together as the queen gripped her hands tightly.

"As am I," Hygd said softly. "I am afraid that when you ride through those gates you will not return."

Beowulf wanted to reassure her, as she had so many times before. Each time in the twelve years they had been together, when monsters or war had called her away, she had always promised to return. Even with her survival being uncertain, she had always made that promise, knowing she could at least do her utmost to uphold it. This time she could make no oath when she was certain that it would be broken. She wanted desperately to give her word, but she knew deep down it would be a lie, and the promise could not leave her lips.

Beowulf said more with her silence than if she had spoken, and Hygd let go of her hands to wrap her arms tightly around the warrior. The queen's breath came unsteadily, her shoulders shaking slightly as she clung to Beowulf. Hygd leaned back enough to look her in the eyes, and the sight of tears on her cheeks broke what remained of Beowulf's resolve. Her own vision blurred, and her eyes burned slightly. She kept her breath and her voice steady as she spoke.

"You would not stop me?" she asked.

Hygd gave a small, heartbroken smile. "Would that I could, but it is not my place. You choose the path you walk and the destiny you carve for yourself. I would not ask you not to do this, because it goes against your nature." She let out a mirthless laugh. "I always said you were one of the most noble warriors I'd met, and I feel cruel to wish it was not so. You have always protected your people, you have always been a shield against the darkness of the world, and I know you could not rest or live peacefully if you did not act as such."

Beowulf gave a genuine smile, however small, and blinked as a few tears streamed down her cheeks. She could disagree with nothing Hygd said, but she could hear the pain in her voice, and she wished desperately that there might yet be another way. She had a choice, she knew that, but her heart was set on its path. She had to make peace with the consequences.

"I am not afraid of dying," Beowulf said in a voice so quiet it was barely a whisper. "I do not fear the end of my days, for I have lived by my code for all of them. But..."

She trailed off, feeling something tighten in her throat.

"I am afraid of losing you." She barely managed to get the words out before her voice broke. Hygd leaned forward and pulled her into an embrace, and the two of them held each other so tightly Beowulf could barely breathe.

She wished she could slow time as she tried to preserve in her mind the feel of Hygd's arms around her, the sweet smell of her hair, the sound of her heartbeat. There was no choice to make. Hygd had been right, and Beowulf knew that she would not be able to find rest or peace until she had done all she could to protect her people. Twelve years seemed, in that instant, to have passed in the blink of an eye. She could not help but think back to the fateful night when she had asked for Hygd's hand, when they were still strangers to each other. Everything that had passed between them since, every kiss and every word spoken, seemed to slip like sand through her fingers. When Beowulf spoke again, it took all her strength to not drop to her knees in the queen's arms.

"I am so sorry."

Hygd pulled away from their embrace to cup Beowulf's face in her hands, sorrow in her eyes but a faltering smile on her lips as she spoke.

"Do not be. You would not be yourself if it was any other way, and if you were anyone else, I would not love you the way I do." She took a shuddering breath. "The way I always will."

She kissed Beowulf, fiercely and deeply. They wrapped their arms around each other once more and pulled close together, holding each other until the sound of horses and the shouts of the war party drifted through from outside. Hygd slowly relinquished her grip, and Beowulf stood savoring every second as she looked at the woman she loved.

After a moment, Beowulf turned to the nearby table where Naegling and her armor rested. Hygd helped her in silence. It was a task Beowulf could have done herself, but one that the queen undertook with quiet care. It gave them time.

Hygd pulled Beowulf's tunic over her head and wrapped her belt around her waist. Her fingers worked carefully, lacing the warrior's bracers with precision before pulling a heavy fur-mantled cloak around her wife's broad shoulders. Beowulf reached out and took the queen's hands once more.

"I will see you again," Beowulf said softly. "I cannot say when, or where, but I know in my heart I *will* see you again."

Hygd merely nodded, tears streaming silently down her face as she gave Beowulf's hands a final squeeze. Beowulf turned, not daring to look over her shoulder as her strides carried her back through the hall and past the great doors.

Her heart ached as she forced her legs to move, her mind blank as she stepped out into the morning. Dawn had broken; the light shone dimly through clouds that covered the sun. Thunderheads loomed near the mountains, and the wind blew cold and clear, banners snapping in the breeze.

The horses had been gathered, Beowulf's among them, and roughly two dozen warriors had assembled there. Just beyond them gather a larger crowd made of a smattering of other fighters, guards and villagers. Amid the two groups, conversation was lulled and quiet, uneasiness settling in. The calls of the ravens that perched on the roof of the hall seemed deafening in the hushed air. Beowulf stood just past the doorway, taking her time to look over the warriors who had volunteered. Almost all of them she recognized, save perhaps one or two whose visage was hidden by their helms.

"Tyr's favor be upon all those brave enough to join me in this hunt." She spoke clearly, her breath turning to steam in the chilled autumn air. "There is no bond beholden to any of you to make you take this journey unless you so choose."

Several nods passed amid the warriors, and the crowd of observers fell silent. Beowulf took a deep breath and placed a hand around Naegling as it hung at her waist.

"You know we face a creature of legend, a firebreather and a destroyer that would wipe all that we hold dear from this earth. To victory or death." She raised her voice as she spoke, her words carrying through the clear air.

"Victory or death! For Beowulf!" shouted one of the warriors at the back, and the rest of those assembled echoed him in a thunderous roar as weapons were raised and shields shaken. Life flooded back into the air as the roar went up, and even the ones who had come simply to watch shouted their support, pointing their weapons toward the sky as the cheer rippled outward.

Beowulf pulled herself up into the saddle as the other warriors mounted on all sides. She paused only long enough to look back to the great doors of the hall, where Hygd had emerged with Heardred and Halga by her side. Heardred looked livid, and Beowulf knew that being left behind angered him, but sending one of her heirs to almost certain destruction was a risk she could not take, and a heartbreak she wanted to spare the queen. Beowulf smiled at both the prince and princess, before looking once more at Hygd.

A thousand words were carried in the queen's gaze, and Beowulf did her utmost to speak them back with only a look and the raise of a hand. The cheer surged in volume, and she smiled with all the love and sorrow in her heart, then gripped the reins and urged her steed down the path away from the hall.

The other warriors fell in behind, and the roar of the crowd followed them as they descended into the village at a trot and passed beyond the gates into the open lands beyond. Thunder rumbled in the distance as they picked up pace, their path taking them along the rough beaten track toward the east as the sky darkened above them and the wind picked up. Beowulf kept her jaw tight and her eyes on the land before them, not daring to turn back. The wind dried her tears as quickly as they fell, her cheeks kissed by the air of the coming storm. She whispered a quiet prayer for the well-being of those she loved and urged her horse onwards.

Chapter 18

They had seen the destruction of the villages, all three of them. Even the very soil was blackened, and all had been turned to ash and cinders, buildings now little more than charred husks. The war party tracked the dragon from the third village, and scouts rode out into the mountains while the rest of the group made a makeshift camp not far from the ruins. There was a stream there, higher up and unspoiled by ash and corpses, and the small grove through which it ran gave them suitable cover off the roads.

Night had already begun to fall, and though Beowulf had hoped they might find the creature on their first day, she had underestimated the distance it could cover on the wing. They resigned to camp out of sight, resting themselves and their horses with the hopes that the scouts might find their quarry before morning. Mounts were tied, sleeping furs unfurled on the ground, and small fires kindled against the cold of the coming night as the stars winked awake above them.

The storm had passed away to the west, and thankfully no rain or snow had fallen. A light frost was already beginning to gather on the ground as the light faded. Thunder still rumbled in the distance, low and quiet, and the warriors took their meal in relative silence and prepared to bed down for the night.

Beowulf had already laid her fur on the grass to sleep, when something caught her eye.

One of the warriors moved in a way that was troublingly familiar as he spread his belongings on the ground for the night several yards away. He was at the edge of their camp, near the stream, as far to the opposite side of their gathered crowd from Beowulf as could be. She watched him for a moment as he moved in the light of the three small fires they had kindled, then she stood and slowly moved across their campsite toward him.

Beowulf threaded her way between the bodies of those already asleep, and those who still sat and talked in hushed tones, as an occasional warrior offered her a nod. The young fighter she had seen was rolling out his fur when she approached him from behind and spoke in a voice slightly louder than conversation tones.

"You there."

The warrior startled slightly, and he turned around. Beneath his helm she could see the thin beard on his jaw and the brightness of his eyes. She looked at him for a moment, then sucked her teeth and stepped past him toward the edge of camp.

"Walk with me," she said quietly, and after a moment's hesitation, he followed.

They passed out of the light of the fires and walked all the way to the the small stream near the perimeter of the clearing. The sound of wind in the evergreens above and the burbling of the stream over the rocks dampened all noise. Once they were far enough removed from the camp for privacy, Beowulf turned abruptly, bringing her hand up to slap against the side of the warrior's helm. She checked her strength, no more than jostling him slightly as he flinched and swore.

"Wiglaf! What in the nine realms are you doing here?" she hissed, quietly cursing herself for not noticing his presence among them any sooner. He jerked his helmet off, half flustered by her blow and half angry.

"What do you think I'm doing?" he hissed back. "You're going to fight a *dragon*, and I am damn well coming with you." He squared his shoulders and crossed his arms tightly over his chest.

She sighed heavily. "This is too dangerous. Go home." She stared at him a moment longer before stepping back past him toward the camp.

"No."

She turned slowly.

"You disobey your queen?" Her tone was dangerous and her gaze calculating, and her words were like the knocking of an arrow before the bowstring is pulled taught.

"I am just as capable as any of the warriors here, and just as able to make my own choices where my fate is concerned."

"It's too dangerous, I already told you—"

"And yet you allowed any warriors to volunteer to join you. Why can't I be counted among them?"

She let out a small grunt of frustration as she faced him squarely, hands on her hips. "It's not the same."

"Why not? You think I'm less capable? You yourself trained me!" His voice rose, not high enough to yet be heard by the camp, but the edge in it was sharp as his hands balled into fists.

"This is not about your capability." She kept her voice level but dropped none of the warning in it. "I'll not have you risk your life so recklessly; this is no simple hill troll or border skirmish. You don't—"

"I can make my own choices!" he bit back, and she stepped forward to grip him firmly by the shoulders. Had it been any other day she might have held fast to her position of authority, but her heart had done nothing but ache since she left the hall, and she felt somehow too weary.

"Wiglaf." She spoke slowly, fighting to keep her voice from breaking. "I can't protect you."

He stopped, his shoulders slowly dropping as he looked at her. Some of the anger drained from his face as the two of them regarded each other. Wiglaf sighed as her hands slid from his shoulders, and he reached out to take one of them in his own.

"You can't protect me from everything." He smiled, small and sad. "You cannot protect anyone from everything."

His words pained her, and she knew it showed on her face. She did not have the strength in her heart to hide it. He saw it, and gave an apologetic shrug before he spoke.

"You chose not to stay at the hall and send riders out. You chose to hunt this thing, regardless of the consequences, because of the danger it poses to the people you love."

Beowulf nodded slowly, wishing she could argue against him. She knew it was his choice to make, and for a strange moment she wondered if she felt some fraction of what Hygd had felt when the two of them had parted.

Wiglaf looked her in the eyes, and spoke with a quiet voice.

"Please. Let me do the same."

Beowulf sighed heavily, still feeling the oppressive weariness that hung about her shoulders. There was a fire in his eyes she could not ignore, and she knew there would be no changing his mind.

"I curse your stubbornness," she said, scrubbing her face with her free hand. "If you insist on staying, so be it. But please, be careful."

He nodded vigorously, before reaching down to his belt and removing the long dagger that was sheathed there.

"Here," he said, holding it out. "For luck, and as a thank you."

She regarded the blade for a moment, the simple design of the pommel, too long for a dagger but too short for a sword. He had always carried it with him; back when he was so small it seemed a perfectly sized sword for him. He had been holding it the day she'd found him, clutching it white-knuckled and hiding in a barrel after everything he had known was destroyed. It was more than simply a blade, and the gesture brought a small measure of warmth to her heart. She reached out and took the long knife, tucking it carefully into her own belt.

"Thank you. I hope I won't need it."

He nodded in agreement, his expression becoming slightly stony as both of their minds drifted to what awaited them.

"Thank you for letting me stay."

I pray I won't regret it, Beowulf thought as she nodded to him. She felt only defeat, weight still pressing down on her shoulders as she released his hand and turned back toward the camp and trudged through the frosty grass. Wiglaf followed, keeping his helm tucked under his arm. With his identity exposed but his presence allowed, he moved his belongings a bit closer to the fire. Beowulf walked back to her own fur where it was spread across the ground, and lay down heavily.

Given the events of the day and what likely lay ahead, she would have expected sleep to be elusive. But sorrow had somehow turned to weariness, and she felt so tired that even the worries that swam through her head went quiet before too long. She did not dream of fire that night. Instead, she dreamt of the meadow and the great tree she had seen so many years ago when she had been dragged down beneath the icy waves. This time she carried Naegling in her hand, and the gaping hole in the tree was empty. The goddess, waiting for her as always, held an open palm toward her into which Beowulf placed her sword. Freya's other hand took Beowulf's in her own, and a warm light cascaded over them.

A noise roused Beowulf from sleep some time before dawn. She snapped awake in the darkness, hearing the warriors stirring around her. Her hand had instinctively gone to the hilt of Naegling at her waist as she peered through the dark. The coals from the fire cast little in the way of light, and the eastern sky had yet to brighten in the predawn. Someone was shouting as they jogged between the sleeping figures. The scout had to peer about in the dark for a time before he found her. By then she had already gotten her feet under her, and the initial spike of panic from her sudden waking had subsided.

"It's here!" he gasped, panting slightly as he came to an unsteady halt before her. Warning prickled into her limbs as the warriors continued to scrabble to their feet around her.

"How close?" she asked.

"Less than a mile," he managed between breaths. "It must have set more fires in the lowlands. We saw it fly down into one of the grottoes here less than an hour past. We think it might be sleeping."

She didn't answer. She had already begun to gather up what little belongings she had, the other warriors following suit. The scout called after her as she tied up her fur and walked to where her horse was tied.

"My queen, it's unlike anything I've seen. Its wings were massive. The wind from it shook the trees as it flew over."

She could feel a ripple of fear around her, and saw a few nervous glances exchanged between the warriors as she finished packing up her things and turned back to the scout.

"Thank you for bringing news. If indeed the beast slumbers, that gives us an advantage we otherwise might not have." She spoke loudly enough that she was sure any others who were listening could hear. The scout gave a shaky nod, then Beowulf turned back to her horse and pulled herself up into the saddle. She didn't have to wait long for the others, and after only a span of minutes the only signs of their passing were the indents in the grass and the ashes from their fires.

She glanced over her shoulder as they went, her eyes on Wiglaf as he rode not far behind her. They set out on the thin game track they had followed from the road. Beowulf let the scout lead the way as they wound up through the foothills near the toes of the mountains, the night still dark around them. Strange sounds whispered about them, the wind filtering through the trees and bringing frost on the air with it. Even the horses seemed restless, and made little sound.

Up through the darkened woods they traveled, as a soft layer of snow began to crunch underfoot and the ground leveled out in a high open space. Here granite crags protruded like teeth from the earth, casting strange shadows as the first gray light brightened the eastern sky. The scout motioned for them to stop, and they tied their mounts before continuing on foot.

They climbed up a small rise, treading silently as they moved between the snow-covered trees, their breath curling steam as the stars slowly began to vanish. The entire area was still open, and the mountains loomed high on their left as they walked carefully toward the gathering glow in the east. Here, where the ground was flat and the trees scarce, there was a small dug-out cavern beneath a granite overhang. It was large enough to resemble a small cave, and even in the faint light they could see an unmistakable trickle of smoke rising from it.

"There." The scout barely whispered as he pointed to the overhang. The other scout was there as well, some hundred yards from the cave and carefully tucked behind a granite crag, doubtless to be sure the creature hadn't fled before they arrived. The warriors slowly fanned out behind Beowulf, swords drawn as they watched the cavern.

Beowulf turned to all those who had followed her. All eyes were upon her as they stood in sight of the cave. She could feel fear rising in her chest, but she breathed deeply and spoke quietly, her voice carrying in the clear gray twilight.

"I make this boast," she began slowly. The tradition of her warrior's promise had never gotten easier, no matter how often she had been called upon to make it. This time, it was about more than her own vow, and for that reason it troubled her less. Much though she would have disliked to admit, she knew she was also stalling, if only a little. She had spent her life as a warrior, and what waited for her in that cave was a truth and an inevitability she had lived with every moment. Now that she suddenly faced it, despite all the courage in her heart, she could not deny the fear she felt.

"To all those here before me," she said quietly, looking at each of them in turn. "I thank you for your courage, your willingness to defend these lands and stand by my side." She saw a few nods among them. Still, there was a fear she could see in the eyes that looked back at her.

"I make this vow, as a warrior and as your queen." She breathed deep, trying to slow her heart where it had begun to flutter nervously against her ribs. Steam left her lips, swirling in the predawn air. "I will do all that I can, give all that I can, to face this monster that threatens our people and our lands."

She turned her gaze briefly earthward, worrying the pommel of her sword with her hand. It took several moments to steady her mind and transmute all that she thought into words.

"Death awaits all of us. It is the one thing that makes us equal, regardless of who we are or what we achieve in our short lives. It is a last gate, and how we choose to cross it is not always up to us. But sometimes it is. Fate is an arrow that comes for all of us, but we each choose if we take that arrow in the back or in the chest."

Beowulf caught a few nods of agreement in the gathering before her, and a few of the warriors hefted their blades or took a few steps closer as she spoke. Her words were only for herself now, that much she knew, but she was grateful there were others there to hear them.

"Valhalla or Fólkvangr await all those who die a noble death, but there is yet a form of immortality to be gleaned here on earth. All who perish may yet live on in the stories that are told about them. And"—her eyes settled on Wiglaf for a moment—"in the hearts of those who we love and who love us."

Another murmur of agreement passed around the circle, and Beowulf drew her blade. Naegling sang a bright clear note as she pulled it from her scabbard and hefted her shield. "I thank all of you who have followed me here, and I vow that this morning will bring this monster's end, or mine."

The warriors held their weapons close and shook them slightly at her words. They might have made more ruckus had they not been afraid to wake their prey. Beowulf turned and pulled her shield in close, Naegling shining by her side as she walked toward the cave. The warriors fanned out as they drew nearer to the entrance, stepping carefully on frosted earth as they went.

Once she was within a stone's throw of the entrance, Beowulf could finally see the creature through the graying predawn. Its body was a deep ruddy color like rust, its massive wings were folded down by its side, and a trickle of smoke rose from its nostrils. A long tail was wrapped around its body in a circular fashion, hiding its rear legs. Even from almost thirty feet away, she could smell the overpowering odor of smoke and sulfur, as well as an almost metallic aroma that wafted from where the creature slumbered. She made it within ten feet before the dragon opened its eyes.

Beowulf could not have guessed if it was aware of them and simply waiting, or if indeed they had caught it by surprise. Either way, its tail suddenly lashed out, and Beowulf barely managed to duck in time. Some of those behind her were not so lucky, and a handful of warriors were thrown back by the force of its strike. The beast lurched up from where it slumbered, raising its head high and opening its wings. Eyes of burnt orange glowed like coals beneath the swept-back horns protruding from its head, and the scales along its throat shimmered where they had been rubbed smooth as it rose to its full height. It gazed down at the warriors who approached and settled its eyes on Beowulf at the forefront as it opened its jaws and let out a roar that seemed to shake the very stones around them.

The smell of blood and death hung heavy on its hot breath as it swept one of its wings forward like an arm, catching Beowulf and a handful of others with the blow. She ducked behind her shield, her legendary strength keeping her upright as she was pushed backward, her feet digging long lines in the dirt as the other warriors around her tumbled like small stones in an avalanche.

Her mind was no longer on those who were with her, save perhaps Wiglaf. The creature before her was the target of her narrowing focus as her body and mind came alive in the flurry of battle. She shook herself and stepped out of the grooves her boots had cut into the earth as the dragon reared its head back and a glow seeped through its chest. Beowulf barely had time to shout a warning and crouch behind her shield before a gout of flame illuminated the entire mountainside.

Not all the warriors had been so lucky, and she could hear someone scream as she brushed a small patch of flame off her shoulder and advanced on the creature once more. The dragon watched her approach, almost seeming to leer as it held its maw wide. It propelled itself forward, using its wings like arms, its powerful legs driving into the ground. Beowulf watched as a warrior threw a spear that bounced harmlessly off its side.

The dragon lunged, and Beowulf threw herself to the side as its jaws closed in the air where she had stood only a moment before. Its tail whipped past, colliding with two other warriors. One of the men had managed to raise his shield, but the barbed spine on the end of the creature's tail shattered it into a rain of splinters. Beowulf watched as long as she dared, before scrambling to her feet and swinging at the dragon's side, close to its wing. Her blade sang as it glanced off the dragon's scales, its armored hide completely unharmed.

She cursed under her breath and ducked as the beast swung a claw-tipped wing toward her head. Its talon grated against her shield as it went over, her legs bracing her beneath the force of the blow. She blew stray hairs from her face and squared her shoulders, hefting her sword in her hand as the creature reared back for another attack. The warriors around her regrouped, their hesitance palpable as they drew near.

"We can't hurt it!" someone shouted above the fray, before the dragon spewed fire again. The warriors scattered as great curls of flame illuminated the coming dawn, sending a wall of heat through the frigid air. Beowulf leaped behind a crag of granite as flames roared by her, the heat plastering her hair to the sides of her face with sweat. Her chest heaved, and the scorching air burned in her throat.

She didn't hesitate. As soon as the flames began to subside, she lunged from behind the rocks and closed the gap between herself and the dragon, this time aiming for its fleshy wing. Her blade glanced off the scales that lined the wing but cut cleanly through the dark rust-colored skin stretched between the bones. Hot blood spattered as the creature let out a shriek that shook the earth and pierced the air.

"The wings! Aim for the wings!" she shouted as it lurched forward, almost head-butting her. She raised her shield at the last moment and felt the crack of its horns against the wood. Its head was bigger than her whole body, and the blow very nearly shattered her shield and sent her tumbling backward. She got her feet beneath her once more, the taste of iron in her mouth as she spat a mix of dirt and blood and lifted her sword again.

That was when she saw it. Someone was running, their back just visible out of the corner of her sight. She kept her body toward the dragon, daring to turn for long enough to see her warriors as they fled. Her heart sank for the briefest moment, before rage bubbled in her veins and made her grit her teeth as she watched them run. Those who hadn't yet been burned or broken by the beast's attack turned and fled down from the plateau. Anger and disappointment vied for dominance within her as she watched, cursing their dishonor beneath her breath as a voice rose above the tumult.

"Cowards!"

She turned to see Wiglaf standing a short distance from her, protected by a crag of granite, his helm off and his hair ringing his face in a dark halo. Blood and dirt were smeared on his cheeks, and he brandished his sword at the backs of their forces as they fled.

The strange mix of love and fear that the sight kindled in her chest only lingered for a moment, before she had to duck behind a nearby rock to avoid another gout of flame. As the flickering fire cleared, she made eye contact with Wiglaf across the gap between where they both crouched. Admiration, gratitude, fear. She wasn't sure what odd mix it was she felt, but she hoped her eyes said what in that moment her lips could not, before she rose to her feet and threw herself once more at her adversary.

The world around her narrowed, her every thought now bent on the creature before her as she narrowly avoided a blow from its talon-tipped wing. It snapped with its jaws, catching the corner of her tunic as she dodged, her sword ringing harmlessly off its scales. Its tail snapped out and caught her side, ripping through leather and mail as she skidded backward. White-hot pain seared along her ribs, and she felt the warmth of her own blood seeping into the cloth.

Wiglaf advanced carefully, as she had, narrowly avoiding blows until he was close enough to strike out with his sword. His blade did nothing, glancing off the dragon as if its skin was harder than steel. But he kept the beast occupied, which was more than she could hope to ask for, and she managed to run beneath its wing to strike the unarmored sinew of its shoulder. Her blade bit a shallow wound into its flesh as it shrieked again and lashed out with its back leg, a talon catching her in the side of her chest as it sent her tumbling backward across the frigid ground.

Dawn was fast approaching, and the faint light from the east washed across the frosty landscape. Beowulf clambered laboriously to her feet in time to see the dragon's tail strike Wiglaf hard enough to shatter his shield and send him tumbling like a ragdoll. She shouted his name, her voice hoarse and barely audible over the creature's roar as it turned to her and lunged forward. She ducked a sweeping strike from its wing and braced her shield as its wicked eyes blazed and its open maw descended.

No ordinary mortal could have withstood that blow from its head, but she held strong beneath the onslaught as its teeth shattered the shield in her left hand, sending splinters sprinkling onto the ground. Before it could raise its head again, she brought her blade down with all her strength. Naegling sang through the air, catching the dragon on the top of its skull. There was a crack like lightning, and the blade she had carried for all those years snapped like ice under the force of the blow. She staggered back, her blade no more than a hilt in her hand, the same gilded prize she had found in the cave where she had bested Grendel's mother so many years ago.

It's time. The thought seemed to come outside of her own mind as she looked down at what was left of that fateful sword. Beowulf breathed deeply, aware of the dragon raising its head once more, as the world around her slowed and steadied. The hilt fell from her hand onto the soft earth, and she reached to her waist to draw Wiglaf's long knife. Her left arm was still numb from where the dragon had broken her defenses, but she still had strength. A cold smirk curled in the corner of her mouth as the blade glinted in her grip. It was just her and the dragon, and its eyes blazed as it let out a mighty roar.

The wind from its lungs tore through her hair, its cry deafening as she stood before it. Mouth open wide, the dragon lunged forward, and Beowulf charged to meet it. The two collided, and her arm drove the blade forward and up as the dragon's jaws closed. Fangs pierced into her right collarbone at the base of her neck, and pain seared through her. The entirety of her right arm seemed to disappear for a moment as she thrust the blade with all her strength, pushing up into the soft flesh of the roof of its mouth.

Blood poured over her hand, and the creature's entire body seemed to spasm and lurch as her blade found its mark. They stood frozen for a moment as she watched blood pool in those orange eyes. The dragon's jaw released, and fangs were pulled free from her neck and shoulder as it reared up toward the sky, its bellow turning to a long wail as flecks of crimson flew from its mouth. Beowulf's arm dropped, pain burning through her as she watched the dragon writhe, its body turning up the earth like a plow as it thudded heavily. It gave one last beat of its massive wings as it trembled into stillness, its eyes rolling back in its great head as a final burble echoed from its throat.

She stood panting, unsteady on her feet. Only when she was sure the dragon was dead did she let her knees buckle and pain drag her to the ground. She had lost all feeling in her right arm, and the agony that radiated from the gaping wounds near her shoulder and the side of her neck clouded her senses. As she rolled onto her back, savoring the sudden quiet around her, she coughed a fine mist of red.

Dawn had finally broken, and the first golden rays of sun struck the earth around her as the faintest snow began to fall from the sky above.

She heard the thud of hurried footsteps, and then something was beneath her shoulders, lifting her slightly. Wiglaf looked down at her, his face streaked with blood and his eyes filled with worry. He wrapped an arm beneath her back to prop her upright, his other hand pressed to the side of her neck. She didn't need to ask after her own wounds. She found answers enough in his eyes, and in her own body as she lost the feeling in her feet. Her blood seemed to burn from the bite, and her limbs felt heavy.

"You did it," he said, his voice almost desperate. "You killed it." He tried to grin, but nothing could hide the sorrow in his eyes. "We'll get you patched up."

"Poison." She coughed, then shook her head and smiled. Wiglaf's expression broke.

"I'm sorry," he gasped.

"Don't be. This wasn't your making." She continued to smile, finding just enough feeling in her left arm that she could raise it to him. He took her hand and held it tightly to his own chest.

"I will see that those cowards are punished for—" he began angrily, but she shook her head.

"They did what most would do. Their knowledge of their cowardice is something they must live with, and that is punishment enough. This beast caused enough hardship. Please let this go."

He frowned, but managed a small nod, and Beowulf's thoughts drifted to Hygd. She felt her own tears begin to slide down her cheeks, and she swallowed hard as the pain in her body gave way to a strange numbness. The queen filled her mind until she was all Beowulf could think about, each new memory that welled within her sending a pang of sorrow through her heart. She felt Wiglaf shift slightly beneath her as he held her tightly, his arm wrapped under her shoulders.

"Please," he said in a small voice. "Please hold on." His hand gripped her own desperately, and as she looked at him, she realized he was crying.

"It's alright," she said softly, giving his hand a small squeeze with what was left of her strength.

"No," he said, his voice thick. "Please don't go where I can't follow. I can't lose you too. You're my family." His words ended in a small gasp as his shoulders hunched and he buckled toward her.

"As you are mine." She gave a soft smile, heaviness settling into her limbs as coldness spread through her body. "You may not be my child by blood, but you are by bond. It's the choices we make that shape our destiny, and the people we love who are our family. I'll always be with you."

Wiglaf nodded, his eyes flooded with tears, his breath coming in great heaving shudders as he held her tightly. He gripped her hand even after her strength left her and darkness began to cloud her vision. Cold shadows seemed to surround her as a steady stillness settled in her mind. It was not unlike sinking into deep waters, as she had done so many times in life. She had expected to feel fear as the world began to fall away, but instead it was love that filled her heart.

Love for the queen who had become her wife, with whom she had shared so many years of peace and prosperity. Love for the children she had never expected but that she considered her own, though none of them were of her blood. Lastly, a love for her path, and that, of all the ways she might have departed this earth, she did so with a blade in her hands, as a bulwark between darkness and those she held dear.

Just as the world seemed fully subsumed in black, a sudden warmth bloomed in her chest, warm and soft like a summer sunrise. Heat flooded through her, and she felt light as a feather as her vision and all around her cleared in a brilliant white-gold light. Someone was leaning over her where she lay in her adopt-ed son's arms, someone she had seen before.

Freya's hawk-feather cape draped from her shoulders as she leaned down over Beowulf, her eyes bright and with a smile on her lips. She regarded Beowulf for a moment, then reached down toward her. Beowulf sat upright, or so it felt, and took

Freya's hand. The goddess pulled her to her feet, and her voice was gentle, echoing slightly as she spoke.

"It's time."

"I know." Beowulf nodded, and the goddess clasped her hand. She took a last look at Wiglaf, where he knelt holding a body she recognized as her own, before the world began to fall away in brilliant light. Her thoughts drifted one last time to Hygd. Unburdened by sadness, she thought of all they had shared, and breathed her last promise before she joined the ranks of the fallen.

"I will see you again, my love."

Chapter 19

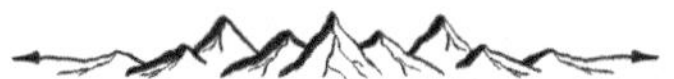

The autumn skies roiled with thunder and a thick mist stretched across the land on the day Beowulf's pyre burned. Angry clouds gathered amid the peaks of the mountains, high above where the lowlands were cloaked in fog like a thick blanket. It was one of the rare days when the view to the sea from the great cliffs was hidden, though the Queen's Hall was still visible in the valley below where it stood just above the mists.

The air was oddly still, only barely stirring the great trees that stood amid the standing stones, the finest layer of powder turning them white. A soft blanket of snow-covered everything, wrapping the world in silence. Smoke from the pyre rose steadily into the air, flames thawing the ground near the edge of the cliffs. It was customary that a crowd would gather to mourn, but so vast was the host that had come to bid farewell to their queen that they stretched nearly halfway down the winding path back to the valley.

Stillness spread across the land, a gloom that settled softly onto the earth and turned the forests quiet and the skies dim. The bustling villages were silent, the forge fires were cold. Even the great Queen's Hall seemed morose where it sat in the rolling lowlands, surrounded by a sea of fog. Out of sight, the distant western ocean perfumed the air that moved ever so faintly through the snow-covered trees.

The mourners had been at their vigil long enough that fallen flakes had gathered in the furs that lined Wiglaf's shoulders where he stood still as a statue. There were more people on that cliffside than ever in recorded memory, but he and three others stood slightly apart from the crowd. The warmth from the pyre did not melt the frost that clung to the edges of his beard, crystallized by the faint cold air. He stood tucked beneath his cloak, staring into the flickering flames that sent a clear column of smoke trailing up to the heavens.

Halga and Heardred flanked Wiglaf, the three children of the queens standing slightly behind the woman closest to the flames. Hygd had her back to the gathered crowd. The snowy furs of her robe rose to her pale cheeks, and her hair had been loosened from its braid to hang wild about her in streaks of near black and gray. She had not said a single word, but stood and watched the flames rise.

Halga, the heir to the realm, was a statue, her pale face drawn tight with sorrow. Her brother, his fists tight by his sides, looked trapped somewhere between anger and grief. Wiglaf watched Heardred as he clenched his jaw and stared into the fire. As he regarded the prince, he felt suddenly lonely, and not for lack of company. The first person to pull him from the hell that nearly killed him so many years ago was gone. Someone who had seemed so permanent, larger than life and somehow endlessly enduring. She had left behind a hole, one that tore through the entire realm.

The world was unlikely to see anyone like her ever again. Stories had followed Beowulf since she was a foundling, until all the realm had known her name. She had been a shield against monsters and invaders alike, and so many had known the stories of her. Stories that doubtless would be told for many years to come, though how well they captured the truth of things couldn't be known. The realm had known her, and the loss of her seemed to still the entire world on that day, as if the mountains themselves shared in the grief of those who dwelt in their shadow.

Wiglaf dwelt on his sadness as the hours passed and the crowd on the cliffs slowly shrank, the pyre burning ever lower. When he finally moved, his body ached with protest both from his recent wounds and how long he had stood as still as the surrounding runestones in the cold. He took a few steps forward and drew alongside the queen, who turned slightly at his approach.

Hygd seemed to have aged a decade in a single night, her face weary and tear stains lining her cheeks as she looked at him. The firelight reflected in her eyes, their brilliant blue turned somehow to a faded gray as she regarded Wiglaf. She reached out a hand and took his own as they stood beside each other. He wanted desperately to say something, but every word he could think of seemed utterly useless.

It was Hygd who finally spoke.

"I am afraid of what awaits you. Of what awaits us." She sighed deeply as she raised her head and looked out across the lowlands.

"What do you foresee?" He shifted slightly, keeping her hand in his.

"She was a shield. Not only by what she did, but by who she was. She protected all these lands with her story and legend as much as with her sword."

"You fear invasion." He didn't speak it as a question, his own thoughts following hers as he realized her meaning. She was right. The Geats had celebrated an unprecedented time of peace under Beowulf's rule alongside Hygd, and word of their new vulnerability would spread like wildfire.

"It will come. I fear for the future of these lands and all those who dwell within." Hygd's voice was brittle.

"As do I," Wiglaf said quietly, "but I will do all I can to protect our people, and to protect my brother and sister."

Hygd looked at him, something fragile and tender in her eyes, before she turned back to the pyre which had begun to burn low.

"You may not be her son by birth, but you have her spirit." Her gentle smile split Wiglaf to his core.

"She was a mother to me," he said, his voice wavering slightly as he struggled to keep it even. "And a teacher. And perhaps a father too."

Wiglaf looked at Hygd, watching her gaze drift skyward following the smoke, fresh tears sliding down her cheeks as she stood by the pyre, the heat making her wild hair dance. Her spirit had always been unbreakable, but there was something about her now that seemed shattered, something past the armor of her poise and the strength of her gaze. She reminded him suddenly of a great tree, still standing proud even when its center has been ripped asunder by lightning and flame.

He sighed, his gaze still settled on her as he spoke. "What was she to you?" he asked softly.

Hygd turned to him, her eyes filled with tears.

"A friend, and a lover." She smiled knowingly. "A queen, and a warrior..." Her voice became hushed. "She was everything to me."

The two of them turned back to the pyre as Heardred and Halga joined them, standing close as the flames burned low and the sky began to darken. Somewhere in the forest behind them a raven called, and a soft snow began to fall from the gloaming skies.

Glossary

Aesir (Ay-seer)

Primary race of gods in Norse mythology. Includes the deities Odin, Thor, Balder, Frigg and Tyr. The Aesir were likely brought with the Germanic tribes that expanded into Scandinavia and are descended from the Indo-European religion of the late Neolithic period. They are more warlike than their counterparts, the Vanir.

Aeschere (Ash-ear)
A councilor and friend to King Hrothgar of Heorot. Aeschere was close to the king from their youth and served him loyally.

Amma (Ah-muh)
Danish shieldmaiden in service to King Hrothgar of Heorot.

All-father
One of the names used for Odin, leader of the Norse pantheon. Associated with wisdom, leadership, and warfare, Odin is associated with the gift of foresight. The leader of the combined Aesir and Vanir races of gods, the one-eyed Odin is often depicted alongside ravens and/or wolves.

Beowulf (Bay-oh-wolf)

A hero from Scandinavian mythology, Beowulf was a legendary warrior who defeated monsters and ruled the Geatish tribes of Scandinavia.

Braggi (Brag-ee)
A Geatish warrior and close friend to Beowulf; Braggi met her when the two were children and had only just begun their training as warriors.

Breca (Brek-ah)
A Geatish warrior who trained alongside Beowulf for many years.

Danes (Day-ns)
An ethnic group and nationality that originated in Denmark. They also lived in southern Scandinavia during the Viking Age (793 CE until 1066 CE). At the time of the books, the Danes are ruled by King Hrothgar.

Ecgtheow (Egg-thee-ow)
Father of Beowulf. A Geatish warrior who was exiled for starting a blood feud. Despite his status as an outcast, he was welcomed by King Hrothgar and spent time among the Danes.

Ecglaf (Egg-laff)
A Danish warrior. Father of Unferth, a warrior serving as a retainer to King Hrothgar of Heorot.

Einar (Eye-nar)
A warrior loyal to Beowulf; part of her band of Geatish retainers.

Erik (Air-ick)
A servant of an unnamed Geatish lord.

Fenris (Fen-riss)

Also referred to as Fenrir, the Fenris wolf is a monstrous wolf in Norse mythology, imprisoned by the gods with the aid of the warrior god Tyr. Fenris is a representation of the fates, as well as ferocity, and is prophesied to kill Odin during Ragnarök, the mythic battle between gods and giants that leads to the end of all things.

Freya (Fray-uh)
Norse goddess, one of the Vanir, associated with pre-Germanic mythic traditions of Scandinavia. Freya is often associated with women and fertility, as well as magic. In older Nordic traditions she is often depicted as a warrior goddess who presides over the domain of warfare. Freya often takes the form of a hawk and rules over one of the realms of the afterlife. Unlike Valhalla, Fólkvangr is a home for the spirits of the fallen that is more closely tied to nature and is under the open sky.

Fólkvangr (Foke-vang-er)
Ruled over by the goddess Freya, Fólkvangr is one of the Nordic afterlives. A home for those who die noble deaths, it is a wild haven and sanctuary for individuals of all genders who lived and died bravely.

Foundling
A young child raised by individuals who are not their birth parents. Used to describe abandoned children who have been adopted, as well as those removed from their families to be raised as warriors.

Frisia (Free-shia)
A cross-border cultural region in northwestern Europe, encompassing the north of the Netherlands and parts of western Germany. Home to the Frisians, one of the many cultural groups of Scandinavia during the Viking Age, who warred with the Geats and Danes.

Geats (Gheets/Gay-ts)
A north Germanic tribe who lived in southern Sweden during the Viking Age. Divided into Western and Eastern groups respectively, the Geats were at times allied with the Danes, and warred with other nearby cultural groups, including the Swedes and Frisians.

Gaetland (Gheet-land/Gate-land)
The territory of the Geatish people, encompassing much of southern Sweden in a region now known as Götaland, rich in forests and mountains.

Grendel (Gren-dul)
A monstrous creature who haunts the hall of Heorot, home of King Hrothgar. Grendel is a twisted humanoid creature with an appetite for human flesh. The size of nearly three men put together, Grendel is formidable not only for his size but for the fact that no weapon can pierce his skin.

Gunnar (Gun-ahr)
Villager from the town of Vänersborg. Not to be confused with Jarl Gunnar.

Halga (Hall-gah)
Daughter of King Hygelac and Queen Hygd, Halga is the eldest child and heir to the throne.

Heardred (Here-dred)
Son of King Hygelac and Queen Hygd, Heardred is the younger brother to Halga.

Hel
Another of the Norse afterlives, one for those who do not die nobly or in battle. Hel is an underworld realm, one that is cold, dark, and filled with ailment and woe.

Heorot (Here-rot)
The great hall of King Hrothgar, leader of the Danes. Heorot is the pride of Hrothgar's bloodline, one of the finest mead halls ever built and the jewel of the Danish realm.

*Hrethric (Reth-rick)
Son of King Hrothgar and Queen Wealtheow, the youngest of their sons and one of the heirs to the Danish throne.

*Hrothgar (Roth-garr)
King of the Danes, Hrothgar is descended from a long line of leadership and rules from his seat in the great hall, Heorot.

*Hrothmund (Roth-mund)
Son of King Hrothgar and Queen Wealtheow, the eldest of their sons and the first in line for the Danish throne.

*Hrunting (Runt-ing)
The well-crafted sword of Unferth, a warrior and retainer who is also the nephew of King Hrothgar, whom he serves.

Hygd (Hig-d)
Queen of the Geats, and wife to King Hygelac. Hygd's marriage to the king was for the purpose of forging an alliance, as she is of foreign descent.

Hygelac (Hi-gul-ack)
King of the Geats, whom Beowulf serves. Hygelac is married to Hygd, a noblewoman of foreign blood, and together they rule from the Great Hall of the King (The Queen's Hall on the map) in Geatland.

Jarl (Yar-uhl)
A noble title in Scandinavia during the Viking Age, similar to the rank of Duke in Medieval Europe. Jarls ruled territories, managed justice, and lead armies. Higher in rank than a clan chief, but lower than a king.

Jarl Gunnar (Yar-uhl Gun-ahr)
One of the jarls of the Geats.

Jarl Igni (Yar-uhl Ig-nee)
One of the jarls of the Geats.

Naegling (Nay-gling)
Famed sword of the warrior Beowulf. Forged after Beowulf's return to Geatland after aiding King Hrothgar of the Danes.

Njord (Nyor-d)
Nordic god of the oceans and seas; one of the Aesir.

Odin (Oh-din)
Also known as the All-father, leader of the Norse pantheon; one of the Aesir. See "All-father" in the glossary.

Ravna (Rahv-nuh)
One of the warriors of the Geats; retainer and friend to Beowulf and Braggi.

Shieldmaiden (Shield Maiden)
Female warrior, often of higher status in leadership or of famed accomplishments and renown.

Swedes (Swee-ds)
An ethnic group native to Sweden. During the Viking Age, they frequently warred with neighboring groups, including the Danes.

Tordenvejr (Tore-den-vare)
Beowulf's horse. Name translates to "thunderstorm."

Tyr (Teer)
Norse god of war and warriors. One of the Aesir, associated with justice, nobility, and the code of honor as well as battle and conflict.

Unferth (Uhn-fehrt)
Nephew to King Hrothgar of the Danes. Warrior and retainer to his king.

Valhalla (Vahl-hall-ah)
One of the Norse afterlives, reserved for warriors and others who die noble deaths and live honorably. Odin the All-father presides over Valhalla, which takes the form of a great mead hall where the spirits of the deceased enjoy food and drink as well as daily battle.

Vänersborg (Van-ersh-bor)
A large village near the northernmost edge of the Geatish lands near the border of Swedish territory, at the edge of modern Lake Vänern.

Vanir (Va-neer)
The other race of gods in Norse mythology, often considered subservient to their counterparts, the Aesir. The Vanir are associated with wealth, fertility, nature and foresight, unlike the more warlike Aesir. The Vanir possessed magic that the Aesir did not, and only taught the Aesir after the two races intermingled to end their ongoing conflict and warfare. They may have been more closely associated with the tribal groups that existed in the region prior to the arrival of Germanic ethnic groups.

Wealtheow (Well-the-oh)

Queen of the Danes, wife to King Hrothgar and mother to Hrothmund and Hrethric.

Wergild (Where-gild)
Germanic tradition that demanded payment of money as compensation for injury or death. Always paid in equal measure to damage done or life lost. Often used to try to prevent blood feuds.

Wiglaf (Vig-lawf)
Foundling child from Vänersborg; later becomes a warrior of the Geats.

Wulfgar (Wolf-garr)
Warrior and advisor to King Hrothgar who speaks to visitors on his king's behalf.

Yggdrassil (Ig-draw-sill)
Also known as the World Tree. In myth, the worlds of the gods and mortals are all held within its branches, with the afterlife of Hel situated beneath its roots. It is often represented as an ash tree.

*Names that include an "hr" at their start have no equivalent pronunciation in modern English. A more accurate pronunciation includes a very slight "h" sound before immediately pronouncing the next consonant.

Afterword

Main character death is not something I enjoy, as a reader or writer. Nor is it something I intend to use frequently, if at all, in any future works. The story of Beowulf was challenging to write regarding the fate of the main character, and during the writing process I was unsure of how to handle the ending.

So much of who Beowulf is, what the character represents, embodies the Norse notion of fate insofar as the inescapable nature of death. Instead, so much of who we are and the legacy we leave behind (the closest thing to immortality we have) is based on how we meet that end. For Beowulf, their death is one of the most integral aspects of their life. As one who lives honorably, and is willing to die protecting everything they love, death represents an inevitability that they face bravely, while acknowledging their own fear, sorrow and mortality.

Furthermore, in the Norse theology, death is not final in the slightest but rather a door to whatever comes next. There is a sense of attachment to people, places and things that even death cannot touch, chief among them being love and honor.

While I wanted, desperately, to have a more typical happy ending, I could not write it. Such an ending felt like a betrayal of so much that the story of Beowulf represents, and the importance of fate to the hero's narrative.

Acknowledgements

Many thanks to the amazing people who helped bring this project to life.

To my spouse, for their endless patience and advice, as well as my fantastic editor Jane Spencer.

Special thanks to Miranda not only for her edits and feedback, but also her incredible enthusiasm for the book, and to Laurie Fadave, the first person to put a translation of Beowulf in my hands when I was a teen.

I am also incredibly grateful for the artists involved. Thank you Shade of Stars for the beautiful dust jacket art, Josh (Art of Arklin) for the foil cover design, Soldagarius for the stunning interior character art as well as Ramona (Alderdoodle) and Soulafein for the section and chapter heading art.

Lastly, huge thanks to all the backers on Kickstarter who helped make the hardcover print of this book a reality.

www.ingramcontent.com/pod-product-compliance
Lightning Source LLC
Chambersburg PA
CBHW071533110726
47908CB00007B/1867